Feeling Very Strange: The Slipstream Anthology

"Oh, these stories!…Don't stop until all have been read."
—*Booklist*, starred review

"At last we have our definitive collection…And once again, we can rejoice that revolution after revolution will be printed, not televised."
—*The Agony Column*

"Worth buying? Well if you want to be the hippest cat on the block, then yes."
—*SF Crowsnest*

"Leave it to Tachyon, one of the most exhilarating and intellectually probing small presses, to put out a book like this…. This book is a joy, and could easily become a staple of college syllabi in the not-so-distant future."
—*Time Out Chicago*

"…whether you're interested in the boundaries of slipstream or not, *Feeling Very Strange* is a terrific collection of stories."
—*Intergalactic Medicine Show*

Rewired: The Post-Cyberpunk Anthology

"Editors James Patrick Kelly and John Kessel round up sixteen inspiring, mind-altering stories written since cyberpunk's heyday ended and the 'post-cyberpunk' era began…and every story in the bunch is a knockout."
—*Boing Boing*

"…fascinating, and indispensable to any serious SF reader…. *Rewired* is one of the best imaginable anthologies covering what SF is doing right now."
—Andrew Wheeler

"This really is an excellent collection and a reminder that the short story is often the best venue for new ideas in the field."
—*SF Crowsnest*

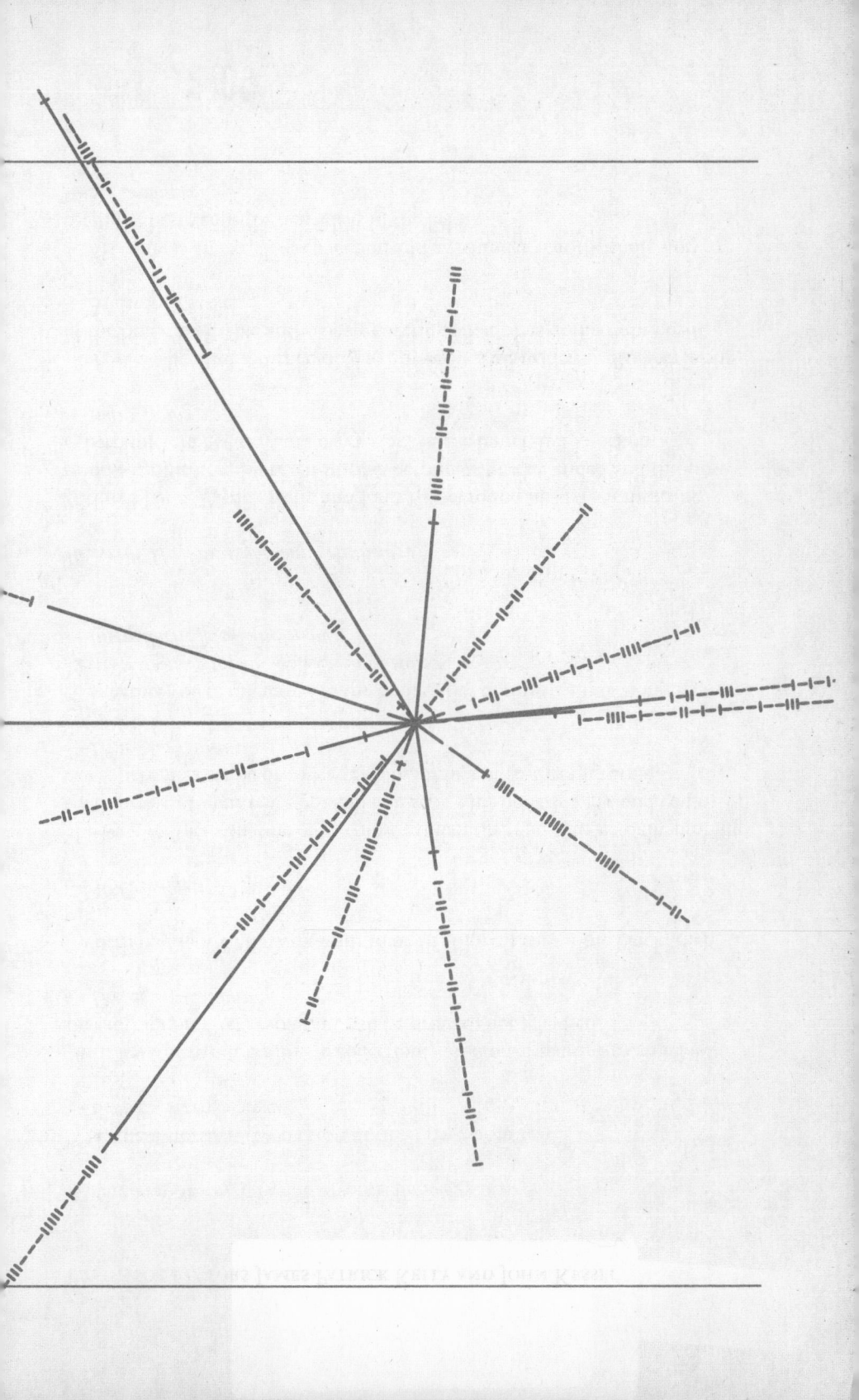

THE SECRET HISTORY
OF SCIENCE FICTION

SEL

THE SECRET HISTORY OF SCIENCE FICTION
COPYRIGHT © 2009 BY JAMES PATRICK KELLY
AND JOHN KESSEL

INTERIOR DESIGN BY JOHN COULTHART
COVER DESIGN BY ANN MONN
COVER ART BY DIGITAL VISION LTD.

TACHYON PUBLICATIONS
1459 18TH STREET #139
SAN FRANCISCO, CA 94107
(415) 285-5615
WWW.TACHYONPUBLICATIONS.COM
TACHYON@TACHYONPUBLICATIONS.COM

SERIES EDITOR: JACOB WEISMAN

ISBN 13: 978-1-892391-93-3
ISBN 10: 1-892391-92-9

PRINTED IN THE UNITED STATES OF AMERICA
BY WORZALLA
FIRST EDITION: 2009
9 8 7 6 5 4 3 2 1

—‖————‖—‖—‖‖‖—‖—‖‖‖———‖‖‖—‖————‖———‖—‖—‖‖—‖‖‖———‖‖‖—‖————‖‖‖—‖

The novel of ideas. The novel of manners. The novel of grim witness. The novel of pure dreaming. The novel of excess. The novel of unreadability. The comic novel. The romance novel. The epistolary novel. The promising first novel. The sad, patchwork, grave-robbing, over-my-dead-body posthumous novel. The suspense novel. The crime novel. The experimental novel. The historical novel. The novel of meticulous observations. The novel of marital revenge. The beach novel. The war novel. The antiwar novel. The postwar novel. The out-of-print novel. The novel that sells to the movies before it is written. The novel that critics like to say they want to throw across the room. The science fiction novel. The metafiction novel. The death of the novel. The novel that changes your life because you are young and open-hearted and eager to take an existential leap.
    —Don DeLillo

Realistic fiction leaves out far, far too much. How old is realistic fiction? How old is fantasy?
    —Gene Wolfe

INTRODUCTION
JAMES PATRICK KELLY
& JOHN KESSEL

IN 1998, THE *Village Voice* published an essay by Jonathan Lethem titled "Close Encounters: The Squandered Promise of Science Fiction" which begins with an alternative history in which Thomas Pynchon's *Gravity's Rainbow* was voted the 1973 Nebula Award by the Science Fiction Writers of America. In fact, though Pynchon's landmark work of postmodern fiction was indeed nominated for the Nebula that year, the award went to Arthur C. Clarke's *Rendezvous with Rama*. Lethem called this moment "a tombstone marking the death of the hope that science fiction was about to merge with the mainstream."

Lethem was not the first to regret the failed *rapprochement* of sf and what we will call mainstream fiction; similar comments have been made by writers from Harlan Ellison to Thomas Disch to Samuel Delany to Barry Malzberg to Carter Scholz (Scholz's 1984 essay "Inside the Ghetto, and Out" was quoted by Lethem in his *Voice* piece). Lethem's essay was reprinted in *The New York Review of Science Fiction* and aroused a number of responses from within the sf field, notably a well considered piece by Ray Davis in that same magazine. Davis pointed out a number of ways that Lethem was rhetorically unfair to the sf genre and its writers.[1]

Lethem was writing in the late 1990s, after two decades of hugely successful films by Spielberg and Lucas and Cameron had cemented the genre's association in the popular mind with explosions, special effects, aliens, and adventure stories. He was writing about a moment in sf's history, however, in the early 1970s, at the end of a decade of writers attempting to claim for sf the mantle

---

1 Readers interested in the details of these arguments would do well to check them out: WWW. VERYSILLY.ORG/LETHEM/LETHEMS _ VISION.HTML and Davis's response at WWW.PSEUDOPODIUM. ORG/KOKONINO/JLVLS.HTML. An email exchange between Davis and Lethem, also reprinted in the *NYRSF* is available at WWW.PSEUDOPODIUM.ORG/REPRESS/SHORTS/DAVIS _ AND _ LETHEM- MISTAKES _ WERE _ MADE.HTML.

of art, for whom the benchmark sf films were Stanley Kubrick's most recent efforts, *Dr. Strangelove, 2001: A Space Odyssey*, and *A Clockwork Orange*. In 1973 it seemed possible that sf might be understood as a form of fiction that could be written by adults, for adults.

We understand why some might say that, after the mid-1970s, sf went back to the playroom, never to be taken seriously again. But they do a vast disservice to the writers and readers of the next thirty years. What we hope to present in this anthology is an alternative vision of sf from the early 1970s to the present, one in which it becomes evident that the literary potential of sf was not squandered. We offer evidence that the developments of the 1960s and early '70s have been carried forth, if mostly outside of the public eye. For years they have been overshadowed by popular media sf and best-selling books that cater to the media audience. And at the same time that, on one side of the genre divide, sf was being written at the highest levels of ambition, on the other side, writers came to use the materials of sf for their own purposes, writing fiction that is clearly science fiction, but not identified by that name.

This is the secret history of science fiction.

The Less Secret History

At a lecture in 1970, one of the editors of this volume heard noted sf writer Theodore Sturgeon compare the history of science fiction to the handle of a suitcase. Like the handle of a suitcase, Sturgeon said, sf had emerged from the body of literature in general, and like the handle, would eventually merge back into it.

The term "science fiction" did not exist until the 1930s. It arose out of the pulp magazines. The first successful all-sf pulp was Hugo Gernsback's *Amazing Stories*, begun in 1926. But sf existed as a widely published form of fiction before Gernsback, much of it written by writers of stature. In fact, in its early years, *Amazing* reprinted all of H. G. Wells's scientific romances, Jules Verne's extraordinary voyages, as well as many stories by Poe. Brian Aldiss identifies the first sf novel as Mary Shelley's *Frankenstein*. H. Bruce Franklin has made a convincing case that every major American fiction writer of the nineteenth century, from Hawthorne through Melville to Twain, wrote stories that we would today call science fiction.

Gernsback's consolidation of sf into a pulp genre created a new culture and ad hoc critical standards for sf. Before then, each writer had to invent the genre for himself. After Gernsback, and especially after John W. Campbell and the rise of a critical fan community, arguments about the definitions of sf, what constituted good and bad sf, plausibility, techniques, specialty publishers, conventions, and call-and-response threads of stories all became hallmarks of the genre. When Mark Twain sat down to write his time travel novel, *A Connecticut Yankee in King Arthur's Court*, he did not have to reckon with the history of such stories. By 1955, within the sf magazines, such a story would have to pass muster with an active community of demanding editors, such as Campbell, H. L. Gold, or Anthony Boucher, astute critics like James Blish and Damon Knight, and fanatical readers who would have read pretty much every time travel yarn ever written. Over a forty-year period a sense of the sf genre developed. Davis suggests this community can be defined by "loose overlapping bundles of marketing techniques (including bookstore placement and publishing imprints), critical communities (including journalistic and awards systems) and interwriterly influence (including career path options and the impetus of 'I can go that one better' challenges)." All of this ghetto culture arose and solidified outside of mainstream canons and notice.

It also led to inbreeding. John Clute has described "hard" science fiction as "an idiom which treats the world as a problem to be solved, for gain." Now it is true that even during the height of the so-called "Golden Age" of the pulps there was sf that was not Campbellian (which treated the world, for instance, as a site for escapist adventure), but the canons of what constituted "good" sf were dominated, within the ghetto, by such formulations as rigorous extrapolation, scientific accuracy, plain-spoken prose, reliable narrators, clear-cut villains and heroes, definite conclusions, a positive attitude toward the future, and a belief in the rationality of the universe.

Even in the '40s and '50s, adherence to this consensus was far from universal. In the 1960s came New Wave science fiction, first in the U.K. and later in the U.S., written by a new generation of writers who brought the methods and materials of literary modernism to sf (John Brunner adapted Dos Passos, Brian Aldiss was influenced by Joyce). Members of this generation were as likely to have been English majors as engineers. The first scholarly journals, *Extrapolation* and *Science Fiction Studies*, began. Damon Knight founded the Milford and Clarion workshops and the Science Fiction Writers of America, which at least at its beginning was interested as much in improving the quality of written sf as in representing sf writers as a trade organization.

So by the early 1970s, *Gravity's Rainbow* could, in the light of the New Wave, be seen as science fiction (it is fiction in which science — ballistics, statistics — and technology — the V2 rocket — play important roles), even if it is not extrapolative future fiction, and does not provide an adventure story, an admirable hero, or a clear-cut resolution. By the standards built up within the pulp tradition, it doesn't look much like sf, but by 1970 those standards were being challenged, if not yet overthrown, within the sf ghetto.

DISTINCTIONS WITHOUT A DIFFERENCE?

Lethem's polemical alternative vision of the Science Fiction Writers of America embracing *Gravity's Rainbow* while kicking *Rendezvous with Rama* to the curb is farfetched but at least possible. However he goes on to imagine an aftermath which serves up hyperbole as breathtaking as that in Swift's "A Modest Proposal." By making common cause with Pynchon and later with Don DeLillo, who published *Ratner's Star* in 1976, science fiction might have begun the process of decertifying itself as a genre. As Lethem puts it, "the notion of science fiction ought to have been gently and lovingly dismantled, and the writers dispersed." As it turned out, there was no consensus on either side — mainstream or science fiction — for ending the Cold War between the genres. Pynchon's hypothetical Nebula would have been an anomaly, not a turning point. In the light of the overwhelming influence of *Star Trek*, of *Star Wars,* and of *E.T.*, it is hard to see how Lethem's vision might have come to pass.

In the years since, however, a vocal minority in science fiction has continued to advocate for writing and reading across the divide. They include some of the genre's strongest writers, whose work has garnered recognition all out of proportion to their numbers. Those who have succeeded in finding a wider readership — or worse, crossing over to *publication* in the mainstream — are viewed in some quarters with suspicion. Conservative fans of the genre regard them as a kind of literary carpetbagger, their work as a betrayal of sacred traditions. Call them the literary wing of science fiction, or as the critic and writer Orson Scott Card had it — punning on the term *sci-fi* — "li-fi writers."

At the same time, writers who have come to prominence in the mainstream have regularly ventured into what has been considered genre territory. Their work has often been greeted with bemusement or, on occasion, hostility. Certain mainstream critics, smug in their assumptions of what science fiction must be, have twisted themselves into knots to avoid endorsing the genre enterprise.

For instance, in a generally favorable 1981 *New York Times* review of Doris Lessing's *Canopus in Argos* series, Robert Alter recapitulates a plot involving galactic empires and then wonders, "Is all this, strictly speaking, science fiction?" Eventually, he decides it must be something completely different:

> Let me suggest that the genre to which this kind of writing most directly belongs is what Northrop Frye has called the "anatomy" — a kind of fiction, as Frye notes, that is "a combination of fantasy and morality" and that "presents us with a vision of the world in terms of a single intellectual pattern." The most familiar instance of the anatomy for English readers, and one particularly apposite to Doris Lessing's project, is *Gulliver's Travels*. The fantastic assumptions of Swift's narrative are an elaborate game of perspectives, exploited, quite obviously but also quite brilliantly, to magnify and expose the pettiness, the savagery, the silliness, the brutality of our supposedly civilized lives.

It is hard to read such a passage without concluding it is an example of either ignorance or bad faith. Anyone with more than a passing knowledge of science fiction can cite innumerable works that share literary DNA with *Gulliver's Travels*, using the perspective of extrapolated futures to examine our supposedly civilized lives. One might as well attempt to separate science fiction writers from non-science fiction writers by how often their work has appeared in *The New Yorker*.[2]

What all such attempts to evade the term "science fiction" share is the desire to separate the mainstream from the history of sf in the pulps. And it is undeniable that over the last forty years, increasing numbers of writers who have no career connections to the sf culture, and no knowledge of or connection to genre sf standards, have written fiction that, by the looser definition of the New Wave, or of the pre-Gernsbackian world before there was "science fiction," fits some definition of the term.

At short lengths this is a little less evident than at longer ones. Such novels as *Fiskadoro*, *The Birth of the People's Republic of Antarctica*, *Ratner's Star*,

---

2 Which, of course, has been done. By this standard the mainstream fiction writers in this anthology are DeLillo, Millhauser, Chabon, Boyle, Lethem, Le Guin, Atwood, and Saunders,

The Handmaid's Tale, Galatea 2.2, The Brief History of the Dead, Oryx and Crake, The Sparrow, Riddley Walker, The Road, The Yiddish Policemen's Union, Slaughterhouse 5, Galapagos, Shikasta, Never Let Me Go, Cloud Atlas, and a dozen others, all recognizably use materials or conventions commonly associated with science fiction.

Because these writers are in many cases blissfully ignorant of sf culture, or their publishers allergic to the label, and for better or worse (and there are disadvantages as well as advantages) free of its constraints, their science fiction sometimes resembles slipstream[3] or magic realism or surrealism or metafiction more than it does sf.

ON THE USELESSNESS OF THE TERM GENRE

But it seems to us that the divide between the mainstream and science fiction is more apparent than real. At its foundation is the problem of defining a genre, any genre. The word means too much, and many of its meanings are at odds with one another. When some use it as a term of commerce, others hear it as a term of art. Is it defined by form, style, or subject matter? Or perhaps by all three? Is it the vision in the mind of the writer as his fingers curl over the keyboard, a specific page in a publisher's spring catalog, or the expectation of the reader as she reads the first sentence of a new story? If science fiction is a genre, is not the mainstream also a genre, if only as defined by its negatives? Might it not be said that mainstream is that genre which does not feature aliens, vampires, cowboys, detectives, or romantic heroines? Unless it does.

The problem of defining science fiction is one which its community of readers and writers has struggled with for the last fifty years. There is a website — there is always a website — which lists fifty different definitions of the genre as proposed by some of its most accomplished writers and astute critics. None are completely

all of whom have appeared in *The New Yorker* more than once. The sf writers are Gloss, Scholz, Wilhelm, McHugh, Disch, Shepard, Willis, Fowler, Kelly, and Kessel, none of whom have ever been published there.

And then there's Gene Wolfe. As far as we can tell, Wolfe, aside from Ursula Le Guin, the most prolific and respected of the "genre" writers represented here, has had one story ("On the Train," 1983) appear in *The New Yorker*.

3 See *Feeling Very Strange: The Slipstream Anthology*, eds. James Patrick Kelly and John Kessel.

satisfactory. In fact, one of the best minds science fiction has ever produced, Damon Knight, famously threw up his hands in resignation over the project and wrote, "Science fiction is what we point to when we say it." This is particularly appropriate given science fiction's current state. The territory of the genre has grown as its borders with neighboring genres — including the mainstream — have become more permeable. It is large and contains such multitudes as would have truly astounded those writers who wrote for *Astounding* back in the '40s and '50s. If those who struggle within its perceived but ineffable constraints can't agree on what it means, then how is it that those who know it only by reputation write with certainty about what it can and cannot accomplish?

In the same way, it is difficult to imagine how one might define the sprawl that is the mainstream genre. And who would dare to draw a boundary line between its two principle subgenres, the literary and the popular novel? It strikes us that we would all be better served to invoke the Knight exception and rely on ad hoc definitions of the mainstream, rather than build elaborate critical structures on the shifting sands of the publishing industry.

For those who resist the notion that the mainstream is a genre, we recommend that they browse the shelves of their local bookstore. For if the mainstream is not a genre, then it must necessarily embrace all kinds of writing: romance, adventure, horror, thriller, crime, and, yes, science fiction.

WHAT WE POINT TO WHEN WE SAY SCIENCE FICTION

The title of this book says "science fiction." So, given our uneasiness about the strictures of genre, in what ways are the stories in this book science fiction?

One standard that has been frequently used to separate mainstream fiction from science fiction is to point to the degree to which the story in question is invested in the examination of individual characters. Wells asserted that "To show how peculiar things struck peculiar people is one peculiarity too many" in order to argue that sf is not fundamentally about character. Many a mainstream critic has agreed with him, with the assumption that "peculiar" (in the sense of individual, unique) character is the center of all literature, and that therefore science fiction is not literature.

But Wells's assertion was never universally true, even about his own fiction. In the last forty years much science fiction has turned to the exploration of character. In this anthology you will find many stories that spend as much time on the people as they do on the premise, that use the sf background as a means to explore human beings who are as individual as any in realistic fiction. Gene Wolfe's "The Ziggurat" turns the intrusion of female time travelers from the future into a psychological study of a lone-wolf male, his troubles with women, issues of masculinity, violence, self-doubt, and self-definition. In this nest of uncertainties, what is really happening? Millhauser, Kelly, Fowler, Willis, McHugh, and Disch's stories are not so much about technology or the future as about the people whose lives are caught up in the anxieties arising from a fantastic premise, and attempts to cope with their existential situations.

The flip side of assertions about science fiction's disregard of character is the assertion that sf is idea fiction. And this is true, for much sf. Here, again, there has been a merging, this time with the mainstream moving toward the genre. In the last thirty years postmodern fiction has challenged the centrality of characterization to literature. A postmodernist doesn't care about characters; William Gass in *Fiction and the Figures of Life* says characters are just black marks on paper. What is important is the game, the satirical effect, the philosophical speculation, the disruption of expectations, the beauty of the result.

So T. C. Boyle's "Descent of Man" plays absurd games with Jane Goodall's studies of primates, and George Saunders' "93990" adopts the dispassion of a scientific report to make a telling point about the inhumanity of human beings. Don DeLillo uses a space station and World War III as setting, but not subject, creating an almost love story out of the language of technology. The stories by Le Guin, Lethem, Scholz, Kessel, and Atwood likewise are not predicated on exploration of character, but instead use sf to explore ideas, make social comments, or play games.

Other modes of writing sf:

The use of the sf premise as a metaphor. In Pynchon's novel, "gravity's rainbow" is the parabola described by a V2 rocket as it is launched in Germany and arcs through the atmosphere to London. This parabolic quality is often present in sf, even in Golden Age sf — but it is increasingly evident in literary sf. Le Guin's "The Ones Who Walk Away from Omelas" uses the sf background to tell a political parable. Connie Willis's "Schwarzschild Radius" uses the physics of black holes as a metaphor for the isolation of men trapped in war, drawn inexorably toward their deaths. Jonathan Lethem's "The Hardened Criminals" literalizes the title's cliché to create a background for the exploration of a son's relationship to his father.

Metafictional games: Carter Scholz's "The Nine Billion Names of God" borrows Arthur C. Clarke's most famous story to mock the possibility of stable linguistic meaning. Michael Chabon's "The Martian Agent, A Planetary Romance" playfully looks over its shoulder at pulp icons, using them self-consciously for his own purposes.

Realism of the future: "Angouleme" by Thomas Disch and "Ladies and Gentlemen, This Is Your Crisis" by Kate Wilhelm give us everyday life in the near future. "Interlocking Pieces" by Molly Gloss brings humanist concerns to biomedical future brain transplant; similarly, McHugh's "Frankenstein's Daughter" shows us a family in the aftermath of a cloning attempt gone wrong.

Social comment: Margaret Atwood's "Homelanding" uses the concept of aliens as access to feminist truths.

The past and the present: "Standing Room Only" is a time travel story turned inside out. Like so much contemporary sf and near-sf, it shows interest in the nineteenth century as an origin and mirror of contemporary society. Likewise, "The Wizard of West Orange" uses an imaginary invention of Edison's laboratory to reveal insights about human character.

SCIENCE FICTION WITHOUT THE FUTURE

You may note something missing from most of these stories, something that has become so associated with science fiction that its absence may seem to disqualify these stories as sf: the future. The future, if it appears in these stories at all, is parsimoniously doled out. "Salvador," published in 1986, at the height of the U.S. involvement in proxy wars in El Salvador and Nicaragua, was set about twenty minutes into the future. Many of these stories take place in what is essentially the present, with the addition of some small technological or social change. Others are set in the past, into which the future may intrude only as time travelers arrive. Still others are speculative only in so far as they propose an alternative history (alternative history has, for reasons that are as much matters of association as of literary theory, been accepted by most readers and publishers as a form of sf, from the time of Philip K. Dick's *The Man in the High Castle* or Ward Moore's *Bring the Jubilee*.)

But pre-pulp science fiction was often set in the present. Shelley's *Frankenstein*, the sf stories of Poe, virtually all of Jules Verne, and even most of Wells are more often than not set in the present day of the author, and involve the intrusion of some fantastic event, justified by technology or science — Captain Nemo's *Nautilus*, Wells's Martian invaders — into the mundane world. It is only in the pulp magazines that the future becomes the preferred home of sf. The public image of sf arises from that future — the *Star Wars* films make a fetish of resuscitating the imagery of '30s pulp magazines — robots, aliens, and above all space travel. Oddly, as this image of sf has come to dominate media popular culture, written sf has moved closer and closer to the present.

The loss of the future as home ground for sf has bothered some writers, readers, and critics who embrace sf culture.[4] It seems to us that one of the consequences of the *rapprochement* between sf and the literary mainstream is this move to set stories in the present, and to reduce the extrapolative element in favor of experimental structure or emphasis on characterization.

Traditional sf is today broken into pieces, just as it was stitched together from pieces by Gernsback, Campbell, and the pulps. They attempted to fuse disparate reactions to the advent of the industrial age and the assaults of the scientific revolution on religion, society, and the place of humanity in the universe, along with the wild adventure and gothic romance of popular fiction, into a single genre. Are any novels more different than Shelley's *Frankenstein*, Poe's *The Narrative of Arthur Gordon Pym*, Verne's *20,000 Leagues Under the Sea*, and Wells's *When the Sleeper Wakes*? For a time, in the darkness of neglect (benign or otherwise) by Literature with the capital "L", and by some procrustean trimming, the pulp magazines seemed to turn science fiction into a single thing. But if "genre" sf ever had a consistent core, a commitment solely to the future, that time has long passed.

WHY ARE WE HERE?

Which brings us back to Jonathan Lethem's essay.

Clearly we are in sympathy with the sentiment behind Lethem's essay. In a clarification following its original publication in the *Village Voice*, he revealed that the editors had, without his knowledge, changed his title from "Why Can't We All Just Live Together?: A Vision of Genre Paradise Lost" to "Close Encounters:

---

4 See "Science Fiction without the Future" by Judith Berman (WWW.JUDITHBERMAN.NET/SF-FUTURE.HTML). Berman, an anthropologist who began publishing sf in the 1990s, noted with some alarm how little of the contents of the leading sf magazines is set in the future, or takes conceptual risks. She has not been the only person to worry about this.

The Squandered Promise of Science Fiction." Instead of being taken as an invitation to tear down walls, as he intended, it was read by many as an indictment of a close-minded genre for failing to acknowledge a work of genius erected on its territory. This impression was reinforced by Lethem's own suspect status in science fiction: although well-published in the genre, he was also finding acceptance in the mainstream. Thus he was perceived as one of the "li-fi" crowd, probably someone who would turn his back on the genre as soon as he got the chance. Nothing of the sort has happened. Indeed, Lethem's career is instructive with regards to the obstacles that remain to getting a fair reading on either side of the divide. A year after he wrote his essay, he won the National Book Critics Circle Award for his novel *Motherless Brooklyn* and in 2003 published *The Fortress of Solitude*, which became a *New York Times* bestseller. And yet, he reports, that for many mainstream readers and reviewers, his work in genre is either invisible or irrelevant.

While many minds still remain closed, the walls that separate the mainstream from science fiction are, in fact, crumbling. The bankruptcy of assertion that mainstream novels set in the future can't be science fiction because they're not written by science fiction writers arises out of a kind of tribalism that does not bear close scrutiny. And it is past time to ignore the likewise tribal howls of genre conservatives who demand that mainstream writers are dilettantes who need to take Remedial Science Fiction 101 before they venture in genre territory. In 2005, three of the twenty stories in *The Best American Short Stories* were by writers primarily known for their science fiction. And in 2008, a writer with impeccable mainstream credentials, Michael Chabon, did win the Science Fiction and Fantasy Writers of America's Nebula Award for *The Yiddish Policemen's Union*.

But these are only the latest developments in what we have decided to call *The Secret History of Science Fiction*. For while the vested interests that resisted rapprochement held sway these many years, there were always those who refused to be constrained either by the strictures of the mainstream genre or of that of science fiction. These writers wrote the stories that came to them in the only way they could; where they were published was, to a large extent, an accident of the times they were conceived in. We offer this collection as proof that their history need be secret no longer.

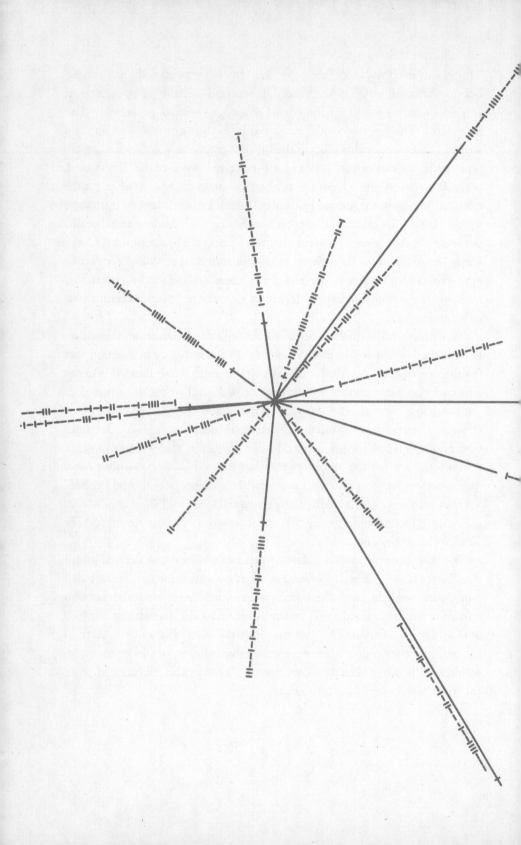

I have a class theory of literature. I come from the wrong neighborhood to sell to *The New Yorker*. No matter how good I am as an artist, they always can smell where I come from. I guess the only one of all of us who ever found her way into *The New Yorker* was Ursula Le Guin, and even then she was like a visiting alien.
—Thomas M. Disch

It's less true of other art forms, but for some reason with writers in particular we want to know where to stick them, where to *shelve* them. There's a general tendency in the world to force people to assume positions that are much more rigid than what comes naturally to them. Once you make what you think is a choice that's going to empower you in some way, often it turns out somewhere down the line that it turned into a trap; you were actually closing out a lot of options to yourself without realizing it.
—Michael Chabon

Angouleme
Thomas M. Disch

THERE WERE SEVEN Alexandrians involved in the Battery plot — Jack, who was the youngest and from the Bronx, Celeste DiCecca, Sniffles and MaryJane, Tancred Miller, Amparo (of course), and *of course,* the leader and mastermind, Bill Harper, better known as Little Mister Kissy Lips. Who was passionately, hopelessly in love with Amparo. Who was nearly thirteen (she would be, fully, by September this year), and breasts just beginning. Very very beautiful skin, like lucite. Amparo Martinez.

Their first, nothing operation was in the East 60's, a broker or something like that. All they netted was cufflinks, a watch, a leather satchel that wasn't leather after all, some buttons, and the usual lot of useless credit cards. He stayed calm through the whole thing, even with Sniffles slicing off buttons, and *soothing.* None of them had the nerve to ask, though they all wondered, how often he'd been through this scene before. What they were about wasn't an innovation. It was partly that, the need to innovate, that led them to think up the plot. The only really memorable part of the holdup was the name laminated on the cards, which was, weirdly enough, Lowen, Richard W. An omen (the connection being that they were all at the Alexander Lowen School), but of what?

Little Mister Kissy Lips kept the cufflinks for himself, gave the buttons to Amparo (who gave them to her uncle), and donated the rest (the watch was a piece of crap) to the Conservation booth outside the Plaza right where he lived.

His father was a teevee executive. In, as he would quip, both senses. They had got married young, his mama and papa, and divorced soon after but not before he'd come to fill out their quota. Papa, the executive, remarried, a man this time and somewhat more happily. Anyhow it lasted long enough that the offspring, the leader and mastermind, had to learn to adjust to the situation, it being permanent. Mama simply went down to the Everglades and disappeared, sploosh.

In short, he was well-to-do. Which is how, more than by overwhelming talent, he got into the Lowen School in the first place. He had the right kind of body though, so with half a desire there was no reason in the city of New York he couldn't grow up to be a professional dancer, even a choreographer. He'd have the connections for it, as Papa was fond of pointing out.

For the time being, however, his bent was literary and religious rather than balletic. He loved, and what seventh grader doesn't, the abstracter foxtrots and more metaphysical twists of a Dostoevsky, a Gide, a Mailer. He longed for the experience of some vivider pain than the mere daily hollowness knotted into his tight young belly, and no weekly stomp-and-holler of group therapy with other jejune eleven-year-olds was going to get him his stripes in the major leagues of suffering, crime, and resurrection. Only a bona fide crime would do that, and of all the crimes available murder certainly carried the most prestige, as no less an authority than Loretta Couplard was ready to attest, Loretta Couplard being not only the director and co-owner of the Lowen School but the author, as well, of two nationally televised scripts, both about famous murders of the 20th Century. They'd even done a unit in social studies on the topic: A History of Crime in Urban America.

The first of Loretta's murders was a comedy involving Pauline Campbell, R.N., of Ann Arbor, Michigan, circa 1951, whose skull had been smashed by three drunken teenagers. They had meant to knock her unconscious so they could screw her, which was 1951 in a nutshell. The eighteen-year-olds, Bill Morey and Max Pell, got life; Dave Royal (Loretta's hero) was a year younger and got off with twenty-two years.

Her second murder was tragic in tone and consequently inspired more respect, though not among the critics, unfortunately. Possibly because her heroine, also a Pauline (Pauline Wichura), though more interesting and complicated, had also been more famous in her own day and ever since. Which made the competition, one bestselling novel and a serious film biography, considerably stiffer. Miss Wichura had been a welfare worker in Atlanta, Georgia, very much into environment and the population problem, this being the immediate pre-Regents period when anyone and everyone was legitimately starting to fret. Pauline decided to do something, *viz.,* reduce the population herself and in the fairest way possible. So whenever any of the families she visited produced one child above the three she'd fixed, rather generously, as the upward limit, she found some unobtrusive way of thinning that family back to the preferred maximal size. Between 1989 and 1993 Pauline's journals (Random House, 1994) record twenty-six murders, plus an additional fourteen failed attempts. In addition she had the highest welfare department record in the U.S. for abortions and sterilizations among the families whom she advised.

"Which proves, I think," Little Mister Kissy Lips had explained one day after school to his friend Jack, "that a murder doesn't have to be of someone *famous* to be a form of idealism."

But of course idealism was only half the story: the other half was curiosity. And beyond idealism *and* curiosity there was probably even another half, the basic childhood need to grow up and kill someone.

They settled on the Battery because, one, none of them ever were there ordinarily; two, it was posh and at the same time relatively, three, uncrowded, at least once the night shift were snug in their towers tending their machines. The night shift seldom ate their lunches down in the park.

And, four, because it was beautiful, especially now at the beginning of summer. The dark water, chromed with oil, flopping against the buttressed shore; the silences blowing in off the Upper Bay, silences large enough sometimes that you could sort out the different noises of the city behind them, the purr and quaver of the skyscrapers, the ground-shivering *mysterioso* of the expressways, and every now and then the strange sourceless screams that are the melody of New York's theme song; the blue-pink of sunsets in a visible sky; the people's faces, calmed by the sea and their own nearness to death, lined up in rhythmic rows on the green benches. Why, even the statues looked beautiful here, as though someone had believed in them once, the way people must have believed in the statues in the Cloisters, so long ago.

His favorite was the gigantic killer-eagle landing in the middle of the monoliths in the memorial for the soldiers, sailors, and airmen killed in World War II. The largest eagle, probably, in all Manhattan. His talons ripped apart what was *surely* the largest artichoke.

Amparo, who went along with some of Miss Couplard's ideas, preferred the more humanistic qualities of the memorial (him on top and an angel gently probing an enormous book with her sword) for Verrazzano, who was not, as it turned out, the contractor who put up the bridge that had, so famously, collapsed. Instead, as the bronze plate in back proclaimed:

IN APRIL 1524
THE FLORENTINE-BORN NAVIGATOR
VERRAZZANO
LED THE FRENCH CARAVEL LA DAUPHINE
TO THE DISCOVERY OF
THE HARBOR OF NEW YORK
AND NAMED THESE SHORES ANGOULEME
IN HONOR OF FRANCIS I KING OF FRANCE

"Angouleme" they all agreed, except Tancred, who favored the more prevalent and briefer name, was much classier. Tancred was ruled out of order and the decision became unanimous.

It was there, by the statue, looking across the bay of Angouleme to Jersey, that they took the oath that bound them to perpetual secrecy. Whoever spoke of what they were about to do, unless he were being tortured by the Police, solemnly called upon his co-conspirators to insure his silence by other means. Death. All revolutionary organizations take similar precautions, as the history unit on Modern Revolutions had made clear.

How he got the name: it had been Papa's theory that what modern life cried out for was a sweetening of old-fashioned sentimentality. Ergo, among all the other indignities this theory gave rise to, scenes like the following: "Who's my Little Mister Kissy Lips!" Papa would bawl out, sweetly, right in the middle of Rockefeller Center (or a restaurant, or in front of the school), and he'd shout right back, "I am!" At least until he knew better.

Mama had been, variously, "Rosebud," "Peg O' My Heart," and (this only at the end) "The Snow Queen." Mama, being adult, had been able to vanish with no other trace than the postcard that still came every Xmas postmarked from Key Largo, but Little Mister Kissy Lips was stuck with the New Sentimentality willy-nilly. True, by age seven he'd been able to insist on being called "Bill" around the house (or, as Papa would have it, "Just Plain Bill"). But that left the staff at the Plaza to contend with, and Papa's assistants, schoolmates, anyone who'd ever heard the name. Then a year ago, aged ten and able to reason, he laid down the new law — that his name *was* Little Mister Kissy Lips, the whole awful mouthful, each and every time. His reasoning being that if anyone would be getting his face rubbed in shit by this it would be Papa, who deserved it. Papa didn't seem to get the point, or else he got it and another point besides, you could never be sure how stupid or how subtle he really was, which is the worst kind of enemy.

Meanwhile at the nationwide level the New Sentimentality had been a rather overwhelming smash. *The Orphans*, which Papa produced and sometimes was credited with writing, pulled down the top Thursday evening ratings for two years. Now it was being overhauled for a daytime slot. For one hour every day our lives were going to be a lot sweeter, and chances were Papa would be a millionaire or more as a result. On the sunny side, this meant that *he'd* be the son of a millionaire. Though he generally had contempt for the way money corrupted everything it touched, he had to admit that in certain cases it didn't have to be a bad thing. It boiled down to this (which he'd always known): that Papa was a necessary evil.

This was why every evening when Papa buzzed himself into the suite he'd shout out, "Where's my Little Mister Kissy Lips," and he'd reply, "Here, Papa!" The cherry on this sundae of love was a big wet kiss, and then one more for their new "Rosebud," Jimmy Ness. (Who drank, and was not in all likelihood going to last much longer.) They'd all three sit down to the nice *family* dinner Jimmyness had cooked, and Papa would tell them about the cheerful, positive things that had happened that day at CBS, and Little Mister Kissy Lips would tell all about the bright fine things that had happened to *him*. Jimmy would sulk. Then Papa and Jimmy would go somewhere or just disappear into the private Everglades of sex, and Little Mister Kissy Lips would buzz himself out into the corridor (Papa knew better than to be repressive about hours), and within half an hour he'd be at the Verrazzano statue with the six other Alexandrians, five if Celeste had a lesson, to plot the murder of the victim they'd all finally agreed on.

No one had been able to find out his name. They called him Alyona Ivanovna, after the old pawnbroker woman that Raskolnikov kills with an ax.

The spectrum of possible victims had never been wide. The common financial types of the area would be carrying credit cards like Lowen, Richard W., while the generality of pensioners filling the benches were even less tempting. As Miss Couplard had explained, our economy was being refeudalized and cash was going the way of the ostrich, the octopus, and the moccasin flower.

It was such extinctions as these, but especially seagulls, that were the worry of the first lady they'd considered, a Miss Kraus, unless the name at the bottom of her hand-lettered poster (STOP THE SLAUGHTER of The *Innocents!!* etc.) belonged to someone else. Why, if she were Miss Kraus, was she wearing what seemed to be the old-fashioned diamond ring and gold band of a Mrs.? But the more crucial problem, which they couldn't see how to solve, was: Was the diamond real?

Possibility Number Two was in the tradition of the original *Orphans of the Storm*, the Gish sisters. A lovely semiprofessional who whiled away the daylight pretending to be blind and serenading the benches. Her pathos was rich, if a bit worked-up; her repertoire was archaeological; and her gross was fair, especially when the rain added its own bit of too-much. However: Sniffles (who'd done this research) was certain she had a gun tucked away under the rags.

Three was the least poetic possibility, just the concessionaire in back of the giant eagle selling Fun and Synthamon. His appeal was commercial. But he had a licensed Weimaraner, and though Weimaraners can be dealt with, Amparo liked them.

"You're just a Romantic," Little Mister Kissy Lips said. "Give me one good reason."

"His eyes," she said. "They're amber. He'd haunt us."

They were snuggling together in one of the deep embrasures cut into the stone of Castle Clinton, her head wedged into his armpit, his fingers gliding across the lotion on her breasts (summer was just beginning). Silence, warm breezes, sunlight on water, it was all ineffable, as though only the sheerest of veils intruded between them and an understanding of something (all this) really meaningful. Because they thought it was their own innocence that was to blame, like a smog in their souls' atmosphere, they wanted more than ever to be rid of it at times, like this, when they approached so close.

"Why not the dirty old man, then?" she asked, meaning Alyona.

"Because he *is* a dirty old man."

"That's no reason. He must take in at least as much money as that singer."

"That's not what I mean." What he meant wasn't easy to define. It wasn't as though he'd be too easy to kill. If you'd seen him in the first minutes of a program, you'd know he was marked for destruction by the second commercial. He was the defiant homesteader, the crusty senior member of a research team who understood Algol and Fortran but couldn't read the secrets of his own heart. He was the Senator from South Carolina with his own peculiar brand of integrity but a racist nevertheless. Killing that sort was too much like one of

Papa's scripts to be a satisfying gesture of rebellion.

But what he said, mistaking his own deeper meaning, was: "It's because he deserves it, because we'd be doing society a favor. Don't ask me to give *reasons*."

"Well, I won't pretend I understand that, but do you know what I think, Little Mister Kissy Lips?" She pushed his hand away.

"You think I'm scared."

"Maybe you *should* be scared."

"'Maybe you should shut up and leave this to me. I said we're going to do it. We'll do it."

"To him then?"

"Okay. But for gosh sakes, Amparo, we've got to think of something to call the bastard besides 'the dirty old man'!"

She rolled over out of his armpit and kissed him. They glittered all over with little beads of sweat. The summer began to shimmer with the excitement of first night. They had been waiting so long and now the curtain was rising.

M-Day was scheduled for the first weekend in July, a patriotic holiday. The computers would have time to tend to their own needs (which have been variously described as "confession," "dreaming," and "throwing up"), and the Battery would be as empty as it ever gets.

Meanwhile their problem was the same as any kids face anywhere during summer vacation, how to fill the time.

There were books, there were the Shakespeare puppets if you were willing to queue up for that long, there was always teevee, and when you couldn't stand sitting any longer there were the obstacle courses in Central Park, but the density there was at lemming level. The Battery, because it didn't try to meet anyone's needs, seldom got so overpopulated. If there had been more Alexandrians and all willing to fight for the space, they might have played ball. Well, another summer....

What else? There were marches for the political, and religions at various energy levels for the apolitical. There would have been dancing, but the Lowen School had spoiled them for most amateur events around the city.

As for the supreme pastime of sex, for all of them except Little Mister Kissy Lips and Amparo (and even for them, when it came right down to orgasm) this was still something that happened on a screen, a wonderful hypothesis that lacked empirical proof.

One way or another it was all consumership, everything they might have done, and they were tired, who isn't, of being passive. They were twelve years old, or eleven, or ten, and they couldn't wait any longer. For what? they wanted to know.

So, except when they were just loafing around solo, all these putative resources, the books, the puppets, the sports, arts, politics, and religions, were in the same category of usefulness as merit badges or weekends in Calcutta, which is a name you can still find on a few old maps of India. Their lives were not enhanced, and their summer passed as summers have passed immemorially. They slumped and moped and lounged about and teased each other and complained. They acted out desultory, shy fantasies and had long pointless arguments about the more peripheral facts of existence — the habits of jungle animals or how bricks had been made or the history of World War II.

One day they added up all the names on the monoliths set up for the soldiers, sailors, and airmen. The final figure they got was 4,800.

"Wow," said Tancred.

"But that can't be *all* of them," MaryJane insisted, speaking for the rest. Even that "wow" had sounded half ironic.

"Why not?" asked Tancred, who could never resist disagreeing. "They came from every different state and every branch of the service. It has to be complete or the people who had relatives left off would have protested."

"But so *few?* It wouldn't be possible to have fought more than one battle at that rate."

"Maybe..." Sniffles began quietly. But he was seldom listened to.

"Wars were different then," Tancred explained with the authority of a prime-time news analyst. "In those days more people were killed by their own automobiles than in wars. It's a fact."

"Four thousand, eight *hundred?*"

"...a lottery?"

Celeste waved away everything Sniffles had said or would ever say. "MaryJane is right, Tancred. It's simply a *ludicrous* number. Why, in that same war the Germans gassed seven *million* Jews."

"Six million Jews," Little Mister Kissy Lips corrected. "But it's the same idea. Maybe the ones here got killed in a particular campaign."

"Then it would say so." Tancred was adamant, and he even got them to admit at last that 4,800 was an impressive figure, especially with every name spelled out in stone letters.

One other amazing statistic was commemorated in the park: over a thirty-three-year period Castle Clinton had processed 7.7 million immigrants into the United States.

Little Mister Kissy Lips sat down and figured out that it would take 12,800 stone slabs the size of the ones listing the soldiers, sailors, and airmen in order to write out all the immigrants' names, with country of origin, and an area of five square miles to set that many slabs up in, or all of Manhattan from here to 28th Street. But would it be worth the trouble, after all? Would it be that much different from the way things were already?

Alyona Ivanovna:

An archipelago of irregular brown islands was mapped on the tan sea of his bald head. The mainlands of his hair were marble outcroppings, especially his beard, white and crisp and coiling. The teeth were standard MODICUM issue; clothes, as clean as any fabric that old can be. Nor did he smell, particularly. And yet....

Had he bathed every morning you'd still have looked at him and thought he was filthy, the way floorboards in old brownstones seem to need cleaning moments after they've been scrubbed. The dirt had been bonded to the wrinkled flesh and the wrinkled clothes, and nothing less than surgery or burning would get it out.

His habits were as orderly as a polka dot napkin. He lived at a Chelsea dorm for the elderly, a discovery they owed to a rainstorm that had forced him to take the subway home one day instead of, as usual, walking. On the hottest nights he might sleep over in the park, nesting in one of the Castle windows. He bought his lunches from a Water Street specialty shop, *Dumas Fils:* cheeses, imported fruit, smoked fish, bottles of cream, food for the gods. Otherwise he did without, though his dorm must have supplied prosaic necessities like breakfast. It was a strange way for a panhandler to spend his quarters, drugs being the norm.

His professional approach was out-and-out aggression. For instance, his hand in your face and, "How about it, Jack?" Or, confidingly, "I need sixty cents to get home." It was amazing how often he scored, but actually it wasn't amazing. He had charisma.

And someone who relies on charisma *wouldn't* have a gun.

Agewise he might have been sixty, seventy, seventy-five, a bit more even, or much less. It all depended on the kind of life he'd led, and where. He had an accent none of them could identify. It was not English, not French, not Spanish, and probably not Russian.

Aside from his burrow in the Castle wall there were two distinct places he preferred. One, the wide-open stretch of pavement along the water. This was where he worked, walking up past the Castle and down as far as the concession stand. The passage of one of the great Navy cruisers, the USS *Dana* or the USS *Melville*, would bring him, and the whole Battery, to a standstill, as though a whole parade were going by, white, soundless, slow as a dream. It was a part of history, and even the Alexandrians were impressed, though three of them had taken the cruise down to Andros Island and back. Sometimes, though, he'd stand by the guardrail for long stretches of time without any real reason, just looking at the Jersey sky and the Jersey shore. After a while he might start talking to himself, the barest whisper but very much in earnest, to judge by the way his forehead wrinkled. They never once saw him sit on one of the benches.

The other place he liked was the aviary. On days when they'd been ignored he'd contribute peanuts or breadcrumbs to the cause of the birds' existence. There were pigeons, parrots, a family of robins, and a proletarian swarm of what the sign declared to be chickadees, though Celeste, who'd gone to the library to make sure, said they were nothing more than a rather swank breed of sparrow. Here too, naturally, the militant Miss Kraus stationed herself when she bore testimony. One of her peculiarities (and the reason, probably, she was never asked to move on) was that under no circumstances did she ever deign to argue. Even sympathizers pried no more out of her than a grim smile and a curt nod.

One Tuesday, a week before M-Day (it was the early A.M. and only three Alexandrians were on hand to witness this confrontation), Alyona so far put aside his own reticence as to try to start a conversation going with Miss Kraus.

He stood squarely in front of her and began by reading aloud, slowly, in that distressingly indefinite accent, from the text of STOP THE SLAUGHTER: "The Department of the Interior of the United States Government, under the secret direction of the Zionist Ford Foundation, is *systematically* poisoning the oceans of the World with so-called 'food farms.' Is this 'peaceful application of Nuclear Power'? Unquote, the *New York Times,* August 2, 2024. Or a new

Moondoggle!! *Nature World,* Jan. Can we afford to remain indifferent any longer? Every day 15,000 seagulls die as a direct result of Systematic Genocides while elected Officials falsify and distort the evidence. Learn the facts. Write to the Congressmen. *Make your voice heard!!"*

As Alyona had droned on, Miss Kraus turned a deeper and deeper red. Tightening her fingers about the turquoise broom-handle to which the placard was stapled, she began to jerk the poster up and down rapidly, as though this man with his foreign accent were some bird of prey who'd perched on it.

"Is that what you think?" he asked, having read all the way down to the signature despite her jiggling tactic. He touched his bushy white beard and wrinkled his face into a philosophical expression. "I'd *like* to know more about it, yes, I would. I'd be interested in hearing what *you* think."

Horror had frozen up every motion of her limbs. Her eyes blinked shut but she forced them open again.

"Maybe," he went on remorselessly, "we can discuss this whole thing. Some time when you feel more like talking. All right?"

She mustered her smile, and a minimal nod. He went away then. She was safe, temporarily, but even so she waited till he'd gone halfway to the other end of the sea-front promenade before she let the air collapse into her lungs. After a single deep breath the muscles of her hands thawed into trembling.

M-Day was an oil of summer, a catalog of everything painters are happiest painting — clouds, flags, leaves, sexy people, and in back of it all the flat empty baby-blue of the sky. Little Mister Kissy Lips was the first one there, and Tancred, in a kind of kimono (it hid the pilfered Luger), was the last. Celeste never came. (She'd just learned she'd been awarded the exchange scholarship to Sofia.) They decided they could do without Celeste, but the other nonappearance was more crucial. Their victim had neglected to be on hand for M-Day. Sniffles, whose voice was most like an adult's over the phone, was delegated to go to the Citibank lobby and call the West 16th Street dorm.

The nurse who answered was a temporary. Sniffles, always an inspired liar, insisted that his mother — "Mrs. *Anderson,* of course she lives there, Mrs. Alma F. Anderson" — had to be called to the phone. This was 248 West 16th, wasn't it? Where *was* she if she wasn't there? The nurse, flustered, explained that the residents, all who were fit, had been driven off to a July 4th picnic at Lake Hopatcong as guests of a giant Jersey retirement condominium. If he called bright and early tomorrow they'd be back and he could talk to his mother then.

So the initiation rites were postponed, it couldn't be helped. Amparo passed around some pills she'd taken from her mother's jar, a consolation prize. Jack left, apologizing that he was a borderline psychotic, which was the last that anyone saw of Jack till September. The gang was disintegrating, like a sugar cube soaking up saliva, then crumbling into the tongue. But what the hell — the sea still mirrored the same blue sky, the pigeons behind their wicket were no less iridescent, and trees grew for all of that.

They decided to be silly and made jokes about what the M *really* stood for in M-Day. Sniffles started off with "Miss Nomer, Miss Carriage, and Miss Steak." Tancred, whose sense of humor did not exist or was very private, couldn't do better than "Mnemone, mother of the Muses." Little Mister Kissy Lips said, "Merciful Heavens!" MaryJane maintained reasonably that M was for MaryJane. But Amparo said it stood for "Aplomb" and carried the day.

Then, proving that when you're sailing the wind always blows from behind you, they found Terry Riley's day-long *Orfeo* at 99.5 on the FM dial. They'd studied *Orfeo* in mime class, and by now it was part of their muscle and nerve. As Orpheus descended into a hell that mushroomed from the size of a pea to the size of a planet, the Alexandrians metamorphosed into as credible a tribe of souls in torment as any since the days of Jacopo Peri. Throughout the afternoon little audiences collected and dispersed to flood the sidewalk with libations of adult attention. Expressively they surpassed themselves, both one by one and all together, and though they couldn't have held out till the apotheosis (at 9:30) without a stiff psychochemical wind in their sails, what they had danced was authentic and very much their own. When they left the Battery that night they felt better than they'd felt all summer long. In a sense they had been exorcised.

But back at the Plaza Little Mister Kissy Lips couldn't sleep. No sooner was he through the locks than his guts knotted up into a Chinese puzzle. Only after he'd unlocked his window and crawled out onto the ledge did he get rid of the bad feelings. The city was real. His room was not. The stone ledge was real and his bare buttocks absorbed reality from it. He watched slow movements in enormous distances and pulled his thoughts together.

He knew without having to talk to the rest that the murder would never take place. The idea had never meant for them what it had meant for him. One pill and they were actors again, content to be images in a mirror.

Slowly, as he watched, the city turned itself off. Slowly the dawn divided the sky into an east and a west. Had a pedestrian been going fast on 58th Street and had that pedestrian looked up, he would have seen the bare soles of a boy's feet swinging back and forth, angelically.

He would have to kill Alyona Ivanovna himself. Nothing else was possible.

Back in his bedroom, long ago, the phone was ringing its fuzzy nighttime ring. That would be Tancred (or Amparo?) trying to talk him out of it. He foresaw their arguments. Celeste and Jack couldn't be trusted now. Or, more subtly: they'd all made themselves too visible with their *Orfeo*. If there were even a small investigation, the benches would remember them, remember how well they had danced, and the police would know where to look.

But the real reason, which at least Amparo would have been ashamed to mention now that the pill was wearing off, was that they'd begun to feel sorry for their victim. They'd got to know him too well over the last month and their resolve had been eroded by compassion.

A light came on in Papa's window. Time to begin. He stood up, golden in the sunbeams of another perfect day, and walked back along the foot-wide ledge to his own window. His legs tingled from having sat so long.

He waited till Papa was in the shower, then tippytoed to the old secretaire in his bedroom (W. & J. Sloan, 1952). Papa's keychain was coiled atop the walnut veneer. Inside the secretaire's drawer was an antique Mexican cigar box, and in the cigar box a velvet bag, and in the velvet bag Papa's replica of a French dueling pistol, circa 1790. These precautions were less for his son's sake than on account of Jimmy Ness, who every so often felt obliged to show he was serious with his suicide threats.

He'd studied the booklet carefully when Papa had bought the pistol and was able to execute the loading procedure quickly and without error, tamping the premeasured twist of powder down into the barrel and then the lead ball on top of it.

He cocked the hammer back a single click.

He locked the drawer. He replaced the keys, just so. He buried, for now, the pistol in the stuffs and cushions of the Turkish corner, tilted upright to keep the ball from rolling out. Then with what remained of yesterday's ebullience he bounced into the bathroom and kissed Papa's cheek, damp with the morning's allotted two gallons and redolent of 4711.

They had a cheery breakfast together in the coffee room, which was identical to the breakfast they would have made for themselves except for the ritual of being waited on by a waitress. Little Mister Kissy Lips gave an enthusiastic account of the Alexandrians' performance of *Orfeo,* and Papa made his best effort of seeming not to condescend. When he'd been driven to the limit of this pretense, Little Mister Kissy Lips touched him for a second pill, and since it was better for a boy to get these things from his father than from a stranger on the street, he got it.

He reached the South Ferry stop at noon, bursting with a sense of his own imminent liberation. The weather was M-Day all over again, as though at midnight out on the ledge he'd forced time to go backwards to the point when things had started going wrong. He'd dressed in his most anonymous shorts and the pistol hung from his belt in a dun dittybag.

Alyona Ivanovna was sitting on one of the benches near the aviary, listening to Miss Kraus. Her ring hand gripped the poster firmly, while the right chopped at the air, eloquently awkward, like a mute's first words following a miraculous cure.

Little Mister Kissy Lips went down the path and squatted in the shadow of his memorial. It had lost its magic yesterday, when the statues had begun to look so silly to everyone. They still looked silly. Verrazzano was dressed like a Victorian industrialist taking a holiday in the Alps. The angel was wearing an angel's usual bronze nightgown.

His good feelings were leaving his head by little and little, like aeolian sandstone attrited by the centuries of wind. He thought of calling up Amparo, but any comfort she might bring to him would be a mirage so long as his purpose in coming here remained unfulfilled.

He looked at his wrist, then remembered he'd left his watch home. The gigantic advertising clock on the facade of the First National Citibank said it was fifteen after two. That wasn't possible.

Miss Kraus was *still* yammering away.

There was time to watch a cloud move across the sky from Jersey, over the Hudson, and past the sun. Unseen winds nibbled at its wispy edges. The cloud became his life, which would disappear without ever having turned into rain.

Later, and the old man was walking up the sea promenade toward the Castle. He stalked him, for miles. And then they were alone, together, at the far end of the park.

"Hello," he said, with the smile reserved for grown-ups of doubtful importance.

He looked directly at the dittybag, but Little Mister Kissy Lips didn't lose his composure. He would be wondering whether to ask for money, which would be kept, if he'd had any, in the bag. The pistol made a noticeable bulge but not the kind of bulge one would ordinarily associate with a pistol.

"Sorry," he said coolly. "I'm broke."

"Did I ask?"

"You were going to."

The old man made as if to return in the other direction, so he had to speak quickly, something that would hold him here.

"I saw you speaking with Miss Kraus."

He was held.

"Congratulations — you broke through the ice!"

The old man half-smiled, half-frowned. "You know her?"

"Mm. You could say that we're *aware* of her." The "we" had been a deliberate risk, an hors d'oeuvre. Touching a finger to each side of the strings by which the heavy bag hung from his belt, he urged on it a lazy pendular motion. "Do you mind if I ask you a question?"

There was nothing indulgent now in the man's face. "I probably do."

His smile had lost the hard edge of calculation. It was the same smile he'd have smiled for Papa, for Amparo, for Miss Couplard, for anyone he liked. "Where do you come from? I mean, what country?"

"That's none of your business, is it?"

"Well, I just wanted…to know."

The old man (he had ceased, somehow, to be Alyona Ivanovna) turned away and walked directly toward the squat stone cylinder of the old fortress.

He remembered how the plaque at the entrance — the same that had cited the 7.7 million — had said that Jenny Lind had sung there and it had been a great success.

The old man unzipped his fly and, lifting out his cock, began pissing on the wall.

Little Mister Kissy Lips fumbled with the strings of the bag. It was remarkable how long the old man stood there pissing because despite every effort of the stupid knot to stay tied he had the pistol out before the final sprinkle had been shaken out.

He laid the fulminate cap on the exposed nipple, drew the hammer back two clicks, past the safety, and aimed.

The man made no haste zipping up. Only then did he glance in Little Mister Kissy Lips' direction. He saw the pistol aimed at him. They stood not twenty feet apart, so he must have seen it.

He said, "Ha!" And even this, rather than being addressed to the boy with the gun, was only a parenthesis from the faintly aggrieved monologue he resumed each day at the edge of the water. He turned away, and a moment later he was back on the job, hand out, asking some fellow for a quarter.

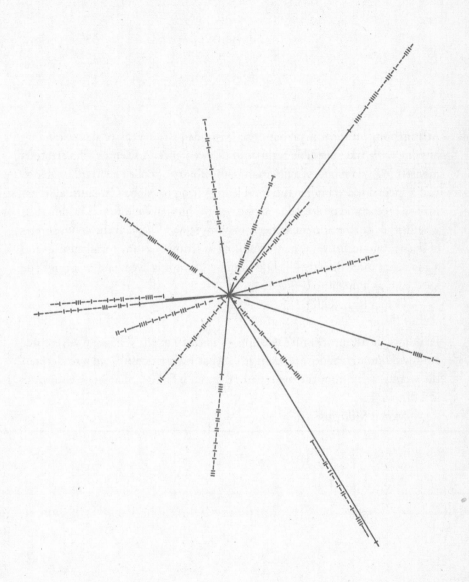

At this point, realism is perhaps the least adequate means of understanding or portraying the incredible realities of our existence. A scientist who creates a monster in his laboratory; a librarian in the library of Babel; a wizard unable to cast a spell; a spaceship having trouble in getting to Alpha Centauri: all these may be precise and profound metaphors of the human condition. The fantasist, whether he uses the ancient archetypes of myth and legend or the younger ones of science and technology, may be talking as seriously as any sociologist — and a good deal more directly — about human life as it is lived, and as it might be lived, and as it ought to be lived.
—Ursula K. Le Guin

Fiction is an adventure or it's nothing — nothing at all. What's an adventure? An invitation to wonder and danger. If what I write doesn't lead a reader into the woods, away from the main path, then it's a failure. Somebody else wrote it. I disown it.
—Steven Millhauser

The Ones Who Walk Away from Omelas
Ursula K. Le Guin

With a clamor of bells that set the swallows soaring, the Festival of Summer came to the city Omelas, bright-towered by the sea. The rigging of the boats in harbor sparkled with flags. In the streets between houses with red roofs and painted walls, between old moss-grown gardens and under avenues of trees, past great parks and public buildings, processions moved. Some were decorous: old people in long stiff robes of mauve and grey, grave master workmen, quiet, merry women carrying their babies and chatting as they walked. In other streets the music beat faster, a shimmering of gong and tambourine, and the people went dancing, the procession was a dance. Children dodged in and out, their high calls rising like the swallows' crossing flights over the music and the singing. All the processions wound towards the north side of the city, where on the great water-meadow called the Green Fields boys and girls, naked in the bright air, with mud-stained feet and ankles and long, lithe arms, exercised their restive horses before the race. The horses wore no gear at all but a halter without bit. Their manes were braided with streamers of silver, gold, and green. They flared their nostrils and pranced and boasted to one another; they were vastly excited, the horse being the only animal who has adopted our ceremonies as his own. Far off to the north and west the mountains stood up half encircling Omelas on her bay. The air of morning was so clear that the snow still crowning the Eighteen Peaks burned with white-gold fire across the miles of sunlit air, under the dark blue of the sky. There was just enough wind to make the banners that marked the racecourse snap and flutter now and then. In the silence of the broad green meadows one could hear the music winding through the city streets, farther and nearer and ever approaching, a cheerful faint sweetness of the air that from time to time trembled and gathered together and broke out into the great joyous clanging of the bells.

Joyous! How is one to tell about joy? How describe the citizens of Omelas?

They were not simple folk, you see, though they were happy. But we do not say the words of cheer much any more. All smiles have become archaic. Given a description such as this one tends to make certain assumptions. Given a description such as this one tends to look next for the King, mounted on a splendid stallion and surrounded by his noble knights, or perhaps in a golden litter borne by great-muscled slaves. But there was no king. They did not use swords, or keep slaves. They were not barbarians. I do not know the rules and laws of their society, but I suspect that they were singularly few. As they did without monarchy and slavery, so they also got on without the stock exchange, the advertisement, the secret police, and the bomb. Yet I repeat that these were not simple folk, not dulcet shepherds, noble savages, bland utopians. They were not less complex than us. The trouble is that we have a bad habit, encouraged by pedants and sophisticates, of considering happiness as something rather stupid. Only pain is intellectual, only evil interesting. This is the treason of the artist: a refusal to admit the banality of evil and the terrible boredom of pain. If you can't lick 'em, join 'em. If it hurts, repeat it. But to praise despair is to condemn delight, to embrace violence is to lose hold of everything else. We have almost lost hold; we can no longer describe a happy man, nor make any celebration of joy. How can I tell you about the people of Omelas? They were not naive and happy children — though their children were, in fact, happy. They were mature, intelligent, passionate adults whose lives were not wretched. O miracle! but I wish I could describe it better. I wish I could convince you. Omelas sounds in my words like a city in a fairy tale, long ago and far away, once upon a time. Perhaps it would be best if you imagined it as your own fancy bids, assuming it will rise to the occasion, for certainly I cannot suit you all. For instance, how about technology? I think that there would be no cars or helicopters in and above the streets; this follows from the fact that the people of Omelas are happy people. Happiness is based on a just discrimination of what is necessary, what is neither necessary nor destructive, and what is destructive. In the middle category, however — that of the unnecessary but undestructive, that of comfort, luxury, exuberance, etc. — they could perfectly well have central heating, subway trains, washing machines, and all kinds of marvelous devices not yet invented here, floating light-sources, fuelless power, a cure for the common cold. Or they could have none of that; it doesn't matter. As you like it. I incline to think that people from towns up and down the coast have been coming in to Omelas during the last days before the Festival on very fast little trains and double-decked trams, and that the train station of Omelas is actually the handsomest building in town, though plainer than the magnificent Farmers' Market. But even granted trains, I fear that Omelas so far strikes some of you as goody-goody. Smiles, bells, parades, horses, bleh. If so, please add an orgy. If an orgy would help, don't hesitate. Let us not, however, have temples from which issue beautiful nude priests and priestesses already half in ecstasy and ready to copulate with any man or woman, lover or stranger, who desires union with the deep godhead of the blood, although that was my first idea. But really it would be better not to have any temples in Omelas — at least, not manned temples. Religion yes, clergy no. Surely the beautiful nudes can just wander about, offering themselves like divine soufflés to the hunger of the needy and the rapture of the flesh. Let them join the processions. Let tambourines be struck above the copulations, and the glory of desire be proclaimed upon the gongs, and (a not unimportant point) let the offspring of these delightful rituals be beloved and looked after by all. One thing I know there is none of in Omelas is guilt. But what else should there be? I thought at first there were not drugs, but that is puritanical. For those who like it, the faint insistent sweetness of *drooz* may perfume the ways of the city, *drooz* which first brings a great lightness and brilliance to the mind and limbs, and then after some hours a dreamy languor, and wonderful visions at last of the very arcane and inmost secrets of the Universe, as well as exciting the pleasure of sex beyond belief; and it is not habit-forming. For more modest tastes I think there ought to be beer. What else, what else belongs in the joyous city? The sense of victory, surely, the celebration of courage. But as we did without clergy, let us do without soldiers. The joy built upon successful slaughter is not the right kind of joy; it will not do; it is fearful and it is trivial. A boundless and generous contentment, a magnanimous triumph felt not against some outer enemy but in communion with the finest and fairest in the souls of all men everywhere and the splendor of the world's summer: this is what swells the hearts of the people of Omelas, and the victory they celebrate is that of life. I really don't think many of them need to take *drooz*.

Most of the procession have reached the Green Fields by now. A marvelous smell of cooking goes forth from the red and blue tents of the provisioners. The faces of small children are amiably sticky; in the benign grey beard of a man a couple of crumbs of rich pastry are entangled. The youths and girls have mounted their horses and are beginning to group around the starting line of the course. An old women, small, fat, and laughing, is passing out flowers from a basket, and tall young men wear her flowers in their shining hair. A child of nine or ten sits at the edge of the crowd, alone, playing on a wooden flute. People pause to listen, and they smile, but they do not speak to him, for he never ceases playing and never sees them, his dark eyes wholly rapt in the sweet, thin magic of the tune.

He finishes, and slowly lowers his hands holding the wooden flute.

As if that little private silence were the signal, all at once a trumpet sounds from the pavilion near the starting line: imperious, melancholy, piercing. The horses rear on their slender legs, and some of them neigh in answer. Sober-faced, the young riders stroke the horses' necks and soothe them, whispering, "Quiet, quiet, there my beauty, my hope...." They begin to form in rank along the starting line. The crowds along the racecourse are like a field of grass and flowers in the wind. The Festival of Summer has begun.

Do you believe? Do you accept the festival, the city, the joy? No? Then let me describe one more thing.

In a basement under one of the beautiful public buildings of Omelas, or perhaps in the cellar of one of its spacious private homes, there is a room. It has one locked door, and no window. A little light seeps in dustily between cracks in the boards, secondhand from a cobwebbed window somewhere across the cellar. In one corner of the little room a couple of mops, with stiff, clotted, foul-smelling heads stand near a rusty bucket. The floor is dirt, a little damp to the touch, as cellar dirt usually is. The room is about three paces long and two wide: a mere broom closet or disused tool room. In the room a child is sitting. It could be a boy or a girl. It looks about six, but actually is nearly ten. It is feeble-minded. Perhaps it was born defective, or perhaps it has become imbecile through fear, malnutrition, and neglect. It picks its nose and occasionally fumbles vaguely with its toes or genitals, as it sits hunched in the corner farthest from the bucket and the two mops. It is afraid of the mops. It finds them horrible. It shuts its eyes, but it knows the mops are still standing there; and the door is locked; and nobody will come. The door is always locked; and nobody ever comes, except that sometimes — the child has no understanding of time or interval — sometimes the door rattles terribly and opens, and a person, or several people, are there. One of them may come in and kick the child to make it stand up. The others never come close, but peer in at it with frightened, disgusted eyes. The food bowl and the water jug are hastily filled, the door is locked, the eyes disappear. The people at the door never say anything, but the child, who has not always lived in the tool room, and can remember sunlight and its mother's voice, sometimes speaks. "I will be good," it says. "Please let me out. I will be good!" They never answer. The child used to scream for help at night, and cry a good deal, but now it only makes a kind of whining, "eh-haa, eh-haa," and it speaks less and less often. It is so thin there are no calves to its legs; its belly protrudes; it lives on a half-bowl of cornmeal and grease a day. It is naked. Its buttocks and thighs are a mass of festered sores, as it sits in its own excrement continually.

They all know it is there, all the people of Omelas. Some of them have come to see it, others are content merely to know it is there. They all know that it has to be there. Some of them understand why, and some do not, but they all understand that their happiness, the beauty of their city, the tenderness of their friendships, the health of their children, the wisdom of their scholars, the skill of their makers, even the abundance of their harvest and the kindly weathers of their skies, depend wholly on this child's abominable misery.

This is usually explained to children when they are between eight and twelve, whenever they seem capable of understanding; and most of those who come to see the child are young people, though often enough an adult comes, or comes back, to see the child. No matter how well the matter has been explained to them, these young spectators are always shocked and sickened at the sight. They feel disgust, which they had thought themselves superior to. They feel anger, outrage, impotence, despite all the explanations. They would like to do some-thing for the child. But there is nothing they can do. If the child were brought up into the sunlight out of that vile place, if it were cleaned and fed and com-forted, that would be a good thing indeed; but if it were done, in that day and hour all the prosperity and beauty and delight of Omelas would wither and be destroyed. Those are the terms. To exchange all the goodness and grace of every life in Omelas for that single, small improvement: to throw away the happiness of thousands for the chance of the happiness of one: that would be to let guilt within the walls indeed.

The terms are strict and absolute; there may not even be a kind word spoken to the child.

Often the young people go home in tears, or in a tearless rage, when they have seen the child and faced this terrible paradox. They may brood over it for weeks or years. But as time goes on they begin to realize that even if the child could be released, it would not get much good of its freedom: a little vague pleasure of warmth and food, no doubt, but little more. It is too degraded and imbecile to know any real joy. It has been afraid too long ever to be free of fear. Its habits are too uncouth for it to respond to humane treatment. Indeed, after so long it would probably be wretched without walls about it to protect it, and darkness for its eyes, and its own excrement to sit in. Their tears at the bitter injustice dry when they begin to perceive the terrible justice of reality, and to accept it. Yet it is their tears and anger, the trying of their generosity and the acceptance of their helplessness, which are perhaps the true source of the splendor of their lives. Theirs is no vapid, irresponsible happiness. They know that they, like the child, are not free. They know compassion. It is the existence of the child, and their knowledge of its existence, that makes possible the nobility of their architecture, the poignancy of their music, the profundity of their science. It is because of the child that they are so gentle with children. They know that if the wretched one were not there sniveling in the dark, the other one, the flute-player, could make no joyful music as the young riders line up in their beauty for the race in the sunlight of the first morning of summer.

Now do you believe in them? Are they not more credible? But there is one more thing to tell, and this is quite incredible.

At times one of the adolescent girls or boys who go to see the child does not go home to weep or rage, does not, in fact, go home at all. Sometimes also a man or woman much older falls silent for a day or two, and then leaves home. These people go out into the street, and walk down the street alone. They keep walking, and walk straight out of the city of Omelas, through the beautiful gates. They keep walking across the farmlands of Omelas. Each one goes alone, youth or girl, man or woman. Night falls; the traveler must pass down village streets, between the houses with yellow-lit windows, and on out into the darkness of the fields. Each alone, they go west or north, towards the mountains. They go on. They leave Omelas, they walk ahead into the darkness, and they do not come back. The place they go towards is a place even less imaginable to most of us than the city of happiness. I cannot describe it at all. It is possible that it does not exist. But they seem to know where they are going, the ones who walk away from Omelas.

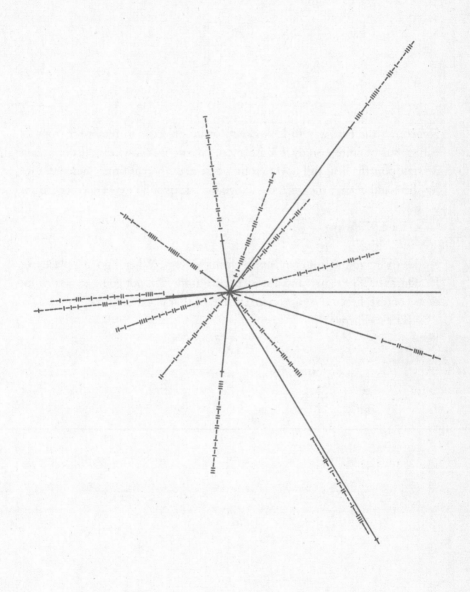

Sometimes the best way to look closely at an object is to remove it from its natural surroundings, study it in isolation. We do that in science fiction; often we transport the here and now to somewhere else, another time. Sometimes we stay here and change the time, or change the background to get a closer, clearer view.

—Kate Wilhelm

Stories spring to me from landscapes, from settings. When I go to a place like Honduras or Nicaragua, and a story occurs to me, I'm not going to take it out of its context, because it's a story particular to that place and time.

—Lucius Shepard

Ladies and Gentlemen, This Is Your Crisis
Kate Wilhem

4 P.M. FRIDAY

LOTTIE'S FACTORY CLOSED early on Friday, as most of them did now. It was four when she got home, after stopping for frozen dinners, bread, sandwich meats, beer. She switched on the wall TV screen before she put her bag down. In the kitchen she turned on another set, a portable, and watched it as she put the food away. She had missed four hours.

They were in the mountains. That was good. Lottie liked it when they chose mountains. A stocky man was sliding down a slope, feet out before him, legs stiff — too conscious of the camera, though. Lottie couldn't tell if he had meant to slide, but he did not look happy. She turned her attention to the others.

A young woman was walking slowly, waist high in ferns, so apparently unconscious of the camera that it could only be a pose this early in the game. She looked vaguely familiar. Her blond hair was loose, like a girl in a shampoo commercial, Lottie decided. She narrowed her eyes, trying to remember where she had seen the girl. A model, probably, wanting to be a star. She would wander aimlessly, not even trying for the prize, content with the publicity she was getting.

The other woman was another sort altogether. A bit overweight, her thighs bulged in the heavy trousers the contestants wore; her hair was dyed black and fastened with a rubber band in a no-nonsense manner. She was examining a tree intently. Lottie nodded at her. Everything about her spoke of purpose, of concentration, of planning. She'd do.

The final contestant was a tall black man, in his forties probably. He wore old-fashioned eyeglasses — a mistake. He'd lose them and be seriously handicapped. He kept glancing about with a lopsided grin.

Lottie had finished putting the groceries away; she returned to the living room to sit before the large unit that gave her a better view of the map, above the sectioned screen. The Andes, she had decided, and was surprised and pleased to find she was wrong. Alaska! There were bears and wolves in Alaska still, and elk and moose.

The picture shifted, and a thrill of anticipation raised the hairs on Lottie's arms and scalp. Now the main screen was evenly divided; one half showed the man who had been sliding. He was huddled against the cliff, breathing very hard. On the other half of the screen was an enlarged aerial view. Lottie gasped. Needle-like snow-capped peaks, cliffs, precipices, a raging stream…The yellow dot of light that represented the man was on the edge of a steep hill covered with boulders and loose gravel. If he got on that, Lottie thought, he'd be lost. From where he was, there was no way he could know what lay ahead. She leaned forward, examining him for signs that he understood, that he was afraid, anything. His face was empty; all he needed now was more air than he could get with his labored breathing.

Andy Stevens stepped in front of the aerial map; it was three feet taller than he. "As you can see, ladies and gentlemen, there is only this scrub growth to Dr. Burnside's left. Those roots might be strong enough to hold, but I'd guess they are shallowly rooted, wouldn't you? And if he chooses this direction, he'll need something to grasp, won't he?" Andy had his tape measure and a pointer. He looked worried. He touched the yellow dot of light. "Here he is. As you can see, he is resting, for the moment, on a narrow ledge after his slide down sixty-five feet of loose dirt and gravel. He doesn't appear to be hurt. Our own Dr. Lederman is watching him along with the rest of us, and he assures me that Dr. Burnside is not injured."

Andy pointed out the hazards of Dr. Burnside's precarious position, and the dangers involved in moving. Lottie nodded, her lips tight and grim. It was off to a good start.

6 P.M. FRIDAY

Butcher got home, as usual, at six. Lottie heard him at the door but didn't get up to open it for him. Dr. Burnside was still sitting there. He had to move. Move, you bastard! Do something!

"Whyn't you unlock the door?" Butcher yelled, yanking off his jacket.

Lottie paid no attention. Butcher always came home mad, resentful because she had got off early, mad at his boss because the warehouse didn't close down early, mad at traffic, mad at everything.

"They say anything about them yet?" Butcher asked, sitting in his recliner. Lottie shook her head. Move, you bastard! Move!

The man began to inch his way to the left and Lottie's heart thumped, her hands clenched.

"What's the deal?" Butcher asked hoarsely, already responding to Lottie's tension.

"Dead end that way," Lottie muttered, her gaze on the screen. "Slide with boulders and junk if he tries to go down. He's gotta go right."

The man moved cautiously, never lifting his feet from the ground but sliding them along, testing each step. He paused again, this time with less room than before. He looked desperate. He was perspiring heavily. Now he could see the way he had chosen offered little hope of getting down. More slowly than before, he began to back up; dirt and gravel shifted constantly.

The amplifiers picked up the noise of the stuff rushing downward, like a waterfall heard from a distance, and now and then a muttered unintelligible word from the man. The volume came up: he was cursing. Again and again he stopped. He was pale and sweat ran down his face. He didn't move his hands from the cliff to wipe it away.

Lottie was sweating too. Her lips moved occasionally with a faint curse or prayer. Her hands gripped the sofa.

7:30 P.M. FRIDAY

Lottie fell back onto the sofa with a grunt, weak from sustained tension. They were safe. It had taken over an hour to work his way to this place where the cliff and steep slope gave way to a gentle hill. The man was sprawled out face down, his back heaving.

Butcher abruptly got up and went to the bathroom. Lottie couldn't move yet. The screen shifted and the aerial view filled the larger part. Andy pointed out the contestants' lights and finally began the recap.

Lottie watched on the portable set as she got out their frozen dinners and heated the oven. Dr. Lederman was talking about Angie Dawes, the young aspiring actress whose problem was that of having been overprotected all her life. He said she was a potential suicide, and the panel of examining physicians had agreed Crisis Therapy would be helpful.

The next contestant was Mildred Ormsby, a chemist, divorced, no children. She had started on a self-destructive course through drugs, said Dr. Lederman, and would be benefited by Crisis Therapy.

The tall black man, Clyde Williams, was an economist; he taught at Harvard and had tried to murder his wife and their three children by burning down their house with them in it. Crisis Therapy had been indicated.

Finally Dr. Edward Burnside, the man who had started the show with such drama, was shown being interviewed. Forty-one, unmarried, living with a woman, he was a statistician for a major firm. Recently he had started to feed the wrong data into the computer, aware but unable to stop himself.

Dr. Lederman's desk was superimposed on the aerial view and he started his taped explanation of what Crisis Therapy was. Lottie made coffee. When she looked again Eddie was still lying on the ground, exhausted, maybe even crying. She wished he would roll over so she could see if he was crying.

Andy returned to explain how the game was played: the winner received one million dollars, after taxes, and all the contestants were undergoing Crisis Therapy that would enrich their lives beyond measure. Andy explained the automatic, air-cushioned, five-day cameras focused electronically on the contestants, the orbiting satellite that made it possible to keep them under observation at all times, the light amplification, infrared system that would keep them visible all night. This part made Lottie's head ache.

Next came the full-screen commercial for the wall units. Only those who had them could see the entire show. Down the left side of the screen were the four contestants, each in a separate panel, and over them a topographical map that showed the entire region, where the exit points were, the nearest roads, towns. Center screen could be divided any way the director chose. Above this picture was the show's slogan: "This Is Your Crisis!" and a constantly running commercial. In the far right corner there was an aerial view of the selected site, with the colored dots of light. Mildred's was red, Angie's was green. Eddie's yellow, Clyde's blue. Anything else larger than a rabbit or squirrel that moved into the viewing area would be white.

The contestants were shown being taken to the site, first by airplane, then helicopter. They were left there on noon Friday and had until midnight Sunday to reach one of the dozen trucks that ringed the area. The first one to report in at one of the trucks was the winner.

Lottie made up her bed on the couch while Butcher opened his recliner full length and brought out a blanket and pillow from the bedroom. He had another beer and Lottie drank milk and ate cookies, and presently they turned off the light and there was only the glow from the screen in the room.

The contestants were settled down for the night, each in a sleeping bag, campfires burning low, the long northern twilight still not faded. Andy began to explain the contents of the backpacks.

Lottie closed her eyes, opened them several times, just to check, and finally fell asleep.

Lottie sat up suddenly, wide awake, her heart thumping. The red beeper had come on. On center screen the girl was sitting up, staring into darkness, obviously frightened. She must have heard something. Only her dot showed on her screen, but there was no way for her to know that. Lottie lay down again, watching, and became aware of Butcher's heavy snoring. She shook his leg and he shifted and for a few moments breathed deeply, without the snore, then began again.

Francine Dumont was the night M.C.; now she stepped to one side of the screen. "If she panics," Francine said in a hushed voice, "it could be the end of the game for her." She pointed out the hazards in the area — boulders, a steep drop-off, the thickening trees on two sides. "Let's watch," she whispered and stepped back out of the way.

The volume was turned up; there were rustlings in the undergrowth. Lottie closed her eyes and tried to hear them through the girl's ears, and felt only contempt for her. The girl was stiff with fear. She began to build up her campfire. Lottie nodded. She'd stay awake all night, and by late tomorrow she'd be finished. She would be lifted out, the end of Miss Smarty Pants Dawes.

Lottie sniffed and closed her eyes, but now Butcher's snores were louder. If only he didn't sound like a dying man, she thought — sucking in air, holding it, holding it, then suddenly erupting into a loud snort that turned into a gurgle. She pressed her hands over her ears and finally slept again.

There were beer cans on the table, on the floor around it. There was half a loaf of bread and a knife with dried mustard and the mustard jar without a top. The salami was drying out, hard, and there were onion skins and bits of brown lettuce and an open jar of pickles. The butter had melted in its dish, and the butter knife was on the floor, spreading a dark stain on the rug.

Nothing was happening on the screen now. Angie Dawes hadn't left the fern patch. She was brushing her hair.

Mildred was following the stream, but it became a waterfall ahead and she would have to think of something else.

The stout man was still making his way downward as directly as possible, obviously convinced it was the fastest way and no more dangerous than any other.

The black man was being logical, like Mildred, Lottie admitted. He watched the shadows and continued in a southeasterly direction, tackling the hurdles as he came to them, methodically, without haste. Ahead of him, invisible to him, but clearly visible to the floating cameras and the audience, were a mother bear and two cubs in a field of blueberries.

Things would pick up again in an hour or so, Lottie knew. Butcher came back. "You have time for a quick shower," Lottie said. He was beginning to smell.

"Shut up." Butcher sprawled in the recliner, his feet bare.

Lottie tried not to see his thick toes, grimy with warehouse dust. She got up and went to the kitchen for a bag, and started to throw the garbage into it. The cans clattered.

"Knock it off, will ya!" Butcher yelled. He stretched to see around her. He was watching the blond braid her hair. Lottie threw another can into the bag.

9 P.M. SATURDAY

Butcher sat on the edge of the chair, biting a fingernail. "See that?" he breathed. "You see it?" He was shiny with perspiration.

Lottie nodded, watching the white dots move on the aerial map, watching the blue dot moving, stopping for a long time, moving again. Clyde and the bears were approaching each other minute by minute, and Clyde knew now that there was something ahead of him.

"You see that?" Butcher cried out hoarsely.

"Just be still, will you?" Lottie said through her teeth. The black man was sniffing the air.

"You can smell a goddam lousy bear a country mile!" Butcher said. "He knows."

"For God's sake, shut up!"

"Yeah, he knows all right," Butcher said softly. "Mother bear, cubs...she'll tear him apart."

"Shut up! Shut up!"

Clyde began to back away. He took half a dozen steps, then turned and ran. The bear stood up; behind her the cubs tumbled in play. She turned her head in a listening attitude. She growled and dropped to four feet and began to amble in the direction Clyde had taken. They were about an eighth of a mile apart. Any second she would be able to see him.

Clyde ran faster, heading for thick trees. Past the trees was a cliff he had skirted earlier.

"Saw a cave or something up there," Butcher muttered. "Betcha. Heading for a cave."

Lottie pressed her hands hard over her ears. The bear was closing the gap; the cubs followed erratically, and now and again the mother bear paused to glance at them and growl softly. Clyde began to climb the face of the cliff. The bear came into view and saw him. She ran. Clyde was out of her reach; she began to climb, and rocks were loosened by her great body. When one of the cubs bawled, she let go and half slid, half fell back to the bottom. Standing on her hind legs, she growled at the man above her. She was nine feet tall. She shook her great head from side to side another moment, then turned and waddled back toward the blueberries, trailed by her two cubs.

"Smart bastard," Butcher muttered. "Good thinking. Knew he couldn't outrun a bear. Good thinking."

Lottie went to the bathroom. She had smelled the bear, she thought. If he had only shut up a minute! She was certain she had smelled the bear. Her hands were trembling.

The phone was ringing when she returned to the living room. She answered, watching the screen. Clyde looked shaken, the first time he had been rattled since the beginning.

"Yeah," she said into the phone. "He's here." She put the receiver down.

"Your sister."

"She can't come over," Butcher said ominously. "Not unless she's drowned that brat."

"Funny," Lottie said, scowling. Corinne should have enough consideration not to make an issue of it week after week.

"Yeah," Butcher was saying into the phone. "I know it's tough on a floor set, but what the hell, get the old man to buy a wall unit. What's he planning to do, take it with him?" He listened. "Like I said, you know how it is. I say okay, then Lottie gives me hell. Know what I mean? I mean, it ain't worth it. You know?" Presently he banged the receiver down.

"Frank's out of town?"

He didn't answer, settled himself down into his chair and reached for his beer.

"He's in a fancy hotel lobby where they got a unit screen the size of a barn and she's got that lousy little portable…"

"Just drop it, will ya? She's the one that wanted the kid, remember. She's bawling her head off but she's not coming over. So drop it!"

"Yeah, and she'll be mad at me for a week, and it takes two to make a kid."

"Jesus Christ!" Butcher got up and went into the kitchen. The refrigerator door banged. "Where's the beer?"

"Under the sink."

"Jesus! Whyn't you put it in the refrigerator?"

"There wasn't enough room for it all. If you've gone through all the cold beers, you don't need any more!"

He slammed the refrigerator door again and came back with a can of beer. When he pulled it open, warm beer spewed halfway across the room. Lottie knew he had done it to make her mad. She ignored him and watched Mildred worm her way down into her sleeping bag. Mildred had the best chance of winning, she thought. She checked her position on the aerial map. All the lights were closer to the trucks now, but there wasn't anything of real importance between Mildred and the goal. She had chosen right every time.

"Ten bucks on yellow," Butcher said suddenly.

"You gotta be kidding! He's going to break his fat neck before he gets out of there!"

"Okay, ten bucks." He slapped ten dollars down on the table, between the TV dinner trays and the coffee pot.

"Throw it away," Lottie said, matching it. "Red."

"The fat lady?"

"Anybody who smells like you better not go around insulting someone who at least takes time out to have a shower now and then!" Lottie cried and swept past him to the kitchen. She and Mildred were about the same size. "And why don't you get off your butt and clean up some of that mess! All I do every weekend is clear away garbage!"

"I don't give a shit if it reaches the ceiling!"

Lottie brought a bag and swept trash into it. When she got near Butcher, she held her nose.

6 A.M. SUNDAY

Lottie sat up. "What happened?" she cried. The red beeper was on. "How long's it been on?"

"Half an hour. Hell, I don't know."

Butcher was sitting tensely on the side of the recliner, gripping it with both hands. Eddie was in a tree, clutching the trunk. Below him, dogs were tearing apart his backpack, and another dog was leaping repeatedly at him.

"Idiot!" Lottie cried. "Why didn't he hang up his stuff like the others?"

Butcher made a noise at her, and she shook her head, watching. The dogs had smelled food, and they would search for it, tearing up everything they found. She smiled grimly. They might keep Mr. Fat Neck up there all day, and even if he got down, he'd have nothing to eat.

That's what did them in, she thought. Week after week it was the same. They forgot the little things and lost. She leaned back and ran her hand through her hair. It was standing out all over her head.

Two of the dogs began to fight over a scrap of something and the leaping dog jumped into the battle with them. Presently they all ran away, three of them chasing the fourth.

"Throw away your money," Lottie said gaily, and started around Butcher. He swept out his hand and pushed her down again and left the room without a backward look. It didn't matter who won, she thought, shaken by the push. That twenty and twenty more would have to go to the finance company to pay off the loan for the wall unit. Butcher knew that; he shouldn't get so hot about a little joke.

"This place looks like a pigpen," Butcher growled. "You going to clear some of this junk away?" He was carrying a sandwich in one hand, beer in the other; the table was littered with breakfast remains, leftover snacks from the morning and the night before.

Lottie didn't look at him. "Clear it yourself."

"I'll clear it." He put his sandwich down on the arm of his chair and swept a spot clean, knocking over glasses and cups.

"Pick that up!" Lottie screamed. "I'm sick and tired of cleaning up after you every damn weekend! All you do is stuff and guzzle and expect me to pick up and clean up."

"Damn right."

Lottie snatched up the beer can he had put on the table and threw it at him. The beer streamed out over the table, chair, over his legs. Butcher threw down the sandwich and grabbed at her. She dodged and backed away from the table into the center of the room. Butcher followed, his hands clenched.

"You touch me again, I'll break your arm!"

"Bitch!" He dived for her and she caught his arm, twisted it savagely and threw him to one side.

He hauled himself up to a crouch and glared at her with hatred. "I'll fix you," he muttered. "I'll fix you!"

Lottie laughed. He charged again, this time knocked her backward and they crashed to the floor together and rolled, pummeling each other.

The red beeper sounded and they pulled apart, not looking at each other, and took their seats before the screen.

"It's the fat lady," Butcher said malevolently. "I hope the bitch kills herself!"

Mildred had fallen into the stream and was struggling in waist-high water to regain her footing. The current was very swift, all white water here. She slipped and went under. Lottie held her breath until she appeared again, downstream, retching, clutching at a boulder. Inch by inch she drew herself to it and clung there trying to get her breath back. She looked about desperately; she was very white. Abruptly she launched herself into the current, swimming strongly, fighting to get to the shore as she was swept down the river.

Andy's voice was soft as he said, "That water is forty-eight degrees, ladies and gentlemen! Forty-eight! Dr. Lederman, how long can a person be immersed in water that cold?"

"Not long, Andy. Not long at all." The doctor looked worried too. "Ten minutes at the most, I'd say."

"That water is reducing her body heat second by second," Andy said solemnly. "When it is low enough to produce unconsciousness…"

Mildred was pulled under again; when she appeared this time, she was much closer to shore. She caught a rock and held on. Now she could stand up, and presently she dragged herself rock by rock, boulder by boulder, to the shore. She was shaking hard, her teeth chattering. She began to build a fire. She could hardly open her waterproof matchbox. Finally she had a blaze and she began to strip. Her backpack, Andy reminded the audience, had been lost when she fell into the water. She had only what she had on her back, and if she wanted to continue after the sun set and the cold evening began, she had to dry her things thoroughly.

"She's got nerve," Butcher said grudgingly.

Lottie nodded. She was weak. She got up, skirted Butcher, and went to the kitchen for a bag. As she cleaned the table, every now and then she glanced at the naked woman by her fire. Steam was rising off her wet clothes.

10 P.M. SUNDAY

Lottie had moved Butcher's chair to the far side of the table the last time he had left it. His beard was thick and coarse, and he still wore the clothes he had put on to go to work Friday morning. Lottie's stomach hurt. Every weekend she got constipated.

The game was between Mildred and Clyde now. He was in good shape, still had his glasses and his backpack. He was farther from his truck than Mildred was from hers, but she had eaten nothing that afternoon and was limping badly. Her boots must have shrunk, or else she had not waited for them to get completely dry. Her face twisted with pain when she moved.

The girl was still posing in the high meadow, now against a tall tree, now among the wild flowers. Often a frown crossed her face and surreptitiously she scratched. Ticks, Butcher said. Probably full of them.

Eddie was wandering in a daze. He looked empty, and was walking in great aimless circles. Some of them cracked like that, Lottie knew. It had happened before, sometimes to the strongest one of all. They'd slap him right in a hospital and no one would hear anything about him again for a long time, if ever. She didn't waste pity on him.

She would win, Lottie knew. She had studied every kind of wilderness they used and she'd know what to do and how to do it. She was strong, and not afraid of noises. She found herself nodding and stopped, glanced quickly at Butcher to see if he had noticed. He was watching Clyde.

"Smart," Butcher said, his eyes narrowed. "That sonabitch's been saving himself for the home stretch. Look at him." Clyde started to lope, easily, as if aware the TV truck was dead ahead.

Now the screen was divided into three parts, the two finalists, Mildred and Clyde, side by side, and above them a large aerial view that showed their red and blue dots as they approached the trucks.

"It's fixed!" Lottie cried, outraged when Clyde pulled ahead of Mildred. "I hope he falls down and breaks his back!"

"Smart," Butcher said over and over, nodding, and Lottie knew he was imagining himself there, just as she had done. She felt a chill. He glanced at her and for a moment their eyes held — naked, scheming. They broke away simultaneously.

Mildred limped forward until it was evident each step was torture. Finally she sobbed, sank to the ground and buried her face in her hands.

Clyde ran on. It would take an act of God now to stop him. He reached the truck at twelve minutes before midnight.

For a long time neither Lottie nor Butcher moved. Neither spoke. Butcher had turned the audio off as soon as Clyde reached the truck, and now there were the usual after-game recaps, the congratulations, the helicopter liftouts of the other contestants.

Butcher sighed. "One of the better shows," he said. He was hoarse.

"Yeah. About the best yet."

"Yeah." He sighed again and stood up. "Honey, don't bother with all this junk now. I'm going to take a shower, and then I'll help you clean up, okay?"

"It's not that bad," she said "I'll be done by the time you're finished. Want a sandwich, doughnut?"

"I don't think so. Be right out." He left. When he came back, shaved, clean, his wet hair brushed down smoothly, the room was neat again, the dishes washed and put away.

"Let's go to bed, honey," he said, and put his arm lightly about her shoulders. "You look beat."

"I am." She slipped her arm about his waist. "We both lost."

"Yeah, I know. Next week."

She nodded. Next week. It was the best money they ever spent, she thought, undressing. Best thing they ever bought, even if it would take them fifteen years to pay it off. She yawned and slipped into bed. They held hands as they drifted off to sleep.

Art is supposed to be unconventional which is why I detest genre writing of all kinds. I mean, it's comforting for the people who read it — but they are morons. (Laughs). Because they know that Joe will get murdered and somebody else will figure out why or how. Or some spy will figure out how to prevent terrorists from taking over the world. I don't really care. It doesn't interest me. I want to be taken away to a different place every time.
　　—T. C. Boyle

The thing I have always liked best about science fiction is that it defies definition. It keeps constantly reinventing itself — and just when you thought stories about robots or time travel or first contact had been done to death, it thinks of some brand-new way to tell an old story, or some brand-new story to tell.
　　—Connie Willis

DESCENT OF MAN
T. C. BOYLE

I WAS LIVING with a woman who suddenly began to stink. It was very difficult. The first time I confronted her she merely smiled. "Occupational hazard," she said. The next time she curled her lip. There were other problems too. Hairs, for instance. Hairs that began to appear on her clothing, sharp and black and brutal. Invariably I would awake to find these hairs in my mouth, or I would glance into the mirror to see them slashing like razor edges across the collars of my white shirts. Then too there was the fruit. I began to discover moldering bits of it about the house — apple and banana most characteristically — but plum and tangelo or even passion fruit and yim-yim were not at all anomalous. These fruit fragments occurred principally in the bedroom, on the pillow, surrounded by darkening spots. It was not long before I located their source: they lay hidden like gems in the long wild hanks of her hair. Another occupational hazard.

Jane was in the habit of sitting before the air conditioner when she came home from work, fingering out her hair, drying the sweat from her face and neck in the cool hum of the machine, fruit bits sifting silently to the carpet, black hairs drifting like feathers. On these occasions the room would fill with the stink of her, bestial and fetid. And I would find my eyes watering, my mind imaging the dark rotting trunks of the rain forest, stained sienna and mandalay and Hooker's green with the excrements dropped from above. My ears would keen with the whistling and crawking of the jungle birds, the screechings of the snot-nosed apes in the branches. And then, slack-faced and tight-boweled, I would step into the bathroom and retch, the sweetness of my own intestinal secrets a balm against the potent hairy stench of her.

One evening, just after her bath (the faintest odor lingered, yet still it was so trenchant I had to fight the impulse to get up and urinate on a tree or a post or something), I lay my hand casually across her belly and was suddenly startled to see an insect flit from its cover, skate up the swell of her abdomen, and bury itself in her navel. "Good Christ," I said.

"Hm?" she returned, peering over the cover of her Yerkish[1] reader.

"That," I said. "That bug, that insect, that vermin."

She sat up, plucked the thing from its cachette, raised it to her lips and popped it between her front teeth. "Louse," she said, sucking. "Went down to the old-age home on Thirteenth Street to pick them up."

I anticipated her: "Not for — ?"

"Why certainly, potpie — so Konrad can experience a tangible gratification of his social impulses during the grooming ritual. You know: you scratch my back, I scratch yours."

I lay in bed that night sweating, thinking about Jane and those slippery-fingered monkeys poking away at her, and listening for the lice crawling across her scalp or nestling their bloody little siphons in the tufts under her arms. Finally, about four, I got up and took three Doriden. I woke at two in the afternoon, an insect in my ear. It was only an earwig. I had missed my train, failed to call in at the office. There was a note from Jane: Pick me up at four. Konrad sends love.

The Primate Center stood in the midst of a macadamized acre or two, looking very much like a school building: faded brick, fluted columns, high mesh fences. Finger paintings and mobiles hung in the windows, misshapen ceramics crouched along the sills. A flag raggled at the top of a whitewashed flagpole. I found myself bending to examine the cornerstone: Asa Priff Grammar School, 1939. Inside it was dark and cool, the halls were lined with lockers and curling watercolors, the linoleum gleamed like a shy smile. I stepped into the BOYS' ROOM. The urinals were a foot and a half from the floor. Designed for little people, I mused. Youngsters. Hardly big enough to hold their little peters without the teacher's help. I smiled, and situated myself over one of the urinals, the strong honest scent of Pine-Sol in my nostrils. At that moment the door wheezed open and a chimpanzee shuffled in. He was dressed in shorts, shirt and bow tie. He nodded to me, it seemed, and made a few odd gestures with his hands as he moved up to the urinal beside mine. Then he opened his fly

---

1 From work of Robert Hearns Yerkes (1875–1956), American psychologist who founded Yale labs of primate biology.

THE SECRET HISTORY OF SCIENCE FICTION

and pulled out an enormous slick red organ like a peeled banana. I looked away, embarrassed, but could hear him urinating mightily. The stream hissed against the porcelain like a thunderstorm, rattled the drain as it went down. My own water wouldn't come. I began to feel foolish. The chimp shook himself daintily, zippered up, pulled the plunger, crossed to the sink, washed and dried his hands, and left. I found I no longer had to go.

Out in the hallway the janitor was leaning on his flathead broom. The chimp stood before him gesticulating with manic dexterity: brushing his forehead and tugging his chin, slapping his hands under his armpits, tapping his wrists, his tongue, his ear, his lip. The janitor watched intently. Suddenly — after a particularly virulent flurry — the man burst into laughter, rich braying globes of it. The chimp folded his lip and joined in, adding his weird nasal snickering to the janitor's barrel-laugh. I stood by the door to the BOYS' ROOM in a quandary. I began to feel that it might be wiser to wait in the car — but then I didn't want to call attention to myself, darting in and out like that. The janitor might think I was stealing paper towels or something. So I stood there, thinking to have a word with him after the chimp moved on — with the expectation that he could give me some grassroots insight into the nature of Jane's job. But the chimp didn't move on. The two continued laughing, now harder than ever. The janitor's face was tear-streaked. Each time he looked up the chimp produced a gesticular flurry that would stagger him again. Finally the janitor wound down a bit, and still chuckling, held out his hands, palms up. The chimp flung his arms up over his head and then heaved them down again, rhythmically slapping the big palms with his own. "Right on! Mastuh Konrad," the janitor said, "Right on!" The chimp grinned, then hitched up his shorts and sauntered off down the hall. The janitor turned back to his broom, still chuckling.

I cleared my throat. The broom began a geometrically precise course up the hall toward me. It stopped at my toes, the ridge of detritus flush with the pinions of my wingtips. The janitor looked up. The pupil of his right eye was fixed in the corner, beneath the lid, and the white was red. There was an ironic gap between his front teeth. "Kin ah do sumfin fo yo, mah good man?" he said.

"I'm waiting for Miss Good."

"Ohhh, Miz *Good*," he said, nodding his head. "Fust ah tought yo was thievin paypuh tow-els outen de Boys' Room but den when ah sees yo standin dere rigid as de Venus de Milo ah thinks to mahsef: he is some kinda new sculpture de stoodents done made is what he is." He was squinting up at me and grinning like we'd just come back from sailing around the world together.

"That's a nice broom," I said.

He looked at me steadily, grinning still. "Yo's wonderin what me and Mastuh Konrad was jivin bout up dere, isn't yo? Well, ah tells yo: he was relatin a hoomerous anecdote, de punch line ob which has deep cosmic implications in dat it establishes a common groun between monks and Ho-mo sapiens despite dere divergent ancestries." He shook his head, chortled. "Yes in-deed, dat Mastuh Konrad is quite de wit."

"You mean to tell me you actually understand all that lip-pulling and finger-waving?" I was beginning to feel a nameless sense of outrage.

"Oh sartinly, mah good man. Dat ASL."

"What?"

"ASL is what we was talkin. A-merican Sign Language. Developed for de deef n dumb. Yo sees, Mastuh Konrad is sumfin ob a genius round here. He can commoonicate de mos esoteric i-deas in bof ASL and Yerkish, re-spond to and translate English, French, German and Chinese. Fack, it was Miz Good was tellin me dat Konrad is workin right now on a Yerkish translation ob Darwin's *De-scent o Man*. He is mainly into anthro-pology, yo knows, but he has cultivated a interess in udder fields too. Dis lass fall he done undertook a Yerkish translation ob Chomsky's *Language and Mind* and Nietzsche's *Jenseits von Gut and Böse*.[2] And dat's some pretty heavy shit, Jackson."

I was hot with outrage. "Stuff," I said. "Stuff and nonsense."

"No sense in feelin personally treated by Mastuh Konrad's chievements, mah good fellow — yo's got to ree-lize dat he is a genius."

A word came to me: "Bullhonk," I said. And turned to leave.

The janitor caught me by the shirtsleeve. "He is now scorin his turd opera," he whispered. I tore away from him and stamped out of the building.

Jane was waiting in the car. I climbed in, cranked down the sunroof and opened the air vents.

At home I poured a water glass of gin, held it to my nostrils and inhaled. Jane sat before the air conditioner, her hair like a urinal mop, stinking. Black hairs

---

2 "Beyond good and evil."

cut the atmosphere, fruit bits whispered to the carpet. Occasionally the tip of my tongue entered the gin. I sniffed and tasted, thinking of plastic factories and turpentine distilleries and rich sulfurous smoke. On my way to the bedroom I poured a second glass.

In the bedroom I sniffed gin and dressed for dinner. "Jane?" I called. "Shouldn't you be getting ready?" She appeared in the doorway. She was dressed in her work clothes: jeans and sweatshirt. The sweatshirt was gray and hooded. There were yellow stains on the sleeves. I thought of the lower depths of animal cages, beneath the floor meshing. "I figured I'd go like this," she said. I was knotting my tie. "And I wish you'd stop insisting on baths every night — I'm getting tired of smelling like a coupon in a detergent box. It's unnatural. Unhealthy."

In the car on the way to the restaurant I lit a cigar, a cheap twisted black thing like half a pepperoni. Jane sat hunched against her door, unwashed. I had never before smoked a cigar. I tried to start a conversation but Jane said she didn't feel like talking: talk seemed so useless, such an anachronism. We drove on in silence. And I reflected that this was not the Jane I knew and loved. Where, I wondered, was the girl who changed wigs three or four times a day and sported nails like a Chinese emperor? — and where was the girl who dressed like an Arabian bazaar and smelled like the trade winds?

She was committed. The project, the study, grants. I could read the signs: she was growing away from me.

The restaurant was dark, a maze of rocky gardens, pancake-leafed vegetation, black fountains. We stood squinting just inside the door. Birds whistled, carp hissed through the pools. Somewhere a monkey screeched. Jane put her hand on my shoulder and whispered in my ear. "Siamang," she said. At that moment the leaves parted beside us: a rubbery little fellow emerged and motioned us to sit on a bench beneath a wicker birdcage. He was wearing a soiled loincloth and eight or ten necklaces of yellowed teeth. His hair flamed out like a brushfire. In the dim light from the braziers I noticed his nostrils — both shrunken and pinched, as if once pierced straight through. His face was of course inscrutable. As soon as we were seated he removed my socks and shoes, Jane's sneakers, and wrapped our feet in what I later learned were plantain leaves. I started to object — I bitterly resent anyone looking at my feet — but Jane shushed me. We had waited three months for reservations.

The maitre d' signed for us to follow, and led us through a dripping stone-walled tunnel to an outdoor garden where the flagstones gave way to dirt and we found ourselves on a narrow plant-choked path. He licked along like an iguana and we hurried to keep up. Wet fronds slapped back in my face, creepers snatched at my ankles, mud sucked at the plantain leaves on my feet. The scents of mold and damp and long-lying urine hung in the air, and I thought of the men's room at the subway station. It was dark as a womb. I offered Jane my hand, but she refused it. Her breathing was fast. The monkey chatter was loud as a zoo afire. "Far out," she said. I slapped a mosquito on my neck.

A moment later we found ourselves seated at a bamboo table overhung with branch and vine. Across from us sat Dr. and Mrs. U-Hwak-Lo, director of the Primate Center and wife. A candle guttered between them. I cleared my throat, and then began idly tracing my finger around the circular hole cut in the table's center. The Doctor's ears were the size of peanuts. "Glad you two could make it," he said. "I've long been urging Jane to sample some of our humble island fare." I smiled, crushed a spider against the back of my chair. The Doctor's English was perfect, pure Martha's Vineyard — he sounded like Ted Kennedy's insurance salesman. His wife's was weak: "Yes," she said, "nussing cook here, all roar." "How exciting!" said Jane. And then the conversation turned to primates, and the Center.

Mrs. U-Hwak-Lo and I smiled at one another. Jane and the Doctor were already deeply absorbed in a dialogue concerning the incidence of anal retention in chimps deprived of Frisbee coordination during the sensorimotor period. I gestured toward them with my head and arched my eyebrows wittily. Mrs. U-Hwak-Lo giggled. It was then that Jane's proximity began to affect me. The close wet air seemed to concentrate her essence, distill its potency. The U-Hwak-Los seemed unaffected. I began to feel queasy. I reached for the fingerbowl and drank down its contents. Mrs. U-Hwak-Lo smiled. It was coconut oil. Just then the waiter appeared carrying a wooden bowl the size of a truck tire. A single string of teeth slapped against his breastbone as he set the bowl down and slipped off into the shadows. The Doctor and Jane were oblivious — they were talking excitedly, occasionally lapsing into what I took to be ASL, ear- and nose- and lip-picking like a manager and his third-base coach. I peered into the bowl: it was filled to the rim with clean-picked chicken bones. Mrs. U-Hwak-Lo nodded, grinning: "No on-tray," she said. "Appeticer." At that moment a simian screamed somewhere close, screamed like death itself. Jane looked up. "Rhesus," she said.

On my return from the men's room I had some difficulty locating the table in the dark. I had already waded through two murky fountains and was preparing to plunge through my third when I heard Mrs. U-Hwak-Lo's voice behind me. "Here," she said. "Make quick, repass now serve." She took my hand and led me back to the table. "Oh, they're enormously resourceful," the Doctor was saying as I stumbled into my chair, pants wet to the knees. "They first employ a general anesthetic — a distillation of the chu-bok root — and then the chef (who logically doubles as village surgeon) makes a circular incision about the macaque's cranium, carefully peeling back the already-shaven scalp, and staunching the blood flow quite effectively with maura-ro, a highly absorbent powder derived from the tamana leaf. He then removes both the frontal and parietal plates to expose the brain…"
I looked at Jane: she was rapt. I wasn't really listening. My attention was directed toward what I took to be the main course, which had appeared in my absence. An unsteady pinkish mound now occupied the center of the table, completely obscuring the circular hole — it looked like cherry vanilla yogurt, a carton and a half, perhaps two. On closer inspection I noticed several black hairs peeping out from around its flaccid edges. And thought immediately of the bush-headed maitre d'. I pointed to one of the hairs, remarking to Mrs. U-Hwak-Lo that the rudiments of culinary hygiene could be a little more rigorously observed among the staff. She smiled. Encouraged, I asked her what exactly the dish was. "Much delicacy," she said. "Very rare find in land of Lincoln." At the moment the waiter appeared and handed each of us a bamboo stick beaten flat and sharpened at one end.
"…then the tribal elders or visiting dignitaries are seated around the table," the Doctor was saying. "The chef has previously of course located the macaque beneath the table, the exposed part of the creature's brain protruding from the hole in its center. After the feast, the lower ranks of the village population divide up the remnants. It's really quite efficient."
"How fascinating!" said Jane. "Shall we try some?"
"By all means…but tell me, how has Konrad been coming with that Yerkish epic he's been working up?"
Jane turned to answer, bamboo stick poised: "Oh I'm so glad you asked — I'd almost forgotten. He's finished his tenth book and tells me he'll be doing two more — out of deference to the Miltonic tradition. Isn't that a groove?"
"Yes," said the Doctor, gesturing toward the rosy lump in the center of the table. "Yes it is. He's certainly — and I hope you won't mind the pun — a brainy fellow. Ho-ho."

"Oh, Doctor," Jane laughed, and plunged her stick into the pink. Beneath the table, in the dark, a tiny fist clutched at my pantleg.

I missed work again the following day. This time it took five Doriden to put me under. I had lain in bed sweating and tossing, listening to Jane's quiet breathing, inhaling her fumes. At dawn I dozed off, dreamed briefly of elementary school cafeterias swarming with knickered chimps and weltered with trays of cherry vanilla yogurt, and woke stale-mouthed. Then I took the pills. It was three-thirty when I woke again. There was a note from Jane: *Bringing Konrad home for dinner. Vacuum rug and clean toilet.*

Konrad was impeccably dressed — long pants, platform wedgies, cufflinks. He smelled of eau de cologne, Jane of used litter. They arrived during the seven o'clock news. I opened the door for them. "Hello, Jane," I said. We stood at the door, awkward, silent.

"Well?" she said. "Aren't you going to greet our guest?" "Hello, Konrad," I said. And then: "I believe we met in the boys' room at the Center the other day?" He bowed deeply, straight-faced, his upper lip like a halved cantaloupe. Then he broke into a snicker, turned to Jane and juggled out an impossible series of gestures. Jane laughed. Something caught in my throat. "Is he trying to say something?" I asked. "Oh potpie," she said, "it was nothing — just a little quote from Yeats."

"Yeats?"

"Yes, you know: 'An aged man is but a paltry thing.'"[3]

Jane served watercress sandwiches and animal crackers as hors d'oeuvres. She brought them into the living room on a cut-glass serving tray and set them down before Konrad and me, where we sat on the sofa, watching the news. Then she returned to the kitchen. Konrad plucked up a tiny sandwich and swallowed it like a communion wafer, sucking the tips of his fingers. Then he lifted the tray and offered it to me. I declined. "No, thank you," I said. Konrad shrugged, set the plate down in his lap, and carefully stacked all the sandwiches in its center. I pretended to be absorbed with the news: actually I studied him, half-face. He was filling the gaps in his sandwich-construction with animal crackers. His lower lip protruded, his ears were rubbery, he was balding. With both hands he crushed the heap of crackers and sandwiches together and began kneading it until it took

---

3 From "Sailing to Byzantium" by William Butler Yeats (1856–1939), Irish poet.

on the consistency of raw dough. Then he lifted the whole thing to his mouth and swallowed it without chewing. There were no whites to his eyes.

Konrad's only reaction to the newscast was a burst of excitement over a war story — the reporter stood against the wasteland of treadless tanks and recoilless guns in Thailand or Syria or Chile; huts were burning, old women weeping. "Wow-wow! Eeeeeeee! Er-er-er-er," Konrad said. Jane appeared in the kitchen doorway, hands dripping. "What is it, Konrad?" she said. He made a series of violent gestures. "Well?" I asked. She translated: "Konrad says that 'the pig oppressors' genocidal tactics will lead to their mutual extermination and usher in a new golden age...'" — here she hesitated, looked up at him to continue (he was springing up and down on the couch, flailing his fists as though they held whips and scourges) — "'...of freedom and equality for all, regardless of race, creed, color — or genus.' I wouldn't worry," she added, "it's just his daily slice of revolutionary rhetoric. He'll calm down in a minute — he likes to play Che,[4] but he's basically nonviolent."

Ten minutes later Jane served dinner. Konrad, with remarkable speed and coordination, consumed four cans of fruit cocktail, thirty-two spareribs, half a dozen each of oranges, apples and pomegranates, two cheeseburgers and three quarts of chocolate malted. In the kitchen, clearing up, I commented to Jane about our guest's prodigious appetite. He was sitting in the other room, listening to *Don Giovanni*,[5] sipping brandy. Jane said that he was a big, active male and that she could attest to his need for so many calories. "How much does he weigh?" I asked. "Stripped," she said, "one eighty-one. When he stands up straight he's four eight and three quarters." I mulled over this information while I scraped away at the dishes, filed them in the dishwasher, neat ranks of blue china. A few moments later I stepped into the living room to observe Jane stroking Konrad's ears, his head in her lap. I stand five seven, one forty-three.

When I returned from work the following day, Jane was gone. Her dresser drawers were bare, the closet empty. There were white rectangles on the wall where her Rousseau[6] reproductions had hung. The top plank of the bookcase was ribbed with the dust-prints of her Edgar Rice Burroughs[7] collection. Her

---

4 Che Guevara (1928–1967), Cuban revolutionary killed in Bolivia.
5 Opera (1787) by Mozart.
6 Henri Rousseau (1844–1910), French painter.
7 Popular American novelist (1875–1950), author of the Tarzan books.

girls' softball trophy, her natural foods cookbook, her oaken cudgel, her moog, her wok: all gone. There were no notes. A pain jabbed at my sternum, tears started in my eyes. I was alone, deserted, friendless. I began to long even for the stink of her. On the pillow in the bedroom I found a fermenting chunk of pineapple. And sobbed.

By the time I thought of the Primate Center the sun was already on the wane. It was dark when I got there. Loose gravel grated beneath my shoes in the parking lot; the flag snapped at the top of its pole; the lights grinned lickerishly from the Center's windows. Inside the lighting was subdued, the building hushed. I began searching through the rooms, opening and slamming doors. The linoleum glowed all the way up the long corridor. At the far end I heard someone whistling "My Old Kentucky Home." It was the janitor. "Howdedo," he said. "Wut kin ah do fo yo at such a inauspicious hour ob de night?"

I was candid with him. "I'm looking for Miss Good."

"Ohhh, she leave bout fo-turdy evy day — sartinly yo should be well apprised ob dat fack."

"I thought she might be working late tonight."

"Noooo, no chance ob dat." He was staring at the floor.

"Mind if I look for myself?"

"Mah good man, ah trusts yo is not intimatin dat ah would diskise de troof...far be it fum me to pre-varicate just to proteck a young lady wut run off fum a man dat doan unnerstan her needs nor 'low her to spress de natchrul inclination ob her soul."

At that moment a girlish giggle sounded from down the hall. Jane's girlish giggle. The janitor's right hand spread itself across my chest. "Ah wooden insinooate mahself in de middle ob a highly sinificant speriment if ah was yo, Jackson," he said, hissing through the gap in his teeth. I pushed by him and started down the corridor. Jane's laugh leaped out again. From the last door on my left. I hurried. Suddenly the Doctor and his wife stepped from the shadows to block the doorway. "Mr. Horne," said the Doctor, arms folded against his chest, "take hold of yourself. We are conducting a series of experiments here that I simply cannot allow you to —"

"A fig for your experiments," I shouted. "I want to speak to my, my — roommate." I could hear the janitor's footsteps behind me. "Get out of my way, Doctor," I said. Mrs. U-Hwak-Lo smiled. I felt panicky. Thought of the Tong

Wars. "Is dey a problem here, Doc?" the janitor said, his breath hot on the back of my neck. I broke. Grabbed the Doctor by his elbows, wheeled around and shoved him into the janitor. They went down on the linoleum like spastic skaters. I applied my shoulder to the door and battered my way in, Mrs. U-Hwak-Lo's shrill in my ear: "You make big missake, Misser!" Inside I found Jane, legs and arms bare, pinching a lab smock across her chest. She looked puzzled at first, then annoyed. She stepped up to me, made some rude gestures in my face. I could hear scrambling in the hallway behind me. Then I saw Konrad — in a pair of baggy BVDs. I grabbed Jane. But Konrad was there in an instant — he hit me like a grill of a Cadillac and I spun across the room, tumbling desks and chairs as I went. I slumped against the chalkboard. The door slammed: Jane was gone. Konrad swelled his chest, swayed toward me, the fluorescent lights hissing overhead, the chalkboard cold against the back of my neck. And I looked up into the black eyes, teeth, fur, rock-ribbed arms.

Technology is our fate, our truth. It is what we mean when we call ourselves the only superpower on the planet. The materials and methods we devise make it possible for us to claim the future. We don't have to depend on God or the prophets or other astonishments. We are the astonishment. The miracle is what we ourselves produce, the systems and networks that change the way we live and think.

—Don DeLillo

What we now normally consider the mainstream — so called realistic fiction — is a small literary genre, fairly recent in origin, which is likely to be relatively short lived.... It's a matter of whether you're content to focus on everyday events or whether you want to try to encompass the entire universe. If you go back to the literature written in ancient Greece or Rome, or during the Middle Ages and much of the Renaissance, you'll see writers trying to write not just about everything that exists but about everything that could exist.

—Gene Wolfe

Human Moments in World War III
Don DeLillo

A NOTE ABOUT Vollmer. He no longer describes the earth as a library globe or a map that has come alive, as a cosmic eye staring into deep space. This last was his most ambitious fling at imagery. The war has changed the way he sees the earth. The earth is land and water, the dwelling place of mortal men, in elevated dictionary terms. He doesn't see it anymore (storm-spiraled, sea-bright, breathing heat and haze and color) as an occasion for picturesque language, for easeful play or speculation.

At two hundred and twenty kilometers we see ship wakes and the larger airports. Icebergs, lightning bolts, sand dunes. I point out lava flows and cold-core eddies. That silver ribbon off the Irish coast, I tell him, is an oil slick.

This is my third orbital mission, Vollmer's first. He is an engineering genius, a communications and weapons genius, and maybe other kinds of genius as well. As mission specialist I'm content to be in charge. (The word "specialist," in the peculiar usage of Colorado Command, refers here to someone who does not specialize.) Our spacecraft is designed primarily to gather intelligence. The refinement of the quantum burn technique enables us to make frequent adjustments of orbit without firing rockets every time. We swing out into high wide trajectories, the whole earth as our psychic light, to inspect unmanned and possibly hostile satellites. We orbit tightly, snugly, take intimate looks at surface activities in untraveled places.

The banning of nuclear weapons has made the world safe for war.

I try not to think big thoughts or submit to rambling abstractions. But the urge sometimes comes over me. Earth orbit puts men into philosophical temper. How can we help it? We see the planet complete, we have a privileged vista. In our attempts to be equal to the experience, we tend to meditate importantly on subjects like the human condition. It makes a man feel *universal*, floating over the continents, seeing the rim of the world, a line as clear as a compass arc, knowing it is just a turning of the bend to Atlantic twilight, to sediment plumes and kelp beds, an island chain glowing in the dusky sea.

I tell myself it is only scenery. I want to think of our life here as ordinary, as a housekeeping arrangement, an unlikely but workable setup caused by a housing shortage or spring floods in the valley.

Vollmer does the systems checklist and goes to his hammock to rest. He is twenty-three years old, a boy with a longish head and close-cropped hair. He talks about northern Minnesota as he removes the objects in his personal preference kit, placing them on an adjacent Velcro surface for tender inspection. I have a 1901 silver dollar in my personal preference kit. Little else of note. Vollmer has graduation pictures, bottle caps, small stones from his backyard. I don't know whether he chose these items himself or whether they were pressed on him by parents who feared that his life in space would be lacking in human moments.

Our hammocks are human moments, I suppose, although I don't know whether Colorado Command planned it that way. We eat hot dogs and almond crunch bars and apply lip balm as part of the presleep checklist. We wear slippers at the firing panel. Vollmer's football jersey is a human moment. Outsized, purple and white, of polyester mesh, bearing the number 79, a big man's number, a prime of no particular distinction, it makes him look stoop-shouldered, abnormally long-framed.

"I still get depressed on Sundays," he says.

"Do we have Sundays here?"

"No, but they have them there and I still feel them. I always know when it's Sunday."

"Why do you get depressed?"

"The slowness of Sundays. Something about the glare, the smell of warm grass, the church service, the relatives visiting in nice clothes. The whole day kind of lasts forever."

"I didn't like Sundays either."

"They were slow but not lazy-slow. They were long and hot, or long and cold. In summer my grandmother made lemonade. There was a routine. The whole day was kind of set up beforehand and the routine almost never changed. Orbital routine is different. It's satisfying. It gives our time a shape and substance. Those Sundays were shapeless despite the fact you knew what was coming, who was coming, what we'd all say. You knew the first words out of the mouth of each person before anyone spoke. I was the only kid in the group. People were happy to see me. I used to want to hide."

"What's wrong with lemonade?" I ask.

A battle management satellite, unmanned, reports high-energy laser activity in orbital sector Dolores. We take out our laser kits and study them for half an hour. The beaming procedure is complex and because the panel operates on joint control only we must rehearse the sets of established measures with the utmost care.

A note about the earth. The earth is the preserve of day and night. It contains a sane and balanced variation, a natural waking and sleeping, or so it seems to someone deprived of this tidal effect.

This is why Vollmer's remark about Sundays in Minnesota struck me as interesting. He still feels, or claims he feels, or thinks he feels, that inherently earthbound rhythm.

To men at this remove, it is as though things exist in their particular physical form in order to reveal the hidden simplicity of some powerful mathematical truth. The earth reveals to us the simple awesome beauty of day and night. It is there to contain and incorporate these conceptual events.

Vollmer in his shorts and suction clogs resembles a high-school swimmer, all but hairless, an unfinished man not aware he is open to cruel scrutiny, not aware he is without devices, standing with arms folded in a place of echoing voices and chlorine fumes. There is something stupid in the sound of his voice. It is too direct, a deep voice from high in the mouth, well back in the mouth, slightly insistent, a little loud. Vollmer has never said a stupid thing in my presence. It is just his voice that is stupid, a grave and naked bass, a voice without inflection or breath.

We are not cramped here. The flight deck and crew quarters are thoughtfully designed. Food is fair to good. There are books, videocassettes, news and music. We do the manual checklists, the oral checklists, the simulated firings with no sign of boredom or carelessness. If anything, we are getting better at our tasks all the time. The only danger is conversation.

I try to keep our conversations on an everyday plane. I make it a point to talk about small things, routine things. This makes sense to me. It seems a sound tactic, under the circumstances, to restrict our talk to familiar topics, minor matters. I want to build a structure of the commonplace. But Vollmer has a tendency to bring up enormous subjects. He wants to talk about war and the weapons of war. He wants to discuss global strategies, global aggressions. I tell him now that he has stopped describing the earth as a cosmic eye, he wants to see it as a game board or computer model. He looks at me plain-faced and tries to get me in a theoretical argument: selection space-based attacks versus long drawn-out well-modulated land-sea-air engagements. He quotes experts, mentions sources. What am I supposed to say? He will suggest that people are disappointed in the war. The war is dragging into its third week. There is a sense in which it is worn out, played out. He gathers this from the news broadcasts we periodically receive. Something in the announcer's voice hints at a let-down, a fatigue, a faint bitterness about — *something*. Vollmer is probably right about this. I've heard it myself in the tone of the broadcaster's voice, in the voice of Colorado Command, despite the fact that our news is censored, that they are not telling us things they feel we shouldn't know, in our special situation, our exposed and sensitive position. In his direct and stupid-sounding and uncannily perceptive way, young Vollmer says that people are not enjoying this war to the same extent that people have always enjoyed and nourished themselves on war, as a heightening, a periodic intensity. What I object to in Vollmer is that he often shares my deep-reaching and most reluctantly held convictions. Coming from that mild face, in that earnest resonant run-on voice, these ideas unnerve and worry me as they never do when they remain unspoken. Vollmer's candor exposes something painful.

It is not too early in the war to discern nostalgic references to earlier wars. All wars refer back. Ships, planes, entire operations are named after ancient battles, simpler weapons, what we perceive as conflicts of nobler intent. This recon-interceptor is called Tomahawk II. When I sit at the firing panel I look at a photograph of Vollmer's granddad when he was a young man in sagging khakis and a shallow helmet, standing in a bare field, a rifle strapped to his shoulder. This is a human moment and it reminds me that war, among other things, is a form of longing.

We dock with the command station, take on food, exchange videocassettes. The war is going well, they tell us, although it isn't likely they know much more than we do.

Then we separate.

The maneuver is flawless and I am feeling happy and satisfied, having resumed human contact with the nearest form of the outside world, having traded quips and manly insults, traded voices, traded news and rumors — buzzes, rumbles, scuttlebutt. We stow our supplies of broccoli and apple cider and fruit cocktail and butterscotch pudding. I feel a homey emotion, putting away the colorfully packaged goods, a sensation of prosperous well-being, the consumer's solid comfort.

Volmer's T-shirt bears the word *Inscription*.

"People had hoped to be caught up in something bigger than themselves," he says. "They thought it would be a shared crisis. They would feel a sense of shared purpose, shared destiny. Like a snowstorm that blankets a large city — but lasting months, lasting years, carrying everyone along, creating fellow-feeling where there was only suspicion and fear. Strangers talking to each other, meals by candlelight when the power fails. The war would ennoble everything we say and do. What was impersonal would become personal. What was solitary would be shared. But what happens when the sense of shared crisis begins to dwindle much sooner than anyone expected? We begin to think the feeling lasts longer in snowstorms."

A note about selective noise. Forty-eight hours ago I was monitoring data on the mission console when a voice broke in on my report to Colorado Command. The voice was unenhanced, heavy with static. I checked my headset, checked the switches and lights. Seconds later the command signal resumed and I heard our flight dynamics officer ask me to switch to the redundant sense frequencer. I did this but it only caused the weak voice to return, a voice that carried with it a strange and unspecifiable poignancy. I seemed somehow to recognize it. I don't mean I knew who was speaking. It was the tone I recognized, the touching quality of some half-remembered and tender event, even through the static, the sonic mist.

In any case, Colorado Command resumed transmission in a matter of seconds.

"We have a deviate, Tomahawk."

"We copy. There's a voice."

"We have gross oscillation here."

"There's some interference. I have gone redundant but I'm not sure it's helping."

"We are clearing an outframe to locate source."

"Thank you, Colorado."

"It is probably just selective noise. You are negative red on the step-function quad."

"It was a voice," I told them.

"We have just received an affirm on selective noise."

"I could hear words, in English."

"We copy selective noise."

"Someone was talking, Colorado."

"What do you think selective noise is?"

"I don't know what it is."

"You are getting a spill from one of the unmanneds."

"If it's an unmanned, how could it be sending a voice?"

"It is not a voice as such, Tomahawk. It is selective noise. We have some real firm telemetry on that."

"It sounded like a voice."

"It is supposed to sound like a voice. But it is not a voice as such. It is enhanced."

"It sounded unenhanced. It sounded human in all sorts of ways."

"It is signals and they are spilling from geosynchronous orbit. This is your deviate. You are getting voice codes from twenty-two thousand miles. It is basically a weather report. We will correct, Tomahawk. In the meantime, advise you stay redundant."

About ten hours later Vollmer heard the voice. Then he heard two or three other voices. They were people speaking, people in conversation. He gestured to me as he listened, pointed to the headset, then raised his shoulders, held his hands apart to indicate surprise and bafflement. In the swarming noise (as he said later), it wasn't easy to get the drift of what people were saying. The static was frequent, the references were somewhat elusive, but Vollmer mentioned how intensely affecting these voices were, even when the signals were at their weakest. One thing he did know: it wasn't selective noise. A quality of purest, sweetest sadness issued from remote space: He wasn't sure but he thought there was also a background noise integral to the conversation. Laughter. The sound of people laughing.

In other transmissions we've been able to recognize theme music, an announcer's introduction, wisecracks and bursts of applause, commercials for products whose long-lost brand names evoke the golden antiquity of great cities buried in sand and river silt.

Somehow we are picking up signals from radio programs of forty, fifty, sixty years ago.

Our current task is to collect imagery data on troop deployment. Vollmer surrounds his Hasselblad, engrossed in some microadjustment. There is a seaward bulge of stratocumulus. Sunglint and littoral drift. I see blooms of plankton in a blue of such Persian richness it seems an animal rapture, a color-change to express some form of intuitive delight. As the surface features unfurl, I list them aloud by name. It is the only game I play in space, reciting the earth-names, the nomenclature of contour and structure. Glacial scour, moraine debris. Shatter-coning at the edge of a multi-ring impact site. A resurgent caldera, a mass of castellated rimrock. Over the sand seas now. Parabolic dunes, star dunes, straight dunes with radial crests. The emptier the land, the more luminous and precise the names for its features. Vollmer says the thing science does best is name the features of the world.

He has degrees in science and technology. He was a scholarship winner, an honors student, a research assistant. He ran science projects, read technical papers in the deep-pitched earnest voice that rolls off the roof of his mouth. As mission specialist (generalist), I sometimes resent his nonscientific perceptions, the glimmerings of maturity and balanced judgment. I am beginning to feel slightly preempted. I want him to stick to systems, onboard guidance, data parameters. His human insights make me nervous.

"I'm happy," he says.

These words are delivered with matter-of-fact finality and the simple statement affects me powerfully. It frightens me in fact. What does he mean he's happy? Isn't happiness totally outside our frame of reference? How can he think it is possible to be happy here? I want to say to him, "This is just a housekeeping arrangement, a series of more or less routine tasks. Attend to your tasks, do your testing, run through your checklists." I want to say, "Forget the measure of our vision, the sweep of things, the war itself, the terrible death. Forget the overarching night, the stars as static points, as mathematical fields. Forget the cosmic solitude, the upwelling awe and dread."

I want to say, "Happiness is not a fact of this experience, at least not to the extent that one is bold enough to speak of it."

Laser technology contains a core of foreboding and myth. It is a clean sort of lethal package we are dealing with, a well-behaved beam of photons, an engineered coherence, but we approach the weapon with our minds full of ancient warnings and fears. (There ought to be a term for this ironic condition: primitive fear of the weapons we are advanced enough to design and produce.) Maybe this is why the project managers were ordered to work out a firing procedure that depends on the coordinated actions of two men — two temperaments, two souls — operating the controls together. Fear of the power of light, the pure stuff of the universe.

A single dark mind in a moment of inspiration might think it liberating to fling a concentrated beam at some lumbering humpbacked Boeing making its commercial rounds at thirty thousand feet.

Vollmer and I approach the firing panel. The panel is designed in such a way that the joint operators must sit back to back. The reason for this, although Colorado Command never specifically said so, is to keep us from seeing each other's face. Colorado wants to be sure that weapons personnel in particular are not influenced by each other's tics and perturbations. We are back to back, therefore, harnessed in our seats, ready to begin. Vollmer in his purple and white jersey, his fleeced pad-abouts.

This is only a test.

I start the playback. At the sound of a prerecorded voice command, we each insert a modal key in its proper slot. Together we count down from five and then turn the keys one-quarter left. This puts the system in what is called an open-minded mode. We count down from three. The enhanced voice says, *You are open-minded now.*

Vollmer speaks into his voiceprint analyzer.

"This is code B for bluegrass. Request voice identity clearance."

We count down from five and then speak into our voiceprint analyzers. We say whatever comes into our heads. The point is simply to produce a voiceprint that matches the print in the memory bank. This ensures that the men at the panel are the same men authorized to be there when the system is in an open-minded mode.

This is what comes into my head: "I am standing at the corner of Fourth and Main, where thousands are dead of unknown causes, their scorched bodies piled in the street."

We count down from three. The enhanced voice says, *You are cleared to proceed to lock-in position.*

We turn our modal keys half right. I activate the logic chip and study the numbers on my screen. Vollmer disengages voiceprint and puts us in voice circuit rapport with the onboard computer's sensing mesh. We count down from five. The enhanced voice says, *You are locked in now.*

"Random factor seven," I say. "Problem seven. Solution seven."

Vollmer says, "Give me an acronym."

"BROWN, for Bearing Radius Oh White Nine."

My color-spec lights up brown. The numbers on my display screen read 2, 18, 15, 23, 14. These are the alphanumeric values of the letters in the acronym BROWN as they appear in unit succession.

The logic-gate opens. The enhanced voice says, *You are logical now.*

As we move from one step to the next, as the colors, numbers, characters, lights and auditory signals indicate that we are proceeding correctly, a growing satisfaction passes through me — the pleasure of elite and secret skills, a life in which every breath is governed by specific rules, by patterns, codes, controls. I try to keep the results of the operation out of my mind, the whole point of it, the outcome of these sequences of precise and esoteric steps. But often I fail. I let the image in, I think the thought, I even say the word at times. This is confusing, of course. I feel tricked. My pleasure feels betrayed, as if it had a life of its own, a childlike or intelligent-animal existence independent of the man at the firing panel.

We count down from five. Vollmer releases the lever that unwinds the systems-purging disc. My pulse marker shows green at three-second intervals. We count down from three. We turn the modal keys three-quarters right. I activate the beam sequencer. We turn the keys one-quarter right. We count down from three. Bluegrass music plays over the squawk box. The enhanced voice says, *You are moded to fire now.*

We study our world map kits.

"Don't you sometimes feel a power in you?" Vollmer says. "An extreme state of good health, sort of. An *arrogant* healthiness. That's it. You are feeling so good you begin thinking you're a little superior to other people. A kind of life-strength."

An optimism about yourself that you generate almost at the expense of others. Don't you sometimes feel this?"

(Yes, as a matter of fact.)

"There's probably a German word for it. But the point I want to make is that this powerful feeling is so — I don't know — *delicate*. That's it. One day you feel it, the next day you are suddenly puny and doomed. A single little thing goes wrong, you feel doomed, you feel utterly weak and defeated and unable to act powerfully or even sensibly. Everyone else is lucky, you are unlucky, hapless, sad, ineffectual and doomed."

(Yes, yes.)

By chance we are over the Missouri River now, looking toward the Red Lakes of Minnesota. I watch Vollmer go through his map kit, trying to match the two worlds. This is a deep and mysterious happiness, to confirm the accuracy of a map. He seems immensely satisfied. He keeps saying, *"That's it, that's it."*

Vollmer talks about childhood. In orbit he has begun to think about his early years for the first time. He is surprised at the power of these memories. As he speaks he keeps his head turned to the window. Minnesota is a human moment. Upper Red Lake, Lower Red Lake. He clearly feels he can see himself there.

"Kids don't take walks," he says. "They don't sunbathe or sit on the porch."

He seems to be saying that children's lives are too well-supplied to accommodate the spells of reinforced being that the rest of us depend on. A deft enough thought but not to be pursued. It is time to prepare for a quantum burn.

We listen to the old radio shows. Light flares and spreads across the blue-banded edge, sunrise, sunset, the urban grids in shadow. A man and woman trade well-timed remarks, light, pointed, bantering. There is a sweetness in the tenor voice of the young man singing, a simple vigor that time and distance and random noise have enveloped in eloquence and yearning. Every sound, every lilt of strings has this veneer of age. Vollmer says he remembers these programs, although of course he has never heard them before. What odd happenstance, what flourish or grace of the laws of physics, enables us to pick up these signals? Traveled voices, chambered and dense. At times they have the detached and surreal quality of aural hallucination, voices in attic rooms, the complaints of dead relatives. But the sound effects are full of urgency and verve. Cars turn dangerous corners, crisp gunfire fills the night. It was, it is, wartime. Wartime for Duz and Grape-Nuts Flakes. Comedians make fun of the way the enemy talks. We hear hysterical mock German, moonshine Japanese. The cities are in light, the listening millions, fed, met comfortably in drowsy rooms, at war, as the night comes softly down. Vollmer says he recalls specific moments, the comic inflections, the announcer's fat-man laughter. He recalls individual voices rising from the laughter of the studio audience, the cackle of a St. Louis businessman, the brassy wail of a high-shouldered blonde, just arrived in California, where women wear their hair this year in aromatic bales.

Vollmer drifts across the wardroom, upside-down, eating an almond crunch.

He sometimes floats free of his hammock, sleeping in a fetal crouch, bumping into walls, adhering to a corner of the ceiling grid.

"Give me a minute to think of the name," he says in his sleep.

He says he dreams of vertical spaces from which he looks, as a boy, at — *something*. My dreams are the heavy kind, the kind that are hard to wake from, to rise out of. They are strong enough to pull me back down, dense enough to leave me with a heavy head, a drugged and bloated feeling. There are episodes of faceless gratification, vaguely disturbing.

"It's almost unbelievable when you think of it, how they live there in all that ice and sand and mountainous wilderness. Look at it," he says. "Huge barren deserts, huge oceans. How do they endure all those terrible things? The floods alone. The earthquakes alone make it crazy to live there. Look at those fault systems. They're so big, there's so many of them. The volcanic eruptions alone. What could be more frightening than a volcanic eruption? How do they endure avalanches, year after year, with numbing regularity? It's hard to believe people live there. The floods alone. You can see whole huge discolored areas, all flooded out, washed out. How do they survive, where do they go? Look at the cloud buildups. Look at that swirling storm center. What about the people who live in the path of a storm like that? It must be packing incredible winds. The lightning alone. People exposed on beaches, near trees and telephone poles. Look at the cities with their spangled lights spreading in all directions. Try to imagine the crime and violence. Look at the smoke pall hanging low. What does that mean in terms of respiratory disorders? It's crazy. Who would live there? The deserts, how they encroach. Every year they claim more and more arable land. How enormous those snowfields are. Look at the massive storm fronts over the ocean. There are ships down there, small craft some of them. Try to imagine the waves, the rocking. The hurricanes alone. The tidal waves. Look at those coastal communities exposed to tidal waves. What could be more frightening than a tidal wave? But they live there, they stay there. Where could they go?"

I want to talk to him about calorie intake, the effectiveness of the earplugs and nasal decongestants. The earplugs are human moments. The apple cider and the broccoli are human moments. Vollmer himself is a human moment, never more so than when he forgets there is a war.

The close-cropped hair and longish head. The mild blue eyes that bulge slightly. The protuberant eyes of long-bodied people with stooped shoulders. The long hands and wrists. The mild face. The easy face of a handyman in a panel truck that has an extension ladder fixed to the roof and a scuffed license plate, green and white, with the state motto beneath the digits. That kind of face.

He offers to give me a haircut. What an interesting thing a haircut is, when you think of it. Before the war there were time slots reserved for such activities. Houston not only had everything scheduled well in advance but constantly monitored us for whatever meager feedback might result. We were wired, taped, scanned, diagnosed, and metered. We were men in space, objects worthy of the most scrupulous care, the deepest sentiments and anxieties.

Now there is a war. Nobody cares about my hair, what I eat, how I feel about the spacecraft's decor, and it is not Houston but Colorado we are in touch with. We are no longer delicate biological specimens adrift in an alien environment. The enemy can kill us with its photons, its mesons, its charged particles faster than any calcium deficiency or trouble of the inner ear, faster than any dusting of micrometeoroids. The emotions have changed. We've stopped being candidates for an embarrassing demise, the kind of mistake or unforeseen event that tends to make a nation grope for the appropriate response. As men in war we can be certain, dying, that we will arouse uncomplicated sorrows, the open and dependable feelings that grateful nations count on to embellish the simplest ceremony.

A note about the universe. Vollmer is on the verge of deciding that our planet is alone in harboring intelligent life. We are an accident and we happened only once. (What a remark to make, in egg-shaped orbit, to someone who doesn't want to discuss the larger questions.) He feels this way because of the war.

The war, he says, will bring about an end to the idea that the universe swarms, as they say, with life. Other astronauts have looked past the star-points and imagined infinite possibility, grape-clustered worlds teeming with higher forms. But this was before the war. Our view is changing even now, his and mine, he says, as we drift across the firmament.

Is Vollmer saying that cosmic optimism is a luxury reserved for periods between world wars? Do we project our current failure and despair out toward the star clouds, the endless night? After all, he says, where are they? If they exist, why has there been no sign, not one, not any, not a single indication that serious people might cling to, not a whisper, a radio pulse, a shadow? The war tells us it is foolish to believe.

Our dialogues with Colorado Command are beginning to sound like computer-generated tea-time chat. Vollmer tolerates Colorado's jargon only to a point. He is critical of their more debased locutions and doesn't mind letting them know. Why, then, if I agree with his views on this matter, am I becoming irritated by his complaints? Is he too young to champion the language? Does he have the experience, the professional standing to scold our flight dynamics officer, our conceptual paradigm officer, our status consultants on waste-management systems and evasion-related zonal options? Or is it something else completely, something unrelated to Colorado Command and our communications with them? Is it the sound of his voice? Is it just his *voice* that is driving me crazy?

Vollmer has entered a strange phase. He spends all his time at the window now, looking down at the earth. He says little or nothing. He simply wants to look, do nothing but look. The oceans, the continents, the archipelagos. We are configured in what is called a cross-orbit series and there is no repetition from one swing around the earth to the next. He sits there looking. He takes meals at the window, does checklists at the window, barely glancing at the instruction sheets as we pass over tropical storms, over grass fires and major ranges. I keep waiting for him to return to his prewar habit of using quaint phrases to describe the earth. It's a beach ball, a sun-ripened fruit. But he simply looks out the window, eating almond crunches, the wrappers floating away. The view clearly fills his consciousness. It is powerful enough to silence him, to still the voice that rolls off the roof of his mouth, to leave him turned in the seat, twisted uncomfortably for hours at a time.

The view is endlessly fulfilling. It is like the answer to a lifetime of questions and vague cravings. It satisfies every childlike curiosity, every muted desire, whatever there is in him of the scientist, the poet, the primitive seer, the watcher of fire and shooting stars, whatever obsessions eat at the night side of his mind, whatever sweet and dreamy yearning he has ever felt for nameless places faraway, whatever earth-sense he possesses, the neural pulse of some wilder awareness, a sympathy for beasts, whatever belief in an immanent vital force, the Lord of Creation, whatever secret harboring of the idea of human oneness, whatever wishfulness and simple-hearted hope, whatever of too much and not enough, all at once and little by little, whatever burning urge to escape responsibility and routine, escape his own overspecialization, the circumscribed and inward-spiraling self, whatever remnants of his boyish longing to fly, his dreams of strange spaces and eerie heights, his fantasies of happy death, whatever indolent and sybaritic leanings, lotus-eater, smoker of grasses and herbs, blue-eyed gazer into space — all these are satisfied, all collected and massed in that living body, the sight he sees from the window.

"It is just so interesting," he says at last. "The colors and all."

The colors and all.

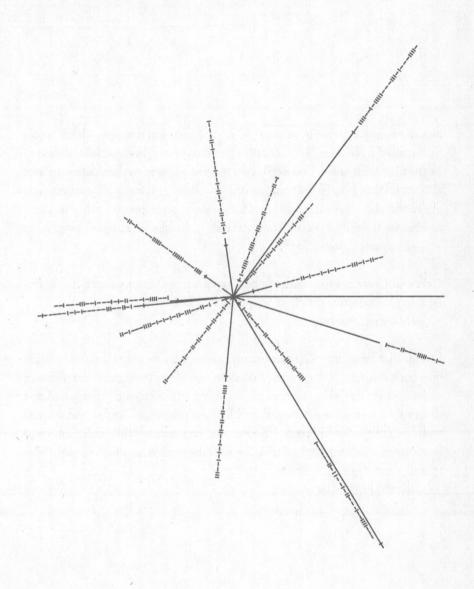

Not all of science fiction is "science" — science occurs in it as a plot-driver, a tool — but all of it is fiction. This narrative form has always been with us: it used to be the kind with angels and devils in it. It's the gateway to the shadowiest and also the brightest part of our human imaginative world; a map of what we most desire and also what we most fear. That's why it's an important form. It points to what we'd do if we could. And increasingly, thanks to "science," we can.

—Margaret Atwood

Oryx and Crake is a speculative fiction, not a science fiction proper. It contains no intergalactic space travel, no teleportation, no Martians.

—Margaret Atwood

I think that there are still a great many people who wouldn't seek out or pick up a book if it were in the science fiction section of the book store, but if it were shelved somewhere else, and they picked it up and read it, and nobody had told them that it was science fiction, they'd have no problem. They've read *Beloved* and *The Lovely Bones*. People have become very comfortable with fantastical literature, which seems to be shelved all over the place now. But if you ask them to read science fiction, they would balk.

—Karen Joy Fowler

Homelanding
Margaret Atwood

1. WHERE SHOULD I begin? After all, you have never been there; or if you have, you may not have understood the significance of what you saw, or thought you saw. A window is a window, but there is looking out and looking in. The native you glimpsed, disappearing behind the curtain, or into the bushes, or down the manhole in the mainstreet — my people are shy — may have been only your reflection in the glass. My country specializes in such illusions.

2. Let me propose myself as typical. I walk upright on two legs, and have in addition two arms, with ten appendages, that is to say, five at the end of each. On the top of my head, but not on the front, there is an odd growth, like a species of seaweed. Some think this is a kind of fur, others consider it modified feathers, evolved perhaps from scales like those of lizards. It serves no functional purpose and is probably decorative.

My eyes are situated in my head, which also possess two small holes for the entrance and exit of air, the invisible fluid we swim in, and one larger hole, equipped with bony protuberances called teeth, by means of which I destroy and assimilate certain parts of my surroundings and change them into my self. This is called eating. The things I eat include roots, berries, nuts, fruits, leaves, and the muscle tissues of various animals and fish. Sometimes I eat their brains and glands as well. I do not as a rule eat insects, grubs, eyeballs or the snouts of pigs, though these are eaten with relish in other countries.

3. Some of my people have a pointed but boneless external appendage, in the front, below the navel or midpoint. Others do not. Debate about whether the possession of such a thing is an advantage or disadvantage is still going on. If this item is lacking, and in its place there is a pocket or inner cavern in which fresh members of our community are grown, it is considered impolite to mention it openly to strangers. I tell you this because it is the breach of etiquette most commonly made by tourists.

In some of our more private gatherings, the absence of cavern or prong is politely overlooked, like club feet or blindness. But sometimes a prong and a cavern will collaborate in a dance, or illusion, using mirrors and water, which is always absorbing for the performers but frequently grotesque for the observers. I notice that you have similar customs.

Whole conventions and a great deal of time have recently been devoted to discussions of this state of affairs. The prong people tell the cavern people that the latter are not people at all and are in reality more akin to dogs or potatoes, and the cavern people abuse the prong people for their obsession with images of poking, thrusting, probing and stabbing. Any long object with a hole at the end, out of which various projectiles can be shot, delights them.

I myself — I am a cavern person — find it a relief not to have to worry about climbing over barbed wire fences or getting caught in zippers.

But that is enough about our bodily form.

4. As for the country itself, let me begin with the sunsets, which are long and red, resonant, splendid and melancholy, symphonic you might almost say; as opposed to the short boring sunsets of other countries, no more interesting than a lightswitch. We pride ourselves on our sunsets. "Come and see the sunset," we say to one another. This causes everyone to rush outdoors or over to the window.

Our country is large in extent, small in population, which accounts for our fear of large empty spaces, and also our need for them. Much of it is covered in water, which accounts for our interest in reflections, sudden vanishings, the dissolution of one thing into another. Much of it however is rock, which accounts for our belief in Fate.

In summer we lie about in the blazing sun, almost naked, covering our skins with fat and attempting to turn red. But when the sun is low in the sky and faint, even at noon, the water we are so fond of changes to something hard and white and cold and covers up the ground. Then we cocoon ourselves, become lethargic, and spend much of our time hiding in crevices. Our mouths shrink and we say little.

Before this happens, the leaves on many of our trees turn blood red or lurid yellow, much brighter and more exotic than the interminable green of jungles. We find this change beautiful. "Come and see the leaves," we say, and jump into our moving vehicles and drive up and down past the forests of sanguinary trees, pressing our eyes to the glass.

We are a nation of metamorphs.

Anything red compels us.

5. Sometimes we lie still and do not move. If air is still going in and out of our breathing holes, this is called sleep. If not, it is called death. When a person has achieved death a kind of picnic is held, with music, flowers and food. The person so honoured, if in one piece, and not, for instance, in shreds or falling apart, as they do if exploded or a long time drowned, is dressed in becoming clothes and lowered into a hole in the ground, or else burnt up.

These customs are among the most difficult to explain to strangers. Some of our visitors, especially the young ones, have never heard of death and are bewildered. They think that death is simply one more of our illusions, our minor tricks; they cannot understand why, with so much food and music, the people are sad.

But you will understand. You too must have death among you. I can see it in your eyes.

6. I can see it in your eyes. If it weren't for this I would have stopped trying long ago, to communicate with you in this halfway language which is so difficult for both of us, which exhausts the throat and fills the mouth with sand; if it weren't for this I would have gone away, gone back. It's this knowledge of death, which we share, where we overlap. Death is our common ground. Together, on it, we can walk forward.

By now you must have guessed: I come from another planet. But I will never say to you, *Take me to your leader*s. Even I — unused to your ways though I am — would never make that mistake. We ourselves have such beings among us, made of cogs, pieces of paper, small disks of shiny metal, scraps of coloured cloth. I do not need to encounter more of them.

Instead I will say, take me to your trees. Take me to your breakfasts, your sunsets, your bad dreams, your shoes, your nouns. Take me to your fingers; take me to your deaths.

These are worth it. These are what I have come for.

Ghettos are typically domains of the exiled. Certainly I felt exiled. My art school had been across the street from Brown University, and I had friends there, and when I ventured to speak of my reading with them, I was embarrassed. I didn't have their vocabulary. But I felt equally exiled at Clarion. I saw that the others were bright, introverted, and devoted, like myself. But their devotions were not mine. There were no aspirant Kafkas, not even an aspirant Disch. These students had read and loved more science fiction than I imagined existed. Even the science fiction writers I admired were considered peripheral. How, I wondered, could anyone read both Philip Dick and Thomas Disch, and think Dick the better writer? How could anyone read A. E. van Vogt at all?
  —Carter Scholz

Dylan and Dick, by their own unwillingness to hide their clumsiness and variability, or to protect me from an awareness of the fallible processes behind even their masterpieces, seduced me into sympathy.
  —Jonathan Lethem

It's true that I sometimes make deliberate use of existing stories, though it's also true that I very often don't. Insofar as I do, it is, yes, one way of maintaining a necessary distance, for the paradoxical sake of closeness. But I think something else is also at work. When I make use of an existing story, I take pleasure in participating in something beyond myself that is much greater than myself, and equal pleasure in striking a variation. I take pleasure, you might say, in acknowledging the past and then sharply departing from it. And there is something to be said for releasing oneself from the obligations of relentless novelty; a certain kind of insistent originality is nothing but the attempt of mediocrity to appear interesting to itself.
  —Steven Millhauser

THE NINE BILLION NAMES OF GOD
CARTER SCHOLZ

Dear Mr. Scholz,

Regarding your submission, "The Nine Billion Names of God": I shouldn't even bother to respond, but I don't want you to think that I'm gullible. Plagiarism occurs in science fiction as elsewhere, but I've never before seen anyone submit a word-for-word copy of another story, let alone a story as well-known as Arthur C. Clarke's "The Nine Billion Names of God." For you to imagine that any editor could fail to recognize this story implies a real ignorance of, and contempt for, our field. In the future I will not welcome your submissions.

Sincerely,

Robert Sales

Editor

NOVUS Science Fiction

Dear Mr. Sales,

Well, this is what comes of submitting without a cover letter. Of course I knew you would recognize Clarke's story, and I hoped that you would infer the reasoning behind my story, which I freely admit is word-for-word the same as Clarke's. Nonetheless, there are important differences, which I shall explain.

First, this story could not have been written today. Too much of the internal evidence is against it. If a reader recognizes the story, the clue is obvious, and the disorientation is instant. Otherwise, an uneasiness will grow at mention of the "Mark V computer" with its "thousands of calculations a second," the "electromatic typewriters," "Sam Jaffe," and other obvious anachronisms.

I have avoided using the conventional meanings of words. For example, when I use "machine," I intend "a vast and barren expanse of land" or "an outmoded philosophical system." Naturally this presents difficulties. The invention (or redefinition) of words is nothing new to science fiction, but I doubt if it has ever been done on this scale, where every single word in a story has a meaning unique to that story. (The new meanings are all tabulated in a glossary that I chose not to submit, economy being the first virtue of art; a short story with explanatory notes the length of a novel would be ridiculous.)

So there is enough depth here to interest a reader. There is the "mask" of the Clarke narrative, behind which lurks my own narrative, told in my "invented" language, and behind that is the story of my story: how a contemporary work of prose came to resemble superficially a science fiction story of the 1950s. These are deep questions of context; as the identical arrangement of letters (such as *elf* or *pain*) may mean differently in different languages, so my arrangement of words "means" very differently than Clarke's.

There is more, but I think this sufficient for now. The story is difficult, I admit, but not inaccessible. I think your readers are intelligent enough to deal with it.

Of course, I understand your reluctance. After all, if I may say so, your publication has gained a certain reputation for stodginess, and your more conservative readers would probably find "The Nine Billion Names of God" too avant-garde. I shall try another market.

Yours,
Carter Scholz

Dear Mr. Scholz,

Are you for real? Are you saying you've used the words of Clarke's story to stand in, one-for-one, for other words, like a cryptograph? It's absurd. I don't believe a word of it. Even the idea is derivative. I'm sure I've seen it in Borges. In its most basic form this notion of changing the context of an artifact might make a readable story, but certainly not this way.

There's no need to blame my "conservative" readers for the rejection. Just blame me.

Sincerely,
Robert Sales

Dear Mr. Sales,

Since you ask, here is the revised ms. As you can see, no words have been changed, but experience should teach you to look further. I have revised my glossary and appendices, and changed some rules of grammar, along with quite a lot of the history of the world from which this artifact purports to come. Also — a nice touch, I think — the articles in the story have all been restored to their original meanings. "A" is "a," "the" is "the," etc.

There is so much information in the world already that I find it more revealing to create new contexts for existing artifacts than to create more artifacts. It would be more accurate to compare my work to Warhol or Duchamp than Clarke or Borges, whom in any case I have not read.

Sincerely,
Carter Scholz

Dear Mr. Scholz,

Incredible. I had no idea you would resubmit "your" story — with "revisions," no less! I am re-returning it. I don't want to see it again, ever. I don't care if it's "really" derivative of Duchamp or Warhol or Gustave Flaubert. Just leave me alone.

RS

Dear Mr. Sales,

This time I'm lowering my sights a little. I think you'll find this story really funny. It's a kind of "parody-by-repetition." This kind of parody is effective with works of a "baroque" nature, that is, works based on the logical, exhaustive permutations of a few principles. Science fiction stories are "baroque" because they are the intellectual children of empiricism, so they tend to offer explanations, and they tend to exhaust a limited repertoire of materials. The ambition of explanations is to be complete, so such systems tend to be closed, and this closure leads naturally to repetition and counterfeiting, endlessly evident in rack after rack of books about plucky young wizards or wisecracking starship tailgunners. The sportive élan of early science fiction has spiraled into an abortive ennui, and its writers face an endgame situation, where the remaining moves are few and predictable. Clarke's monks naming the names of God from AAAAAAAAA to ZZZZZZZZZ (with the help of a computer) no more surely faced the end of their world. My "counterfeit" of Clarke is more interesting, more purely "speculative" than this other sort of plagiarism. Here, the very act of quoting becomes parody, much like the act of moving a soup can from the supermarket to a gallery. It makes ridiculous the soup, the gallery, the audience, and the artist. It unites them.

Sincerely,

Carter Scholz

P. S. There are several refinements in this draft. I hope you don't think I'm overworking it. Since each time I submit it its context is changed, of course you are not really seeing the "same" "story" "again." There are no "agains" in this game.

Dear Mr. Scholz,

No! I see no changes in the story, but you are definitely overworking me!

You seem to have a good mind. Why not do something constructive with your time? Save yourself postage and save me grief.

Yours, again, still, and for the last time,

Bob Sales

"Dear" "Mr." "Sales,"

A "text" "admits of" numerous "interpretations." The "interpretations" "become" more numerous as "time" "passes." Most "important," "it" seems to "me," is the "act" of "reprinting" "The Nine Billion Names of God" "today." "Presenting" it in that "context" "sets up" a series of "speculations" more "interesting" than those "raised" by most of the "stories" "you" "publish." This "matter" of "context" is a kind of "Last Question" for "art," "literature," and "ultimately" "science fiction." The "real" "story" always "lies" "outside" the "words" — in "context," "implication," and "association" — in what is "not" "written." "Surely" "you" can "see" "that"? Let "us" be "brave," and "pursue" the "implications" of "our" "activities."

"Sincerely,"

"Carter Scholz"

Dear Mr. Scholz,

How would it be if I bought the story and didn't publish it? Would that get you off my back? The quotes in your last letter gave me eyestrain, and I'm beginning to dread opening my mail.

Yours,

Sales

Dear Mr. Sales,

Since I am obviously among friends, since you understand that words mean only what we are conditioned to think they mean (legitimated in dictionaries according to the biases of lexicographers), I will dispense with the quotes. And I will tell you something which I previously withheld. My story, "The Nine Billion Names of God," was generated by a computer. But let me approach this new development by stages.

Like any number of people (your mailbox must be jammed with their efforts), I once thought I would like to write science fiction. For several years I worked at it, until the notion had passed from a hobby to an avocation to a passion to an obsession. Never has so much energy been turned to such small account. I failed, utterly, exhaustively, repeatedly; daily, yearly, by degrees and in large lots, I failed. I collected a tower of rejections informing me it had all been done better, and probably with less effort, by Clifford Simak or Curt Siodmak in 1947. And in truth, looking over my millions of failed words, I could no longer tell whether they were very much better, very much worse, or about the same as the published works I had set out to emulate.

By now I was not in my right mind. Have you ever lain awake at night, repeating a simple word like "clown" over and over, until it loses its meaning? Entire stories reached that insane pitch for me. In my sleep I would get rejection letters about my own dreams. Only a long course of therapy brought me back to a point where I could, more or less, construct sentences.

So I gave it up and went back to school.

My graduate studies were about randomness. In one course I made a random number program to simulate the motion of gas molecules in a closed space. By varying the "temperature" of the space I could control the degree of randomness. I used the numbers to select words from a dictionary, and generate random texts; late at night I found their incoherence soothing. But one night, in the midst of this placid gibberish, the machine suddenly gave out the complete text of "The Nine Billion Names of God."

As in cliché fiction, the hackles did stand on my neck. I printed the pages. I checked the network in vain for any sign of a prankster.

I shut down the machine and went home. There I compared my printout to the published Clarke text. Word for word it was the same. There was nothing strange about it, except for where and how it had appeared. After a few stiff drinks, I began to feel lighthearted. For there it was, at last, the product of my labors, a vindication, a light at the end of a closed universe, the abnihilisation of the etym, the big bang. I had produced a real science fiction story, and a certified classic, at that! However obliquely, I had become a science fiction writer; I had, in fact, with exactly the same words, achieved more subtlety, depth, and irony than Clarke himself. How could I doubt it? For, unlike Clarke's story, mine could be verified at the atomic level.

Well, I thought to give myself the Fields Prize for math and a Nebula Award for best story. In a fever I devised my histories, glossaries, and so on, as I have previously explained. I created a unique context for an extant text, a story as commonplace in the world of science fiction as Campbell's soup is to *tout le monde*.

Running the program backwards, by the way, produced Asimov's "The Last Question."

But this brings me to the central problem. If gas molecules (or their stand-ins), capering at random, can produce a pattern equivalent to the pattern of words in "The Nine Billion Names of God," or "The Last Question," or indeed in time any text, even those not yet written — then why write? An author publishes from doubt, I think; he wants the world to regard him as real, substantial, genuine. But in this case, does such confirmation matter? Can one persuade molecules?

The pattern of any story can be found in the random phenomena of nature. The air hums. Daily the ten thousand things recite all nine billion names. A rainstorm, a gust of wind, the bending of a tree, heat waves, all are instinct with a wisdom beyond signs, more engaging than any story because they encompass and can engender all stories. You may find a story in a tree, but never a tree in a story, only the constellation of letters *tree*, and the crushed remains of one in the paper. Why tell stories if all the stories that ever could be are told constantly in the wind and the rain? That is the real last question: do we need fiction? do we need science? I think we do not, most of us.

I labored years with my ambition, and have learned that it is pointless. The end of ambition is to end ambition, just as the point of a fiction is to subsume lesser fictions, and the end point of all fiction is to reach that supreme fiction, the world. Though not without a journey.

But we have taken that journey before. In our stories we have gone past Mercury and Pluto; inclined in worshipful orbit to our great gods Speed and Death, those creators and annihilators of meaning, we have turned a thousand times in a thousand tales. We have seen the engines of our imagination actually built and lifted into space, and they have not meliorated our plight. I think we may never reach a plain sense of things as long as we have either science or fiction to hide behind.

The story of the story of my story ends here. Believing this, I must withdraw my manuscript from submission. I hope you understand. I'd rather not see any more stories published anywhere.

Thank you for your interest.

Sincerely,

Carter Scholz

Dear Contributor:

We are returning your manuscript because publication of *NOVUS Science Fiction* has been discontinued. Thank you for your interest.

The Editor

But I'd begun to read science fiction, and I realized that I could probably write science fiction that would allow me to explore some of the same questions [as in western fiction]. You can put people on unpopulated landscapes and give then pioneer-like situations — it just maybe wouldn't be on this planet.... I wrote a number of science fiction short stories, all of which got published pretty rapidly.... When I wrote *The Jump-Off Creek*...I thought I was taking a big jump to write a book about a woman in the west...[Then] I went to work on...a science fiction novel, and that became *The Dazzle of Day*. When *The Jump-Off Creek* came out and made a splash, people would ask me what I was working on, and when I'd tell them their faces would turn white; they'd be taken aback.... It didn't come out until 1996, and it pretty much sank like a stone because people who liked *Jump-Off Creek* weren't willing to follow me into science fiction.
—Molly Gloss

The positive side of the ghettoization of the fantastic is that writers within that ghetto have done a lot of exploring and defining. Jazz was not invented by the high culture — it was a popular, low art form fermented in a ghetto. Art as a whole gains new forms when artists create schools, defining themselves as a thing apart, gaining strength and coherence by finding their literary ancestors and their literary opponents, inventing their craft. I think both movements — the separation into schools and the breaking down of walls between them — can be useful to artists.... But you know, can we blame a black man for looking a little sideways when a white liberal tells him he ought to get the chip off his shoulder, realize he isn't any different from anyone else, and embrace his white brothers, forgetting that there is any black and white — when he has evidence every day of his life that his blackness is a fact that the vast majority of the world cannot and does not ignore? It's easy for the white liberal to say that race doesn't matter.... Who has the most work to do in tearing down these irrational barriers? I know a hell of a lot more about Herman Melville and Virginia Woolf than the average literary intellectual knows about China Miéville and Gene Wolfe.
—John Kessel

Interlocking Pieces
Molly Glass

For Teo, there was never a question of abandoning the effort. After the last refusal — the East European Minister of Health sent her his personal explanation and regrets — it became a matter of patience and readiness and rather careful timing.

A uniformed policeman had been posted beside her door for reasons, apparently, of protocol. At eight-thirty, when he went down the corridor to the public lavatory, Teo was dressed and waiting, and she walked out past the nurses' station. It stood empty. The robo-nurse was still making the eight-o'clock rounds of the wing's seventy or eighty rooms. The organic nurse, just come on duty, was leaning over the vid display in the alcove behind the station, familiarizing herself with the day's new admissions.

Because it was the nearest point of escape, Teo used the staircase. But the complex skill of descending stairs had lately deserted her, so she stepped down like a child, one leg at a time, grimly clutching the metal banister with both hands. After a couple of floors she went in again to find a public data terminal in a ward that was too busy to notice her.

They had not told her even the donor's name, and a straightforward computer request met a built-in resistance: DATA RESTRICTED***KEY IN PHYSICIAN IDENT CODE. So she asked the machine for the names of organ donors on contract with the regional Ministry of Health, then a list of the hospital's terminal neurological patients, the causes and projected times of their deaths, and the postmortem neurosurgeries scheduled for the next morning. And, finally, the names of patients about whom information was media-restricted. Teo's own name appeared on the last list. She should have been ready for that but found she was not, and she sat staring until the letters grew unfamiliar, assumed strange juxtapositions, became detached and meaningless — the name of a stranger.

The computer scanned and compared the lists for her, extrapolated from the known data, and delivered only one name. She did not ask for hard copy. She looked at the vid display a moment, maybe longer than a moment, and then punched it off and sat staring at the blank screen.

Perhaps not consciously, she had expected a woman. The name, a man's name, threw her off balance a little. She would have liked a little time to get used to the sound of it, the sound it made in her head and on her lips. She would have liked to know the name before she knew the man. But he would be dead in the morning. So she spoke it once, only once, aloud, with exactness and with care. "Dhavir Stahl," she said. And then went to a pneumo-tube and rode up.

In the tube there were at first several others, finally only one. Not European, perhaps North African, a man with eyebrows in a thick straight line across a beetled brow. He watched her sidelong — clearly recognized her — and he wore a physician's ID badge. In a workplace as large as this one the rumor apparatus would be well established. He would know of her admission, maybe even the surgery that had been scheduled. Would, at the very least, see the incongruity of a VIP patient, street-dressed and unaccompanied, riding up in the public pneumo-tube. So Teo stood imperiously beside him with hands cupped together behind her back and eyes focused on the smooth center seam of the door while she waited for him to speak, or not. When the tube opened at the seventy-eighth floor he started out, then half-turned toward her, made a stiff little bow, and said, "Good health, Madame Minister," and finally exited. If he reported straightaway to security, she might have five minutes, or ten, before they reasoned out where she had gone. And standing alone now in the pneumo-tube, she began to feel the first sour leaking of despair — what could be said, learned, shared in that little time?

There was a vid map beside the portal on the ninety-first floor. She searched it until she found the room and the straightest route, then went deliberately down the endless corridors, past the little tableaux of sickness framed where a door here or there stood open, and finally to the designated door, closed.

She would have waited. She wanted to wait, to gather up a few dangling threads, reweave a place or two that had lately worn through. But the physician in the pneumo-tube had stolen that possibility. So she took in a thin new breath and touched one thumb to the admit disk. The door opened, waited for her, closed behind her. She stood just inside, stood very straight, with her hands open beside her thighs.

The man whose name was Dhavir Stahl was fitting together the pieces of a masters-level holoplex, sitting cross-legged, bare-kneed, on his bed, with the scaffolding of the puzzle in front of him on the bed table and its thousands of tiny elements jumbled around him on the sheets. He looked at Teo from under the ledge of his eyebrows while he worked. He had that vaguely anxious quality all East Europeans seemed to carry about their eyes. But his mouth was good, a wide mouth with creases lapping around its corners, showing the places where his smile would fit. And he worked silently, patiently.

"I…would speak with you," Teo said.

He was tolerant, even faintly apologetic. "Did you look at the file, or just the door code? I've already turned down offers from a priest and a psychiatrist and, this morning, somebody from narcotics. I just don't seem to need any deathbed comforting."

"I am Teo."

"What is that? One of the research divisions?"

"My name."

His mouth moved, a near smile, perhaps embarrassment, or puzzlement.

"They hadn't told you my name, then," she said.

And finally he took it in. His face seemed to tighten, all of it pulling back toward his scalp as the skin shrinks from the skull of a corpse, so that his mouth was too wide and there was no space for smiling. Or too much.

"They…seem to have a good many arbitrary rules," Teo said. "They refused me this meeting, your name even. And you, mine, it appears. I could not — I had a need to know."

She waited raggedly through a very long silence. Her palms were faintly damp, but she continued to hold them open beside her legs. Finally Dhavir Stahl moved, straightened a little, perhaps took a breath. But his eyes stayed with Teo.

"You look healthy," he said. It seemed a question.

She made a slight gesture with one shoulder, a sort of shrugging off. "I have…lost motor skills." And in a moment, because he continued to wait, she added, "The cerebellum is evidently quite diseased. They first told me I would die. Then they said no, maybe not, and they sent me here."

He had not moved his eyes from her. One of his hands lightly touched the framework of the puzzle as a blind man would touch a new face, but he never took his eyes from Teo. Finally she could not bear that, and her own eyes skipped out to the window and the dark sheets of rain flapping beneath the overcast.

"You are...not what I expected," he said. When her eyes came round to him again, he made that near smile and forced air from his mouth — not a laugh, a hard sound of bleak amusement. "Don't ask! God, I don't know what I expected." He let go the puzzle and looked away finally, looked down at his hands, then out to the blank vid screen on the wall, the aseptic toilet in the corner. When he lifted his face to her again, his eyes were very dark, very bright. She thought he might weep, or that she would. But he said only, "You are Asian." He was not quite asking it.

"Yes."

"Pakistani?"

"Nepalese."

He nodded without surprise or interest. "Do you climb?"

She lifted her shoulders again, shrugging. "We are not all Sherpa bearers," she said with a prickly edge of impatience. There was no change at his mouth, but he fell silent and looked away from her. Belatedly she felt she might have shown more tolerance. Her head began to ache a little from a point at the base of the skull. She would have liked to knead the muscles along her shoulders. But she waited, standing erect and stiff and dismal, with her hands hanging, while the time they had together went away quickly and ill used.

Dhavir Stahl raised his arms, made a loose, meaningless gesture in the air, then combed back his hair with the fingers of both hands. His hair and his hands seemed very fine. "Why did you come?" he said, and his eyelashes drew closed, shielding him as he spoke.

There were answers that would have hurt him again. She sorted through for one that would not. "To befriend you," she said, and saw his eyes open slowly. In a moment he sighed. It was a small sound, dry and sliding, the sound a bare foot makes in sand. He looked at the puzzle, touched an element lying loose on the bed, turned it round with a fingertip. And round.

Without looking toward her, he said, "Their computer has me dead at four-oh-seven-fourteen. They've told you that, I guess. There's a two percent chance of miscalculation. Two or three, I forget. So anyway, by four-thirty..." His mouth was drawn out thin.

"They would have given you another artificial heart."

He lifted his face, nearly smiled again. "They told you that? Yes. Another one. I wore out my own and one of theirs." He did not explain or justify. He simply raised his shoulders, perhaps shrugging, and said, "That's enough." He was looking toward her, but his eyes saw only inward. She waited for him. Finally he stirred, turned his palms up, studied them.

"Did they—I wasn't expecting a woman. Men and women move differently. I didn't think they'd give a man's cerebellum to a woman." He glanced at Teo, at her body. "And you're small. I'm, what, twenty kilos heavier, half a meter taller? I'd think you'd have some trouble getting used to…the way I move. Or anyway the way my brain tells my body to move." He was already looking at his hands again, rubbing them against one another with a slight papery sound.

"They told me I would adapt to it," Teo said. "Or the…new cerebellum could be retaught."

His eyes skipped up to her as if she had startled or frightened him. His mouth moved too, sliding out wide to show the sharp edge of his teeth. "They didn't tell me that," he said from a rigid grin.

It was a moment before she was able to find a reason for his agitation. "It won't…they said it wouldn't…reduce the donor's…sense of self."

After a while, after quite a while, he said, "What word did they use? They wouldn't have said 'reduce.' Maybe 'correct' or 'edit out.'" His eyes slid sideways, away from her, then back again. His mouth was still tight, grimacing, shaping a smile that wasn't there. "They were at least frank about it. They said the cerebellum only runs the automatic motor functions, the skilled body movements. They said they would have expected — no, they said they would have liked — a transplanted cerebellum to be mechanical. A part, like a lung or a kidney. The 'mind' ought to be all in the forebrain. They told me there wouldn't be any donor consciousness, none at all, if they could figure out how to stop it."

In the silence after, as if speaking had dressed the wound, his mouth began to heal. In a moment he was able to drop his eyes from Teo. He sat with his long, narrow hands cupped on his knees and stared at the scaffolding of his puzzle. She could hear his breath sliding in and out, a contained and careful sound. Finally he selected an element from among the thousands around him on the bed, turned it solemnly in his hands, turned it again, then reached to fit it into the puzzle, deftly finding a place for it among the multitude of interlocking pieces. He did not look at Teo. But in a moment he said, "You don't look scared. I'd be scared if they were putting bits of somebody else inside my head." He slurred the words a little at the end and jumped his eyes white-edged to Teo.

She made a motion to open her hands, to shrug, but then, irresistibly, turned her palms in, chafed them harshly against her pants legs. She chose a word from among several possible. "Yes," she said. And felt it was she who now wore the armored faceplate with its stiff and fearful grin.

Dhavir's eyes came up to her again with something like surprise, and certainly with tenderness. And then Teo felt the door behind her opening, its cushioned quiet, and there were three security people there, diminishing the size of the room with their small crowd, their turbulence. The first one extended her hand but did not quite touch Teo's arm. "Minister Teo," she said. Formal. Irritated.

Dhavir seemed not to register the formal address. Maybe he would remember it later, maybe not, and Teo thought probably it wouldn't matter. They watched each other silently, Teo standing carefully erect with her hands, the hands that no longer brushed teeth nor wrote cursive script, the hands she had learned to distrust, hanging open beside her thighs, and Dhavir sitting cross-legged amid his puzzle, with his forearms resting across those frail, naked knees. Teo waited. The security person touched her elbow, began to draw her firmly toward the door, and then finally Dhavir spoke her name. "Teo," he said. And she pulled her arm free, turned to stand on the door threshold, facing him.

"I run lopsided," he said, as if he apologized for more than that. "I throw my heels out or something." There were creases beside his mouth and his eyes, but he did not smile.

In a moment, with infinite, excruciating care, Teo opened her hands palms outward, lifting them in a gesture of acceptance. "You and I," she said. "We shall learn to live with it."

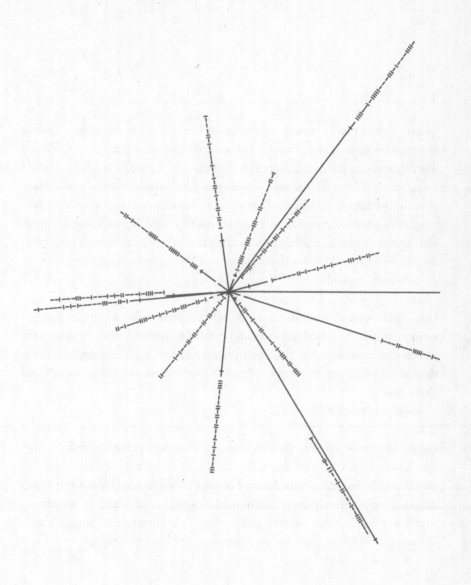

As to whether I may be considered a moralist, I feel this is the sort of question best answered by an objective observer. I'm not even sure what a moralist is. Viewed through a post-modern lens, a moralist might well be seen to be an idiot...a label I would resist. When told that my stories display a preoccupation with "...the means by which some core of individual integrity can be defended etc.," I wouldn't deny it out of hand. At the same time, I believe that to a large degree people are actors playing themselves, thus it's entirely possible that at heart I am utterly pragmatic, unromantic, unconcerned with the human condition, and self-deluding.

 —Lucius Shepard

How comfortable are we, thinking of ourselves as artists? There's no question that we're artists, but it's something we're uncomfortable thinking about because of the pulp fiction creation myth "It Came from the Gutter." We were raised out of the mud of the pulps and have yet to achieve the same status as Updike, Joyce Carol Oates, and all.

 —James Patrick Kelly

Lately I've been intrigued by the idea of using science-fictional or fantasy backdrops against which to set stories that have nothing to do with those backdrops, that are essentially mainstreamish. Most of us are intently focused on our immediate surround, on problems that distract us from observation, so inured to the ordinary rhythms of our days that we often remain more or less unaware of the great shapes of history that enfold us, and often unaware as well of simpler things.

 —Lucius Shepard

Salvador
Lucius Shepard

THREE WEEKS BEFORE they wasted Tecolutla, Dantzler had his baptism of fire. The platoon was crossing a meadow at the foot of an emerald-green volcano, and being a dreamy sort, he was idling along, swatting tall grasses with his rifle barrel and thinking how it might have been a first-grader with crayons who had devised this elementary landscape of a perfect cone rising into a cloudless sky, when cap-pistol noises sounded on the slope. Someone screamed for the medic, and Dantzler dove into the grass, fumbling for his ampules. He slipped one from the dispenser and popped it under his nose, inhaling frantically; then, to be on the safe side, he popped another — "A double helpin' of martial arts," as DT would say — and lay with his head down until the drugs had worked their magic. There was dirt in his mouth, and he was very afraid.

Gradually his arms and legs lost their heaviness, and his heart rate slowed. His vision sharpened to the point that he could see not only the pinpricks of fire blooming on the slope, but also the figures behind them, half-obscured by brush. A bubble of grim anger welled up in his brain, hardened to a fierce resolve, and he started moving towards the volcano. By the time he reached the base of the cone, he was all rage and reflexes. He spent the next forty minutes spinning acrobatically through the thickets, spraying shadows with bursts of his M-18; yet part of his mind remained distant from the action, marveling at his efficiency, at the comic-strip enthusiasm he felt for the task of killing. He shouted at the men he shot, and he shot them many more times than was necessary, like a child playing soldier.

"Playin' my ass!" DT would say. "You just actin' natural."

DT was a firm believer in the ampules; though the official line was that they contained tailored RNA compounds and pseudoendorphins modified to an inhalant form, he held the opinion that they opened a man up to his inner nature. He was big, black, with heavily muscled arms and crudely stamped features, and he had come to the Special Forces direct from prison, where he had done a stretch for attempted murder; the palms of his hands were covered by jail tattoos — a pentagram and a horned monster. The words DIE HIGH were painted on his helmet. This was his second tour in Salvador, and Moody — who was Dantzler's buddy — said the drugs had addled DT's brains, that he was crazy and gone to hell.

"He collects trophies," Moody had said. "And not just ears like they done in 'Nam."

When Dantzler had finally gotten a glimpse of the trophies, he had been appalled. They were kept in a tin box in DT's pack and were nearly unrecognizable; they looked like withered brown orchids. But despite his revulsion, despite the fact that he was afraid of DT, he admired the man's capacity for survival and had taken to heart his advice to rely on the drugs.

On the way back down the slope they discovered a live casualty, an Indian kid about Dantzler's age, nineteen or twenty. Black hair, adobe skin, and heavy-lidded brown eyes. Dantzler, whose father was an anthropologist and had done fieldwork in Salvador, figured him for a Santa Ana tribesman; before leaving the States, Dantzler had pored over his father's notes, hoping this would give him an edge, and had learned to identify the various regional types. The kid had a minor leg wound and was wearing fatigue pants and a faded COKE ADDS LIFE T-shirt. This T-shirt irritated DT no end.

"What the hell you know 'bout Coke?" he asked the kid as they headed for the chopper that was to carry them deeper into Morazán Province. "You think it's funny or somethin'?" He whacked the kid in the back with his rifle butt, and when they reached the chopper, he slung him inside and had him sit by the door. He sat beside him, tapped out a joint from a pack of Kools, and asked, "Where's Infante?"

"Dead," said the medic.

"Shit!" DT licked the joint so it would burn evenly. "Goddamn beaner ain't no use 'cept somebody else know Spanish."

"I know a little," Dantzler volunteered.

Staring at Dantzler, DT's eyes went empty and unfocused. "Naw," he said. "You don't know no Spanish."

Dantzler ducked his head to avoid DT's stare and said nothing; he thought he understood what DT meant, but he ducked away from the understanding as well. The chopper bore them aloft, and DT lit the joint. He let the smoke out his nostrils and passed the joint to the kid, who accepted gratefully.

"*Qué sabor!*" he said, exhaling a billow; he smiled and nodded, wanting to be friends.

Dantzler turned his gaze to the open door. They were flying low between the hills, and looking at the deep bays of shadow in their folds acted to drain away the residue of the drugs, leaving him weary and frazzled. Sunlight poured in, dazzling the oil-smeared floor.

"Hey, Dantzler!" DT had to shout over the noise of the rotors. "Ask him whass his name!"

The kid's eyelids were drooping from the joint, but on hearing Spanish he perked up; he shook his head, though, refusing to answer. Dantzler smiled and told him not to be afraid.

"Ricardo Quu," said the kid.

"Kool!" said DT with false heartiness. "Thass my brand!" He offered his pack to the kid.

"*Gracias,* no." The kid waved the joint and grinned.

"Dude's named for a goddamn cigarette," said DT disparagingly, as if this were the height of insanity.

Dantzler asked the kid if there were more soldiers nearby, and once again received no reply; but, apparently sensing in Dantzler a kindred soul, the kid leaned forward and spoke rapidly, saying that his village was Santander Jiménez, that his father was — he hesitated — a man of power. He asked where they were taking him. Dantzler returned a stony glare. He found it easy to reject the kid, and he realized later this was because he had already given up on him.

Latching his hands behind his head, DT began to sing — a wordless melody. His voice was discordant, barely audible above the rotors; but the tune had a familiar ring and Dantzler soon placed it. The theme from *Star Trek.* It brought back memories of watching TV with his sister, laughing at the low-budget aliens and Scotty's Actors' Equity accent. He gazed out the door again. The sun was behind the hills, and the hillsides were unfeatured blurs of dark green smoke. Oh, God, he wanted to be home, to be anywhere but Salvador! A couple of the guys joined in the singing at DT's urging, and as the volume swelled, Dantzler's emotion peaked. He was on the verge of tears, remembering tastes and sights, the way his girl Jeanine had smelled, so clean and fresh, not reeking of sweat and perfume like the whores around Ilopango — finding all this substance in the banal touchstone of his culture and the illusions of the hillsides rushing past. Then Moody tensed beside him, and he glanced up to learn the reason why.

In the gloom of the chopper's belly, DT was as unfeatured as the hills — a black presence ruling them, more the leader of a coven than a platoon. The other two guys were singing their lungs out, and even the kid was getting into the spirit of things. *"Música!"* he said at one point, smiling at everybody, trying to fan the flame of good feeling. He swayed to the rhythm and essayed a "la-la" now and again. But no one else was responding.

The singing stopped, and Dantzler saw that the whole platoon was staring at the kid, their expressions slack and dispirited.

"Space!" shouted DT, giving the kid a little shove. "The final frontier!"

The smile had not yet left the kid's face when he toppled out the door. DT peered after him; a few seconds later he smacked his hand against the floor and sat back, grinning. Dantzler felt like screaming, the stupid horror of the joke was so at odds with the languor of his homesickness. He looked to the others for reaction. They were sitting with their heads down, fiddling with trigger guards and pack straps, studying their bootlaces, and seeing this, he quickly imitated them.

Morazán Province was spook country. Santa Ana spooks. Flights of birds had been reported to attack patrols; animals appeared at the perimeters of campsites and vanished when you shot at them; dreams afflicted everyone who ventured there. Dantzler could not testify to the birds and animals, but he did have a recurring dream. In it the kid DT had killed was pinwheeling down through a golden fog, his T-shirt visible against the roiling back-drop, and sometimes a voice would boom out of the fog, saying, "You are killing my son." No, no, Dantzler would reply, it wasn't me, and besides, he's already dead. Then he would wake covered with sweat, groping for his rifle, his heart racing.

But the dream was not an important terror, and he assigned it no significance. The land was far more terrifying. Pine-forested ridges that stood out against the sky like fringes of electrified hair; little trails winding off into thickets and petering out, as if what they led to had been magicked away; gray rock faces along which they were forced to walk, hopelessly exposed to ambush. There were innumerable booby traps set by the guerrillas, and they lost several men to rockfalls. It was the emptiest place of Dantzler's experience. No people, no animals, just a few hawks circling the solitudes between the ridges. Once in a while they found tunnels, and these they blew with the new gas grenades; the gas ignited the rich concentrations of hydrocarbons and sent flame sweeping through the entire system. DT would praise whoever had discovered the tunnel and would estimate in a loud voice how many beaners they had "refried." But Dantzler knew they were traversing pure emptiness and burning empty holes. Days, under debilitating heat, they humped the mountains, traveling seven, eight, even ten klicks up trails so steep that frequently the feet of the guy ahead of you would be on a level with your face; nights, it was cold, the darkness absolute, the silence so profound that Dantzler imagined he could hear the great humming vibration of the earth. They might have been anywhere or nowhere. Their fear was nourished by the isolation, and the only remedy was "martial arts."

Dantzler took to popping the pills without the excuse of combat. Moody cautioned him against abusing the drugs, citing rumors of bad side effects and DT's madness; but even he was using them more and more often. During basic training, Dantzler's DI had told the boots that the drugs were available only to the Special Forces, that their use was optional; but there had been too many instances of lackluster battlefield performance in the last war, and this was to prevent a reoccurrence.

"The chickenshit infantry take 'em," the DI had said. "You bastards are brave already. You're born killers, right?"

"Right, sir!" they had shouted.

"What are you?"

"Born killers, sir!"

But Dantzler was not a born killer; he was not even clear as to how he had been drafted, less clear as to how he had been manipulated into the Special Forces, and he had learned that nothing was optional in Salvador, with the possible exception of life itself.

The platoon's mission was reconnaissance and mop-up. Along with other Special Forces platoons, they were to secure Morazán prior to the invasion of Nicaragua; specifically, they were to proceed to the village of Tecolutla, where a Sandinista patrol had recently been spotted, and following that they were to join up with the First Infantry and take part in the offensive against León, a provincial capital just across the Nicaraguan border. As Dantzler and Moody walked together, they frequently talked about the offensive, how it would be good to get down into flat country; occasionally they talked about the possibility of reporting DT, and once, after he had led them on a forced night march, they toyed with the idea of killing him. But most often they discussed the ways of the Indians and the land, since this was what had caused them to become buddies.

Moody was slightly built, freckled, and red-haired; his eyes had the "thousand-yard stare" that came from too much war. Dantzler had seen winos with such vacant, lusterless stares. Moody's father had been in 'Nam, and Moody said it had been worse than Salvador because there had been no real commitment to win; but he thought Nicaragua and Guatemala might be the worst of all, especially if the Cubans sent in troops as they had threatened. He was adept at locating tunnels and detecting booby traps, and it was for this reason Dantzler had cultivated his friendship. Essentially a loner, Moody had resisted all advances until learning of Dantzler's father; thereafter he had buddied up, eager to hear about the field notes, believing they might give him an edge.

"They think the land has animal traits," said Dantzler one day as they climbed along a ridgetop. "Just like some kinds of fish look like plants or sea bottom, parts of the land look like plain ground, jungle...whatever. But when you enter them, you find you've entered the spirit world, the world of *Sukias*."

"What's *Sukias?*" asked Moody.

"Magicians." A twig snapped behind Dantzler, and he spun around, twitching off the safety of his rifle. It was only Hodge — a lanky kid with the beginnings of a beer gut. He stared hollow-eyed at Dantzler and popped an ampule.

Moody made a noise of disbelief. "If they got magicians, why ain't they winnin'? Why ain't they zappin' us off the cliffs?"

"It's not their business," said Dantzler. "They don't believe in messing with worldly affairs unless it concerns them directly. Anyway, these places — the ones that look like normal land but aren't — they're called..." He drew a blank on the name. "*Aya*-something. I can't remember. But they have different laws. They're where your spirit goes to die after your body dies."

"Don't they got no Heaven?"

"Nope. It just takes longer for your spirit to die, and so it goes to one of these places that's between everything and nothing."

"Nothin'," said Moody disconsolately, as if all his hopes for an afterlife had been dashed. "Don't make no sense to have spirits and not have no Heaven."

"Hey," said Dantzler, tensing as wind rustled the pine boughs. "They're just a bunch of damn primitives. You know what their sacred drink is? Hot chocolate! My old man was a guest at one of their funerals, and he said they carried cups of hot chocolate balanced on these little red towers and acted like drinking it was going to wake them to the secrets of the universe." He laughed, and the laughter sounded tinny and psychotic to his own ears. "So you're going to worry about fools who think hot chocolate's holy water?"

"Maybe they just like it," said Moody. "Maybe somebody dyin' just give 'em an excuse to drink it."

But Dantzler was no longer listening. A moment before, as they emerged from pine cover onto the highest point of the ridge, a stony scarp open to the winds and providing a view of rumpled mountains and valleys extending to the horizon, he had popped an ampule. He felt so strong, so full of righteous purpose and controlled fury, it seemed only the sky was around him, that he was still ascending, preparing to do battle with the gods themselves.

Tecolutla was a village of whitewashed stone tucked into a notch between two hills. From above, the houses — with their shadow-blackened windows and doorways — looked like an unlucky throw of dice. The streets ran uphill and down, diverging around boulders. Bougainvilleas and hibiscuses speckled the hillsides, and there were tilled fields on the gentler slopes. It was a sweet, peaceful place when they arrived, and after they had gone it was once again peaceful; but its sweetness had been permanently banished. The reports of Sandinistas had proved accurate, and though they were casualties left behind to recuperate, DT had decided their presence called for extreme measures. Fu gas, frag grenades, and such. He had fired an M-60 until the barrel melted down, and then had manned the flamethrower. Afterward, as they rested atop the next ridge, exhausted and begrimed, having radioed in a chopper for resupply, he could not get over how one of the houses he had torched had come to resemble a toasted marshmallow.

"Ain't that how it was, man?" he asked, striding up and down the line. He did not care if they agreed about the house; it was a deeper question he was asking, one concerning the ethics of their actions.

"Yeah," said Dantzler, forcing a smile. "Sure did."

DT grunted with laughter. "You *know* I'm right, don'tcha man?"

The sun hung directly behind his head, a golden corona rimming a black oval, and Dantzler could not turn his eyes away. He felt weak and weakening, as if threads of himself were being spun loose and sucked into the blackness. He had popped three ampules prior to the firefight, and his experience of Tecolutla had been a kind of mad whirling dance through the streets, spraying erratic bursts that appeared to be writing weird names on the walls. The leader of the Sandinistas had worn a mask — a gray face with a surprised hole of a mouth and pink circles around the eyes. A ghost face. Dantzler had been afraid of the mask and had poured round after round into it. Then, leaving the village, he had seen a small girl standing beside the shell of the last house, watching them, her colorless rag of a dress tattering in the breeze. She had been a victim of that malnutrition disease, the one that paled your skin and whitened your hair and left you retarded. He could not recall the name of the disease — things like names were slipping away from him — nor could he believe anyone had survived, and for a moment he had thought the spirit of the village had come out to mark their trail.

That was all he could remember of Tecolutla, all he wanted to remember. But he knew he had been brave.

Four days later, they headed up into a cloud forest. It was the dry season, but dry season or not, blackish gray clouds always shrouded these peaks. They were shot through by ugly glimmers of lightning, making it seem that malfunctioning neon signs were hidden beneath them, advertisements for evil. Everyone was jittery, and Jerry LeDoux — a slim dark-haired Cajun kid — flat-out refused to go.

"It ain't reasonable," he said. "Be easier to go through the passes."

"We're on recon, man! You think the beaners be waitin' in the passes, wavin' their white flags?" DT whipped his rifle into firing position and pointed it at LeDoux. "C'mon, Louisiana man. Pop a few, and you feel different."

As LeDoux popped the ampules, DT talked to him.

"Look at it this way, man. This is your big adventure. Up there it be like all them animal shows on the tube. The savage kingdom, the unknown. Could be like Mars or somethin'. Monsters and shit, with big red eyes and tentacles. You wanna miss that, man? You wanna miss bein' the first grunt on Mars?"

Soon LeDoux was raring to go, giggling at DT's rap.

Moody kept his mouth shut, but he fingered the safety of his rifle and glared at DT's back. When DT turned to him, however, he relaxed. Since

Tecolutla he had grown taciturn, and there seemed to be a shifting of lights and darks in his eyes, as if something were scurrying back and forth behind them. He had taken to wearing banana leaves on his head, arranging them under his helmet so the frayed ends stuck out the side like strange green hair. He said this was camouflage, but Dantzler was certain it bespoke some secretive irrational purpose. Of course DT had noticed Moody's spiritual erosion, and as they prepared to move out, he called Dantzler aside.

"He done found someplace inside his head that feel good to him," said DT. "He's tryin' to curl up into it, and once he do that he ain't gon' be responsible. Keep an eye on him."

Dantzler mumbled his assent, but was not enthused.

"I know he your fren', man, but that don't mean shit. Not the way things are. Now me, I don't give a damn 'bout you personally. But I'm your brother-in-arms, and thass somethin' you can count on...y'understand."

To Dantzler's shame, he did understand.

They had planned on negotiating the cloud forest by nightfall, but they had underestimated the difficulty. The vegetation beneath the clouds was lush — thick, juicy leaves that mashed underfoot, tangles of vines, trees with slick, pale bark and waxy leaves — and the visibility was only about fifteen feet. They were gray wraiths passing through grayness. The vague shapes of the foliage reminded Dantzler of fancifully engraved letters, and for a while he entertained himself with the notion that they were walking among the half-formed phrases of a constitution not yet manifest in the land. They barged off the trail, losing it completely, becoming veiled in spiderwebs and drenched by spills of water; their voices were oddly muffled, the tag ends of words swallowed up. After seven hours of this, DT reluctantly gave the order to pitch camp. They set electric lamps around the perimeter so they could see to string the jungle hammocks; the beam of light illuminated the moisture in the air, piercing the murk with jeweled blades. They talked in hushed tones, alarmed by the eerie atmosphere. When they had done with the hammocks, DT posted four sentries — Moody, LeDoux, Dantzler, and himself. Then they switched off the lamps.

It grew pitch-dark, and the darkness was picked out by plips and plops, the entire spectrum of dripping sounds. To Dantzler's ears they blended into a gabbling speech. He imagined tiny Santa Ana demons talking about him, and to stave off paranoia he popped two ampules. He continued to pop them, trying to limit himself to one every half hour; but he was uneasy, unsure where to train his rifle in the dark, and he exceeded his limit. Soon it began to grow light again, and he assumed that more time had passed than he had thought. That often happened with the ampules — it was easy to lose yourself in being alert, in the wealth of perceptual detail available to your sharpened senses. Yet on checking his watch, he saw it was only a few minutes after two o'clock. His system was too inundated with the drugs to allow panic, but he twitched his head from side to side in tight little arcs to determine the source of the brightness. There did not appear to be a single source; it was simply that filaments of the cloud were gleaming, casting a diffuse golden glow, as if they were elements of a nervous system coming to life. He started to call out, then held back. The others must have seen the light, and they had given no cry; they probably had a good reason for their silence. He scrunched down flat, pointing his rifle out from the campsite.

Bathed in the golden mist, the forest had acquired an alchemic beauty. Beads of water glittered with gemmy brilliance; the leaves and vines and bark were gilded. Every surface shimmered with light…everything except a fleck of blackness hovering between two of the trunks, its size gradually increasing. As it swelled in his vision, he saw it had the shape of a bird, its wings beating, flying toward him from an inconceivable distance — inconceivable, because the dense vegetation did not permit you to see very far in a straight line, and yet the bird was growing larger with such slowness that it must have been coming from a long way off. It was not really flying, he realized; rather, it was as if the forest were painted on a piece of paper, as if someone were holding a lit match behind it and burning a hole, a hole that maintained the shape of a bird as it spread. He was transfixed, unable to react. Even when it had blotted out half the light, when he lay before it no bigger than a mote in relation to its huge span, he could not move or squeeze the trigger. And then the blackness swept over him. He had the sensation of being borne along at incredible speed, and he could no longer hear the dripping of the forest.

"Moody!" he shouted. "DT!"

But the voice that answered belonged to neither of them. It was hoarse, issuing from every part of the surrounding blackness, and he recognized it as the voice of his recurring dream.

"You are killing my son," it said. "I have led you here, to this *ayahuamaco*, so he may judge you."

Dantzler knew to his bones the voice was that of the Sukia of the village of Santander Jiménez. He wanted to offer a denial, to explain his innocence, but all he could manage was, "No." He said it tearfully, hopelessly, his forehead resting on his rifle barrel. Then his mind gave a savage twist, and his soldiery self regained control. He ejected an ampule from his dispenser and popped it.

The voice laughed — malefic, damning laughter whose vibrations shuddered Dantzler. He opened up with the rifle, spraying fire in all directions. Filigrees of golden holes appeared in the blackness, tendrils of mist coiled through them. He kept on firing until the blackness shattered and fell in jagged sections toward him. Slowly. Like shards of black glass dropping through water. He emptied the rifle and flung himself flat, shielding his head with his arms, expecting to be sliced into bits; but nothing touched him. At last he peeked between his arms; then — amazed, because the forest was now a uniform lustrous yellow — he rose to his knees. He scraped his hands on one of the crushed leaves beneath him, and blood welled from the cut. The broken fibers of the leaf were as stiff as wires. He stood, a giddy trickle of hysteria leaking up from the bottom of his soul. It was no forest, but a building of solid gold worked to resemble a forest — the sort of conceit that might have been fabricated for the child of an emperor. Canopied by golden leaves, columned by slender golden trunks, carpeted by golden grasses. The water beads were diamonds. All the gleam and glitter soothed his apprehension; here was something out of a myth, a habitat for princesses and wizards and dragons. Almost gleeful, he turned to the campsite to see how the others were reacting.

Once, when he was nine years old, he had sneaked into the attic to rummage through the boxes and trunks, and he had run across an old morocco-bound copy of *Gulliver's Travels*. He had been taught to treasure old books, and so he had opened it eagerly to look at the illustrations, only to find that the centers of the pages had been eaten away, and there, right in the heart of the fiction, was a nest of larvae. Pulpy, horrid things. It had been an awful sight, but one unique in his experience, and he might have studied those crawling scraps of life for a very long time if his father had not interrupted. Such a sight was now before him, and he was numb with it.

They were all dead. He should have guessed they would be; he had given no thought to them while firing his rifle. They had been struggling out of their hammocks when the bullets hit, and as a result they were hanging half-in, half-out, their limbs dangling, blood pooled beneath them. The veils of golden mist made them look dark and mysterious and malformed, like monsters killed as they emerged from their cocoons. Dantzler could not stop staring, but he was shrinking inside himself. It was not his fault. That thought kept swooping in and out of a flock of less acceptable thoughts; he wanted it to stay put, to be true, to alleviate the sick horror he was beginning to feel.

"What's your name?" asked a girl's voice behind him.

She was sitting on a stone about twenty feet away. Her hair was a tawny shade of gold, her skin a half-tone lighter, and her dress was cunningly formed out of the mist. Only her eyes were real. Brown heavy-lidded eyes — they were at variance with the rest of her face, which had the fresh, unaffected beauty of an American teenager.

"Don't be afraid," she said, and patted the ground, inviting him to sit beside her.

He recognized the eyes, but it was no matter. He badly needed the consolation she could offer; he walked over and sat down. She let him lean his head against her thigh.

"What's your name?" she repeated.

"Dantzler," he said. "John Dantzler." And then he added, "I'm from Boston. My father's…" It would be too difficult to explain about anthropology. "He's a teacher."

"Are there many soldiers in Boston?" She stroked his cheek with a golden finger.

The caress made Dantzler happy. "Oh, no," he said. "They hardly know there's a war going on."

"This is true?" she said, incredulous.

"Well, they *do* know about it, but it's just news on the TV to them. They've got more pressing problems. Their jobs, families."

"Will you let them know about the war when you return home?" she asked. "Will you do that for me?"

Dantzler had given up hope of returning home, of surviving, and her assumption that he would do both acted to awaken his gratitude. "Yes," he said fervently. "I will."

"You must hurry," she said. "If you stay in the *ayahuamaco* too long, you will never leave. You must find the way out. It is a way not of directions or trails, but of events."

"Where is this place?" he asked, suddenly aware of how much he had taken it for granted.

She shifted her leg away, and if he had not caught himself on the stone, he would have fallen. When he looked up, she had vanished. He was surprised that her disappearance did not alarm him; in reflex he slipped out a couple of ampules, but after a moment's reflection he decided not to use them. It was impossible to slip them back into the dispenser, so he tucked them into the interior webbing of his helmet for later. He doubted he would need them, though. He felt strong, competent and unafraid.

Dantzler stepped carefully between the hammocks; not wanting to brush against them; it might have been his imagination, but they seemed to be bulged down lower than before, as if death had weighed out heavier than life. That heaviness was in the air, pressuring him. Mist rose like golden steam from the corpses, but the sight no longer affected him — perhaps because the mist gave the illusion of being their souls. He picked up a rifle with a full magazine and headed off into the forest.

The tips of the golden leaves were sharp, and he had to ease past them to avoid being cut; but he was at the top of his form, moving gracefully, and the obstacles barely slowed his pace. He was not even anxious about the girl's warning to hurry; he was certain the way out would soon present itself. After a minute or so he heard voices, and after another few seconds he came to a clearing divided by a stream, one so perfectly reflecting that its banks appeared to enclose a wedge of golden mist. Moody was squatting to the left of the stream, staring at the blade of his survival knife and singing under his breath — a wordless melody that had the erratic rhythm of a trapped fly. Beside him lay Jerry LeDoux, his throat slashed from ear to ear. DT was sitting on the other side of the stream; he had been shot just above the knee, and though he had ripped up his shirt for bandages and tied off the leg with a tourniquet, he was not in good shape. He was sweating, and a gray chalky pallor infused his skin. The entire scene had the weird vitality of something that had materialized in a magic mirror, a bubble of reality enclosed within a gilt frame.

DT heard Dantzler's footfalls and glanced up. "Waste him!" he shouted, pointing to Moody.

Moody did not turn from contemplation of the knife. "No," he said, as if speaking to someone whose image was held in the blade.

"Waste him, man!" screamed DT. "He killed LeDoux!"

"Please," said Moody to the knife. "I don't want to."

There was blood clotted on his face, more blood on the banana leaves sticking out of his helmet.

"Did you kill Jerry?" asked Dantzler; while he addressed the question to Moody, he did not relate to him as an individual, only as part of a design whose message he had to unravel.

"Jesus Christ! Waste him!" DT smashed his fist against the ground in frustration.

"Okay," said Moody. With an apologetic look, he sprang to his feet and charged Dantzler, swinging the knife.

Emotionless, Dantzler stitched a line of fire across Moody's chest; he went sideways into the bushes and down.

"What the hell was you waitin' for!" DT tried to rise, but winced and fell back. "Damn! Don't know if I can walk."

"Pop a few," Dantzler suggested mildly.

"Yeah. Good thinkin', man." DT fumbled for his dispenser.

Dantzler peered into the bushes to see where Moody had fallen. He felt nothing, and this pleased him. He was weary of feeling.

DT popped an ampule with a flourish, as if making a toast, and inhaled. "Ain't you gon' to do some, man?"

"I don't need them," said Dantzler. "I'm fine."

The stream interested him; it did not reflect the mist, as he had supposed, but was itself a seam of the mist.

"How many you think they was?" asked DT.

"How many what?"

"Beaners, man! I wasted three or four after they hit us, but I couldn't tell how many they was."

Dantzler considered this in light of his own interpretation of events and Moody's conversation with the knife. It made sense. A Santa Ana kind of sense.

"Beats me," he said. "But I guess there's less than there used to be."

DT snorted. "You got *that* right!" He heaved to his feet and limped to the edge of the stream. "Gimme a hand across."

Dantzler reached out to him, but instead of taking his hand, he grabbed his wrist and pulled him off-balance. DT teetered on his good leg, then toppled and vanished beneath the mist. Dantzler had expected him to fall, but he surfaced instantly, mist clinging to his skin. Of course, thought Dantzler; his body would have to die before his spirit would fall.

"What you doin', man?" DT was more disbelieving than enraged.

Dantzler planted a foot in the middle of his back and pushed him down until his head was submerged. DT bucked and clawed at the foot and managed to come to his hands and knees. Mist slithered from his eyes, his nose, and he choked out the words "...kill you...." Dantzler pushed him down again; he got into pushing him down and letting him up, over and over. Not so as to torture him. Not really. It was because he had suddenly understood the nature of the *ayahuamaco*'s laws, that they were approximations of normal laws, and he further understood that his actions had to approximate those of someone jiggling a key in a lock. DT was the key to the way out, and Dantzler was jiggling him, making sure all the tumblers were engaged.

Some of the vessels in DT's eyes had burst, and the whites were occluded by films of blood. When he tried to speak, mist curled from his mouth. Gradually his struggles subsided; he clawed runnels in the gleaming yellow dirt of the bank and shuddered. His shoulders were knobs of black land foundering in a mystic sea.

For a long time after DT sank from view. Dantzler stood beside the stream, uncertain of what was left to do and unable to remember a lesson he had been taught. Finally he shouldered his rifle and walked away from the clearing. Morning had broken, the mist had thinned, and the forest had regained its usual coloration. But he scarcely noticed these changes, still troubled by his faulty memory. Eventually, he let it slide — it would all come clear sooner or later. He was just happy to be alive. After a while he began to kick the stones as he went, and to swing his rifle in a carefree fashion against the weeds.

When the First Infantry poured across the Nicaraguan border and wasted León, Dantzler was having a quiet time at the VA hospital in Ann Arbor, Michigan; and at the precise moment the bulletin was flashed nationwide, he was sitting in the lounge, watching the American League playoffs between Detroit and Texas. Some of the patients ranted at the interruption, while others shouted them down, wanting to hear the details. Dantzler expressed no reaction whatsoever. He was solely concerned with being a model patient; however, noticing that one of the staff was giving him a clinical stare, he added his weight on the side of the baseball fans. He did not want to appear too controlled. The doctors were as suspicious of that sort of behavior as they were of its contrary. But the funny thing was — at least it was funny to Dantzler — that his feigned annoyance at the bulletin was an exemplary proof of his control, his expertise at moving through life the way he had moved through the golden leaves of the cloud forest. Cautiously, gracefully, efficiently. Touching nothing, and being touched by nothing. That was the lesson he had learned — to be as perfect a counterfeit of a man as the *ayahuamaco* had been of the land; to adopt the various stances of a man, and yet, by virtue of his distance from things human, to be all the more prepared for the onset of crisis or a call to action. He saw nothing aberrant in this; even the doctors would admit that men were little more than organized pretense. If he was different from other men, it was only that he had a deeper awareness of the principles on which his personality was founded.

When the battle of Managua was joined, Dantzler was living at home. His parents had urged him to go easy in readjusting to civilian life, but he had immediately gotten a job as a management trainee in a bank. Each morning he would drive to work and spend a controlled, quiet eight hours; each night he would watch TV with his mother, and before going to bed, he would climb to the attic and inspect the trunk containing his souvenirs of war — helmet, fatigues, knife, boots. The doctors had insisted he face his experiences, and this ritual was his way of following their instructions. All in all, he was quite pleased with his progress, but he still had problems. He had not been able to force himself to venture out at night, remembering too well the darkness in the cloud forest, and he had rejected his friends, refusing to see them or answer their calls — he was not secure with the idea of friendship. Further, despite his methodical approach to life, he was prone to a nagging restlessness, the feeling of a chore left undone.

One night his mother came into his room and told him that an old friend, Phil Curry, was on the phone. "Please talk to him, Johnny," she said. "He's been drafted, and I think he's a little scared."

The word *drafted* struck a responsive chord in Dantzler's soul, and after brief deliberation he went downstairs and picked up the receiver.

"Hey," said Phil. "What's the story, man? Three months, and you don't even give me a call."

"I'm sorry," said Dantzler. "I haven't been feeling so hot."

"Yeah, I understand." Phil was silent a moment. "Listen, man. I'm leavin', y'know, and we're havin' a big send-off at Sparky's. It's goin' on right now. Why don't you come down?"

"I don't know."

"Jeanine's here, man. Y'know, she's still crazy 'bout you, talks 'bout you alla time. She don't go out with nobody."

Dantzler was unable to think of anything to say.

"Look," said Phil, "I'm pretty weirded out by this soldier shit. I hear it's pretty bad down there. If you got anything you can tell me 'bout what it's like, man, I'd 'preciate it."

Dantzler could relate to Phil's concern, his desire for an edge, and besides, it felt right to go. Very right. He would take some precautions against the darkness.

"I'll be there," he said.

It was a foul night, spitting snow, but Sparky's parking lot was jammed. Dantzler's mind was flurried like the snow, crowded like the lot — thoughts whirling in, jockeying for position, melting away. He hoped his mother would not wait up, he wondered if Jeanine still wore her hair long, he was worried because the palms of his hands were unnaturally warm. Even with the car windows rolled up, he could hear loud music coming from inside the club. Above the door the words SPARKY'S ROCK CITY were being spelled out a letter at a time in red neon, and when the spelling was complete, the letters flashed off and on and a golden neon explosion bloomed around them. After the explosion, the entire sign went dark for a split second, and the big ramshackle building seemed to grow large and merge with the black sky. He had an idea it was watching him, and he shuddered — one of those sudden lurches downward of the kind that take you just before you fall asleep. He knew the people inside did not intend him any harm, but he also knew that places have a way of changing people's intent, and he did not want to be caught off-guard. Sparky's might be such a place, might be a huge black presence camouflaged by neon, its true substance one with the abyss of the sky, the phosphorescent snowflakes, jittering in his headlights, the wind keening through the side vent. He would have liked very much to drive home and forget about his promise to Phil; however, he felt a responsibility to explain about the war. More than a responsibility, an evangelistic urge. He would tell them about the kid falling out of the chopper, the white-haired girl in Tecolutla, the emptiness. God, yes! How you went down chock-full of ordinary American thoughts and dreams, memories of smoking weed and chasing tail and hanging out and freeway flying with a case of something cold, and how you smuggled back a human-shaped container of pure Salvadorian emptiness. Primo grade. Smuggled it back to the land of silk and money, of mindfuck video games and topless tennis matches and fast-food solutions to the nutritional problem. Just a taste of Salvador would banish all those trivial obsessions. Just a taste. It would be easy to explain.

Of course, some things beggared explanation.

He bent down and adjusted the survival knife in his boot so the hilt would not rub against his calf. From the coat pocket he withdrew the two ampules he had secreted in his helmet that long-ago night in the cloud forest. As the neon explosion flashed once more, glimmers of gold coursed along their shiny surfaces. He did not think he would need them; his hand was steady, and his purpose was clear. But to be on the safe side, he popped them both.

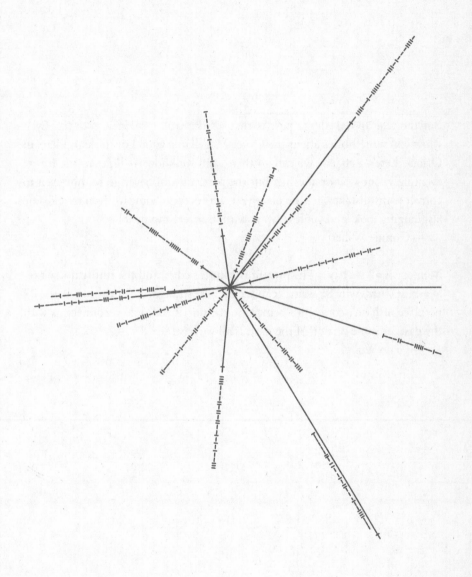

But the real appeal of the past is that it's the true forbidden country. Even when you write stories about the Outer Magellanic Cloud or the star pillars in Orion, there's a chance we can go there, and we know we'll get to the future eventually, one way or another, but the past you can never go to, not even to correct your mistakes. It's the place you can't ever go home to, even to take one last longing look, and yet it's always with us, every moment.
 —Connie Willis

Memory is all we have. The present is a knife's edge, and the future doesn't really exist (that's why SF writers can set all these strange stories there, because it's no place, it hasn't come into being). So memory's ability to reconnect us with the past, or some version of the past, is all we have.
 —Gene Wolfe

Schwarzschild Radius
Connie Willis

"When a star collapses, it sort of falls in on itself." Travers curved his hand into a semicircle and then brought the fingers in. "And sometimes it reaches a kind of point of no return where the gravity pulling in on it is stronger than the nuclear and electric forces, and when it reaches that point nothing can stop it from collapsing and it becomes a black hole." He closed his hand into a fist. "And that critical diameter, that point where there's no turning back, is called the Schwarzschild radius." Travers paused, waiting for me to say something.

He had come to see me every day for a week, sitting stiffly on one of my chairs in an unaccustomed shirt and tie, and talked to me about black holes and relativity, even though I taught biology at the university before my retirement, not physics. Someone had told him I knew Schwarzschild, of course.

"The Schwarzschild radius?" I said in my quavery, old man's voice, as if I could not remember ever hearing the phrase before, and Travers looked disgusted. He wanted me to say, "The Schwarzschild radius! Ah, yes, I served with Karl Schwarzschild on the Russian front in World War I!" and tell him all about how he had formulated his theory of black holes while serving with the artillery, but I had not decided yet what to tell him. "The event horizon," I said.

"Yeah. It was named after Schwarzschild because he was the one who worked out the theory," Travers said. He reminded me of Muller with his talk of theories. He was the same age as Muller, with the same shock of stiff yellow hair and the same insatiable curiosity, and perhaps that was why I let him come every day to talk to me, though it was dangerous to let him get so close.

"I have drawn up a theory of the stars," Muller says while we warm our hands over the Primus stove so that they will get enough feeling in them to be able to hold the liquid barretter without dropping it. "They are not balls of fire, as the scientists say. They are frozen."

"How can we see them if they are frozen?" I say. Muller is insulted if I do not argue with him. The arguing is part of the theory.

"Look at the wireless!" he says, pointing to it sitting disemboweled on the table. We have the back off the wireless again, and in the barretter's glass tube is a red reflection of the stove's flame. "The light is a reflection off the ice of the star."

"A reflection of what?"

"Of the shells, of course."

I do not say that there were stars before there was this war, because Muller will not have an answer to this, and I have no desire to destroy his theory, and besides, I do not really believe there was a time when this war did not exist. The star shells have always exploded over the snow-covered craters of No Man's Land, shattering in a spray of white and red, and perhaps Muller's theory is true.

"At that point," Travers said, "at the event horizon, no more information can be transmitted out of the black hole because gravity has become so strong, and so the collapse appears frozen at the Schwarzschild radius."

"Frozen," I said, thinking of Muller.

"Yeah. As a matter of fact, the Russians call black holes 'frozen stars.' You were at the Russian front, weren't you?"

"What?"

"In World War I."

"But the star doesn't really freeze," I said. "It goes on collapsing."

"Yeah, sure," Travers said. "It keeps collapsing in on itself until even the atoms are stripped of their electrons and there's nothing left except what they call a naked singularity, but we can't see past the Schwarzschild radius, and nobody inside a black hole can tell us what it's like in there because they can't get messages out, so nobody can ever know what it's like inside a black hole."

"I know," I said, but he didn't hear me.

He leaned forward. "What was it like at the front?"

It is so cold we can only work on the wireless a few minutes at a time before our hands stiffen and grow clumsy, and we are afraid of dropping the liquid barretter. Muller holds his gloves over the Primus stove and then puts them on. I jam my hands in my ice-stiff pockets.

We are fixing the wireless set. Eisner, who had been delivering messages between the sectors, got sent up to the front when he could not fix his motorcycle. If we cannot fix the wireless we will cease to be telegraphists and become soldiers and we will be sent to the front lines.

We are already nearly there. If it were not snowing we could see the barbed wire and pitted snow of No Man's Land, and the big Russian coalboxes sometimes land in the communication trenches. A shell hit our wireless hut two weeks ago. We are ahead of our own artillery lines, and some of the shells from our guns fall on us, too, because the muzzles are worn out. But it is not the front, and we guard the liquid barretter with our lives.

"Eisner's unit was sent up on wiring fatigue last night," Muller says, "and they have not come back. I have a theory about what happened to them."

"Has the mail come?" I say, rubbing my sore eyes and then putting my cold hands immediately back in my pockets. I must get some new gloves, but the quartermaster has none to issue. I have written my mother three times to knit me a pair, but she has not sent them yet.

I have a theory about Eisner's unit," he says doggedly. "The Russians have a magnet that has pulled them into the front."

"Magnets pull iron, not people," I say.

I have a theory about Muller's theories. Littering the communications trenches are things that the soldiers going up to the front have discarded: water bottles and haversacks and bayonets. Hans and I sometimes tried to puzzle out why they would discard such important things.

"Perhaps they were too heavy," I would say, though that did not explain the bayonets or the boots.

"Perhaps they know they are going to die," Hans would say, picking up a helmet.

I would try to cheer him up. "My gloves fell out of my pocket yesterday when I went to the quartermaster's. I never found them. They are in this trench somewhere."

"Yes," he would say, turning the helmet, round and round in his hands, "perhaps as they near the front, these things simply drop away from them."

My theory is that what happens to the water bottles and helmets and bayonets is what has happened to Muller. He was a student in university before the war, but his knowledge of science and his intelligence have fallen away from him, and now we are so close to the front, all he has left are his theories. And his curiosity, which is a dangerous thing to have kept.

"Exactly. Magnets pull iron, but *they* were carrying barbed wire!" he says triumphantly, "and so they were pulled in to the magnet."

I put my hands practically into the Primus flame and rub them together, trying to get rid of the numbness. "We had better get the barretter in the wireless again or this magnet of yours will suck it in, too."

I go back to the wireless. Muller stays by the stove, thinking about his magnet. The door bangs open. It is not a real door, only an iron humpie tied to the beam that reinforces the dugout and held with a wedge, and when someone pushes against it, it flies inward, bringing the snow with it.

Snow swirls in, and light, and the sound from the front, a low rumble like a dog growling. I clutch the liquid barretter to my chest and Muller flings himself over the wireless as if it were a wounded comrade. Someone bundled in a wool coat and mittens, with a wool cap pulled over his ears, stands silhouetted against the reddish light in the doorway, blinking at us.

"Is Private Rottschieben here? I have come to see him about his eyes," he says, and I see it is Dr. Funkenheld.

"Come in and shut the door," I say, still carefully protecting the liquid barretter, but Muller has already jammed the metal back against the beam.

"Do you have news?" Muller says to the doctor, eager for new facts to spin his theories from. "Has the wiring fatigue come back? Is there going to be a bombardment tonight?"

Dr. Funkenheld takes off his mittens. "I have come to examine your eyes," he says to me. His voice frightens me. All through the war he has kept his quiet bedside voice, speaking to the wounded in the dressing station and at the stretcher bearers' posts as if they were in his surgery in Stuttgart, but now he sounds agitated and I am afraid it means a bombardment is coming and he will need me at the front.

When I went to the dressing station for medicine for my eyes, I foolishly told him I had studied medicine with Dr. Zuschauer in Jena. Now I am afraid he will ask me to assist him, which will mean going up to the front. "Do your eyes still hurt?" he says.

I hand the barretter to Muller and go over to stand by the lantern that hangs from a nail in the beam.

"I think he should be invalided home, Herr Doktor," Muller says. He knows it is impossible, of course. He was at the wireless the day the message came through that no one was to be invalided out for frostbite or "other noncontagious diseases."

"Can you find me a better light?" the doctor says to him.

Muller's curiosity is so strong that he cannot bear to leave any place where something interesting is happening. If he went up to the front I do not think he would be able to pull himself away, and now I expect him to make some excuse to stay, but I have forgotten that he is even more curious about the wiring fatigue. "I will go see what has happened to Eisner's unit," he says, and opens the door. Snow flies in, as if it had been beating against the door to get in, and the doctor and I have to push against the door to get it shut again.

"My eyes have been hurting," I say, while we are still pushing the metal into place, so that he cannot ask me to assist him. "They feel like sand has gotten into them."

"I have a patient with a disease I do not recognize," he says. I am relieved, though disease can kill us as easily as a trench mortar. Soldiers die of pneumonia and dysentery and blood poisoning every day in the dressing station, but we do not fear it the way we fear the front.

"The patient has fever, excoriated lesions, and suppurating bullae," Dr. Funkenheld says.

"Could it be boils?" I say, though of course he would recognize something so simple as boils, but he is not listening to me, and I realize that it is not a diagnosis from me that he has come for.

"The man is a scientist, a Jew named Schwarzschild, attached to the artillery," he says, and because the artillery are even farther back from the front lines than we are, I volunteer to go and look at the patient, but he does not want that either.

"I must talk to the medical headquarters in Bialystok," he says.

"Our wireless is broken," I say, because I do not want to have to tell him why it is impossible for me to send a message for him. We are allowed to send only military messages, and they must be sent in code, tapped out on the telegraph key. It would take hours to send his message, even if it were possible. I hold up the dangling wire. "At any rate, you must clear it with the commandant," but he is already writing out the name and address on a piece of paper, as if this were a telegraph office.

"You can send the message when you get the wireless fixed. I have written out the symptoms."

I put the back on the wireless. Muller comes in, kicking the door open, and snow flies everywhere, picking up Dr. Funkenheld's message and sending it circling around the dugout. I catch it before it spirals into the flame of the Primus stove.

"The wiring fatigue was pinned down all night," Muller says, setting down a hand lamp. He must have gotten it from the dressing station. "Five of them frozen to death, the other eight have frostbite. The commandant thinks there may be a bombardment tonight." He does not mention Eisner, and he does not say what has happened to the rest of the thirty men in Eisner's unit, though I know. The front has gotten them. I wait, holding the message in my stiff fingers, hoping Dr. Funkenheld will say, "I must go attend to their frostbite."

"Let me examine your eyes," the doctor says, and shows Muller how to hold the hand lamp. Both of them peer into my eyes. "I have an ointment for you to use twice daily," he says, getting a flat jar out of his bag. "It will burn a little."

"I will rub it on my hands then. It will warm them," I say, thinking of Eisner frozen at the front, still holding the roll of barbed wire, perhaps.

He pulls my bottom eyelid down and rubs the ointment on with his little finger. It does not sting, but when I have blinked it into my eye, everything has a reddish tinge. "Will you have the wireless fixed by tomorrow?" he says.

"I don't know. Perhaps."

Muller has not put down the hand lamp. I can see by its light that he has forgotten all about the wiring fatigue and the Russian magnet and is wondering what the doctor wants with the wireless.

The doctor puts on his mittens and picks up his bag. I realize too late I should have told him I would send the message in exchange for them. "I will come check your eyes tomorrow," he says and opens the door to the snow. The sound of the front is very close.

As soon as he is gone, I tell Muller about Schwarzschild and the message the doctor wants to send. He will not let me rest until I have told him, and we do not have time for his curiosity. We must fix the wireless.

"If you were on the wireless, you must have sent messages for Schwarzschild," Travers said eagerly. "Did you ever send a message to Einstein? They've got the letter Einstein sent to him after he wrote him his theory, but if Schwarzschild sent him some kind of message, too, that would be great. It would make my paper."

"You said that no message can escape a black hole?" I said. "But they could escape a collapsing star. Is that not so?"

"Okay," Travers said impatiently and made his fingers into a semicircle again. "Suppose you have a fixed observer over here." He pulled his curved hand back and held the forefinger of his other hand up to represent the fixed observer, "and you have somebody in the star. Say when the star starts to collapse, the person in it shines a light at the fixed observer. If the star hasn't reached the Schwarzschild radius, the fixed observer will be able to see the light, but it will take longer to reach him because the gravity of the black hole is pulling on the light, so it will seem as if time on the star has slowed down and the wavelengths will have been lengthened, so the light will be redder. Of course that's just a thought problem. There couldn't really be anybody in a collapsing star to send the messages."

"We sent messages," I said. "I wrote my mother asking her to knit me a pair of gloves."

There is still something wrong with the wireless. We have received only one message in two weeks. It said, "Russian opposition collapsing," and there was so much static we could not make out the rest of it. We have taken the wireless apart twice. The first time we found a loose wire but the second time we could not find anything. If Hans were here he would be able to find the trouble immediately.

"I have a theory about the wireless," Muller says. He has had ten theories in as many days: The magnet of the Russians is pulling our signals in to it; the northern lights, which have been shifting uneasily on the horizon, make a curtain the wireless signals cannot get through; the Russian opposition is not collapsing at all. They are drawing us deeper and deeper into a trap.

I say, "I am going to try again. Perhaps the trouble has cleared up," and put the headphones on so I do not have to listen to his new theory. I can hear nothing but a rumbling roar that sounds like the front.

I take out the folded piece of paper Dr. Funkenheld gave me and lay it on the wireless. He comes nearly every night to see if I have gotten an answer to his message, and I take off the headphones and let him listen to the static. I tell him that we cannot get through, but even though that is true, it is not the real reason I have not sent the message. I am afraid of the commandant finding out. I am afraid of being sent to the front.

I have compromised by writing a letter to the professor that I studied medicine with in Jena, but I have not gotten an answer from him yet, and so I must go on pretending to the doctor.

"You don't have to do that," Muller says. He sits on the wireless, swinging his leg. He picks up the paper with the symptoms on it and holds it to the flame of the Primus stove. I grab for it, but it is already burning redly. "I have sent the message for you."

"I don't believe you. Nothing has been getting out."

"Didn't you notice the northern lights did not appear last night?"

I have not noticed. The ointment the doctor gave to me makes everything look red at night, and I do not believe in Muller's theories. "Nothing is getting out now," I say, and hold the headphones out to him so he can hear the static. He listens, still swinging his leg. "You will get us both in trouble. Why did you do it?"

"I was curious about it." If we are sent up to the front, his curiosity will kill us. He will take apart a land mine to see how it works. "We cannot get in trouble for sending military messages. I said the commandant was afraid it was a poisonous gas the Russians were using." He swings his leg and grins because now I am the curious one.

"Well, did you get an answer?"

"Yes," he says maddeningly and puts the headphones on. "It is not a poisonous gas."

I shrug as if I do not care whether I get an answer or not. I put on my cap and the muffler my mother knitted for me and open the door, "I am going out to see if the mail has come. Perhaps there will be a letter there from my professor."

"Nature of disease unknown," Muller shouts against the sudden force of the snow. "Possibly impetigo or glandular disorder."

I grin back at him and say, "If there is a package from my mother I will give you half of what is in it."

"Even if it is your gloves?"

"No, not if it is my gloves," I say, and go to find the doctor.

At the dressing station they tell me he has gone to see Schwarzschild and give me directions to the artillery staff's headquarters. It is not very far, but it is snowing and my hands are already cold. I go to the quartermaster's and ask him if the mail has come in.

There is a new recruit there, trying to fix Eisner's motorcycle. He has parts spread out on the ground all around him in a circle. He points to a burlap sack and says, "That is all the mail there is. Look through it yourself."

Snow has gotten into the sack and melted. The ink on the envelopes has run, and I squint at them, trying to make out the names. My eyes begin to hurt. There is not a package from my mother or a letter from my professor, but there is a letter for Lieutenant Schwarzschild. The return address says *Doctor*. Perhaps he has written to a doctor himself.

"I am delivering a message to the artillery headquarters," I say, showing the letter to the recruit. "I will take this up, too." The recruit nods and goes on working.

It has gotten dark while I was inside, and it is snowing harder. I jam my hands in the ice-stiff pockets of my coat and start to the artillery headquarters in the rear. It is pitch-dark in the communication trenches, and the wind twists the snow and funnels it howling along them. I take off my muffler and wrap it around my hands like a girl's muff.

A band of red shifts uneasily all along the horizon, but I do not know if it is the front or Muller's northern lights, and there is no shelling to guide me. We are running out of shells, so we do not usually begin shelling until nine o'clock. The Russians start even later. Sometimes I hear machine-gun fire, but it is distorted by the wind and the snow, and I cannot tell what direction it is coming from.

The communication trench seems narrower and deeper than I remember it from when Hans and I first brought the wireless up. It takes me longer than I think it should to get to the branching that will lead north to the headquarters. The front has been contracting, the ammunition dumps and officer's billets and clearing stations moving up closer and closer behind us. The artillery headquarters has been moved up from the village to a dugout near the artillery line, not half a mile behind us. The nightly firing is starting. I hear a low rumble, like thunder.

The roar seems to be ahead of me, and I stop and look around, wondering if I can have gotten somehow turned around, though I have not left the trenches. I start again, and almost immediately I see the branching and the headquarters.

It has no door, only a blanket across the opening, and I pull my hands free of the muffler and duck through it into a tiny space like a rabbit hole, the timber balks of the earthen ceiling so low I have to stoop. Now that I am out of the roar of the snow, the sound of the front separates itself into the individual crack of a four-pounder, the whine of a star shell, and under it the almost continuous rattle of machine guns. The trenches must not be as deep here. Muller and I can hardly hear the front at all in our wireless hut.

A man is sitting at an uneven table spread with papers and books. There is a candle on the table with a red glass chimney, or perhaps it only looks that way to me. Everything in the dugout, even the man, looks faintly red. He is wearing a uniform but no coat, and gloves with the finger ends cut off, even though there is no stove here. My hands are already cold.

A trench mortar roars, and clods of frozen dirt clatter from the roof onto the table. The man brushes the dirt from the papers and looks up.

"I am looking for Dr. Funkenheld," I say.

"He is not here." He stands up and comes around the table, moving stiffly, like an old man, though he does not look older than forty. He has a moustache, and his face looks dirty in the red light.

"I have a message for him."

An eight-pounder roars, and more dirt falls on us. The man raises his arm to brush the dirt off his shoulder. The sleeve of his uniform has been slit into ribbons. All along the back of his raised hand and the side of his arm are red sores running with pus. I look back at his face. The sores in his moustache and around his nose and mouth have dried and are covered with a crust. Excoriated lesions. Suppurating bullae. The gun roars again, and dirt rains down on his raw hands.

"I have a message for him," I say, backing away from him. I reach in the pocket of my coat to show him the message, but I pull out the letter instead. "There was a letter for you, Lieutenant Schwarzschild." I hold it out to him by one corner so he will not touch me when he takes it.

He comes toward me to take the letter, the muscles in his jaw tightening, and I think in horror that the sores must be on his legs as well. "Who is it from?" he says. "Ah, Herr Professor Einstein. Good," and turns it over. He puts his fingers on the flap to open the letter, and cries out in pain. He drops the letter.

"Would you read it to me?" he says, and sinks down into the chair, cradling his hand against his chest. I can see there are sores in his fingernails.

I do not have any feeling in my hands. I pick the envelope up by its corners and turn it over. The skin of his finger is still on the flap. I back away from the table. "I must find the doctor. It is an emergency."

"You would not be able to find him," he says. Blood oozes out of the tip of his finger and down over the blister in his fingernail. "He has gone up to the front."

"What?" I say, backing and backing until I run into the blanket. "I cannot understand you."

"He has gone up to the front," he says, more slowly, and this time I can puzzle out the words, but they make no sense. How can the doctor be at the front? This is the front.

He pushes the candle toward me. "I order you to read me the letter."

I do not have any feeling in my fingers. I open it from the top, tearing the letter almost in two. It is a long letter, full of equations and numbers, but the words are warped and blurred. "'My Esteemed Colleague! I have read your paper with the greatest interest. I had not expected that one could formulate the exact solution of the problem so simply. The analytical treatment of the problem appears to me splendid. Next Thursday I will present the work with several explanatory words, to the Academy!'"

"Formulated so simply," Schwarzschild says, as if he is in pain. "That is enough. Put the letter down. I will read the rest of it."

I lay the letter on the table in front of him, and then I am running down the trench in the dark with the sound of the front all around me, roaring and shaking the ground. At the first turning, Muller grabs my arm and stops me. "What are you doing here?" I shout. "Go back! Go back!"

"Go back?" he says. "The front's that way." He points in the direction he came from. But the front is not that way. It is behind me, in the artillery headquarters. "I told you there would be a bombardment tonight. Did you see the doctor? Did you give him the message? What did he say?"

"So you actually held the letter from Einstein?" Travers said. "How exciting that must have been! Only two months after Einstein had published his theory of general relativity. And years before they realized black holes really existed. When was this exactly?" He took out a notebook and began to scribble notes. "My esteemed colleague..." he muttered to himself. "Formulated so simply. This is great stuff. I mean, I've been trying to find out stuff on Schwarzschild for my paper for months, but there's hardly any information on him. I guess because of the war."

"No information can get out of a black hole once the Schwarzschild radius has been passed," I said.

"Hey, that's great!" he said, scribbling. "Can I use that in my paper?"

Now I am the one who sits endlessly in front of the wireless sending out messages to the Red Cross, to my professor in Jena, to Dr. Einstein. I have frostbitten the forefinger and thumb of my right hand and have to tap out the letters with my left. But nothing is getting out, and I must get a message out. I must find someone to tell me the name of Schwarzschild's disease.

"I have a theory," Muller says. "The Jews have seized power and have signed a treaty with the Russians. We are completely cut off."

"I am going to see if the mail has come," I say, so that I do not have to listen to any more of his theories, but the doctor stops me on my way out the hut.

I tell him what the message said. "Impetigo!" the doctor shouts. "You saw him! Did that look like impetigo to you?"

I shake my head, unable to tell him what I think it looks like.

"What are his symptoms?" Muller asks, burning with curiosity. I have not told him about Schwarzschild. I am afraid that if I tell him, he will only become more curious and will insist on going up to the front to see Schwarzschild himself.

"Let me see your eyes," the doctor says in his beautiful calm voice. I wish he would ask Muller to go for a hand lamp again so that I could ask him how Schwarzschild is, but he has brought a candle with him. He holds it so close to my face that I cannot see anything but the red flame.

"Is Lieutenant Schwarzschild worse? What are his symptoms?" Muller says, leaning forward.

His symptoms are craters and shell holes, I think. I am sorry I have not told Muller, for it has only made him more curious. Until now I have told him everything, even how Hans died when the wireless hut was hit, how he laid the liquid barretter carefully down on top of the wireless before he tried to cough up what was left of his chest and catch it in his hands. But I cannot tell him this.

"What symptoms does he have?" Muller says again, his nose almost in the candle's flame, but the doctor turns from him as if he cannot hear him and blows the candle out. The doctor unwraps the dressing and looks at my fingers. They are swollen and red. Muller leans over the doctor's shoulder. "I have a theory about Lieutenant Schwarzschild's disease," he says.

"Shut up," I say. "I don't want to hear any more of your stupid theories," and do not even care about the wounded look on Muller's face or the way he goes and sits by the wireless. For now I have a theory, and it is more horrible than anything Muller could have dreamt of.

We are all of us — Muller, and the recruit who is trying to put together Eisner's motorcycle, and perhaps even the doctor with his steady bedside voice — afraid of the front. But our fear is not complete, because unspoken in it is our belief that the front is something separate from us, something we can keep away from by keeping the wireless or the motorcycle fixed, something we can survive by flattening our faces into the frozen earth, something we can escape altogether by being invalided out.

But the front is not separate. It is inside Schwarzschild, and the symptoms I have been sending out, suppurative bullae and excoriated lesions, are not what is wrong with him at all. The lesions on his skin are only the barbed wire and shell holes and connecting trenches of a front that is somewhere farther in.

The doctor puts a new dressing of crepe paper on my hand. "I have tried to invalid Schwarzschild out," the doctor says, and Muller looks at him, astounded. "The supply lines are blocked with snow."

"Schwarzschild cannot be invalided out," I say. "The front is inside him."

The doctor puts the roll of crepe paper back in his kit and closes it. "When the roads open again, I will invalid you out for frostbite. And Muller too."

Muller is so surprised he blurts, "I do not have frostbite."

But the doctor is no longer listening. "You must both escape," he says — and I am not sure he is even listening to himself — "while you can."

"I have a theory about why you have not told me what is wrong with Schwarzschild," Muller says as soon as the doctor is gone.

"I am going for the mail."

"There will not be any mail," Muller shouts after me. "The supply lines are blocked," but the mail is there, scattered among the motorcycle parts. There are only a few parts left. As soon as the roads are cleared, the recruit will be able to climb on the motorcycle and ride away.

I gather up the letters and take them over to the lantern to try to read them, but my eyes are so bad I cannot see anything but a red blur. "I am taking them back to the wireless hut," I say, and the recruit nods without looking up.

It is starting to snow. Muller meets me at the door, but I brush past him and turn the flame of the Primus stove up as high as it will go and hold the letters up behind it.

"I will read them for you," Muller says eagerly, looking through the envelopes I have discarded. "Look, here is a letter from your mother. Perhaps she has sent your gloves."

I squint at the letters one by one while he tears open my mother's letter to me. Even though I hold them so close to the flame that the paper scorches, I cannot make out the names.

"'Dear son,'" Muller reads, "'I have not heard from you in three months. Are you hurt? Are you ill? Do you need anything?'"

The last letter is from Professor Zuschauer in Jena. I can see his name quite clearly in the corner of the envelope, though mine is blurred beyond recognition. I tear it open. There is nothing written on the red paper.

I thrust it at Muller. "Read this," I say.

"I have not finished with your mother's letter yet," Muller says, but he takes the letter and reads: "'Dear Herr Rottschieben, I received your letter yesterday. I could hardly decipher your writing. Do you not have decent pens at the front? The disease you describe is called Neumann's disease or pemphigus —'"

I snatch the letter out of Muller's hands and run out the door. "Let me come with you!" Muller shouts.

"You must stay and watch the wireless!" I say joyously, running along the communication trench. Schwarzschild does not have the front inside him. He has pemphigus, he has Neumann's disease, and now he can be invalided home to hospital.

I go down and think I have tripped over a discarded helmet or a tin of beef, but there is a crash, and dirt and revetting fall all around me. I hear the low buzz of a daisy cutter and flatten myself into the trench, but the buzz does not become a whine. It stops, and there is another crash and the trench caves in.

I scramble out of the trench before it can suffocate me and crawl along the edge toward Schwarzschild's dugout, but the trench has caved in all along its length, and when I crawl up and over the loose dirt, I lose it in the swirling snow.

I cannot tell which way the front lies, but I know it is very close. The sound comes at me from all directions, a deafening roar in which no individual sounds can be distinguished. The snow is so thick I cannot see the burst of flame from the muzzles as the guns fire, and no part of the horizon looks redder than any other. It is all red, even the snow.

I crawl in what I think is the direction of the trench, but as soon as I do, I am in barbed wire. I stop, breathing hard, my face and hands pressed into the snow. I have come the wrong way. I am at the front. I hear a sound out of the barrage of sound, the sound of tires on the snow, and I think it is a tank, and cannot breathe at all. The sound comes closer, and in spite of myself I look up and it is the recruit who was at the quartermaster's.

He is a long way away, behind a coiled line of barbed wire, but I can see him quite clearly in spite of the snow. He has the motorcycle fixed, and as I watch, he flings his leg over it and presses his foot down. "Go!" I shout. "Get out!" The motorcycle jumps forward. "Go!"

The motorcycle comes toward me, picking up speed. It rears up, and I think it is going to jump the barbed wire, but it falls instead, the motorcycle first and then the recruit, spiraling slowly down into the iron spikes. The ground heaves, and I fall too.

I have fallen into Schwarzschild's dugout. Half of it has caved in, the timber balks sticking out at angles from the heap of dirt and snow, but the blanket is still over the door, and Schwarzschild is propped in a chair. The doctor is bending over him. Schwarzschild has his shirt off. His chest looks like Hans's did.

The front roars and more of the roof crumbles. "It's all right! It's a disease!" I shout over it. "I have brought you a letter to prove it," and hand him the letter which I have been clutching in my unfeeling hand.

The doctor grabs the letter from me. Snow whirls down through the ruined roof, but Schwarzschild does not put on his shirt. He watches uninterestedly as the doctor reads the letter.

"'The symptoms you describe are almost certainly those of Neumann's disease, or pemphigus vulgaris. I have treated two patients with the disease, both Jews. It is a disease of the mucous membranes and is not contagious. Its cause is unknown. It always ends in death.'" Dr. Funkenheld crumples up the paper. "You came all this way in the middle of a bombardment to tell me there is no hope?" he shouts in a voice I do not even recognize, it is so unlike his steady doctor's voice. "You should have tried to get away. You should have —" and then he is gone under a crashing of dirt and splintered timbers.

I struggle toward Schwarzschild through the maelstrom of red dust and snow. "Put your shirt on!" I shout at him. "We must get out of here!" I crawl to the door to see if we can get out through the communication trench.

Muller bursts through the blanket. He is carrying, impossibly, the wireless. The headphones trail behind him in the snow. "I came to see what had happened to you. I thought you were dead. The communication trenches are shot to pieces."

It is as I had feared. His curiosity has got the best of him, and now he is trapped, too, though he seems not to know it. He hoists the wireless onto the table without looking at it. His eyes are on Schwarzschild, who leans against the remaining wall of the dugout, his shirt in his hands.

"Your shirt!" I shout and come around to help Schwarzschild put it on over the craters and shell holes of his blasted skin. The air screams and the mouth of the dugout blows in. I grab at Schwarzschild's arm, and the skin of it comes off in my hands. He falls against the table, and the wireless goes over. I can hear the splintering tinkle of the liquid barretter breaking, and then the whole dugout is caving in and we are under the table. I cannot see anything.

"Muller!" I shout. "Where are you?"

"I'm hit," he says.

I try to find him in the darkness, but I am crushed against Schwarzschild. I cannot move. "Where are you hit?"

"In the arm," he says, and I hear him try to move it. The movement dislodges more dirt, and it falls around us, shutting out all sound of the front. I can hear the creak of wood as the table legs give way.

"Schwarzschild?" I say. He doesn't answer, but I know he is not dead. His body is as hot as the Primus stove flame. My hand is underneath his body, and I try to shift it, but I cannot. The dirt falls like snow, piling up around us. The darkness is red for a while, and then I cannot see even that.

"I have a theory," Muller says in a voice so close and so devoid of curiosity it might be mine. "It is the end of the world."

"Was that when Schwarzschild was sent home on sick leave?" Travers said.

"Or validated, or whatever you Germans call it? Well, yeah, it had to be, because he died in March. What happened to Muller?"

I had hoped he would go away as soon as I had told him what had happened to Schwarzschild, but he made no move to get up. "Muller was invalided out with a broken arm. He became a scientist."

"The way you did." He opened his notebook again. "Did you see Schwarzschild after that?"

The question makes no sense.

"After you got out? Before he died?"

It seems to take a long time for his words to get to me. The message bends and curves, shifting into the red, and I can hardly make it out. "No," I say, though that is a lie.

Travers scribbles. "I really do appreciate this, Dr. Rottschieben. I've always been curious about Schwarzschild, and now that you've told me all this stuff I'm even more interested," Travers says, or seems to say. Messages coming in are warped by the gravitational blizzard into something that no longer resembles speech. "If you'd be willing to help me, I'd like to write my thesis on him."

Go. Get out. "It was a lie," I say. "I never knew Schwarzschild. I saw him once, from a distance — your fixed observer."

Travers looks up expectantly from his notes as if he is still waiting for me to answer him.

"Schwarzschild was never even in Russia," I lie. "He spent the whole winter in hospital in Göttingen. I lied to you. It was nothing but a thought problem."

He waits, pencil ready.

"You can't stay here!" I shout. "You have to get away. There is no safe distance from which a fixed observer can watch without being drawn in, and once you are inside the Schwarzschild radius you can't get out. Don't you understand? We are still there!"

We are still there, trapped in the trenches of the Russian front, while the dying star burns itself out, spiraling down into that center where time ceases to exist, where everything ceases to exist except the naked singularity that is somehow Schwarzschild.

Muller tries to dig the wireless out with his crushed arm so he can send a message that nobody can hear — "Help us! Help us!" — and I struggle to free the hands that in spite of Schwarzschild's warmth are now so cold I cannot feel them, and in the very center Schwarzschild burns himself out, the black hole at his center imploding him cell by cell, carrying him down into darkness, and us with him.

"It is a trap!" I shout at Travers from the center, and the message struggles to escape and then falls back.

"I wonder how he figured it out?" Travers says, and now I can hear him clearly. "I mean, can you imagine trying to figure out something like the theory of black holes in the middle of a war and while you were suffering from a fatal disease? And just think, when he came up with the theory, he didn't have any idea that black holes even existed."

I think it's difficult for a novelist nowadays to write without irony about a way of life that's fulfilling or satisfying. I think that in America today it's not easy to see that way of life without being grossly sentimental or blocking out certain realities. It's a paradox. I suppose if we knew it, we'd all be living it. But I do think it's necessary to try to imagine that. It's extremely difficult.

—John Kessel

Genre writers and readers share a common stock of concepts, icons, images, manners, patterns, precisely as the musicians and audiences of Haydn's and Mozart's time shared a *materia musica* which the composer was expected not to shatter or transcend, but to use and make variations on. "The Pattern," says Roberts,[1] "has to be fixed, partly because that's enjoyable in itself, partly because that makes it possible to be surprised and delighted by a diversion from the pattern." Transcendence, as in the case of Mozart, may of course occur; it's wonderful, but it really isn't the point.... [Literature] works through accreting a tradition. A genre is a formal tradition.

—Ursula K. Le Guin

1 Thomas Roberts, *An Aesthetics of Junk Fiction*

Buddha Nostril Bird
John Kessel

After we killed the guard, Glaucon and I ran down the corridor away from the Well. Glaucon had been seriously aged in the fight. He limped and cursed, a piece of dying meat and he knew it. I brushed my hand along the wall looking for a door.

"We'll make it," I said.

"Sure," he said. He held his arm against his side.

We ran past a series of ontological windows: a forest fire, a sun in space, a factory refashioning children into flowers. I worried that the corridor might be a loop. For all I knew, the sole purpose of such corridors was to confuse and recapture escapees. Or maybe the corridors were just for fun. The Relativists delight in such absurdities.

More windows: a snowstorm, a cloudy seascape, a corridor exactly like the one we were in, in which two men wearing yellow robes — prison kosodes like ours — searched for a way out. Glaucon stopped. The hand of his double reached out to meet his. The face of mine stared at me angrily; a strong face, an intelligent one. "It's just a mirror," I said.

"Mirror?"

"A mirror," a voice said. Protagoras appeared ahead of us in the corridor. "Like sex, it reproduces human beings."

An old joke, and typical of Protagoras to quote it without attribution.

Glaucon raised his clock. In the face of Protagoras' infinite mutability it was less than useless: There was no way Glaucon would even get a shot off. My spirit sank as I watched the change come over him. Protagoras dripped fellowship. Glaucon liked him. Nobody but a maniac could dislike Protagoras.

It took all my will to block the endorphin assault, but Glaucon was never as strong as I. A lot of talk about brotherhood had passed between us, but if I'd had my freedom I would have crisped him on the spot. Instead I hid myself from Protagoras' blue eyes, as cold as chips of aquamarine in a mosaic.

"Where are you going?" Protagoras said.

"We were going —" Glaucon started.

"— nowhere," I said.

"A hard place to get to," said Protagoras.

Glaucon's head bobbed like a dog's.

"I know a short way," Protagoras said. "Come along with me."

"Sure," said Glaucon.

I struggled to maintain control. If you had asked him, Protagoras would have denied controlling anyone: "The Superior Man rules by humility." Another sophistry.

We turned back down the corridor. If I stayed with them until we got to the center, there would be no way I could escape. Desperation forced me to test the reality of one of the windows. As we passed the ocean scene, I pushed Glaucon into Protagoras and threw my shoulder against the glass. The window shattered; I was falling. My kosode flapped like the melting wings of Icarus as sky and sea whirled around me, and I hit the water. My breath exploded from me. I flailed and tumbled. At last I found the surface. I sputtered and gasped, my right arm in agony; my ribs ached. I kicked off my slippers and leaned onto my back. The waves rolled me up and down. The sky was low and dark. At the top of each swell I could see to the storm-clouded horizon, flat as a psychotic's affect — but in the other direction was a beach.

I swam. The bad shoulder made it hard, but at that moment I would not have traded places with Glaucon for all the enlightenment of the ancients.

When they sent me to the penal colony they told me, "Prisons ought to be places where people are lodged only temporarily, as guests are. They must not become dwelling places."

Their idea of temporary is not mine. Temporary doesn't mean long enough for your skin to crack like the dry lakebed outside your window, for the memory of your lover's touch to recede until it's only a torment in your dreams, as distant as the mountains that surround the prison. These distinctions are lost on Relativists, as are all distinctions. Which, I suppose, is why I was sent there.

They keep you alone, mostly. I don't mind the isolation — it gave me time to understand exactly how many ways I had been betrayed. I spent hours thinking of Areté, etching her ideal features in my mind. I remembered how they'd ripped me away from her. I wondered if she still lived, and if I would ever see her again. Eventually, when memory had faded, I conquered the passage of time itself: I reconstructed her image from incorruptible ideas and planned the revenge I would take once I was free again, so that the past and the future became more real to me than the endless, featureless present. Such is the power of idea over reality. To the guards I must have looked properly meditative. Inside I burned.

Each day at dawn we would be awakened by the rapping of sticks on our iron bedsteads. In the first hour we drew water from the Well of Changes. In the second we were encouraged to drink (I refused). In the third we washed floors with the water. From the fourth through the seventh we performed every other function that was necessary to maintain the prison. In the eighth we were tortured. At the ninth we were fed. At night, exhausted, we slept.

The torture chamber is made of ribbed concrete. It is a cold room, without windows. In its center is a chair, and beside the chair a small table, and on the table the hood. The hood is black and appears to be made of ordinary fabric, but it is not. The first time I held it, despite the evidence of my eyes I thought it had slipped through my fingers. The hood is not a material object: You cannot feel it, and it has no texture, and although it absorbs all light it is neither warm nor cold.

Your inquisitor invites you to sit in the chair and slip the hood over your head. You do so. He speaks to you. The room disappears. Your body melts away, and you are made into something else. You are an animal. You are one of the ancients. You are a stone, a drop of rain in a storm, a planet. You are in another time and place. This may sound intriguing, and the first twenty times it is. But it never ends. The sessions are indiscriminate. They are deliberately pointless. They continue to the verge of insanity.

I recall one of these sessions, in which I lived in an ancient city and worked a hopeless routine in a store called the "World of Values." The values we sold were merchandise. I married, had children, grew old, lost my health and spirit. I worked forty years. Some days were happy, others sad; most were neither. The last thing I remembered was lying in a hospital bed, unable to see, dying, and hearing my wife talk with my son about what they should have for dinner. When I came out from under the hood, Protagoras yanked me from the chair and told me this poem:

> *Out from the nostrils of the Great Buddha*
> *Flew a pair of nesting swallows.*

I could still hear my phantom wife's cracking voice. I was in no mood for riddles. "Tell me what it means."

"Drink from the Well and I'll tell you."

I turned my back on him.

It was always like that. Protagoras had made a career out of tormenting me. I had known him for too many years. He put faith in nothing, was totally without honor, yet he had power. His intellect was available for any use. He wasted years on banalities. He would argue any side of a case, not because he sought advantage, but because he did not care about right or wrong. He was intolerably lucky. Irresponsible as a child. Inconstant as the wind. His opaque blue gaze could be as witless as a scientist's.

And he had been my first teacher. He had introduced me to Areté, offered me useless advice throughout our stormy relationship, given ambiguous testimony at my trial, and upon the verdict abandoned the university in order to come to the prison and become my inquisitor. The thought that I had once idolized him tormented me more than any session under the hood.

After my plunge through the window into the sea, I fought my way through the surf to the beach. For an unknown time I lay gasping on the wet sand. When I opened my eyes I saw a flock of gulls had waddled up to me. An arm's length away the lead gull, a great bull whose ragged feathers stood out from his neck in a ruff, watched me with beady black eyes. Others of various sizes and markings stood in a wedge behind him. I raised my head; the gulls retreated a few steps, still holding formation. I understood immediately that they were ranked according to their stations in the flock. Thus does nature shadow forth fundamental truth: the rule of the strong over the weak, the relation of one to many in hierarchical order.

Off to the side stood a single scrawny gull, quicker than the rest, but separate, aloof. I supposed him to be a gullish philosopher. I saluted him, my brother.

A sandpiper scuttled along the edge of the surf. Dipping a handful of seawater, I washed sand and pieces of shell from my cheek. Up the slope, saw grass and sea oats held the dunes against the tides. The scene was familiar. With wonder and some disquiet I understood that the window had dumped me into the Great Water quite near the Imperial City.

I stumbled up the sand to the crest of the dunes. In the east, beneath piled thunderheads, lightning flashed over the dark water. To the west, against the sunset's glare, the sand and scrub turned into fields. I started inland. Night fell swiftly. From behind me came clouds, strong winds, then rain. I trudged on, singing into the downpour. The thunder sang back. Water streamed down the creases of my face, the wet kosode weighed on my chest and shoulders, the rough grass cut my feet. In the profound darkness I could continue only by memorizing the landscape revealed by flashes of lightning. Exhilarated, I hurried toward my lover. I shouted at the raindrops, any one of which might be one of my fellow prisoners under the hood. "I'm free!" I told them. I forded the swollen River of Indifference. I stumbled through Iron Tree Forest. Throughout the night I put one foot before the other, and some hours before dawn, in a melancholy drizzle, passed through the Heron's Gate into the city.

In the Processor's Quarter I found a doorway whose overhang kept out the worst of the rain. Above hung the illuminated sign of the Rat. In the corner of this doorway, under this sign, I slept.

I was awakened by the arrival of the owner of the communications shop in whose doorway I had slept.

"I am looking for the old fox," I said. "Do you know where I can find him?"

"Who are you?"

"You may call me the little fox."

He pushed open the door. "Well, Mr. Fox, I can put you in touch with him instantly. Just step into one of our booths."

He must have known I had no money. "I don't want to communicate. I want to see him."

"Communication is much better," the shop owner said. He took a towel, a copper basin, and an ornamental blade from the cupboard beneath his terminal. "No chance of physical violence. No distress other than psychological. Completely accurate reproduction. Sensory enhancement: olfactory, visual, auditory." He opened a cage set into the wall and seized a docile black rat by the scruff of the neck. "Recordability. Access to a network of supporting information services. For slight additional charge we offer intelligence augmentation and instant semiotic analysis. We make the short man tall. Physical presence has nothing to compare."

"I want to speak with him in private."

Not looking at me, he took the rat to the stone block. "We are bonded."

"I don't question your integrity."

"You have religious prejudices against communication? You are a Traveler?"

He would not rest until he forced me to admit I was penniless. I refrained from noting that, if he was such a devout communicator, he could easily have stayed home. Yet he had walked to his shop in person. Swallowing my rage, I said, "I have no money."

He sliced the rat's neck open. The animal made no sound.

After he had drained the blood and put the carcass into the display case, he washed his hands and turned to me. He seemed quite pleased with himself. He took a small object from a drawer. "He is to be found at the university. Here is a map of the maze." He slipped it into my hand.

For this act of gratuitous charity, I vowed that one day I would have revenge. I left.

The streets were crowded. Dusty gold light filtered down between the ranks of ancient buildings. Too short to use the moving ways, I walked. Orange-robed messengers threaded their way through the crowd. Sweating drivers in loincloths pulled pedicabs; I imagined the perfumed lottery winners who reclined behind the opaqued glass of their passenger compartments. In the Medical Quarter, street-side surgeons hawked their services in front of racks of breasts and penises of prodigious size. As before, the names of the streets changed hourly to mark the progress of the sun across the sky. All streets but one, and I held my breath when I came to it: the Way of Enlightenment, which ran between the reform temple and the Imperial Palace. As before, metamorphs entertained the faithful on the stage outside the temple. One of them changed shape as I watched, from a dog-faced man wearing the leather skirt of an athlete to a tattooed CEO in powered suit. "Come drink from the Well of Changes!" he called ecstatically to passersby. "Be reformed!"

The Well he spoke of is both literal and symbolic. The prison Well was its brother; the preachers of the temple claim that all the Wells are one Well. Its water has the power to transform both body and mind. A scientist could tell you how it is done: viruses, brain chemistry, hypnosis, some insane combination of the three. But that is all a scientist could tell you. Unlike a scientist, I could tell you why its use is morally wrong. I could explain that some truths are eternal and ought to be held inviolate, and why a culture that accepts change indiscriminately is rotten at its heart. I could demonstrate, with inescapable logic, that reason is better than emotion. That spirit is greater than flesh. That Relativism is the road to hell.

Instead of relief at being home, I felt distress. The street's muddle upset me, but it was not simply that: The city was exactly as I had left it. The wet morning that dawned on me in the doorway might have been the morning after I was sent away. My absence had made no discernible difference. The tyranny of the Relativists that I and my friends had struggled against had not culminated in the universal misery we had predicted. Though everything changed minute to minute, it remained the same. The one thing that ought to remain constant, Truth, was to them as chimerical as the gene-changers of the temple.

They might have done better, had they had teachers to tell them good from bad.

Looking down the boulevard, in the distance, at the heart of the city, I could see the walls of the palace. By midday I had reached it. Vendors of spiced cakes pushed their carts among the petitioners gathered beneath the great red lacquered doors. One, whose cakes each contained a free password, did a superior business. That the passwords were patent frauds was evident by the fact that the gatekeeper ignored those petitioners who tried using them. But that did not hurt sales. Most of the petitioners were halflings, and a dim-witted rabbit could best them in a deal.

I wept for my people, their ignorance and illogic. I discovered that I was clutching the map in my fist so tightly that the point of it had pierced my skin. I turned from the palace and walked away, and did not feel any relief until I saw the towers of the university rising above Scholars' Park. I remembered my first sight of them, a young boy down from the hills, the smell of cattle still about me, come to study under the great Protagoras. The meticulously kept park, the calm proportions of the buildings, spoke to the soul of that innocent boy: Here you'll be safe from blood and passion. Here you can lose yourself in the world of the mind.

The years had worn the polish off that dream, but I can't say that, seeing it now, once more a fugitive from a dangerous world, I did not feel some of the same joy. I thought of my mother, a loutish farmer who would whip me for reading; of my gentle father, brutalized by her, trying to keep the flame of truth alive in his boy.

On the quadrangle I approached a young woman wearing the topknot and scarlet robe of a humanist. Her head bounced to some inner rhythm, and as I imagined she was pursuing some notion of the Ideal, my heart went out to her. I was about to ask her what she studied when I saw the pin in her temple. She was listening to transtemporal music: her mind eaten by puerile improvisations played on signals picked up from the death agonies of the cosmos. Generations of researchers had devoted their lives to uncovering these secrets, only to have their efforts used by "artists" to erode people's connections with reality. I spat on the walk at her feet; she passed by, oblivious.

At the entrance to the humanities maze I turned on the map and followed it into the gloom. Fifteen minutes later it guided me into the Department of Philosophy. It was the last place I expected to find the fox — the nest of our enemies, the place we had plotted against tirelessly. The secretary greeted me pleasantly.

"I'm looking for a man named Socrates," I said. "Some call him 'the old fox.'"

"Universe of Discourse 3," she said.

I walked down the hall, wishing I had Glaucon's clock. The door to the hall stood open. In the center of the cavelike room, in a massive support chair, sat Socrates. At last I had found a significant change: He was grossly obese. The ferretlike features I remembered were folded in fat. Only the acute eyes remained. I was profoundly shaken. As I approached, his eyes followed me.

"Socrates."

"Blume."

"What happened to you?"

Socrates lifted his dimpled hand, as if to wave away a triviality. "I won."

"You used to revile this place."

"I reviled its usurpers. Now I run it."

"You run it?"

"I'm the dean."

I should have known Socrates had turned against our cause, and perhaps at some level I had. If he had remained true, he would have ended up in a cell next to mine. "You used to be a great teacher," I said.

"Right. Let me tell what happens when a man starts claiming he's a great teacher. First he starts wearing a brocade robe. Then he puts lifts in his sandals. The next thing you know the department's got a nasty paternity suit on its hands."

His senile chuckle was like the bubbling of water in an opium pipe.

"How did you get to be dean?"

"I performed a service for the Emperor."

"You sold out!"

"Blume the dagger," he said. Some of the old anger shaded his voice. "So sharp. So rigid. You always were a prig."

"And you used to have principles."

"Ah, principles," he said. "I'll tell you what happened to my principles. You heard about Philomena the Bandit?"

"No. I've been somewhat out of touch."

Socrates ignored the jab. "It was after you left. Philomena invaded the system, established her camp on the moon, and made her living raiding the empire. The city was at her mercy. I saw my opportunity. I announced that I would reform her. My students outfitted a small ship, and Areté and I launched for the moon."

"Areté!"

"We landed in a lush valley near the camp. Areté negotiated an audience for me. I went, alone. I described to Philomena the advantages of politic behavior. The nature of truth. The costs of living in the world of shadows and the glory of moving into the world of light. How, if she should turn to Good, her story would be told for generations. Her fame would spread throughout the world and her honor outlast her lifetime by a thousand years.

"Philomena listened. When I was finished she drew a knife and asked me, 'How long is a thousand years?'

"Her men stood all around, waiting for me to slip. I started to speak, but before I could she pulled me close and pushed the blade against my throat.

"'A thousand years,' Philomena said, 'is shorter than the exposure of a neutrino passing through a world. How long is life?'

"I was petrified. She smiled. 'Life,' she said, 'is shorter than this blade.'

"I begged for mercy. She threw me out. I ran to the ship, in fear for my life. Areté asked what happened: I said nothing. We set sail for home.

"We landed amid great tumult. I first thought it was riot but soon found it celebration. During our voyage back Philomena had left the moon. People assumed I had convinced her. The Emperor spoke. Our enemies in philosophy were shortened, and the regents stretched me into dean.

"Since then," Socrates said, "I have had trouble with principles."

"You're a coward," I said.

Despite the mask of suet, I could read the ruefulness in Socrates' eyes. "You don't know me," he said.

"What happened to Areté?"

"I have not seen her since."

"Where is she?"

"She's not here." He shifted his bulk, watching the screen that encircled the room. "Turn yourself in, Blume. If they catch you, it will only go harder."

"Where is she?"

"Even if you could get to her, she won't want to see you."

I seized his arm, twisted. "Where is Areté!"

Socrates inhaled sharply. "In the palace," he said.

"She's a prisoner?"

"She's the Empress."

That night I took a place among the halflings outside the palace gate. Men and women regrown from seed after their deaths, imprinted with stored files of their original personalities, all of them had lost resolution, for no identity file could encapsulate human complexity. Some could not speak, others displayed features too stiff to pass for human, and still others had no personalities at all. Their only chance for wholeness was to petition the Empress to perform a transfinite extrapolation from their core data. To be miraculously transformed.

An athlete beside me showed me his endorsements. An actress showed me her notices. A banker showed me his lapels. They asked me my profession. "I am a philosopher," I said.

They laughed. "Prove it," the actress said.

"In the well-ordered state," I told her, "there will be no place for you." To the athlete I said, "Yours is a good and noble profession." I turned to the banker. "Your work is more problematical," I said. "Unlike the actress, you fulfill a necessary function, but unlike the athlete, by accumulating wealth you are likely to gain more power than is justified by your small wisdom."

This speech was beyond them: The actress grumbled and went away. I left the two men and walked along below the battlements. Two bartizans framed the great doors, and archers strolled along the ramparts or leaned through the embrasures to spit on the petitioners. For this reason the halflings camped as far back from the walls as they might without blocking the street. The archers, as any educated man knew, were there for show: The gates were guarded only by a single gatekeeper, a monk who could open the door if bested in a battle of wits, but without whose acquiescence the door could not be budged.

He sat on his stool beside the gate, staring quietly ahead. Those who tried to talk to him could not tell whether they'd get a cuff on the ear or a friendly conversation. His flat, peasant's face was so devoid of intellect that it was some time before I recognized him as Protagoras.

His disguised presence could be one of his whims. Or it could be he was being punished for letting me escape; it could be that he waited for me. I felt an urge to run. But I would not duplicate Socrates' cowardice. If Protagoras recognized me he did not show it, and I resolved to get in or get caught. I was not some half-wit, and I knew him. I approached. "I wish to see the Empress," I said.

"You must wait."

"I've been waiting for years."

"That doesn't matter."

"I have no more time."

He studied me. His manner changed. "What will you pay?"

"I'll pay you a story that will make you laugh until your head aches."

He smiled. I saw that he recognized me; my stomach lurched. "I know many such stories," he said.

"Not like mine."

"Yes. I can see you are a great breeder of headaches."

Desperation drove me forward. "Listen, then: Once there was a warlord who discovered that someone had stolen his most precious possession, a jewel of power. He ordered his servants to scour the fortress for strangers. In the bailey they found a beggar heading for the gate. The lord's men seized him and carried him to the well. 'The warlord's great jewel is lost,' they said to him. They thrust the beggar's head beneath the water. He struggled. They pulled him up and asked, 'Where is the jewel?'

"'I don't know,' he said.

"They thrust him down again, longer this time. When they pulled him up he sputtered like an old engine. 'Where is the jewel?' they demanded. 'I don't know!' he replied.

"Furious at his insolence, fearful for their lives if they should rouse their lord's displeasure, the men pushed the beggar so far into the well that a bystander thought, 'He will surely drown.' The beggar kicked so hard it took three strong men to hold him. When at last they pulled him up he coughed and gasped, face purple, struggling to speak. They pounded him on the back. Finally he drew breath enough for words.

"'I think you should get another diver,' the beggar said. 'I can't see it anywhere down there.'"

Protagoras smiled. "That's not funny."

"What?"

"Maybe for us, but not for the beggar. Or the bystander. Or the servants. The warlord probably had them shortened."

"Don't play games. What do you really think?"

"I think of poor Glaucon. He misses you."

Then I saw that Protagoras only meant to torment me, as he had so many times before. He would answer my desperate need with feeble jokes until I wept or went mad. A fury more powerful than the sun itself swept over me, and I lost control. I fell on him, kicking, biting. The petitioners looked on in amazement. Shouts echoed from the ramparts. I didn't care. I'd forgotten everything but my rage; all I knew was that at last I had him in my hands. I scratched at his eyes, I beat his head against the pavements. Protagoras struggled to speak. I pulled him up and slammed his head against the doors. The tension went out of his muscles. Cross-legged, as if preparing to meditate, he slid to the ground. Blood glistened in the torchlight on the lacquered doors. "Now that's funny," he whispered, and died.

The weight of his body against the door pushed it ajar. It had been open all along.

No one came to arrest me. Across the inner ward, at the edge of an ornamental garden, a person stood in the darkness beneath a plane tree. Most of the lights of the palace were unlit, but radiance from the clerestory above heightened the shadows. Hesitantly I drew closer, too unsteady after my sudden fit of violence to hide. In my confusion I could think to do no more than approach the figure in the garden, who stood patiently as if in long expectation of me. From ten paces away I saw it was a woman dressed as a clown. From five I saw it was Areté.

Her laughter, like shattering crystal, startled me. "How serious you look!"

My head was full of questions. She pressed her fingers against my lips, silencing them. I embraced her. Red circles were painted on her cheeks, and she wore a crepe beard, but her skin was still smooth, her eyes bright, her perfume the same. She was not a day older.

The memory of dead Protagoras' slack mouth marred my triumph. She ducked out of my arms, laughing again. "You can't have me unless you catch me!"

"Areté!"

She darted through the trees. I ran after her. My heart was not in it, and I lost her until she paused beneath a tree, hands on knees, panting. "Come on! I'm not so hard to catch."

The weight was lifted from my heart. I dodged after her. Beneath the trees, through the hedge maze, among the night-blooming jasmine and bougainvillea, the silver moon tipping the edges of the leaves, I chased her. At last she let herself be caught; we fell together into a damp bed of ivy. I rested my head on her breast. The embroidery of her costume was rough against my cheek.

She took my head in her hands and made me look her in the face. Her teeth were pearly white, breath sweet as the scented blossoms around us.

We kissed, through the ridiculous beard (I could smell the spirit gum she'd used to affix it), and the goal they had sought to instill in me at the penal colony was attained: My years of imprisonment vanished into the immediate moment as if they had never existed.

That kiss was the limit of our contact. I expected to spend the night with her; instead, she had a slave take me to a guesthouse for visiting dignitaries, where I was quartered with three minor landholders from the mountains. They were already asleep. After my day of confusion, rage, desire, and fear, I lay there weary but hard awake, troubled by the sound of my own breathing. My thoughts were jumbled white noise. I had killed him. I had found her. Two of the fantasies of my imprisonment fulfilled in a single hour. Yet no peace. The murder of Protagoras would not long go unnoticed. I assumed Areté already knew but did not care. But if she was truly the Empress, why had he not been killed years before? Why had I rotted in prison under him?

I had no map for this maze and eventually fell asleep.

In the morning the slave, Pismire, brought me a wig of human hair, a green kimono, a yellow silk sash, and solid leather sandals: the clothes of a prosperous nonentity. My roommates appeared to be barely lettered country bumpkins, little better than my parents, come to court seeking a judgment against a neighbor or a place for a younger child or protection from some bandit. One of them wore the colors of an inferior upland collegium; the others no colors at all.

I suspected at least one of them was Areté's spy; they might have thought me one as well. We looked enough alike to be brothers.

We ate in a dining room attended by machines. I spent the day studying the public rooms of the palace, hoping to get some information. At the tolling of sixth hour Pismire found me in the vivarium. He handed me a message under the Imperial seal, and left. I turned it on.

"You are invited to an important meeting," the message said.

"With whom?" I asked. "For what purpose?"

The message ignored me. "The meeting begins promptly at ninth hour. Prepare yourself." There followed directions to the place.

When I arrived, the appointed room was empty. A long oak table, walls lined with racks of document spindles. At the far end, French doors gave onto a balcony overlooking an ancient city of glass and metal buildings. I could hear the faint sounds of traffic below.

A side door opened and a woman in the blue suit of the Lawyer entered, followed by a clerk. The woman's glossy black hair was stranded with gray, but her face was smooth. She wore no makeup. She stood at the end of the table, back to the French doors, and set down a leather box. The clerk sat at her right hand. I realized that this forbidding figure was Areté. She had become as mutable as Protagoras.

"Be seated," she said. "We are here to take your deposition."

"Deposition?"

"Your statement on the matter at hand."

"What matter?"

"Your escape from the penal colony. Your murder of the gatekeeper, the honored philosopher Protagoras."

The injustice of this burned through my dismay. "Not murder. Self-defense. Or better still, euthanasia."

"Don't quibble with us. We are deprived of his presence."

"Grow a duplicate. Bring him back to life."

For reply she merely stared at me across the table. The air tasted stale, and I felt a bead of sweat run down my breast beneath my robe. "Is this some game?"

"You may well wish it a game."

"Areté!"

"I am not Areté. I am a Lawyer." She leaned toward me. "Why were you sent to prison?"

"You were with me! You know."

"We are taking your version of events for the record."

"You know as well as I that I was imprisoned for seeking the Truth."

"Which truth?"

There was only one. "The one that people don't want to hear," I said.

"You had access to a truth people did not acknowledge?"

"They are blinded by custom and self-interest."

"You were not?"

"I had, through years of self-abnegation and study, risen above them. I had broken free of the chains of prejudice, climbed out of the cave of shadows that society lives in, and looked at the sun direct."

The clerk smirked as I made this speech. It was the first expression he'd shown.

"And you were blinded by it," Areté said.

"I saw the truth. But when I came back they said I was blind. They would not listen, so they put me away."

"The trial record says that you assisted in the corruption of youth."

"I was a teacher."

"The record says you refused to listen to your opponents."

"I refuse to listen to ignorance and illogic. I refuse to submit to fools, liars, and those who let passion overcome reason."

"You have never been fooled?"

"I was, but not now."

"You never lie?"

"If I do, I still know the difference between a lie and the truth."

"You never act out of passion?"

"Only when supported by reason."

"You never suspect your own motives?"

"I know my motives."

"How?"

"I examine myself. Honestly, critically. I apply reason."

"Spare me your colossal arrogance, your revolting self-pity. Eyewitnesses say you killed the gatekeeper in a fit of rage."

"I had reason. Do you presume to understand my motives better than I? Do you understand your own?"

"No. But that's because I am dishonest. And totally arbitrary." She opened the box and took out a clock. Without hesitation she pointed it at the clerk. His smugness punctured, he stumbled back, overturning his chair. She pressed the trigger. The weapon must have been set for maximum entropy: Before my eyes the clerk aged ten, twenty, fifty years. He died and rotted. In less than a minute he was a heap of bones and gruel on the floor.

"You've been in prison so long you've invented a harmless version of me," Areté said. "I am capable of anything." She laid the clock on the table, turned, and opened the doors to let in a fresh night breeze. Then she climbed onto the table and crawled toward me. I sat frozen. "I am the Destroyer," she said, loosening her tie as she approached. Her eyes were fixed on mine. When she reached me she pushed me over backward, falling atop me. "I am the force that drives the blood through your dying body, the nightmare that wakes you sweating in the middle of the night. I am the fiery caldron within whose heat you are reduced to a vapor, extended from the visible into the invisible, dissipated on the winds of time, of fading memory, of inevitable human loss. In the face of me, you are incapable of articulate speech. About me you understand nothing."

She wound the tie around my neck, drew it tight. "Remember that," she said, strangling me.

I passed out on the floor of the interview room and awoke the next morning in a bed in a private chamber. Pismire was drawing the curtains on a view of an ocean beach: Half-asleep, I watched the tiny figure of a man materialize in a spray of glass, in midair, and fall precipitously into the sea.

Pismire brought me a breakfast of fruit and spiced coffee. Touching the bruises on my neck, I watched the man resurface in the sea and swim ashore. He collapsed on the sand. A flock of gulls came to stand by his head. If I broke through this window, I could warn him. I could say: Socrates is fat. Watch out for the gatekeeper. Areté is alive, but she is changed.

But what could I tell him for certain? Had Areté turned Relativist, like Socrates? Was she free, or being made to play a part? Did she intend to prosecute me for the murder of Protagoras? But if so, why not simply return me to the penal colony?

I did not break through the window, and the man eventually moved up the beach toward the city.

That day servants followed me everywhere. Minor lords asked my opinions. Evidently I was a taller man than I had been the day before. I drew Pismire aside and asked him what rumors were current. He was a stocky fellow with a topknot of coarse black hair and shaved temples, silent, but when I pressed him he opened up readily enough. He said he knew for a fact that Protagoras had set himself up to be killed. He said the Emperor was dead and the Empress was the focus of a perpetual struggle. That many men had sought to make Areté theirs, but none had so far succeeded. That disaster would surely follow any man's success.

"Does she always change semblance from day to day?"

He said he had never noticed any changes.

In midafternoon, at precisely the same time I had yesterday received the summons to the deposition, a footman with the face of a frog handed me an invitation to dine with the Empress that evening.

Three female expediters prepared a scented bath for me; a fourth laid out a kimono of blue crepe embroidered with gold fishing nets. The mirror they held before me showed a man with wary eyes. At the tolling of ninth hour I was escorted to the banquet hall. The room was filled with notables in every finery. A large, low table stretched across the tessellated floor, surrounded by cushions. Before each place was an enamel bowl, and in the center of the table was a large three-legged brass caldron. Areté, looking no more than twenty, stood talking to an extremely handsome man near the head of the table.

"I thank you for your courtesy," I told her.

The man watched me impassively. "No more than is your due," Areté replied. She wore a bright costume of synthetics with pleated shoulders and elbows. She looked like a toy. Her face was painted into a hard mask.

She introduced me to the man, whose name was Meno. I drew her away from him. "You frightened me last night," I said. "I thought you had forgotten me."

Only her soft brown eyes showed she wasn't a pleasure surrogate. "What makes you think I remember?"

"You could not forget and still be the one I love."

"That's probably true. I'm not sure I'm worth such devotion."

Meno watched us from a few paces away. I turned my back to him and leaned closer to her. "I can't believe you mean that," I said quickly. "I think you say such things because you have been imprisoned by liars and self-aggrandizers.

But I am here for you now. I am an objective voice. Just give me a sign, and I will set you free."

Before she could answer, a bell sounded and the people took their places. Areté guided me to a place beside her. She sat, and we all followed suit.

The slaves stood ready to serve, waiting for Areté's command. She looked around the table. "We are met here to eat together," she said. "To dine on ambrosia, because there has been strife in the city, and ambition, and treachery. But now it is going to stop."

Meno now looked openly angry. Others were worried.

"You are the favored ones," said Areté. She turned to me. "And our friend here, the little fox, is the most favored of all. Destiny's author — our new and most trusted adviser."

Several people started to protest. I seized the opportunity given by their shock. "Am I indeed your adviser?"

"You may test it by deeds."

"You and you —" I beckoned to the guards. "Clear these people from the room."

The guests were in turmoil. Meno tried to speak to Areté, but I stepped between them. The guards came forward and forced the men and women to leave. After they were gone, I had the guards and slaves leave as well. The doors closed and the hall was silent. I turned. Areté had watched it all calmly, sitting cross-legged at the head of the table.

"Now, Areté, you must listen to me. Your commands have been twisted throughout this city. You and I have an instinctive sympathy. You must let me determine who sees you. I will interpret your words. The world is not ready to understand without an interpreter; they need to be educated."

"And you are the teacher."

"I am suited to it by temperament and training."

She smiled meekly.

I told Areté that I was hungry. She rose and prepared a bowl of soup from the caldron. I sat at the head of the table. She came and set the bowl before me, then kneeled and touched her forehead to the floor.

"Feed me," I said.

She took the bowl and a napkin. She blew on the ambrosia to cool it, lips pursed. Like a serving girl, she held the bowl to my lips. Areté fed me all of it, like mother to child, lover to lover. It tasted better than anything I had ever eaten. It warmed my belly and inflamed my desire. When the bowl was empty I pushed it away, knocking it from her hand. It clattered on the marble floor. I would be put off no longer. I took her right there, amid the cushions.

She was indeed the hardest of toys.

It had taken me three days from my entrance to the palace to become Areté's lover and voice. The Emperor over the Empress. On the first day of my reign I had the shopkeeper who had insulted me whipped the length of the Way of Enlightenment. On the second I ordered that only those certified in philosophy be qualified to vote. On the third I banished the poets.

Each evening Areté fed me ambrosia from a bowl. Each night we shared the Imperial bed. Each morning I awoke calmer, in more possession of myself. I moved more slowly. The hours of the day were drained of their urgency. Areté stopped changing. Her face settled with a quiet clarity into my mind, a clarity unlike the burning image I had treasured up during my years in the prison.

On the morning of the third day I awoke fresh and happy. Areté was not there. Pismire entered the room bearing a basin, a towel, a razor, a mirror. He washed and shaved me, then held the mirror before me. For the first time I saw the lines about my eyes and mouth were fading, and realized that I was being reformed.

I looked at Pismire. I saw him clearly: eyes cold as aquamarines.

"It's time for you to come home, Blume," he said.

No anger, no protest, arose in me. No remorse. No frustration. "I've been betrayed," I said. "Some virus, some drug, some notion you've put in my head."

Protagoras smiled. "The ambrosia. Brewed with water from the Well."

Now I am back in the prison. Escape is out of the question. Every step outward would be a step backward. It's all relative.

Instead I draw water from the Well of Changes. I drink. Protagoras says whatever changes will happen to me will be a reflection of my own psyche. That my new form is not determined by the water, but by me. How do I control it? I ask. You don't, he replies.

Glaucon has become a feral dog.

Protagoras and I go for long walks across the dry lake. He seldom speaks. I am not angry. Still, I fear a relapse. I am close to being nourished, but as yet I am not sure I am capable of it. I don't understand, as I never understood, where the penal colony is. I don't understand, as I never understood, how I can live without Areté.

Protagoras sympathizes. "Can't live with her, can't live without her," he says. "She's more than just a woman, Blume. You can experience her, but you can't own her."

Right. When I complain about such gnomic replies, Protagoras only puts me under the hood again. I think he knows some secret he wants me to guess, yet he gives no hints. I don't think that's fair.

After our most recent session, I told Protagoras my latest theory of the significance of the poem about the swallows. The poem, I told him, was an emblem of the ultimate and absolute truth of the universe. All things are determined by the ideas behind them, I said. There are three orders of existence, the Material (represented by the physical statue of the Buddha), the Spiritual (represented by its form), and the highest, which transcends both the Material and the Spiritual, the Ideal (represented by the flight of the birds). Humbly I begged Protagoras to tell me whether my analysis was true.

Protagoras said, "You are indeed an intellectual. But in order for me to reveal the answer to a question of such profound spiritual significance, you must first bow down before the sacred Well."

At last I was to be enlightened. Eyes brimming with tears of hope, I turned to the Well and, with the utmost sincerity, bowed.

Then Protagoras kicked me in the ass.

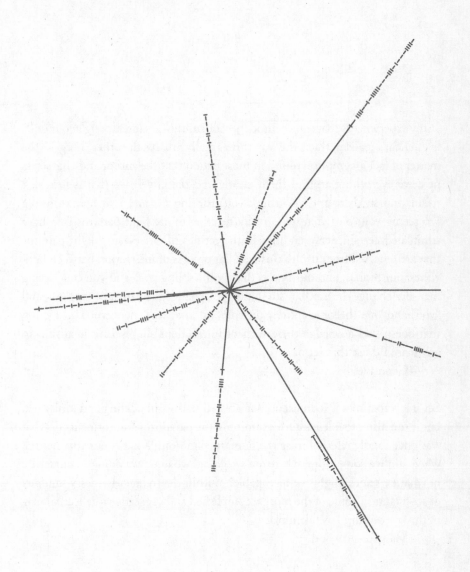

...my experience is that subjects and methods are always interacting in our daily lives. That's realism, that's the way things really are. It's the other thing — the matter of fact assumption found in most fiction that the author and characters perceive everything around them clearly and objectively — that is unreal. I mean, you sit there and you think you're seeing me and I sit here thinking I'm seeing you; but what we're really reacting to are light patterns that have stimulated certain nerve endings in the retinas of our eyes — light patterns that are reflected from us. It's this peculiar process of interaction between light waves, our retinas, and our brains that I call "seeing you" and you call "seeing me." But change the mechanism in my eyes, change the nature of the light, and "you" and "me" become entirely different as far as we're concerned.... Fiction that doesn't acknowledge these sorts of interactions simply isn't "realistic" in any sense I'd use that term.

—Gene Wolfe

Sci-fi is sometimes just an excuse for dressed-up swashbuckling and kinky sex, but it can also provide a kit for examining the paradoxes and torments of what was once fondly referred to as the human condition: What is our true nature, where did we come from, where are we going, what are we doing to ourselves, of what extremes might we be capable? Within the frequently messy sandbox of sci-fi fantasy, some of the most accomplished and suggestive intellectual play of the last century has taken place.

—Margaret Atwood

The Ziggurat
Gene Wolfe

It had begun to snow about one-thirty. Emery Bainbridge stood on the front porch to watch it before going back into the cabin to record it in his journal.

> 13:38 Snowing hard, quiet as owl feathers. Radio says stay off the roads unless you have four-wheel. Probably means no Brook.

He put down the lipstick-red ballpoint and stared at it. With this pen…He ought to scratch out *Brook* and write *Jan* over it.

"To hell with that." His harsh voice seemed loud in the silent cabin. "What I wrote, I wrote. *Quod scripsi* whatever it is."

That was what being out here alone did, he told himself. You were supposed to rest up. You were supposed to calm down. Instead you started talking to yourself. "Like some nut," he added aloud.

Jan would come, bringing Brook. And Aileen and Alayna. Aileen and Alayna were as much his children as Brook was, he told himself firmly. "For the time being."

If Jan could not come tomorrow, she would come later when the county had cleared the back roads. And it was more than possible that she would come, or try to, tomorrow as she had planned. There was that kind of a streak in Jan, not exactly stubbornness and not exactly resolution, but a sort of willful determination to believe whatever she wanted; thus she believed he would sign her papers, and thus she would believe that the big Lincoln he had bought her could go anywhere a Jeep could.

Brook would be all for it, of course. At nine, Brook had tried to cross the Atlantic on a Styrofoam dinosaur, paddling out farther and farther until at last a lifeguard had launched her little catamaran and brought him back, letting the dinosaur float out to sea.

That was what was happening everywhere, Emery thought — boys and men were being brought back to shore by women, though for thousands of years their daring had permitted humanity to survive.

He pulled on his red-plaid double mackinaw and his warmest cap, and carried a chair out onto the porch to watch the snow.

Suddenly it wasn't...He had forgotten the word that he had used before. It wasn't whatever men had. It was something women had, or they thought it was. Possibly it was something nobody had.

He pictured Jan leaning intently over the wheel, her lips compressed to an ugly slit, easing her Lincoln into the snow, coaxing it up the first hill, stern with triumph as it cleared the crest. Jan about to be stranded in this soft and silent wilderness in high-heeled shoes. Perhaps that streak of hers was courage after all, or something so close that it could be substituted for courage at will. Little pink packets that made you think whatever you wanted to be true would be true, if only you acted as if it were with sufficient tenacity.

He was being watched.

"By God, it's that coyote," he said aloud, and knew from the timbre of his own voice that he lied. These were human eyes. He narrowed his own, peering through the falling snow, took off his glasses, blotted their lenses absently with his handkerchief, and looked again.

A higher, steeper hill rose on the other side of his tiny valley, a hill clothed in pines and crowned with wind-swept ocher rocks. The watcher was up there somewhere, staring down at him through the pine boughs, silent and observant.

"Come on over!" Emery called. "Want some coffee?" There was no response.

"You lost? You better get out of this weather!"

The silence of the snow seemed to suffocate each word in turn. Although he had shouted, he could not be certain he had been heard. He stood and made a sweeping gesture: *Come here.*

There was a flash of colorless light from the pines, so swift and slight that he could not be absolutely certain he had seen it. Someone signaling with a mirror — except that the sky was the color of lead above the downward-drifting whiteness of the snow, the sun invisible.

"Come on over!" he called again, but the watcher was gone.

Country people, he thought, suspicious of strangers. But there were no country people around here, not within ten miles; a few hunting camps, a few cabins like his own, with nobody in them now that deer season was over.

He stepped off the little porch. The snow was more than ankle-deep already and falling faster than it had been just a minute before, the pine-clad hill across the creek practically invisible.

The woodpile under the overhang of the south eaves (the woodpile that had appeared so impressive when he had arrived) had shrunk drastically. It was time to cut and split more. Past time, really. The chain saw tomorrow, the ax, the maul, and the wedge tomorrow, and perhaps even the Jeep, if he could get it in to snake the logs out.

Mentally, he put them all away. Jan was coming, would be bringing Brook to stay. And the twins to stay, too, with Jan herself, if the road got too bad.

The coyote had gone up on the back porch!

After a second or two he realized he was grinning like a fool, and forced himself to stop and look instead.

There were no tracks. Presumably the coyote had eaten this morning before the snow started, for the bowl was empty, licked clean. The time would come, and soon, when he would touch the rough yellow-gray head, when the coyote would lick his fingers and fall asleep in front of the little fieldstone fireplace in his cabin.

Triumphant, he rattled the rear door, then remembered that he had locked it the night before. Had locked both doors, in fact, moved by an indefinable dread. Bears, he thought — a way of assuring himself that he was not as irrational as Jan.

There were bears around here, that was true enough. Small black bears, for the most part. But not Yogi Bears, not funny but potentially dangerous park bears who had lost all fear of Man and roamed and rummaged as they pleased. These bears were hunted every year, hunted through the golden days of autumn as they fattened for hibernation. Silver winter had arrived, and these bears slept in caves and hollow logs, in thickets and thick brush, slept like their dead, though slowly and softly breathing like the snow — motionless, dreaming bear-dreams of the last-men years, when the trees would have filled in the old logging roads again and shouldered aside the cracked asphalt of the county road, and all the guns had rusted to dust.

Yet he had been afraid.

He returned to the front of the cabin, picked up the chair he had carried onto the porch, and noticed a black spot on its worn back he could not recall having seen before. It marked his finger, and was scraped away readily by the blade of his pocketknife.

Shrugging, he brought the chair back inside. There was plenty of Irish stew; he would have Irish stew tonight, soak a slice of bread in gravy for the coyote, and leave it in the same spot on the back porch. You could not (as people always said) move the bowl a little every day. That would have been frightening, too fast for any wild thing. You moved the bowl once, perhaps, in a week; and the coyote's bowl had walked by those halting steps from the creek bank where he had glimpsed the coyote in summer to the back porch.

Jan and Brook and the twins might — would be sure to — frighten it. That was unfortunate, but could not be helped; it might be best not to try to feed the coyote at all until Jan and the twins had gone. As inexplicably as he had known that he was being watched, and by no animal, he felt certain that Jan would reach him somehow, bending reality to her desires.

He got out the broom and swept the cabin. When he had expected her, he had not cared how it looked or what she might think of it. Now that her arrival had become problematic, he found that he cared a great deal.

She would have the other lower bunk, the twins could sleep together feet-to-feet in an upper (no doubt with much squealing and giggling and kicking), and Brook in the other upper — in the bunk over his own.

Thus would the family achieve its final and irrevocable separation for the first time; the Sibberlings (who had been and would again be) on one side of the cabin, the Bainbridges on the other: boys here, girls over there. The law would take years, and demand tens of thousands of dollars, to accomplish no more.

Boys here.

Girls over there, farther and farther all the time. When he had rocked and kissed Aileen and Alayna, when he had bought Christmas and birthday presents and sat through solemn, silly conferences with their pleased teachers, he had never felt that he was actually the twins' father. Now he did. Al Sibberling had given them his swarthy good looks and flung them away. He, Emery Bainbridge, had picked them up like discarded dolls after Jan had run the family deep in debt. Had called himself their father, and thought he lied.

There would be no sleeping with Jan, no matter how long she stayed. It was why she was bringing the twins, as he had known from the moment she said they would be with her.

He put clean sheets on the bunk that would be hers, with three thick wool blankets and a quilt.

Bringing her back from plays and country-club dances, he had learned to listen for them; silence had meant he could return and visit Jan's bed when he had driven the sitter home. Now Jan feared that he would want to bargain — his name on her paper for a little more pleasure, a little more love before they parted for good. Much as she wanted him to sign, she did not want him to sign as much as that. Girls here, boys over there. Had he grown so hideous?

Women need a reason, he thought, men just need a place.

For Jan the reason wasn't good enough, so she had seen to it that there would be no place. He told himself it would be great to hug the twins again — and discovered that it would.

He fluffed Jan's pillow anyway, and dressed it in a clean white pillowcase.

She would have found someone by now, somebody in the city to whom she was being faithful, exactly as he himself had been faithful to Jan while he was still married, in the eyes of the law, to Pamela.

The thought of eyes recalled the watcher on the hill.

14:12 Somebody is on the hill across the creek with some kind of signaling device.

That sounded as if he were going crazy, he decided. What if Jan saw it? He added, maybe just a flashlight, although he did not believe it had been a flashlight.

A lion's face smiled up at him from the barrel of the red pen, and he stopped to read the minute print under it, holding the pen up to catch the gray light from the window. "The Red Lion Inn/San Jose." A nice hotel. If — when — he got up the nerve to do it, he would write notes to Jan and Brook first with this pen.

The coyote ate the food I put out for him, I think soon after breakfast. More food tonight. Tomorrow morning I will leave the back door cracked open awhile.
14:15 I am going up on the hill for a look around.

He had not known that until he wrote it.

The hillside seemed steeper than he remembered, slippery with snow. The pines had changed; their limbs drooped like the boughs of hemlocks, springing up like snares when he touched them, and throwing snow in his face. No bird sang.

He had brought his flashlight, impelled by the memory of the colorless signal from the hill. Now he used it to peep beneath the drooping limbs. Most of the tracks that the unseen watcher had left would be covered with new snow by this time; a few might remain, in the shelter of the pines.

He had nearly reached the rocky summit before he found the first, and even it was blurred by snow despite its protection. He knelt and blew the drifted flakes away, clearing it with his breath as he had sometimes cleared the tracks of animals; an oddly cleated shoe, almost like the divided hoof of an elk. He measured it against his spread hand, from the tip of his little finger to the tip of his thumb. A small foot, no bigger than size six, if that.

A boy.

There was another, inferior, print beside it. And not far away a blurred depression that might have been left by a gloved hand or a hundred other things. Here the boy had crouched with his little polished steel mirror, or whatever he had.

Emery knelt, lifting the snow-burdened limbs that blocked his view of the cabin. Two small, dark figures were emerging from the cabin door onto the porch, scarcely visible through the falling snow. The first carried his ax, the second his rifle.

He stood, waving the flashlight. "Hey! You there!"

The one holding his rifle raised it, not putting it to his shoulder properly but acting much too quickly for Emery to duck. The flat crack of the shot sounded clearly, snow or no snow.

He tried to dodge, slipped, and fell to the soft snow.

"Too late," he told himself. And then, "Going to do it for me." And last, "Better stay down in case he shoots again." The cold air was like chilled wine, the snow he lay in lovely beyond imagining. Drawing back his coat sleeve, he consulted his watch, resolving to wait ten minutes — to risk nothing.

They were robbing his cabin, obviously. Had robbed it, in fact, while he had been climbing through the pines. Had fired, in all probability, merely to keep him away long enough for them to leave. Mentally, he inventoried the cabin. Besides the rifle, there had not been a lot worth stealing — his food and a few tools; they might take his Jeep if they could figure out how to hot-wire the ignition, and that was pretty easy on those old Jeeps.

His money was in his wallet, his wallet in the hip pocket of his hunting trousers. His watch — a plastic sports watch hardly worth stealing — was on his wrist. His checkbook had been in the table drawer; they might steal that and forge his checks, possibly. They might even be caught when they tried to cash them.

Retrieving his flashlight, he lifted the limbs as he had before. The intruders were not in sight, the door of the cabin half open, his Jeep still parked next to the north wall, its red paint showing faintly through snow.

He glanced at his watch. One minute had passed, perhaps a minute and a half.

They would have to have a vehicle of some kind, one with four-wheel drive if they didn't want to be stranded with their loot on a back road. Since he had not heard it start up, they had probably left the engine running. Even so, he decided, he should have heard it pull away.

Had they parked some distance off and approached his cabin on foot? Now that he came to think of it, it seemed possible they had no vehicle after all. Two boys camping in the snow, confident that he would be unable to follow them to their tent, or whatever it was. Wasn't there a Boy Scout badge for winter camping? He had never been a Scout, but thought he remembered hearing about one, and found it plausible.

Still no one visible. He let the branches droop again.

The rifle was not really much of a loss, though its theft had better be reported to the sheriff. He had not planned on shooting anyway — had been worried, as a matter of fact, that the twins might get it down and do something foolish, although both had shot at tin cans and steel silhouettes with it before he and Jan had agreed to separate.

Now, with his rifle gone, he could not...

Neither had been particularly attracted to it; and their having handled and fired it already should have satisfied the natural curiosity that resulted in so many accidents each year. They had learned to shoot to please him, and stopped as soon as he had stopped urging them to learn.

Four minutes, possibly five. He raised the pine boughs once more, hearing the muted growl of an engine; for a second or two he held his breath. The Jeep or Bronco or whatever it was, was coming closer, not leaving. Was it possible that the thieves were coming back? Returning with a truck to empty his cabin?

Jan's big black Lincoln hove into view, roared down the gentle foothill slope on which his cabin stood, and skidded to a stop. Doors flew open, and all three kids piled out. Jan herself left more sedately, shutting the door on the driver's side behind her almost tenderly, tall and willowy as ever, her hair a golden helmet beneath a blue-mink pillbox hat.

Her left hand held a thick, black attaché case that was probably his.

Brook was already on the porch. Emery stood and shouted a warning, but it was too late; Brook was inside the cabin, with the twins hard on his heels. Jan looked around and waved, and deep inside Emery something writhed in agony.

By the time he had reached the cabin, he had decided not to mention that the intruders had shot at him. Presumably the shooter had chambered a new round, ejecting the brass cartridge case of the round just fired into the snow; but it might easily be overlooked, and if Brook or the twins found it, he could say that he had fired the day before to scare off some animal.

"Hello," Jan said as he entered. "You left your door open. It's cold as Billy-o in here." She was seated in a chair before the fire.

"I didn't." He dropped into the other, striving to look casual. "I was robbed."

"Really? When?"

"A quarter hour ago. Did you see another car coming in?"

Jan shook her head.

They had been on foot, then; the road ended at the lake. Aloud he said, "It doesn't matter. They got my rifle and my ax." Remembering his checkbook, he pulled out the drawer of the little table. His checkbook was still there; he took it out and put it into an inner pocket of his mackinaw.

"It was an old rifle anyhow, wasn't it?"

He nodded. "My old thirty-thirty."

"Then you can buy a new one, and you should have locked the door. I —"

"You weren't supposed to get here until tomorrow," he told her brusquely. The mere thought of another gun was terrifying.

"I know. But they said a blizzard was coming on TV, so I decided I'd better move it up a day, or I'd have to wait for a week — that was what it sounded like. I told Doctor Gibbons that Aileen would be in next Thursday, and off we went. This shouldn't take long." She opened his attaché case on her lap. "Now here —"

"Where are the kids?"

"Out back getting more wood. They'll be back in a minute."

As though to confirm her words, he heard the clink of the maul striking the wedge. He ventured, "Do you really want them to hear it?"

"Emery, they *know*. I couldn't have hidden all this from them if I tried. What was I going to say when they asked why you never came home anymore?"

"You could have told them I was deer-hunting."

"That's for a few days, maybe a week. You left in August, remember? Well, anyway, I didn't. I told them the truth." She paused, expectant. "Aren't you going to ask how they took it?"

He shook his head.

"The girls were hurt. I honestly think Brook's happy. Getting to live with you out here for a while and all that."

"I've got him signed up for Culver," Emery told her. "He starts in February."

"That's best, I'm sure. Now listen, because we've got to get back. Here's a letter from your —"

"You're not going to sleep here? Stay overnight?"

"Tonight? Certainly not. We've got to start home before this storm gets serious. You always interrupt me. You always have. I suppose it's too late to say I wish you'd stop."

He nodded. "I made up a bunk for you."

"Brook can have it. Now right —"

The back door opened and Brook himself came in. "I showed them how you split the wood, and 'Layna split one. Didn't you, 'Layna?"

"Right here." Behind him, Alayna held the pieces up.

"That's not ladylike," Jan told her.

Emery said, "But it's quite something that a girl her age can swing that maul — I wouldn't have believed she could. Did Brook help you lift it?"

Alayna shook her head.

"*I* didn't want to." Aileen declared virtuously.

"Right here," Jan was pushing an envelope into his hands, "is a letter from your attorney. It's sealed, see? I haven't read it, but you'd better take a look at it first."

"You know what's in it, though," Emery said, "or you think you do."

"He told me what he was going to write to you, yes."

"Otherwise you would have saved it." Emery got out his pocketknife and slit the flap. "Want to tell me?"

Jan shook her head, her lips as tight and ugly as he had imagined them earlier.

Brook put down his load of wood. "Can I see?"

"You can read it for me," Emery told him. "I've got snow on my glasses." He found a clean handkerchief and wiped them. "Don't read it out loud. Just tell me what it says."

"Emery, you're doing this to get even!"

He shook his head. "This is Brook's inheritance that our lawyers are arguing about."

Brook stared.

"I've lost my company," Emery told him. "Basically, we're talking about the money and stock I got as a consolation prize. You're the only child I've got, probably the only one I'll ever have. So read it. What does it say?"

Brook unfolded the letter; it seemed quieter to Emery now, with all five of them in the cabin, than it ever had during all the months he had lived there alone.

Jan said, "What they did was perfectly legal, Brook. You should understand that. They bought up a controlling interest and merged our company with theirs. That's all that happened."

The stiff, parchment-like paper rattled in Brook's hands. Unexpectedly Alayna whispered, "I'm sorry, Daddy."

Emery grinned at her. "I'm still here, honey."

Brook glanced from him to Jan, then back to him. "He says — it's Mister Gluckman. You introduced me one time."

Emery nodded.

"He says this is the best arrangement he's been able to work out, and he thinks it would be in your best interest to take it."

Jan said, "You keep this place and your Jeep, and all your personal belongings, naturally. I'll give you back my wedding and engagement rings —"

"You can keep them," Emery told her.

"No, I want to be fair about this. I've always tried to be fair, even when you didn't come to the meetings between our attorneys. I'll give them back, but I get to keep all the rest of the gifts you've given me, including my car."

Emery nodded.

"No alimony at all. Naturally no child support. Brook stays with you, Aileen and Alayna with me. My attorney says we can force Al to pay child support."

Emery nodded again.

"And I get the house. Everything else we divide equally. That's the stock and any other investments, the money in my personal accounts, your account, and our joint account." She had another paper. "I know you'll want to read it over, but that's what it is. You can follow me into Voylestown in your Jeep. There's a notary there who can witness your signature."

"I had the company when we were married."

"But you don't have it anymore. We're not talking about your company. It's not involved at all."

He picked up the telephone, a diversion embraced at random that might serve until the pain ebbed. "Will you excuse me? This is liable to go on awhile, and I should report the break-in." He entered the sheriff's number from the sticker on the telephone.

The distant clamor — it was not the actual ringing of the sheriff's telephone at all, he knew — sounded empty as well as artificial, as if it were not merely far away but high over the earth, a computer-generated instrument that jangled and buzzed for his ears alone upon some airless asteroid beyond the moon.

Brook laid Phil Gluckman's letter on the table where he could see it.

"Are you getting through?" Jan asked. "There's a lot of ice on the wires. Brook was talking about it on the way up."

"I think so. It's ringing."

Brook said, "They've probably got a lot of emergencies, because of the storm." The twins stirred uncomfortably, and Alayna went to a window to look at the falling snow.

"I should warn you," Jan said, "that if you won't sign, it's war. We spent hours and hours —"

A voice squeaked, *"Sheriff Ron Wilber's Office."*

"My name is Emery Bainbridge. I've got a cabin on Route Eighty-five, about five miles from the lake." The tinny voice spoke unintelligibly.

"Would you repeat that, please?"

"It might be better from the cellular phone in my car," Jan suggested.

"What's the problem, Mister Bainbridge?"

"My cabin was robbed in my absence." There was no way in which he could tell the sheriff's office that he had been shot at without telling Jan and the twins as well; he decided it was not essential. "They took a rifle and my ax. Those are the only things that seem to be missing."

"Could you have mislaid them?"

This was the time to tell the sheriff about the boy on the hill; he found that he could not.

"Can you hear me, Mister Bainbridge?" There was chirping in the background, as if there were crickets on the party line.

He said, "Barely. No, I didn't mislay them. Somebody was in here while I was away — they left the door open, for one thing." He described the rifle and admitted he did not have a record of its serial number, then described the ax and spelled his name.

"We can't send anyone out there now, Mister Bainbridge. I'm sorry."

It was a woman. He had not realized until then that he had been talking to a woman. He said, "I just wanted to let you know, in case you picked somebody up."

"We'll file a report. You can come here and look at the stolen goods whenever you want to, but I don't think there's any guns right now."

"The theft just occurred. About three or a little later." When the woman at the sheriff's office did not speak again, he said, "Thank you," and hung up.

"You think they'll come back tonight, Dad?"

"I doubt very much that they'll come back at all." Emery sat down, unconsciously pushing his chair a little farther from Jan's. "Since you kids went out and split that wood, don't you think you ought to put some of it on the fire?"

"I put mine on," Aileen announced. "Didn't I, Momma?"

Brook picked up several of the large pieces he had carried and laid them on the feeble flames.

"I founded the company years before we got married," Emery told Jan. "I lost control when Brook's mother and I broke up. I had to give her half of my stock, and she sold it."

"It's not —"

"The stock you're talking about dividing now is the stock I got for mine. Most of the money in our joint account, and my personal account, came from the company before we were taken over. You can hang on to everything in your personal accounts. I don't want your money."

"Well, that's kind of you! That's extremely kind of you, Emery!"

"You're worried about the snow, you say, and I think you should be. If you and the twins want to stay here until the weather clears up, you're welcome to. Maybe we can work out something."

Jan shook her head, and for a moment Emery allowed himself to admire her clear skin and the clean lines of her profile. It was so easy to think of all that he wanted to say to her, so hard to say what he had to: "In that case, you'd better go."

"I'm entitled to half our community property!"

Brook put in, "The house's worth ten times more than this place."

Boys here, Emery thought. Girls over there. "You can have the house, Jan. I'm not disputing it — not now. Not yet. But I may, later, if you're stubborn. I'm willing to make a cash settlement…" Even as he said it, he realized that he was not.

"This is what we negotiated. Phil Gluckman represented you! He said so, and so did you. It's all settled."

Emery leaned forward in his chair, holding his hands out to the rising flames. "If everything's settled, you don't need my signature. Go back to the city."

"I — Oh, *God!* I should have known it was no use to come out here."

"I'm willing to give you a cash settlement in the form of a trust fund for the twins. A generous settlement, and you can keep the house, your car, your money, and your personal things. That's as far as I'll go, and it's further than I ought to go. Otherwise, we fight it out in court."

"We negotiated this!"

She shoved her paper at him, and he was tempted to throw it into the fire. Forcing himself to speak mildly, he said, "I know you did, and I know that you negotiated in good faith. So did we. I wanted to see what Phil Gluckman could come up with. And to tell you the truth, I was pretty sure that it would be something I could accept. I'm disappointed in him."

"It's snowing harder," Alayna told them.

"He didn't —" Emery stiffened. "Did you hear something?"

"I haven't heard a thing! I don't have to listen to this!"

It had sounded like a shot, but had probably been no more than the noise of a large branch breaking beneath the weight of the snow. "I've lost my train of thought," he admitted, "but I can make my position clear in three short affirmations. First, I won't sign that paper. Not here, not in Voylestown, and not in the city. Not anywhere. You might as well put it away."

"This is completely unfair!"

"Second, I won't go back and haggle. That's Phil's job."

"Mister high-tech himself, roughing it in the wilderness."

Emery shook his head. "I was never the technical brains of the company, Jan. There were half a dozen people working for me who knew more about the equipment than I did."

"Modest, too. I hope you realize that I'm going to have something to say after you're through."

"Third, I'm willing to try again if you are." He paused, hoping to see her glare soften. "I realize I'm not easy to live with. Neither are you. But I'm willing to try — hard — if you'll let me."

"You really and truly think that you're a great lover, don't you?"

"You married a great lover the first time," he told her.

She seethed. He watched her clench her perfect teeth and take three deep breaths as she forced herself to speak calmly. "Emery, you say that unless I settle for what you're willing to give we'll fight it out in open court. If we do, the public — every acquaintance and business contact you've got — will hear how you molested my girls."

Unwilling to believe what he had heard, he stared at her.

"You didn't think I'd do it, did you? You didn't think I'd expose them to that, and I don't want to. But —"

"It's not true!"

"Your precious Phil Gluckman has questioned them, in my presence and my attorney's. Call him up right now. Ask him what he thinks."

Emery looked at the twins; neither would meet his eyes.

"Do you want to see what a court will give me when the judge hears that? There are a lot of women judges. Do you want to find out?"

"Yes." He spoke slowly. "Yes, Jan. I do."

"It'll ruin you!"

"I'm ruined already." He stood up. "That's what you're refusing to understand. I think you'd better leave now. You and the twins."

She stood too, jumping to her feet with energy he envied. "You set up one company. You could start another one, but not when this gets around."

He wanted to say that he had seen a unique opportunity and taken it — that he'd had his chance in life and made the best of it, and finished here. All that he could manage was, "I'm terribly sorry it's come to this. I never wanted it to, or…" His throat shut, and he felt the sick hopelessness of a fighter whose worst enemies are his own instincts. How would it feel and taste, how would it look, the cold, oiled steel muzzle in his mouth? He could cut a stick in the woods, or even use the red pen to press the trigger.

"Come on, girls, we're going. Goodbye, Brook."

Brook muttered something.

For a brief moment Emery felt Alayna's hand in his; then she was gone. The cabin door slammed behind her.

Brook said, "Don't freak out. She's got it coming."

"I know she does," Emery told him. "So do I, and we're both going to get it. I don't mind for my sake, but I mind terribly for hers. It was my job — my duty — to —"

On the front porch Jan exclaimed, *"Hey!"* Presumably she was speaking to one of the twins.

"I thought you handled yourself really well," Brook said.

Emery managed to smile. "That's another thing. It's my job to teach you how that sort of thing's done, and I didn't. Don't you see that I let her leave — practically made her go — before she'd agreed to what I wanted? I should have moved heaven and earth to keep her here until she did, but I pushed her out the door instead. That's not how you win, that's how you lose."

"You think the sheriff might get your gun back?"

"I hope not." Emery took off his coat and hung it on the peg nearest the front door. For Brook's sake he added, "I like to shoot, but I've never liked shooting animals."

Outside, the sound diminished by distance and the snow, Jan screamed.

Emery was first out of the door, but was nearly knocked off the porch by Brook. Beyond the porch's meager shelter, half obscured by blowing snow, the black Lincoln's hood was up. Jan sprawled in the snow, screaming. One of the twins grappled a small, dark figure; the other was not in sight.

Brook charged into the swirling snow, snow so thick that for a moment he vanished completely. Emery floundered through shin-high snow after him, saw a second small stranger appear — as it seemed — from the Lincoln's engine compartment, and a third emerge from the interior with his rifle in its hand, the dome light oddly spectral in the deepening gloom. For a moment he received the fleeting impression of a smooth, almond-shaped brown face.

The rifle came up. The diminutive figure (shorter than Brook, hardly larger than the twins) jerked at its trigger. Brook grabbed it and staggered backward, falling in the snow. The struggling twin cried out, a childish shriek of pain and rage.

Then their attackers fled — fled preposterously slowly through snow that was for them knee high, but fled nonetheless, the three running clumsily together in a dark, packed mass that almost vanished before they had gone twenty feet.

One turned, wrestled the rifle's lever, jerked the rifle like an unruly dog, and ran again.

Emery knelt in the snow beside Jan. "Are you all right?"

She shook her head, sobbing like a child.

The twin embraced him, gasping, "She hit me, she hit me." He tried to comfort both, an arm for each.

Later — though it seemed to him not much later — Brook draped his shoulders with his double mackinaw, and he realized how cold he was. He stood, lifting the twin, and pulled Jan to her feet. "We'd better get back inside."

"No!"

He dragged her after him, hearing Brook shut the Lincoln's passenger's-side door behind them.

By the time they reached the cabin, Jan was weeping again. Emery put her back in the chair she had occupied a few minutes before. "Listen! Listen here, even if you can't stop bawling. One of the twins is gone. Do you know where she is?"

Sobbing, Jan shook her head.

"That girl with the hood? She hit Mama, and Aileen ran away." The remaining twin pointed.

Brook gasped, "They didn't hurt her, 'Layna?"

"They hurt *me*. They hit my arm." She pushed back her sleeve, wincing.

Emery turned to Brook. "What happened to you?"

"Got it in the belly." Brook managed a sick smile. "He had a gun. Was it the one they stole from you?"

"I think so."

"Well — I grabbed the barrel," Brook paused, struggling to draw breath, "and I tried to push it up," he demonstrated, "so he couldn't shoot. I guess he hit me with the other end. Knocked my wind out."

Emery nodded.

"It happened one time when I was a little kid. We were playing kick-ball. I fell down and another kid kicked me."

The image glimpsed through falling snow returned: Brook floundering toward the small hooded figure with the leveled rifle. Emery felt weak, half sick with fright. "You damned fool kid," he blurted, "you could've been killed!" It sounded angry and almost vicious, although he had not thought himself angry.

"Yeah, I guess I could of."

Jan stopped crying long enough to say, "Emery, don't be mean."

"What were you being when you made the girls say I had molested them?"

"Well, you did!"

Brook said, "He tried to shoot me. I saw him. I think the safety was on. I tried to get to him fast before he wised up."

"That rifle doesn't have one, just the half-cock."

Brook was no longer listening. Under his breath, Emery explained, "He was short-stroking it, pulling down the lever a reasonable distance instead of all the way. You can't do that with a lever-action — it will eject, but it won't load the next round. He'll learn to do it right pretty soon, I'm afraid."

Jan asked querulously, "What about Aileen? Aren't you going to look for Aileen?"

"Alayna, you pointed toward the lake when I asked which way your sister went. Are you sure?"

Alayna hesitated. "Can I look out the window?"

"Certainly. Go ahead."

She crossed the cabin to the front window and looked out, standing on tiptoe. "I never said you felt us and everything like Mama said. I just said all right, all right, I see, and yes, yes, because she was there listening." Alayna's voice was almost inaudible; her eyes were fixed upon the swirling snow beyond the windowpane.

"Thank you, Alayna." Emery spoke rapidly, keeping his voice as low as hers. "You're a good girl, a daughter to be proud of, and I am proud of you. Very proud. But listen — are you paying attention?"

"Yes, Daddy."

"What you tell your mama —" he glanced at Jan, but she was taking off her coat and lecturing Brook, "isn't important. If you've got to lie to her about that so she won't punish you, do what you did. Nod and say yes. What you tell the lawyers is more important, but not very important. They lie all the time, so they've got no business complaining when other people lie to them. But when you're in court, and you've sworn to tell the truth, everything will be terribly important. You *have* to tell the truth then. The plain unvarnished truth, and nothing else. Do you understand?"

Alayna nodded solemnly, turning to face him.

"Not to me, because my life's nearly over. Not to God, because we can't really hurt God, only pain him by our spite and ingratitude. But because if you lie then, it's going to hurt you for years, maybe for the rest of your life."

"When God tells us not to lie, and not to cheat or steal, it's not because those things hurt him. You and I can no more harm God than a couple of ants could hurt this mountain. He does it for the same reason that your mama and I tell you not to play with fire — because we know it can hurt you terribly, and we don't want you to get hurt.

"Now, which way did Aileen run?"

"That way." Alayna pointed again. "I know because of the car. There was a lady at the front looking at the motor, and she sort of tried to catch her, but she got away."

"You say — Never mind." Emery stood. "I'd better go after her."

"Comin' with," Brook announced.

"No, you're not. You're going to see about Alayna's arm." Emery put on his coat. His gloves were in the pockets and his warmest cap on a peg. "There's plenty of food here. Fix some for the three of you — maybe Alayna and her mother will help. Make coffee, too. I'll want some when I get back."

Outside, the creek and the hill across it had disappeared in blowing snow. It would have been wise, Emery reflected, for Jan to have turned the car around before she stopped. It was typical of her that she had not.

He squinted at it through the snow. The hood was still up. The intruders — the boys who had robbed his cabin — had no doubt intended to strip it, stealing the battery and so on, or perhaps hot-wire it and drive it someplace where it could be stripped at leisure. There were three, it seemed — three at least, and perhaps more.

Reaching the Lincoln, he peered into the crowded engine compartment. The battery was still there; although he could not be sure, nothing seemed to be missing. Jan, who had told him he should have locked the cabin door, should have locked the doors; but then Jan seldom did, even in the city, and who would expect trouble way out here during a blizzard?

Emery slammed down the hood. Now that he came to think of it, Jan left her keys in the car more often than not. If she had, he could turn it around for her before the snow got any deeper. Briefly he vacillated, imagining Aileen hiding behind a tree, cold and frightened. But Aileen could not be far, and might very well come out of hiding if she heard the Lincoln start.

As he had half expected, the keys were in the ignition. He started the engine and admired the luxurious interior until warm air gushed from the heater, then allowed the big car to creep forward. Alayna felt certain her twin had run toward the lake, and he had to go in that direction anyway to turn around.

He switched on the headlights.

Aileen might come running when she saw her mother's car. Or he might very well meet her walking back toward the cabin, if she had sense enough to stick to the road; if he did, she could get in and warm up at once.

The Lincoln's front-wheel drive, assisted by its powerful engine, seemed to be handling the snow well so far. At about two miles an hour, he topped the gentle rise beyond the cabin and began the descent to the lake.

Aileen had run down this road toward the lake; but in what direction had the boys run? Emery found that though he could picture them vividly as they fled — three small, dark figures bunched together, one carrying his rifle (somehow carrying away his death while fleeing from him) — he could not be certain of the direction in which they had run. Toward town, or this way? Their tracks would be obscured by snow now in either case.

Had they really fled, as he'd assumed? Wasn't it possible that they'd been pursuing Aileen? It was a good thing —

He took his eyes off the snow-blanketed road for a second to stare at Jan's keys. The doors had been unlocked, the keys in the ignition. If the boys had wanted to strip this car, why hadn't they driven it away?

He stopped, switched on the emergency blinkers, and blew the horn three times. Aileen might, perhaps, have run as far as this — call it three-quarters of a mile, although it was probably a little less. It was hard to believe that she would have run farther, though no doubt a healthy eleven-year-old could run farther than he, and faster, too. Not knowing what else to do, he got out, leaving the lights on and the engine running.

"Aileen! Aileen, honey!"

She had told Phil Gluckman that he, Emery Bainbridge, her foster father, had molested her. Had she believed it, too? He had read somewhere that young children could be made to believe that such things had happened when they had not. What about a bright eleven-year-old?

He made a megaphone of his hands. *"Aileen! Aileen!"*

There was no sound but the song of the rising wind and the scarcely audible purr of the engine.

He got back in and puffed fine snow off his glasses before it could melt. When he had left the cabin, he had intended to search on foot — to tramp along this snow-covered road calling Aileen. Perhaps that would have been best after all.

Almost hesitantly, he put the automatic transmission into first, letting the Lincoln idle forward at a speed that seemed no faster than a slow walk. When a minute or more had passed, he blew the horn again.

That had been a shot he had heard as he sat arguing with Jan; he felt sure of it now. The boy had been trying out his new rifle, experimenting with it.

He blew the horn as he had before, three short beeps.

That model held seven cartridges, but he couldn't remember whether it had been fully loaded. Say that it had. One shot fired at him on the hill, another in the woods (where?) to test the rifle. Five left. Enough to kill him, to kill Jan, and to kill Brook and both twins, assuming Aileen wasn't dead already. Quite possibly the boy with the rifle was waiting in the woods now, waiting for Jan's big black Lincoln to crawl just a little bit closer.

All right, let him shoot. Let the boy shoot at him now, while he sat behind the wheel. The boy might miss him as he sat here, alone in the dark behind tinted safety glass. The boy with his rifle could do nothing worse to him than he had imagined doing to himself, and if he missed, somebody — Jan or Brook, Aileen or Alayna — might live. And living, recall him someday with kindness.

The big Lincoln crept past the dark, cold cabin of his nearest neighbor, a cabin whose rather too-flat roof already wore a peaked cap of snow.

He blew the horn, stopped, and got out as before, wishing that he had remembered to bring the flashlight. As far as he could tell, the snow lay undisturbed everywhere, save for the snaking track behind the Lincoln.

He would continue to the lake, he decided; he could go no farther. There was a scenic viewpoint there with parking for ten or twelve cars. It would be as safe to turn around there as to drive on the road as he had been doing — not that the road, eighteen inches deep in snow already, with drifts topping three feet, was all that safe.

Kicking snow from his boots and brushing it from his coat and trousers, he got back into the car, took off his cap, and cleaned his glasses, then eased the front wheels into the next drift.

When Jan and the twins had left the cabin, they must have seen the boys, perhaps at about the time they were raising the hood. Jan had shouted at them — he had heard her — and gone to her car to make them stop, followed by the twins. What had she said, and what had the boys said in reply? He resolved to question her about it when he returned to the cabin. Somebody had knocked her down; he tried to remember whether her face had been bruised, and decided it had not.

The Lincoln had pushed through the drift, and was already approaching another; here, where the road ran within a hundred feet of Haunted Lake, the snow swirled more wildly than ever. Was there still open water at the deepest part of the lake? He peered between the burdened trees, seeing nothing.

When one of the boys had hit their mother, Aileen had run; Alayna had attacked him. Aileen had acted sensibly and Alayna foolishly, yet it was Alayna he admired. The world would be a better place if more people were as foolish as Alayna and fewer as sensible as Aileen.

Alayna had said something peculiar about their attacker. *The boy with the hood. He hit Mama and Aileen ran away.*

That wasn't exactly right, but close enough, perhaps. The boy had worn a hood, perhaps a hooded sweatshirt underneath his coat, the coat and sweatshirt both black or brown; something of that kind.

For a moment it seemed the Lincoln would stall in the next drift. He backed out and tried again. Returning, he could go through the breaks he had already made, of course; and it would probably be a good idea to turn around, if he could, and return now.

Two dark figures stepped out of the trees at the edge of his lights. Between them was a terrified child nearly as tall as they. One waved, pointing to Aileen and to him.

He braked too hard, sending the crawling Lincoln into a minor skid that left it at an angle to the road. The one who had waved gestured again — and he, catching a glimpse of the smooth young face beneath the hood, realized that it was not a boy's at all, but a woman's.

He got out and found his own rifle pointed at him.

Aileen moaned, "Daddy, Daddy..."

The smooth-faced young woman who had waved shoved her at him, then patted the Lincoln's fender, speaking in a language he could not identify.

Emery nodded. "You'll give her to me if I'll give you the car."

The women stared at him without comprehension.

He dropped to his knees in the snow and hugged Aileen, and made a gesture of dismissal toward the Lincoln.

Both women nodded.

"We'll have to walk it," he told Aileen. "A little over two miles, I guess. But we can't go wrong if we stay on the road."

She said nothing, sobbing.

He stood, not bothering to clean the snow from his knees and thighs. "The keys are in there."

If they understood, they gave no sign of it.

"The engine's running. You just can't hear it."

The freezing wind whipped Aileen's dark hair. He tried to remember how the twins had been dressed when he had seen them getting out of the Lincoln in front of his cabin. She'd had on a stocking cap, surely — long white stocking caps on both the twins. If so, it was gone now. He indicated his own head, and realized that he had left his cap in the car; he started to get it, stopping abruptly when the woman with his rifle lifted it to her shoulder.

She jabbed the rifle in the direction he had come.

"I just want to get my cap," he explained.

She raised the rifle again, putting it to her shoulder without sighting along the barrel. He backed away, saying, "Come on, Aileen."

The other woman produced something that looked more like a tool than a weapon, a crooked metal bar with what seemed to be a split pin at one end.

"I don't want to fight." He took another step backward. He pointed to Aileen's head. "Just let me get my cap and give it to her."

The shot was so sudden and unexpected that there was no time to be afraid. Something tugged violently at his mackinaw.

He tried to rush the woman with the rifle, slipped in the snow, and fell. She took his rifle from her shoulder, pulled down and pushed up its lever almost as dexterously as he could have himself, and pointed it again.

"No, no!" He raised his hands. "We'll go, I swear." He crawled away from her, backward through the snow on his hands and knees, conscious that Aileen was watching with the blank, horror-stricken expression of a child who has exhausted tears.

When he was ten yards or more behind the Lincoln, he stood up and called, "Come here, Aileen. We're going back."

She stared at the women, immobile until one motioned to her, then waded slowly to him through the snow. His right side felt as though it had been scorched with a soldering iron; he wondered vaguely how badly he had been wounded. Catching her hand, he turned his back on the woman and began to trudge away, trying to brace himself against the bullet that he more than half expected.

"Daddy?"

He scarcely dared to speak, but managed, "What is it?"

"Can you carry me?"

"No." He felt he should explain, but could think only of the rifle pointed at his back. "We've got to walk. You're a big girl now. Come on, honey." It was easier to walk in the curving tracks of the Lincoln's tires, and he did so.

"I want to go home."

"So do I, honey. That's where we're going. Come on, it can't be far." He risked a glance toward the lake, and this time caught sight of ice lit by blue lights far away. More to himself than to the doleful, shivering child beside him, he muttered, "Somebody's out there on a boat." No one — no sane, normal person at least — would have a boat in the lake at this time of year. The boats had been drawn up on shore, where they would stay until spring.

He took off his glasses and dropped them into a pocket of his mackinaw, and looked behind him. Jan's Lincoln would have been invisible if it were not for the blinking red glow of its taillights. They winked out together as he watched. "They're stripping it," he told Aileen. "They just got the alternator or the battery."

She did not reply; and he began to walk again, turning up his collar and pulling it close about his ears. The wind was from his left; the warmth on the other side was blood, soaking his clothes and warming the skin under them, however briefly. Slow bleeding, or so it seemed — in which case he might not be wounded too badly and might live. A soft-nosed hunting bullet, but expansion required a little distance, and it could not have had much, probably had not been much bigger than thirty caliber when it had passed through his side.

Which meant that life would continue, at least for a time. He might be tempted to give his body to the lake — to walk out on its tender ice until it gave way and his life, begun in warm amniotic fluid, should terminate in freezing lake water. He might be tempted to lie down in the snow and bleed or freeze to death. But he could not possibly leave Aileen or any other child out here alone, although he need only tell her to follow the road until she reached his cabin.

"Look," she said, "there's a house."

She released his hand to point, and he realized that he was not wearing his gloves, which were in his pockets. "It's closed up, honey." (He had fallen into the habit of calling both the twins "honey" to conceal his inability to distinguish them.) "Have you got gloves?"

"I don't know."

He forced himself to be patient. "Well, look. If you've got gloves or mittens, put them on." This girl, he reminded himself, was the wonder of her class, writing themes that would have done credit to a college student and mastering arithmetic and the rudiments of algebra with contemptuous ease.

"I guess those ladies didn't give them back."

"Then put on mine." He handed them to her.

"Your hands will get cold."

"I'll put one in my pocket, see? And I'll hold your hand with my other one, so the one glove will keep us both warm."

She gave a glove back to him. "My hand won't go around yours, Daddy, but yours will go around mine."

He nodded, impressed, and put the glove on.

It might be possible to get into his neighbor's lightless cabin, closed or not. "I'm going to try to break in," he told Aileen. "There ought to be firewood and matches in there, and there may even be a phone."

But the doors were solid, and solidly locked; and there were grilles over the small windows, as over his own. "We've had a lot of break-ins," he confided, "ever since they paved the road. People drive out to the lake, and they see these places."

"Is it much farther?"

"Not very far. Maybe another mile." He remembered his earlier speculations. "Did you run this far, honey?"

"I don't think so."

"I didn't think that you would." Somewhat gratified, he returned to her and the road. It was darker than ever now, and the tire tracks, obscured by advancing night as well as new-fallen snow, were impossible to follow. Pushing up his sleeve, he looked at his watch: it was almost six o'clock.

"I don't like them," Aileen said. "Those ladies."

"It would surprise me if you did."

"They took my clothes off. I said I'd do it, but they didn't pay any attention, and they didn't know how to do it. They just pulled and pulled till things came off."

"Out here? In the snow?" He was shocked.

"In the ziggurat, but it was pretty cold in there, too."

He found the point in a drift at which the Lincoln had bulldozed its way through, and led her to it. "What did you say? A ziggurat?"

"Uh-huh. Is it much farther?"

"No," he said.

"I could sit down here. You could come back for me in your Jeep."

"No," he repeated. "Come on. If we walk faster, we'll keep warm."

"I'm really tired. They didn't give me hardly anything to eat, either. Just a piece of bread."

He nodded absently, concentrating on walking faster and pulling her along. He was tired too — nearly exhausted. What would he say when he wrote his journal? To take his mind off his weariness and the burning pain in his right side — off his fear, as he was forced to concede — he attempted to compose the entry in his mind.

"I got in the sleeper thing, but it was so cold. My feet got really cold, and I couldn't pull them up. I guess I slept a little."

He looked down at her, blinking away snow; it was too dark for him to gauge her expression. "Those women took you into a ziggurat —"

"Not really, Daddy. That was a kind of temple they had in Babylon. This one just looks like the picture in the book."

"They caught you," he continued doggedly, "and took you there, and undressed you?"

If she nodded, he failed to see the motion. "Did they or didn't they?"

"Yes, Daddy."

"And they fed you, and you slept a little, or anyway tried to sleep. Then you got dressed again and they brought you back here. Is that what you want me to believe?"

"They showed me some pictures, too, but I didn't know what lots of the things were."

"Aileen, you can't possibly have been gone more than a couple of hours at the outside. I doubt it was that long."

He had thought her beyond tears, but she began to sob, not loudly, but with a concentrated wretchedness that tore at his heart. "Don't cry, honey." He picked her up, ignoring the fresh pain in his side.

The wind, which had been rising all afternoon, was blowing hard enough to whistle, an eerie moan among the spectral trees. "Don't cry," he repeated. He staggered forward, holding her over his left shoulder, desperately afraid that he would slip and fall again. Her plastic snow boots were stiff with ice, the insulated trousers above them stiff too.

He could not have said how far he had walked; it seemed miles before a lonely star gleamed through the darkness ahead. "Look," he said, and halted — then turned around so that his daughter, too, could see the golden light. "That's our cabin. Has to be. We're going to make it."

Then (almost at once, it seemed) Brook was running through the snow with the flashlight, he had set Aileen upon her feet, and they were all three stumbling into the warmth and light of the cabin, where Jan knelt and clasped Aileen to her and cried and laughed and cried again, and Alayna danced and jumped and demanded over and over, "Was she lost, Daddy? Was she lost in the woods?"

Brook put a plate of hot corned-beef hash in his lap and pushed a steaming mug of coffee at him.

"Thank you." Emery sighed. "Thank you very much, son." His face felt frozen; merely breathing the steam from the mug was heavenly.

"The car get stuck?"

He shook his head.

"I fixed stuff like you said. 'Layna helped, and Jan says she'll do the dishes. If she won't, I will." Brook had called her Mother for the length of the marriage; but it was over now, emotionally if not legally. Emery's thoughts turned gratefully from the puzzle of Aileen's captivity to that.

"I could toast you some bread in the fireplace," Brook offered. "You want ketchup? I like ketchup on mine."

"A fork," Emery told him, and sipped his coffee.

"Oh. Yeah."

"Was she lost?" Alayna demanded. "I bet she was!"

"I'm not going to talk about that." Emery had come to a decision. "Aileen can tell you herself, as much or as little as she wants."

Jan looked up at him. "I called the sheriff. The number was on your phone." Emery nodded.

"They said they couldn't do anything until she'd been gone for twenty-four hours. It's the law, apparently. They — this woman I talked to — suggested we get our friends and neighbors to search. I told her that you were searching already. Maybe you ought to call and tell them you found her."

He shook his head, accepting a fork from Brook.

"You came back on foot? You walked?"

Aileen said, "From way down by the lake." She had taken off her boots, stockings, and snow pants, and was sitting on the floor rubbing her feet.

"Where's my car?"

"I traded it for Aileen."

Alayna stared at Aileen, wide-eyed. Aileen nodded.

"You *traded* it?"

He nodded too, his mouth full of corned-beef hash.

"Who to?"

He swallowed. "To whom, Jan."

"You are the most irritating man in the world!" If Jan had been standing, she would have stamped.

"He did, Mama. He said they could have the car if they'd give me to him, but they shot him anyway, and he fell down."

"That's right," Emery said. "We ought to have a look at that. It's pretty much stopped bleeding, and I think it's just a flesh wound." Setting his plate and mug on the hearth, he unbuttoned his mackinaw. "If it got the intestine, I suppose I'll have hash all over in there, and it will probably kill me. But there would have been food in my gut anyway. I had pork and beans for lunch."

"They *shot* you?" Jan stared at his blood-stiffened shirt.

He nodded, savoring the moment. *It's nothing, sir. I set the bone myself.* Danny Kaye in some old movie. He cleared his throat, careful to keep his face impassive. "I'm going to have to take this off, and my undershirt and pants, too. Probably my shorts. Maybe you could have the girls look the other way."

Both twins giggled.

"Look at the fire," she told them. "He's hurt. You don't want to embarrass him, do you?"

Brook had gotten the first-aid kit. "This is stuck." He pulled gingerly at the waistband of Emery's trousers. "I ought to cut it off."

"Pull it off," Emery told him. "I'm going to wash those pants and wear them again. I need them." He had unbuckled his belt, unbuttoned his trousers, and unzipped his fly.

"Just above the belt," Brook told him. "An inch, inch and a half lower, and it would have hit your belt."

Jan snapped her fingers. "Oil! Oil will soften the dried blood. Wesson Oil. Have you got any?"

Brook pointed at the cabinet above the sink. Emery said, "There's a bottle of olive oil up there, or there should be."

"'Leen's peeking," Brook told Jan, who told Aileen, "Do that again, young lady, and I'll smack your face!

"Emery, you really ought to make two rooms out of this. This is ridiculous."

"It was designed for four men," he explained, "a hunting party, or a fishing party. You women always insist on being included, then complain about what you find when you are."

She poured olive oil on his caked blood and rubbed it with her fingertips. "I had to get you to sign."

"You could have sent your damned paper to my box in town. I'd have picked it up on Saturday and sent it back to you."

"She couldn't mail me," Brook said. "Are we going to get the car back? My junk was in the trunk."

Emery shrugged. "They're stripping it, I think. We may be able to take back what's left. Maybe they won't look in the trunk."

"They're bound to."

Jan asked, "How are we supposed to get home?"

"I'll drive you to town in the Jeep. There's bus service to the city. If the buses aren't running because of the storm, you can stay in a motel. There are two motels, I think. There could be three." He rubbed his chin. "You'll have to anyway, unless you want to reconsider and stay here. I think the last bus was at five."

Brook was scrutinizing Emery's wound. "That bullet sort of plowed through your skin. It might've got some muscles at your waist, but I don't think it hit any organs."

Emery made himself look down. "Plowed through the fat, you mean. I ought to lose twenty pounds, and if I had, she would have missed."

"A girl?"

Emery nodded.

Jan said, "No wonder you hate us so much," and pulled his bloodstained trousers free.

"I don't hate you. Not even now, when I ought to. Brook, would you give me my coffee? That's good coffee you made, and there's no reason I shouldn't drink it while you bandage that."

Brook handed it to him. "I scrubbed out the pot."

"Good for you. I'd been meaning to."

Alayna interposed, "I make better coffee than Brook does, Daddy, but Mama says I put in too much."

"You should have stitches, Emery. Is there a hospital in town?"

"Just a clinic, and it'll be closed. I've been hurt worse and not had stitches."

Brook filled a pan with water. "Why'd they shoot you, Dad?"

Emery started to speak, thought better of it, and shook his head.

Jan said, "If you're going to drive us into town in the Jeep, you could drive us into the city just as easily."

Setting his water on the stove, Brook hooted.

"You've got money, and you and Brook could stay at a hotel and come back tomorrow."

Emery said, "We're not going to, however."

"Why won't you?"

"I don't have to explain, and I won't."

She glared. "Well, you should!"

"That won't do any good." Privately he wondered which was worse, a woman who had never learned how to get what she wanted or a woman who had.

"You actually proposed that we patch it up. Then you act like this?"

"I'm trying to keep things pleasant."

"Then do it!"

"You mean you want to be courted while you're divorcing me. That's what's usually meant by a friendly divorce, from what I've been able to gather." When she said nothing, Emery added, "Isn't that water hot enough yet, Brook?"

"Not even close."

"I shouldn't explain," Emery continued, "but I will. In the first place, Brook and the twins are going to have about as much elbow room as live bait in the back of the Jeep. It will be miserable for even a short drive. If we so much as try to make it into the city in this weather, they'll be tearing each other to bits before we stop."

Brook put in, "I'll stay here, Dad. I'll be all right."

Emery shook his head. "So would we, Jan. In the second, I think the women who shot me will be back as soon as the storm lets up. If no one's here, they'll break in or burn this place down. It's the only home I've got, and I intend to defend it."

"Sure," Brook said. "Let me stay. I can look after things while you're gone."

"No," Emery told him. "It would be too dangerous."

Emery turned back to Jan. "In the third place, I won't do it because I want to so much. If —"

"You were the one that gave those people my car."

"To get Aileen back. Yes, I did. I'd do it again."

"And you took it without my permission! I trusted you, Emery. I left my keys in the ignition, and you took my car."

He nodded wearily. "To look for Aileen, and I'd do that again too. I suppose you're already planning to bring it up in court."

"You bet I am!"

"I suggest you check the title first."

Aileen herself glanced at him over her shoulder. "I'm really hungry. Can I have the rest of your hash?"

Brook said, "There's more here, 'Leen. You said you weren't, but I saved —"

"I haven't had anything since yesterday except some bread stuff."

Jan began, "Aileen, you know perfectly well —"

Emery interrupted her. "It's only been a couple of hours since they caught you, honey. Remember? We talked about that before we got here."

"I was in there, in the sleep thing —"

Jan snapped, "Aileen, be quiet! I told you not to look around like that."

"It's only Daddy in his underwear. I've seen him like that lots."

"Turn around!"

Trying to weigh each word with significance, Emery said, "Your mama told you to be quiet, honey. That wasn't simply an order. It was good advice."

Brook brought her a plate of corned-beef hash and a fork. "There's bread, too. Want some?"

"Sure. And milk or something."

"There isn't any."

"Water, then." Raising her voice slightly, Aileen added, "I'd get up and get it for myself, but Mama won't let me."

Jan said, "You see what you've started, Emery?"

He nodded solemnly. "I didn't start it, but I'm quite happy about it."

Brook washed his wound and bandaged it, applying a double pad of surgical gauze and so much Curity Wet-Pruf adhesive tape that Emery winced at the mere thought of removing it.

"I might be a doctor," Brook mused, "big money, and this is fun."

"You're a pretty good one already," Emery said gratefully. He kicked off his boots, emptied his pockets onto the table, and stuffed his trousers into a laundry bag, following it with his shirt. "Want to do me a favor, Brook? Scrape my plate into that tin bowl on the drainboard and set it on the back porch."

Jan asked, "Are you well enough to drive, Emery? Forget the fighting. You wouldn't want to see any of us killed. I know you wouldn't."

He nodded, buttoning a fresh shirt.

"So let me drive. I'll drive us into town, and you can drive Brook back here if you feel up to it."

"You'd put us into the ditch," Emery told her. "If I start feeling too weak, I'll pull over and —"

Brook banged the rear door shut behind him and held up a squirrel. "Look at this! It was right up on the porch." The tiny body was stiff, its gray fur powdered with snow.

"Poor little thing!" Jan went over to examine it. "It must have come looking for something to eat, and froze. Have you been feeding them, Emery?"

"It's a present from a friend," he told her. Something clutched his throat, leaving him barely able to speak. "You wouldn't understand."

The Jeep started without difficulty. As he backed it out onto the road, he wondered whether the dark-faced women who had Jan's Lincoln had been unable to solve the simple catches that held the Jeep's hood. Conceivably, they had not seen the Jeep when they had been in his cabin earlier. He wished now that he had asked Aileen how many women she had seen, when the two of them had been alone.

"Drafty in here," Jan remarked. "You should buy yourself a real car, Emery."

The road was visible only as an opening between the trees; he pulled onto it with all four wheels hub-deep in virgin snow, keeping the transmission in second and nudging the accelerator only slightly. Swirling snow filled the headlights. "Honey," he said, "your boots had ice on them. So did your snow pants. Did you wade in the lake?"

From the crowded rear seat, Aileen answered, "They made me, Daddy."

The road was visible only as an open space between trees. To people in a — Emery fumbled mentally for a word and settled on *aircraft*.

To an aircraft, the frozen lake might have looked like a paved helicopter pad or something of that kind, a more or less circular pavement. The black-looking open water at its center might have been taken for asphalt.

Particularly by a pilot not familiar with woods and lakes.

"Emery, you hardly ever answer a direct question. It's one of the things I dislike most about you."

"That's what men say about women," he protested mildly.

"Women are being diplomatic. Men are rude."

"I suppose you're right. What did you ask me?"

"That isn't the point. The point is that you ignore me until I raise my voice."

That seemed to require no reply, so he did not offer one. How high would you have to be and how fast would you have to be coming down before a frozen lake looked like a landing site?

"So do the girls," Jan added bitterly, "they're exactly the same way. So is Brook."

"That ought to tell you something."

"You don't have to be rude!"

One of the twins said, "She wanted to know how long it would take to get to town, Daddy."

It had probably been Alayna, Emery decided. "How long would you like it to take, honey?"

"Real quick!"

That had been the other one, presumably Aileen. "Well," he told her, "we'll be there real quick."

Jan said, "Don't try to be funny."

"I'm being diplomatic. If I wasn't, I'd point out that it's twenty-two miles and we're going about fifteen miles an hour. If we can keep that up all the way, it should take us about an hour and a half."

Jan turned in her seat to face the twins. "Never marry an engineer, girls. Nobody ever told me that, but I'm telling you now. If you do, don't say you were never warned."

One twin began, "You said that about —"

The other interrupted. "Only, it wasn't an engineer that time. It was a tennis player. Did you do it in your head, Daddy? I did too, only it took me longer. One point four and two-thirds, so six six seven. Is that right?"

"I have no idea. Fifteen is smaller than twenty-two, and that's an hour. Seven over, and seven's about half of fifteen. Most real calculations outside school are like that, honey."

"Because it doesn't matter?"

Emery shook his head. "Because the data's not good enough for anything more. It's about twenty-two miles to town on this Jeep's odometer. That could be off by as much as —" Something caught his eye, and he fell silent.

From the rear seat, Brook asked, "What's the matter, Dad?" He sounded half suffocated.

Emery was peering into the rear view mirror, unable to see anything except a blur of snow. "There was a sign back there. What did it say?"

"Don't tell me you're lost, Emery."

"I'm not lost. What did it say, Brook?"

"I couldn't tell, it was all covered with snow."

"I think it was the historical marker sign. I'm going to stop there on the way back."

"Okay, I'll remind you."

"You won't have to. I'll stop."

One of the twins asked, "What happened there?"

Emery did not reply; Brook told her, "There used to be a village there, the first one in this part of the state. Wagon trains would stop there. One time there was nobody there. The log cabins and their stuff was okay, only there wasn't anybody home."

"The Pied Piper," the twin suggested.

"He just took rats and kids. This got everybody."

Jan said, "I don't think that's much of a mystery. An early settlement? The Indians killed them."

The other twin said, "Indians would have scalped them and left the bodies, Mama, and taken things."

"All right, they were stolen by fairies. Emery, this hill looks so steep! Are you sure this is the right road?"

"It's the only road there is. Hills always look steeper covered with snow." When Jan said nothing, he added, "Hell, they *are* steeper."

"They should plow this."

"The plows will be out on the state highway," Emery told her. "Don't worry, only three more mountains."

They let Jan and the twins out in front of the Ramada Inn, and Brook climbed over the back of the front seat. "I'm glad they're gone. I guess I shouldn't say it — she's been pretty nice to me — but I'm glad."

Emery nodded.

"You could've turned around back there." Brook indicated the motel's U-shaped drive. "Are we going into town?"

Emery nodded again.

"Want to tell me what for? I might be able to help."

"To buy two more guns. There's a sporting-goods dealer on Main Street. We'll look there first."

"One for me, huh? What kind?"

"What kind do you want?"

"A three-fifty-seven, I guess."

"No handguns, there's a five-day waiting period. But we can buy rifles or shotguns and take them with us, and we may need them when we get back to the cabin."

"One rifle and one shotgun," Brook decided. "Pumps or semis. You want the rifle or the scattergun, Dad?"

Emery did not reply. Every business that they drove past seemed to be dark and locked. He left the Jeep to rattle and pound the door of the sporting-goods store, but no one appeared to unlock it.

Brook switched off the radio as he got back in. "Storm's going to get worse. They say the main part hasn't even gotten here yet."

Emery nodded.

"You knew, huh?"

"I'd heard a weather report earlier. We're due for two, possibly three days of this."

The gun shop was closed as well. There would be no gun with which to kill the woman who had shot him, and none with which to kill himself. He shrugged half-humorously and got back into the Jeep. Brook said, "We're going to fight with what we've got, huh?"

"A hammer and a hunting knife against my thirty-thirty?" Emery shook his head emphatically. "We're not going to fight at all. If they come around again, we're to do whatever they want, no questions and no objections. If they like anything — this Jeep would be the most likely item, I imagine — we're going to give it to them."

"Unless I get a chance to grab the gun again."

Emery glanced at him. "The first time you tried that, she hadn't learned to use it. She was a lot better when she shot me. Next time she'll be better yet. Am I making myself clear?"

Brook nodded. "I've got to be careful."

"You've got to be more than just careful," Emery told him, "because if you're not, you're going to die. I was ten feet or more from her when she shot at me, and backing away. She fired anyway, and she hit me."

"I got it."

"When you dressed my wound," Emery continued, "you said that if her shot had been an inch or two lower it would have hit my belt. If it had been an inch or two to the left, it would have killed me. Did you think of that?"

"Sure. I just didn't want to say it." Brook pointed to a small dark building. "There's the last store, Rothschild's Records and CDs. It's pretty good. I used to have you drop me there sometimes when you were going into town, remember?"

Intent upon his thoughts and the snow-covered road, Emery did not even nod.

"Those girls have got to be either camping or living in somebody's cabin out here. If we can find out where, we could get some guns when the town's open again and go out there and make them give our stuff back."

Emery muttered, "This is the last trip until the county clears the road."

"We're doing okay now."

"This is a state highway. It's been plowed at least once, most likely within the past couple of hours. The road to the cabin won't have been plowed at all, and we barely made it out."

"I'd like to look at the other car and see if they left any of my stuff."

"All right, if we can drive as far as the cabin, we'll do that. But after that, I'm not taking the Jeep out until the road's been plowed."

"They really were girls? I thought you and 'Leen might have been stringing Jan."

"Two of them were." Emery studied the road. "The one who shot me, and another one who was with her. I imagine the third was as well, she seemed to be about the same size."

Brook nodded to himself. "You never can tell what girls are going to do, I guess."

"Obviously it's harder to predict the actions of someone whose psychology differs from your own. Once you've learned what a woman values, though, you ought to be right most of the time — say, seven out of ten." Emery chuckled. "How's that for a man being divorced for the second time? Do I sound like an expert?"

"Sure. What does a woman value?"

"It varies from woman to woman, and sometimes it changes. You have to learn for each, or guess. With a little experience you ought to be able to make pretty good guesses after you've talked with the woman for a few minutes. You've got to listen to what she says, and listen harder for what she doesn't. All this is true for men as well, of course. Fortunately, men are easier — for other men."

"Okay if I throw you a softball, Dad? I'm leading up to something."

"Go ahead."

"What does Jan value?"

"First of all, the appearance of wealth. She doesn't value money itself, but she wants to impress people with her big car, her mink coat, and so on. Have I missed the turn?"

"I don't think so. We've been going pretty slow."

"I don't either — I don't see how I could have — but I keep worrying about it."

"Money has a poetry of its own, Brook. Women are fond of telling us that we don't get it, but the poetry of money is one of the things that they rarely get. One of a dozen or more, I suppose. Are you going to ask why I married Jan? Is that what you're leading up to?"

"Uh-huh. Why did you?"

"Because I was lonely and fell in love with her. Looking back, I can see very clearly that I wanted to prove to myself that I could make a woman happy, too. I felt I could make Jan happy, and I was right. But after a while — after I lost the company, particularly — it no longer seemed worth the effort."

"I'm with you. Did she love you too? Or did you think she did?"

Emery sighed. "Women don't love in the same way that men do, Brook. I said the psychology was different, and that's one of the main differences. Men are dogs. Women are cats — they love conditionally. For example, I love you. If you were to try to kill me —"

"I wouldn't do that!"

"I'm constructing an extreme example," Emery explained patiently. "Say that I was to try to kill you. You'd fight me off if you could. You might even kill me doing it. But you'd love me afterward, just the same; you may not think so, but you would."

Brook nodded, his face thoughtful.

"When you love a woman, you'll love her in the same way; but women love *as long as* — as long as you have a good job, as long as you don't bring home your friends, and so on. You shouldn't blame them for that, because it's as much a part of their natures as the way you love is of yours. For women, love is a spell that can be broken by picking a flower or throwing a ring into the sea. Love is magic, which is why they frequently use the language of fairy tales when they talk about it."

"We're coming up on the turn." Brook aimed his forefinger at the darkness and the blowing snow. "It's right along here someplace."

"About another half mile. Throw your fastball."

"This woman that shot you. Why did she do it?"

"I've been thinking about that."

"I figured you had."

"Why does anyone, robbing someone else, shoot them?"

"No witnesses?"

Emery shook his head. "A thief doesn't merely shoot to silence a witness, he kills. After she had shot me she let me go. I was still conscious, still able to walk and to talk. Perfectly capable of giving the sheriff a description of her. But she let me go. Why?"

"You were there, Dad. What do you think?"

"You're starting to sound like me." Emery slowed the Jeep from ten miles an hour to six, searching the road to his left.

"I know."

"Because she was frightened, I think. Afraid of me, and afraid she couldn't do it, too. When she shot me, she proved to herself that she could, and I was able to show her — by my actions, because she couldn't understand what I was saying — that I wasn't somebody she had to be afraid of."

The road to the cabin was deep in snow, so deep that they inched and churned their way through it foot by foot. Caution, and speeds scarcely faster than a walk, soon became habitual, and Emery's mind turned to other things. First of all, to the smoothly oval face behind the threatening muzzle of his rifle. Large, dark eyes above a tiny mouth narrowed by determination; a small — slightly flattened? — nose.

Small and slender hands; the thirty-thirty had looked big in them, which meant that they had been hardly larger than the twins'. He did not remember seeing hair, but with that face it would be black, surely. Straight or curled? Not Japanese or Chinese, possibly a small, light-complexioned Afro-American. A mixture of Black and White with Oriental? Filipino? Almost anything seemed possible.

The coal-black hair he had imagined merged with the shadow of her hood. "Brownies," he said aloud.

"What?"

"Brownies. Don't they call those little girls who sell cookies Brownies?"

"Sure. Like Girl Scouts, only littler. 'Leen and 'Layna used to be Brownies."

Emery nodded. "That's right. I remember." But brownies were originally English fairies, small and dark — brown-faced, presumably — mischievous and sometimes spiteful, but often willing to trade their work for food and clothing. Fairies sufficiently feminine that giving their name to an organization for young girls was not ridiculous, as it would have been to call the same little girls gnomes, for example.

Stolen by fairies, Jan had said, referring to villagers of the eighteen-forties.... He tried to remember the precise date, and failed.

Because brownies did not merely trade their labor for the goods they wanted. Often they stole. Milked your cow before you woke up. Snatched your infant from its crib. Lured your children to a place where time ran differently, too fast or too slow. Aileen, who had been gone for no more than two hours at most, had thought she had been gone for a day — had been taken to the ziggurat and shown pictures she had not understood, had slept or at least tried to sleep, had been made to wade into the lake, where blue lights shone.

Where was fairyland?

"Why're you stopping?"

"Because I want to get out and look at something. You stay here."

Flashlight in hand, he shut the Jeep's flimsy vinyl flap. Later — by next morning, perhaps — the snow might be easier to walk on. Now it was still uncompacted, as light as down; he sank above his knees at every step.

The historical marker protruded above the blank whiteness, its size amplified by the snow it wore. He considered brushing off the bronze plaque and reading it, but the precise date and circumstances, as specified by some historian more interested in plausibility than truth, did not matter.

He waded past it, across what would be green and parklike lawn in summer, reminding himself that there was a ditch at its end before the ranch's barbed-wire fence, and wishing he had a stick or staff with which to probe the snow. The body — if he had in fact seen what he had thought he had seen — would be covered by this time, invisible save as a slight mound.

When he stood in the ditch, the snow was above his waist. His gloved hands found the wire, then the almost-buried locust post, which he used to pull himself up, breaching the snow like some fantastic, red-plaid dolphin.

The coyote lay where he had glimpsed it on the drive to town. It had frozen as stiff as the squirrel it had left him, its face twisted in a snarl of pain and surprise. Negotiating the ditch again with so much difficulty that he feared for a few seconds that he would have to call for Brook to rescue him, he stowed the body on the narrow floor behind the Jeep's front seats.

Brook said, "That's a dead coyote."

Emery nodded as he got back behind the wheel and put the Jeep in gear. "Cyanide gun."

"What do you want with that?"

"I don't know. I haven't decided yet."

Brook stared, then shrugged. "I hope you didn't start yourself bleeding again, doing all that."

"I may bury him. Or I might have him stuffed and mounted. That sporting-goods dealer has a taxidermy service. They could do it. Probably wouldn't cost more than a hundred or so."

"You didn't kill it," Brook protested.

"Oh yes, I did," Emery told him.

What they could see of the cabin through the falling snow suggested that it was as they had left it. Emery did not stop, and it would have been difficult to make the Jeep push its way through the banks more slowly than it already was. The world before the windshield was white, framed in black; and upon that blank sheet his mind strove to paint the country from which the small brown women had come, a country that would send forth an aircraft (if the ziggurat in the lake was in fact an aircraft or something like one) crewed by young women more alike than sisters. A country without men, perhaps, or one in which men were hated and feared.

What had they thought of Jan, a woman almost a foot taller than they? Jan with her creamy complexion and yellow hair? Of Aileen and Alayna, girls of their own size, nearly as dark as they, and alike as two peas? The first had run from, the second fought them; and both reactions had quite likely baffled them. From their own perspective, they had crashed in a wilderness of snow and wind and bitter cold — a howling wilderness strangely and dangerously inhabited.

"We could've stopped at the cabin," Brook said. "We can go look for my stuff tomorrow, when there's daylight."

Emery shook his head. "We wouldn't be able to get through tomorrow. The snow will be too deep."

"We could try."

Brook had presumably confirmed their worst fears, as he had himself; and although they'd had his rifle, they had fled at his approach. They had recognized the rifle as a weapon when they had entered and searched his empty, unlocked cabin — empty because he had seen something flash high up on the hill across the creek....

"Is it much farther, Dad?" Brook was peering through the wind-driven snow into the black night again, trying to catch a glimpse of Jan's Lincoln.

"Quite a bit, I believe." Apologetically, Emery added, "We're not going very fast."

The flash from the hill had left a shallow burn on the oak back of his chair. Had it been a laser — a laser weapon? Had they been shooting at him even then? A laser that could do no more than scorch the surface of the chair-back would not kill a man, surely, though it might blind him if it struck his eyes. Not a weapon, perhaps, but a laser tool of some kind that they had tried to employ as a weapon. He recalled the lasers used to engrave steel in the company he had left to found his own.

"Nobody's in that cabin back there now, I guess."

He shook his head. "Been closed since early November. There's nobody out here really, except us and them."

"What do you think they're trying to do out here?"

"Leave." His tone, he hoped, would notify Brook that he was not in the mood for conversation.

"They could've gone in the Lincoln. It wasn't out of gas. I'd been watching the gauge, because she never does."

"They can't drive. If they could, they'd have driven it away from the cabin the first time, when Jan left the keys in it. Besides, the Lincoln couldn't take them where they want to go."

"Dad —"

"That's enough questions for now. I'll tell you more when I've got more of it figured out."

"You must be really tired. I wish we'd stopped at the cabin. There won't be any of my stuff left anyhow."

Was he really as tired as Brook suggested? He considered the matter and

THE SECRET HISTORY OF SCIENCE FICTION

decided he was. Wading through the snow past the historical marker had consumed what little strength he had left after losing blood and slogging home with Aileen through snow that no longer seemed particularly deep. He was operating now on whatever it was that remained when the last strength was gone. On stubbornness and desperation.

"Your grandfather used to tell a story," he remarked to Brook, "about a jackrabbit, a coyote, and a jay. Did I ever tell you that?"

"No." Brook grinned, glad that he was not angry. "What is it?"

"A jay will yell and warn the other animals if there's a coyote around. You know that?"

"Uh-huh."

"Well, this jay was up on a mesquite, with a jackrabbit sleeping in the shade. The jay spotted a coyote stalking the jackrabbit and yelled a warning. The coyote sprang, and the jackrabbit ran, scooting past the mesquite and hooking left, with the coyote after it.

"The jay felt a little guilty about not having spotted the coyote sooner, so he shouted to the jackrabbit, 'You okay? You going to make it?'

"And the jackrabbit called back, 'I'll make it!'

"They went around the mesquite eight or ten times, and it seemed to the jay that the coyote was gaining at every pass. He got seriously worried then, and he shouted down, 'You sure you're going to make it?'

"The jackrabbit called back, 'I'm going to make it!'

"A few more passes, and the coyote was snapping at the jackrabbit's tail. The jay was worried sick by then, and he shouted, 'Rabbit, how do you *know* you're going to make it?' And the jackrabbit called back, 'Hell, I've *got* to make it!'"

Brook said, "You mean you're like that rabbit."

"Right." Emery put the transmission into neutral and set the parking brake. "I've got to make it, and I will."

"Why are we stopping?"

"Because we're here." He opened his flap and got out.

"I don't see the car."

"You will in a minute. Bring the flash."

They had to climb a drift before they found it, nearly buried in snow with its hood still up. Emery reached inside, took Jan's keys out of the ignition lock, and handed them to Brook. "Here, check the trunk. They may not have noticed the keyhole behind the medallion."

A moment later, as he leaned against the snow-covered side of the car, he heard Brook say, "It's here! Everything's still here!"

"I'll help you." He forced himself to walk.

"Just a couple little bags. I can carry them." Brook slammed down the trunk lid so that he would not see whatever was being left behind. A stereo, Emery decided. Possibly a TV. He hated TV, and decided to say nothing.

"You want the keys?"

"You keep them."

"I guess we'll have to call a tow truck when the road's clear. They've taken a lot of stuff out of here." Brook was at the front of the Lincoln, shining the flashlight into its engine compartment.

"Sure," Emery said, and started back to the Jeep.

When he woke the next morning, bacon was frying and coffee perking on the little propane stove. He sat up, discovering that his right side was stiff and painful. "Brook?"

There was no answer.

The cabin was cold, in spite of the blue flames and the friendly odors. He pulled the wool shirt he had put on after Brook had bandaged his wound over the Duofold underwear he had slept in, pushed his legs into the trousers he had dropped on the floor beside his bunk, and stood up. His boots were under the little table, the stockings he had worn beside them. He put the stockings into his laundry bag, got out a clean pair and pulled them on, then tugged on, laced, and tied his boots.

The coffee had perked enough. He turned off the burner and transferred the bacon onto the cracked green plate Brook had apparently planned to use. The bacon still smelled good; he felt that he should eat a piece, but had no appetite.

Had Brook set off on foot to fetch whatever it was that he had left in the Lincoln's trunk? Not with food on the stove. Brook would have turned down the fire under the coffeepot and drunk a cup before he left, taken up the bacon and eaten half of it, probably with bread, butter, and jam.

There was no toaster, but Brook had offered to toast bread in front of the fire the night before. That fire was nearly out, hardly more than embers. Brook had gotten up, started the coffee and put on the bacon, and gone outside for firewood.

Lord, Emery thought, you don't owe me a thing — I know that. But please.

They had taken Aileen and had, perhaps, been bringing her back when they had encountered him. They might very well have taken Brook as well; if they had, they might bring him back in a day or two.

He found that he was staring at the plate of bacon. He set it on the table and put on his mackinaw and second-best cap. Had his best one — the one that the women had not let him retrieve — been on the front seat of Jan's Lincoln? He had not even looked.

Snow had reached the sills of the windows, but it was not snowing as hard as it had the day before. The path plowed by Brook's feet and legs showed plainly, crossing the little back porch, turning south for the stacked wood under the eaves, then retraced for a short distance. Brook had seen something; or more probably, had heard a noise from the cabin's north side, where the Jeep was parked. It was difficult, very difficult, for Emery to step off the porch, following the path that Brook had broken through the deep snow.

Brook's body sprawled before the front bumper, a stick of firewood near its right hand. The blood around its head might, Emery told himself, have come from a superficial scalp wound. Brook might be alive, though unconscious. Even as he crouched to look more closely, he knew it was not true.

He closed his eyes and stood up. They had taken his ax as well as his rifle; he had worried about the rifle and had scarcely given a thought to the ax, yet the ax had done this.

The dead coyote still lay in back of the front seat of the plundered Jeep. He carried it to the south side of the cabin; and where firewood had been that autumn, contrived a rough bier from half a dozen sticks. Satisfied with the effect, he built a larger bier of the same kind for his son, arranged the not-yet-frozen body on it, and covered it with a clean sheet that he weighted with a few more sticks. It would be necessary to call the sheriff if the telephone was still working, and the sheriff might very well accuse him of Brook's murder.

Inside, after a momentary hesitation, he bolted the doors. A calendar hung the year before provided the number of the only undertaker in Voylestown.

"You have reached Merton's Funeral Parlor. We are not able to be with you at this time..."

He waited for the tone, then spoke quickly. "This's Emery Bainbridge." They could get his address from the directory, as well as his number. "My son's dead. I want you to handle the arrangements. Contact me when you can." A second or two of silence, as if in memory of Brook, and then the dial tone. He pressed in the sheriff's number.

"Sheriff Ron Wilber's office."

"This is Emery Bainbridge again. My son, Brook, has been killed."

"Address?"

"Five zero zero north, twenty-six seventy-seven west — that's on Route E-E, about five miles from Haunted Lake."

"How did it happen, Mister Bainbridge?"

He wanted to say that one of the women had stood against the wall of his cabin, holding his ax, and waited for Brook to come around the corner; it had been apparent from the lines plowed through the deep snow, but mentioning it at this time would merely make the investigating officer suspect him. He said, "He was hit in the head with my ax, I think. They took my ax yesterday."

"Yes, I remember. Don't move the body, we'll get somebody out there as soon as we can."

"I already have. When —"

"Then don't move it any more. Don't touch anything else."

"When will you have someone out here?"

He sensed, rather than heard, her indrawn breath. "This afternoon, Emery. We'll try to get one of the deputies there this afternoon."

If she had not been lying, Emery reflected, she would have called him "Mister Bainbridge." He thanked her and hung up, then leaned back in his chair, looking from the telephone to his journal. He should write up his journal, and there was a great deal to write. There had been a cellular phone in Jan's car. Had they taken it? He had not noticed.

He picked up the telephone again but hung it up without pressing in a number. His black sports watch lay under his bunk. He retrieved it, noting the date and time.

09:17 Jan came yesterday, with Brook and the twins. Three small, dark women in hoods tried to strip her car. There was a tussle with Jan and the children.

He stared down at the pen. It was exactly the color of Brook's blood in the snow.

Aileen ran away. I searched for her in Jan's car, which I was able to trade for her. One of the women shot me. They do not understand English.

The red pen had stopped.

His computer back home — he corrected the thought: his computer at Jan's had a spell checker; this pen had none, yet it had sounded a warning without one. Was it possible that the women spoke English after all? On overseas trips he had met people whose English he could scarcely understand. He tried to recall what the women had said and what he had said, and failed with both.

Yet something, some neglected corner of his subconscious, suspected that the women had in fact been speaking English, of a peculiar variety.

> Whan that Aprille with his shoures soote
> The droghte of March hath perced to the roote.

He had memorized the lines in high school — how long had it been? But no, it had been much longer than that, had been more than six hundred years since a great poet had written in a beautiful rhythmic dialect that had at first seemed as alien as German. "When April, with his sweet breath/The drought of March has pierced to the root."

And the language was still changing, still evolving.

He picked up the telephone, fairly sure that he remembered Jan's cellular number, and pressed it in.

A lonely ringing, far away. In Jan's snow-covered black Lincoln? Could a cellular car phone operate without the car's battery? There were bag phones as well, telephones you could carry in a briefcase, so perhaps it could. If the women had taken it to pieces, there would have been a recorded message telling him that the number was no longer in service.

He had lost count of the rings when someone picked up the receiver. "Hello," he said. "Hello?" Even to him, it sounded inane.

No one spoke on the other end. As slowly and distinctly as he could, he said, "I am the man whose son you killed, and I am coming to kill you. If you want to explain before I do, you have to do it now."

No voice spoke.

"Very well. You can call me if you want." He gave his number, speaking more slowly and distinctly than ever. "But I won't be here much longer."

> Or at least, they do not speak an English that I can understand. I should have said that I was not hurt badly. Brook bandaged it. I have not seen a doctor. Maybe I should.

He felt the bandage and found it was stiff with blood. Changing it, he decided, would waste a great deal of valuable time, and might actually make things worse.

Brook and I took Jan and the twins into town. Before I woke up this morning, the women killed Brook, outside in the snow.

There was a little stand of black-willow saplings down by the creek. He waded through the snow to them, cut six with his hunting knife, and carried them back to the cabin.

There he cut four sticks, each three times as long as his foot, and tied their ends in pairs with twine. Shorter sticks, notched at both ends, spread them; he tied the short sticks in place with more twine, then bound the crude snowshoes that he had made to his boots, wrapping each boot tightly with a dozen turns.

He was eight or ten yards from the cabin — walking over the snow rather than through it — when his ears caught the faint ringing of his telephone. He returned to the cabin to answer it, leaving the maul he had been carrying on the porch.

"*Mister Bainbridge? I'm Ralph Merton.*" Ralph Merton's voice was sepulchral. "*May I extend my sympathy to you and your loved ones?*"

Emery sighed and sat down, his snowshoed feet necessarily flat on the floor. "Yes, Mister Merton. It was good of you to return my call. I didn't think you'd be in today."

"*I'm afraid I'm not, Mister Bainbridge. I have an — ah — device that lets me call my office at the parlor and get my messages. May I ask if your son was under a doctor's care?*"

"No, Brook was perfectly healthy, as far as I know."

"*A doctor hasn't seen your son?*"

"No one has, except me." After a few seconds' silence, Emery added, "And the woman who killed him. I think there was another woman with her, in which case the second woman would have seen him, too. Not that it matters, I suppose."

Ralph Merton cleared his throat. "*A doctor will have to examine your son and issue a death certificate before we can come, Mister Bainbridge.*"

"Of course. I'd forgotten."

"*If you have a family doctor...?*"

"No," Emery said.

"In that case," Ralph Merton sounded slightly more human, *"I could phone Doctor Ormond for you. He's a young man, very active. He'll be there just as soon as he can get through, I'm sure."*

"Thank you," Emery said, "I'd appreciate that very much."

"I'll do it as soon as I hang up. Would you let us know as soon as you have a death certificate, Mister Bainbridge?"

"Certainly."

"Wonderful. Now, as to the — ah — present arrangements? Is your son indoors?"

"Out in the snow. I put a sheet over his body, but I'd think it would be covered with snow by this time."

"Wonderful. I'll call Doctor Ormond the moment I hang up, Mister Bainbridge. When you've got the death certificate, you can rely on Merton's for everything. You have my sympathy. I have two sons myself."

"Thank you," Emery repeated, and returned the receiver to its cradle.

The cabin still smelled faintly of bacon and coffee. It might not be wise to leave with an empty stomach, was certainly unwise to leave with a low flame under the coffeepot, as he had been about to do. He turned the burner off, got a clean mug (somewhat hampered by his home-made snowshoes), poured himself a cup, sipped, and made himself eat two slices of bacon. Three more, between two slices of rye bread, became a crude sandwich; he stuffed it into a pocket of his mackinaw.

The maul waited beside the front door; he locked the door and started off over the snow a second time. When the snow-covered road had led him nearly out of sight of the cabin, he thought he heard the faint and lonely ringing of his telephone again. Presumably that was Doctor Ormond; Emery shrugged and trudged on.

The front door of the dark cabin seemed very substantial; after examining it, Emery circled around to the back. Drifted snow had risen nearly to the level of the hasp and padlock that secured the door. Positioning his feet as firmly as he could in snowshoes, he swung his maul like a golf club at the hasp. At the third blow, the screws tore loose and the door crashed inward.

Clambering through the violated doorway, he reflected that he did not know who owned this cabin now or what he looked like, that he would not recognize the owner he intended to rob if he were to meet him on the street. Robbery would be easier if only he could imagine himself apologizing and explaining, and offering to pay — though no apology or explanation would be feasible if he succeeded. He would be a vigilante then; and the law, which extended every courtesy to murderers, detested and destroyed anyone who killed or even resisted them. He would have to find out this cabin's address, he decided, and send cash by mail.

Of course, it was possible that there were no guns here, in which case Brook's murderers would presumably kill him too, before he could do any such thing. They might kill him, for that matter, even if —

Before he could complete the thought, he saw the gun safe, a steel cabinet painted to look like wood, with a combination lock. Half a dozen blows from the maul knocked off the knob. Two dozen more so battered the three-sixteenths-inch steel door that he could work the claws of the big ripping hammer he found in a toolbox into the opening. The battered mechanism was steel, the hammer-handle fiberglass; for a few seconds that seemed far longer, he felt certain the handle would break.

A rivet somewhere in the gun safe surrendered with a *pop* — the sweetest sound imaginable. A slight repositioning of the hammer and another heave, and the door ground back.

The gun safe held a twelve-gauge over-and-under shotgun, a sixteen-gauge pump, and a sleek scoped Sako carbine; there were shot shells of both sizes and three boxes of cartridges for the carbine in one of the drawers below the guns.

Emery took out the carbine and threw it to his shoulder; the stock felt a trifle small — the cabin's owner was probably an inch or two shorter — but it handled almost as if it had been customized for him. The bolt opened crisply to display an empty chamber.

He loaded five cartridges and dropped more into a pocket of his mackinaw. Reflecting that the women might well arm themselves from this cabin too, once they discovered that the lock on the rear entrance was broken, he threw the shotgun shells outside into the snow.

From a thick stand of pine on the lake shore, he had as good a view of the canted structure that Aileen had called a ziggurat as the gray daylight and blowing snow permitted: an assemblage of cubical modules tapering to a peak in a series of snow-covered terraces.

Certainly not an aircraft; a spacecraft, perhaps. More likely, a space station. Toward the bottom — or rather toward the ice surrounding it, for there had to be an additional forty feet or more of it submerged in the lake — the modules were noticeably crushed and deformed.

Rising, he stepped clumsily out onto the wind-swept ice. A part of this had been open water when the women had brought Aileen from the ziggurat back to the road — water that was open because the ice had been broken when the ziggurat broke through it, presumably. Yet that open water had been shallow enough for Aileen to wade through, although this mountain lake was deep a few feet from shore; such open water made no sense, though things seemed to have happened like that.

There were no windows that he could see, but several of the modules appeared to have rounded doors or hatches. If the women kept a watch, they might shoot him now as he shuffled slowly over the ice; but they would have to open one of those hatches to do it, and he would do his best to shoot first. He rechecked the Sako's safety. It was off, and he knew there was a round in the chamber. He removed the glove from his right hand and stuffed it into his pocket on top of more rounds and his forgotten sandwich.

He had wanted to die; and if they gut-shot him during the minute or two more that he would require to reach the base of the ziggurat, he would die in agony right here upon the ice.

Well, men did. All Men. Every human being died at last, young or old; and he had already lived longer than many of the people he had known and liked in high school and college. Had lived almost three times as long as Brook.

To his right, the tracks of small feet in large-cleated boots left the ziggurat, tracks not yet obscured by snow and thus very recent. He turned toward them to examine them, then traced them back to a circular hatch whose lower edge was no more than an inch above the ice. It was dogged shut with a simple latch large enough that he manipulated it easily with his gloved left hand.

A wave of warmth caressed his face as he pulled the hatch open and stepped into the ziggurat. Heat! They had heat in here, heat from some device that was still functioning, though Aileen had complained of the cold. In that case, heat from a source they had been able to repair since the crash, perhaps with parts from Jan's Lincoln.

Almost absently, he closed the hatch behind him. Before him was a second hatch; beyond it, misty blue light and dark water. Here, then, was the explanation for the ice on Aileen's boots and pants legs; she had waded in the lake, all right, but here inside the ziggurat, where there seemed to be about a foot of water.

Sitting in the hatchway of what he decided must surely be an airlock, he unlaced his boots and tugged them off, crude snowshoes and all, then tied his bootlaces together. It would be convenient, perhaps, to leave boots and snowshoes here in the airlock, but without either he would be confined to the ziggurat; he could not risk it. He took off his stockings and stuffed them into his boots, rolled up his trouser legs, and stepped barefoot into the dark water, the boots and snowshoes in his left hand, the Sako carbine in his right, gripped like a pistol.

The walls and ceiling of the module were thick with dials and unfamiliar devices, and a tilted cabinet whose corner rose above the water promised more; he paused to look at what seemed to be a simple dial, although its pointer shimmered, vanished, and reappeared, apparently a conveniently massless projection. The first number looked like zero, queerly lettered; the last — he squinted — three hundred, perhaps, although he had never seen a 3 quite like that. Pushing a tiny knob at the base to the left increased the height of the numerals until each stood about five thirty-seconds of an inch; the pointer darkened and now seemed quite solid.

There was a slight noise from overhead, as though someone in a higher module had dropped some small object.

He stiffened and looked quickly around. An open hatch in the wall at the opposite side of the half-crushed module gave access to an interior module that should (if the slant of both floors was the same) be somewhat less deeply submerged. He waded across and went in, followed by the dial he had examined, which slid across the metal wall like a hockey puck, dodging other devices in its path, until he caught it and pushed the knob at its base to the right again.

A ladder in the middle of the new module invited him to climb to the one above; he did, although with difficulty, his boots and snowshoes slung behind his back and half choking him with his own bootlaces, and the carbine awkwardly grasped in his right hand. The ladder (of some white metal that did not quite seem to be aluminum) gave dangerously beneath his weight, but held.

The higher module into which he emerged was almost intact, and colder than the one from which he had just climbed; the deep thrumming of the wind beyond its metal walls could be distinctly heard, though no window or porthole revealed the snow he knew must be racing down the lake with it.

"Fey," he muttered to himself. And then, somewhat more loudly, "Eerie." How frightened poor Aileen must have been!

Curious, he put down his boots and snowshoes and the Sako, drew his knife, and shaved a few bits of metal from the topmost rung of the ladder. They were bright where the sharp steel had sheared them, dull on the older surfaces. Tempted to guess, he suspended judgment. A somewhat bigger piece gouged from the floor appeared to be of the same material; he unbuttoned his mackinaw and deposited all his samples in a shirt pocket.

The rectangular furnishing against one wall looked as if it might be a workbench topped with white plastic. Two objects of unfamiliar shape lay on it; he crossed the cubicle, stepping over featureless cabinets and others dotted with strangely shaped screens.

The larger object that he took from the bench changed its form at his touch, developing smooth jaws whose curving inner surfaces suggested parabolas; the smaller object snapped open, revealing a convoluted diagram too large to have been contained within it. Points of orange and green light wandered aimlessly over the diagram. After a bit of fumbling, he shut the object again and put it in the chest pocket of his mackinaw, following it with several small items of interest that he discovered in the swinging, extensible compartments that seemed to serve as drawers, though they were not quite drawers.

Without warning, the face of an angry giantess occupied the benchtop and her shouting voice filled the module. Gongs and bells sounded behind her, a music grotesquely harmonious amplified to deafening intensity. For a half second that was nearly too long, he watched and listened, mesmerized.

She was five feet behind him, ax raised, when he turned. He lunged at her as the blow fell, and the wooden handle struck his shoulder. Struggling together, they rolled over the canted floor, she a clawing, biting fury, he with a hand — then both — grabbing at the ax handle.

Wrenching the ax away, he swung it clumsily, hitting her elbow with the flat. She bit his cheek, and seemed about to tear his face off. Releasing the ax, he drove his thumbs into her eyes. She spat him out (such was his confused recollection later), sprang to her feet, dashed away —

And was gone.

Half stunned by the suddenness and violence of the fight as well as the deafening clamor from the workbench, he sat up and looked around him. His stolen ax lay near his left hand; the brownish smear on its bright edge was presumably Brook's blood. His own trickled from his cheek, dotting the uneven metal floor. His boots and snowshoes, and the sleek carbine, lay where he had left them.

Slowly he got to his feet, stooped to reclaim his ax, then stood up without it; he could only carry so much, the carbine was a better weapon, and the ax had killed Brook.

He shook himself. These women had killed Brook. The ax was his ax, and nothing more: a good piece of steel mounted on a length of hickory, a thing he had bought for thirty or forty dollars in the hardware store in town — as foolish to kick the stone you tripped over as to blame the ax.

He picked it up and wiped the blade on one rough sleeve of his mackinaw until most of Brook's blood was gone. The carbine was a better weapon, but if he left the ax where it was the women would almost certainly find it and use it against him. If he carried it outside, he might be able to chop a hole in the ice and drop it in; but dropping it into the dark water at the bottom of the ladder would probably be almost as effective and a hundred times quicker. Soon, perhaps very soon, the one who had just tried to kill him might try again.

The clamor of the bench continued unabated. Childishly, he told it to be quiet, and when it did not respond, chopped at the huge, female, shouting, shrieking face again and again, until silence fell as suddenly as a curtain and the benchtop was white plastic once more. Had it been a teaching device, as well as a repair bench? One that could, perhaps, instruct and entertain the mechanic while she worked?

He laid the ax on it, found a handkerchief, and pressed it to his cheek.

Curious again, he strode to the nearest wall and touched it; it was not as cold as he had expected, though it seemed distinctly colder than the air around him. "Insulated," he muttered to himself, "but not insulated enough." Did you need a lot of insulation for space? Perhaps not; astronauts stayed outside in their suits for hours. After a little reflection, he concluded that a space station could lose heat to space only by radiation, and a space station at room temperature would not radiate much. The ziggurat was losing heat by convection and conduction now, and convection was almost always the greatest thief of heat.

Retrieving the ax, he carried it to the floor hatch to drop it in, and saw the dead woman's body floating facedown in the shallow water of the cubicle below.

When he left, the marks of his snowshoes coming in were as sharp as if they had just been made, although it was snowing hard. So much snow had accumulated on the ziggurat's terraces already that it seemed almost a rock rising from the ice; if he were to point it out to someone — to Brook, say, although it would be better perhaps to point it out to someone still alive. To Alayna or Jan, say, or even to Pamela, who had been Brook's mother. If he were to point it out to any of those people and say, *That rock over there is hollow, and there are strange and wonderful blue-lit rooms inside, where little brown women will try to kill you,* they would think him not a liar but a madman, or a drunk. For centuries, unheeded men and women in England and Ireland and any number of other countries had reported a diminutive race living in hills where time ran differently, although in Africa, where skins were black, the little people's had been white.

He had made the mistake of turning the dead woman over, and the memory of her livid face and empty, unfocused eyes came back to haunt him. Someone used to jet-black faces would have called that dead face white, almost certainly. He searched his mind for a term he had read a year or two before.

Members of that small, pale African race were *Yumbos,* the people from the hills who crept out to steal cornmeal. Aileen had said the women had given her only bread to eat. Rations were short, perhaps; or rations were being hoarded against an indefinite stay.

If its hood had not been up, Emery would have missed the Lincoln, thinking it just another snowdrift. Both doors were locked (he had locked them out of habit, it seemed, the night before) and the keys were still in Brook's pocket. He broke a window with the butt of the carbine and retrieved his best cap. Brook had left some possession, a TV or home computer, in the trunk; but he would have to shoot out the lock, and he was heavily loaded already with the loot of the ziggurat.

As he passed the lightless cabin he had burglarized, it occurred to him that he ought to find out whether the shotguns had been taken. After a few moments' thought, he rejected the idea. The other two women (if indeed there were only two left) might or might not have the shotguns, and might or might not have shells for them if they did. They were dangerous in any case, which was all he really needed to know.

His own cabin was as dark. He tried to remember whether he had left a light on, then whether he had even turned one on that morning. He had written his journal — had briefly and crassly recorded Brook's death there — so he must certainly have switched on the lamp on the table. He could not remember switching it off.

Would they shoot through the glass, and the Cyclone fence wire with which he had covered his windows? Or would they poke the barrel through first, providing him some warning? There might have been more shells in the other cabin, in some drawer or cupboard, or even in the pockets of the old field coat that had hung from a nail near the front door.

His own front door appeared to be just as he had left it; there were no footprints in the fresh snow banked against it, and its bright Yale lock was unmarred. Could they pick locks? He circled the cabin, careful to go by way of the north side, past his Jeep and the spot where Brook had died, so that he would not have to look at Brook's corpse. Brook was surely buried under snow by this time, as he had told the undertaker; yet he could not help visualizing Brook's contorted, untenanted face. Brook would never go to Purdue now, never utilize his father's contacts at NASA. Brook was dead, and all the dreams (so many dreams) had died with him. Was it Brook or the dreams he mourned?

The rear door looked as sound as the front, and there were no visible footprints in the snow. No doubt he had turned out the table light automatically when he had finished writing his journal. Everyone did such things.

He unlocked the rear door, went inside, stood the Sako in a corner, and emptied his pockets onto the table. Here was the dial that had tracked him, the tool that displayed a diagram larger than itself, the oblong card that might be a book whose pages turned each time the reader's hand approached it, the octopus of light whose center was a ceramic sphere no bigger than a marble. Here, too, were the seven-sided cube; the beads that strung themselves and certainly were not actually beads, whatever they might be; and the dish in which small objects seemed to melt and from which in a few minutes they vanished. With them, cartridges for the carbine, his checkbook, keys, handkerchief, and pocketknife; and the unappetizing sandwich.

Seeing it and feeling his own disappointment, he realized that he was hungry. He lit the gas under the coffeepot and sat down to consider the matter. Should he eat first? Bandage his cheek? Build a new fire? The cabin was cold, though it seemed almost cozy after the winter storm outside.

Or should he write his journal first — set down a factual account of everything he had seen in the ziggurat while it was still fresh in his mind? The sensible thing would be to build a fire; but that would mean going out for wood and trying not to see Brook. His mind recoiled from the thought.

An accurate, detailed account of the ziggurat might be worth millions to him in a few years, and could be written — begun at least — while his food was cooking and the coffee getting hot. He opened a can of Irish stew, dumped it into a clean saucepan, lit the burner under it, then sat down again and pressed the switch of the small lamp on the table.

No light flooded from its shade.

He stared at it, tightened the bulb and pressed the switch twice more, and chuckled. No wonder the cabin had been dark! Either the bulb had burned out in his absence, or the wires were down.

Standing up, he pulled the switch cord of the overhead fixture. Nothing.

How did the old song go? Something about wires down south that wouldn't stand the strain if it snowed. These wires, his wires, the ones that the country had run out to the lake four years ago, had not. He found one of the kerosene lanterns he had used before the wires came, filled it, and lit it.

If the electrical wires were down, it seemed probable that the telephone was out as well — but when he held it to his ear the receiver emitted a reassuring dial tone. The telephone people, Emery reminded himself, always seemed to maintain their equipment a little bit better than the power company.

His cheek next, and he would have to fetch water from the creek as he had in the old days or melt snow. He filled his teakettle with clean snow from behind the cabin. Washing off the dried blood revealed the marks of teeth and a bruise. You could catch all sorts of diseases from human bites — human mouths were as dirty as monkeys' — but there was not much that he could do about that now. Gingerly, he daubed iodine on the marks, sponged that side of his face with hydrogen peroxide, and put on a thin pad of gauze, noting that Brook had depleted his supply in bandaging his wounded side.

Had the woman who had bitten him and tried to kill him with his own ax been the one who had killed Brook? It seemed likely, unless the women were trading off weapons; and if that was the case, Brook was avenged. Let the sheriff take it from here. He debated the advisability of leading the sheriff's investigator to the ziggurat.

He stirred his Irish stew, and decided it was not quite warm enough yet; he'd get it good and hot, and pour it over bread.

He wasn't quite warm enough either, and was in fact still wearing his mackinaw, here inside the cabin. It was time to confront the firewood problem. When he had done it, he could take off his mackinaw and settle in until the storm let up and the snowplows brought a deputy, Doctor What's-his-name — Ormond — and the undertaker.

Outside, on the south side of the cabin, he made himself stare at the place where Brook lay. To the eye at least, it was just a little mound of snow, differing from other graves only in being white and smooth; the coyote lay at Brook's head, his mound not noticeably smaller or larger. Emery found that oddly comforting. Brook would have gloried in a tame coyote. They would have to be separated before long, though — in four or five days at most, and probably sooner. It seemed a shame. Emery filled his arms with wood and carried it back into the cabin.

Newspapers first, with a splash of kerosene on them. Then kindling, and wood only when the kindling was burning well. He set the kerosene can on the hearth and knelt to unfold, crumple up, and arrange his newspapers.

There were tracks, footprints, in the powdery gray ashes.

He blinked and stared and blinked again. Stood up and got the flashlight and looked once more.

There could be no doubt, although these were not the clear and detailed prints he would have preferred; they were scuffed, confused, and peppered with some black substance. He rubbed a speck of it between his thumb and forefinger. Soot, of course.

The prints of two pairs of boots with large cleats; small boots in both cases, but one pair was slightly smaller than the other, and the smaller pair showed — yes — a little less wear at the heels.

They had come down his chimney. He stood up again and looked around. Nothing seemed to be missing.

They had climbed onto the roof (his Jeep, parked against the north wall of the cabin, would have made that easy) and climbed down the chimney. He could not have managed it, and neither could Brook, if Brook were still alive; but the twins could have done it, and these women were scarcely larger. He should have seen their footprints, but they had no doubt been obscured by blowing snow, and he had taken them for the ones the women had left that morning when they killed Brook. He had been looking mostly for fresh tracks outside the doors in any case.

There had been none. He felt certain of that; no tracks newer than the ones he himself had made that morning. Why, then, had the women climbed up the chimney when they left? Anybody knowledgeable enough to work with the equipment he had seen in the ziggurat would have no difficulty in opening either of his doors from the inside. Climbing down the chimney might not be terribly hard for women the twins' size, but climbing back up, even with a rope, would be a great deal harder. Why do it when you could just walk out?

He covered the ashes with twice the amount of newspaper he had intended to use, and doused every ball of paper liberally with kerosene. Should he light the fire first or wait until he had the carbine in his hand?

The latter seemed safer. He got the carbine and pushed off its safety, clamped it under one arm, then struck a match and tossed it into the fireplace.

The tiny tongue of yellow flame grew to a conflagration in a second or two. There was a metallic clank before something black crashed down into the fire and sprang at him like a cat.

"Stop!" He swung the butt of the Sako at her. "Stop, or I'll shoot!"

A hand from nowhere gripped his ankle. He kicked free, and a second woman rolled from beneath the bunk Brook had slept in — the one he had made up for Jan. Awkwardly, he clubbed the forearm of the woman who had dropped from the chimney with the carbine barrel, kicked at her knee and missed. "Get out! Get out, both of you, or I swear to God —"

They rushed at him not quite as one, the taller first, the smaller brandishing his rifle. Hands snatched at the carbine, nearly jerking it from his grasp; for a moment, he wrestled the taller woman for it.

The sound of the shot was deafening in the closed cabin. The carbine leaped in his hands.

He found that he was staring into her soot-smeared brown face; it crumpled like his newspapers, her eyes squinting, her mouth twisted in a grimace of pain.

The woman behind her screamed and turned away, dropping his rifle and clutching her thigh. Blood seeped from between her fingers.

The taller woman took a step toward him — an involuntary step, perhaps, as her reflexes sought to keep her from falling. She fell forward, the crumpled face smacking the worn boards of the cabin floor, and lay motionless.

The other woman was kneeling, still trying to hold back her blood. She looked at Emery, a look of mingled despair and mute appeal.

"I won't," he said.

He was still holding the carbine that had shot her. It belonged to someone else, and its owner presumably valued it; but none of that seemed to matter anymore. He threw it aside. "That's why I quit hunting deer," he told her almost casually. "I gut-shot a buck and trailed him six miles. When I found him, he looked at me like that."

The big plastic leaf bags he used to carry his garbage to the dump were under the sink. He pulled down quilt, blankets, and sheet, and spread two bags over the rumpled bunk that had been Brook's, scooped her up, and stretched her on them. "You shot me, and now I've shot you. I didn't mean to. Maybe you didn't either — I'd like to think so, anyway."

With his hunting knife, he cut away the sooty cloth around her wound. The skin at the back of her thigh was unbroken, but beneath it he could feel the hard outline of the bullet. "I'm going to cut there and take that out," he told her. "It should be pretty easy, but we'll have to sterilize the knife and the needle-nosed pliers first."

He gave her the rest of his surgical gauze to hold against her wound, and tried to fill his largest cooking pot with water from the sink. "I should have remembered the pump was off," he admitted to her ruefully, and went outside to fill the pot with clean snow.

"I'm going to wash your wound and bandage it before I get the bullet out." He spoke slowly and distinctly as he stepped back in and shut the door, hoping that she understood at least a part of what he was saying. "First, I have to get this water hot enough that I'll be cleaning it, not infecting it." He put the pot of snow on the stove and turned down the burner under his stew.

"Let's see what happened here." He knelt beside the dead woman and examined the ragged, blood-soaked tear at the back of her jacket, then wiped his fingers. It took an effort of will to roll her over; but he did it, keeping his eyes off her face. The hole the bullet had left in the front of the jacket was so small and obscure that he had to verify it by poking his pen through it before he was satisfied.

He stood again, reached into his mackinaw to push the pen into his shirt pocket, and found the fragments of white metal he had taken from the ziggurat. For a moment, he looked from them to the newspapers still blazing in the fireplace. "I'm going to lay some kindling on the fire. Getting chilled won't help you. It could even kill you." Belatedly, he drew up her sheet, the blankets, and the quilt.

"You're not going to die. Are you afraid you will?" He had a feeling that if he talked to her enough, she would begin to understand; that was how children learned to speak, surely. "I'm not going to kill you, and neither is that wound in your leg, or at least I don't think so."

She replied, and he saw that she was trying to smile. He pointed to the dead woman and to her, and shook his head, then arranged kindling on the burning newspapers. The water in his biggest pot was scarcely warm, but the Irish stew was hot. He filled a bowl, and gave it to her with a spoon; she sat up to eat, keeping her left hand under the covers to press the pad of gauze to her leg.

The Voylestown telephone directory provided a home number for Doctor Ormond. Emery pressed it in.

"Hello."

"Doctor Ormond? This is Emery Bainbridge."

"Right. Ralph Merton told me about you. I'll try to get out there just as quick as I can."

"This is about another matter, Doctor. I'm afraid we've had a gun go off by accident."

A slight gasp came over the wire as Ormond drew breath. *"Someone was hit. Is it bad?"*

"Both of us were. I hope not too badly, though. We had a loaded rifle — my hunting rifle — standing against the wall. We were nervous, you understand. We still are. Some people — these people — I'm sorry." In the midst of the fabrication, Brook's death had taken Emery by the throat.

"I know your son's dead, Mister Bainbridge. Ralph told me. He was murdered?"

"Yes, with an ax. My ax. You'll see him, of course. I apologize, Doctor. I don't usually lose control."

"Perfectly normal and healthy, Mister Bainbridge. You don't have to tell me about the shooting if you don't want to. I'm a doctor, not a policeman."

"My rifle fell over and discharged," Emery said. "The bullet creased my side — I don't think that's too bad — and hit..." Looking at the wounded woman, he ransacked his memory for a suitable name. "Hit Tamar in the leg. I should explain that Tamar's an exchange student who's been staying with us." Tamar had been Solomon's sister, and King Solomon's mines had been somewhere around the Horn of Africa. "She's from Aden. She speaks very little English, I'm afraid. I know first aid, and I'm doing all I can, but I thought I ought to call you."

"She's conscious?"

"Oh, yes. She's sitting up and eating right now. The bullet hit the outer part of her thigh. I think it missed the bone. It's still in her leg. It didn't exit."

"This just happened?"

"Ten minutes ago, perhaps."

"Don't give her any more food, she may vomit. Give her water. There's no intestinal wound? No wound in the abdomen?"

"No, in her thigh as I said. About eight inches above the knee."

"Then let her have water, as much as she wants. Has she lost much blood?"

Emery glanced at the dead woman. It would be necessary to account for the stains of her blood as well as Tamar's. "It's not easy to estimate, but I'd say at least a pint. It could be a little more."

"I see, I see." Ormond sounded relieved. *"I'd give her a transfusion if I had her in the hospital, Mister Bainbridge, but she may not really need one. At least, not badly. How much would you say she weighs?"*

He tried to remember the effort involved in lifting her. He had been excited, of course — high on adrenaline. "Between ninety and a hundred pounds, at a guess."

Ormond grunted. *"Small. Small bones? Height?"*

"Yes, very small. My wife calls her petite." The lie had come easily, unlooked for. "I'd say she's about five foot one. Delicate."

"What about you, Mister Bainbridge? Have you lost much blood?"

"Less than half as much as she has, I'd say."

"I see. The question is whether your intestine has been perforated —"

"Not unless it's a lot closer to the skin than I think it is, Doctor. It's just a crease, as I say. I was sitting down, she was standing up. The bullet creased my side and went into her leg."

"I'd wait a bit, just the same, before I ate or drank anything, Mister Bainbridge. You haven't eaten or drunk since it happened?"

"No," Emery lied.

"Good. Wait a bit. Can you call me back in two hours?"

"Certainly. Thank you, Doctor."

"I'll be here, unless there's an emergency here in town, someplace I can get to. If I'm not here, my wife will answer the phone. Have you called the police?"

"Not about this. It's an accident, not a police matter."

"I'm required to report any gunshot wounds I treat. You may want to report it yourself first."

"All right, I can tell the officer who investigates my son's death."

"That's up to you, but I'll have to report it. Is there anything else?"

"I don't think so."

"Do you have any antibiotics? A few capsules left from an old prescription?"

"I don't think so."

"Look. If you find anything you think might be helpful, call me back immediately. Otherwise, in two hours."

THE SECRET HISTORY OF SCIENCE FICTION

"Right. Thank you, Doctor." Emery hung up.

The snow water was boiling on the stove. He turned off the burner, noting that the potful of packed snow had become less than a quarter of a pot of water. "As soon as that cools off a little, I'm going to wash your wound and put a proper bandage on it," he said.

She smiled shyly.

"You're from Aden. It's in Yemen, I believe. Your name is Tamar. Can you say *Tamar?*" He spoke slowly, mouthing the sounds. *"Ta-mar.* You say it." He pointed to her.

"Teye-mahr." She smiled again, not quite so frightened.

"Very good! You'd speak Arabic, I suppose, but I've got a few books here, and if I can dig up a more obscure language for you, we'll use it — too many people know Arabic. I wish that you could tell me," he hesitated, "where you really come from. Or when you come from. Because that's what I've been thinking. That's crazy, isn't it?"

She nodded, though it seemed to him she had not understood.

"You were up in space in that thing. In the ziggurat." He laid splits of wood on the blazing kindling. "I've been thinking about that, too, and you just about had to be. How many were there in your crew?"

Sensing her incomprehension, be pointed to the dead woman, then to the living one, and held up three fingers. "This many? Three? Wait a minute."

He found a blank page in his journal and drew the ziggurat with three stick figures beside it. "This many?" He offered her his journal and the pen.

She shook her head and pointed to her leg with her free hand.

"Yes, of course. You'll need both hands."

He cleaned her wound as thoroughly as he could with Q-Tips and the steaming snow-water, and contrived a dressing from a clean undershirt and the remaining tape. "Now we've got to get the bullet out. I think we ought to for your sake anyway — it will have carried cloth into the wound, maybe even tissue from the other woman."

Breaking the plastic of a disposable razor furnished him with a small but extremely sharp blade. "I'd planned to use the pen blade of my jackknife," he explained as he helped her roll over, "but this will be better."

He cut away what remained of her trouser leg. "It's going to hurt. I wish I had something to give you."

Two shallow incisions revealed an edge of the mushroomed carbine bullet.

He fished the pliers out of the hot water with a fork, gripped the ragged lead in them, and worked the bullet free. Rather to his surprise, she bit her pillow and did not cry out.

"Here it is." He held the bullet where she could see it. "It went through your friend's breastbone, and I think it must have gotten her heart. Then it was deflected downward, most likely by a rib; and hit you. If it hadn't been deflected, it might have missed you altogether. Or, killed you. Lie still, please." He put his hand on her back and felt her shrink from his touch. "I want to mop away the blood and look at that with the flashlight. If this fragmented at all, it didn't fragment much. But if it did, we want to get all of the pieces out, and anything else that doesn't belong." Unable to stop himself, he added, "You're afraid, aren't you? All of you were. Afraid of me, and of Brook too. Probably afraid of all males."

He found fibers in the wound that had probably come from her trousers and extracted them one by one, tore strips from a second undershirt, and tied a folded pad made of what remained of it to the new wound at the back of her thigh. "This is what we had to do before they had tape," he confided as he tightened the last knot. "Wind cloth around the wounded leg or whatever it was. That's why we call them wounds. If you were wounded, you got bandages wound around you — all right, you can turn back over now." He helped her.

The flames were leaping high in the fieldstone fireplace. He took the metal fragments out of his shirt pocket and showed them to her, then pointed toward it.

She shook her head emphatically.

"Do you mean they won't burn, or they will?" He grinned. "I think you mean they will. Let's see."

He tossed the smallest sliver from the ladder into the fire. After a second or two, there was a burst of brilliant light and puff of white smoke. "Magnesium. I thought so."

He moved his chair next to the bunk in which she lay and sat down. "Magnesium's strong and very light, but it burns. They use it in flashbulbs. Your ziggurat, your lander or space station or whatever it is, will burn with a flame hot enough to destroy just about anything, and I'm going to burn it tomorrow morning. It's a terrible waste and I hate to do it, but that's what I'm going to do. You don't understand any of this, do you, Tamar?" He got his journal and drew fire and smoke coming from the ziggurat.

She studied the drawing, her face thoughtful, then nodded.

"I'm glad you didn't throw a fit about that," he told her. "I was afraid you would, but maybe you were under orders not to disturb things back here any more than you could help."

When she did not react to that, he took another leaf bag from under the sink; to his satisfaction, it was large enough to contain the dead woman. "I had to do that before she got stiff," he explained to the living one. "She'll stiffen up in an hour or so. It's probably better if we don't have to look at her, anyway."

Tamar made a quick gesture he did not comprehend, folded her hands, and shut her eyes.

"Tomorrow, before the storm lets up, I'm going to drag her back to your space station and burn it." He was talking mostly for his own benefit, to clarify his thoughts. "That's probably a crime, but it's what I'm going to do. You do what you've got to." He picked up the Sako carbine. "I'm going to clean this and leave it in the other cabin on the way, and throw away the bullet. As far as the sheriff's concerned, my gun shot us both by accident. If I have to, I'll say you bit my face while I was tending your wound. But I won't be able to shave there anyhow, and by the time they get here my beard may cover it."

She motioned toward his journal and pen, and when he gave them to her produced a creditable sketch of the third woman.

"Gone," he said. "She's dead too. I'd stuck my thumbs in her eyes — she tried to kill me — and she ran. She must have fallen through the hole in the floor. The water down there was pretty shallow, so she would've hit hard. I think she drowned."

Tamar pointed to the leaf bag that held the dead woman, then sketched her with equal facility, finishing by crossing out the sketch.

Emery crossed out the women in the ziggurat as well, and returned the journal and the pen to Tamar. "You'll have to live the rest of your life here, I'm afraid, unless they send somebody for you. I don't expect you to like it — not many of us do — but you'll have to do the best you can, just like the rest of us."

Suddenly excited, she pointed to the tiny face of the lion on his pen and hummed, waving the pen like a conductor's baton. It took him a minute or more to identify the tune.

It was "God Save the Queen."

Later, when she was asleep, he telephoned an experimental physicist. "David," he asked softly, "do you remember your old boss? Emery Bainbridge?"

David did.

"I've got something here I want to tell you about, David. First, though, I've got to say I can't tell you where I got it. That's confidential — top secret. You've got to accept that. I won't *ever* be able to tell you. Okay?"

It was.

"This thing is a little dish. It looks almost like an ashtray." There was a penny in the clutter on the table; he picked it up. "I'm going to drop a penny into it. Listen."

The penny fell with a clink.

"After a while, that penny will disappear, David. Right now it looks just a little misted, like it had been outside in the cold, and there was condensation on it."

Emery moved the dish closer to the kerosene lantern. "Now the penny is starting to look sort of silvery. I think most of the copper's gone, and what I'm seeing is the zinc underneath. You can barely make out Lincoln's face."

David spoke.

"I've tried that. Even if you hold the dish upside down and shake it, the penny — or whatever it is — won't fall out, and I'm not about to reach in and try to pull it out."

The crackling voice in the receiver sounded louder than Emery's own.

"I wish you could, David. It's not much bigger than the end of a pencil now, and shrinking quickly. Hold on —

"There. It's gone. I think the dish must boil off atoms or molecules by some cold process. That's the only explanation I've come up with. I suppose we could check that by analyzing samples of air above it, but I don't have the equipment here.

"David, I'm going to start a new company. I'm going to do it on a shoestring, because I don't want to let any backers in. I'll have to use my own money and whatever I can raise on my signature. I know you've got a good job now. They're probably paying you half what you're worth, which is a hell of a lot. But if you'll come in with me, I'll give you ten percent.

"Of course you can think it over. I expect you to. Let's say a week. How's that?"

David spoke at length.

"Yes, here too. The lights are off, as a matter of fact. It's just by the grace of God that the phone still works. I'll be stuck out here — I'm in the cabin — for

THE SECRET HISTORY OF SCIENCE FICTION

another three or four days, probably. Then I'll drive into the city, and we'll talk.

"Certainly you can look at it. You can pick it up and try it out, but not take it back to your lab. You understand, I'm sure."

A last, querulous question.

Emery chuckled. "No, it's not from a magic store, David. I think I might be able to guess where it's actually from, but I'm not going to. Top secret, remember? It's technology way in advance of ours. We're medieval mechanics who've found a paper shredder. We may never be able to make another shredder, but we can learn a hell of a lot from the one we've got."

When he had hung up, he moved his chair back to the side of Tamar's bunk. She was lying on her back, her mouth and eyes closed, the soft sigh of her respiration distinct against the howling of the wind beyond the log walls.

"Jan's going to want to come back," Emery told Tamar, his voice less than a whisper. "She'll try to kiss and make up two weeks to a month after she finds out about the new company, I'd say. I'll have to get our divorce finalized before she hears. They'll back off a little on that property settlement when she gets back to the city, and then I'll sign."

Tamar's left hand lay on the quilt; his found it, stroking the back and fingers with a touch that he hoped was too light to wake her. "Because I don't want Jan anymore. I want you, Tamar, and you're going to need me."

The delicate brown fingers curled about his, though she was still asleep.

"You're learning to trust me, aren't you? Well, you can. I won't hurt you." He fell silent. He had taught the coyote to trust him; and because he had, the coyote had not feared the smell of Man on the cyanide gun. He would have to make certain Tamar understood that all men were not to be trusted — that there were millions of men who would rob and rape and kill her if they could.

"How did you reproduce, up there in our future, Tamar? Asexually? My guess is artificial insemination, with a means of selecting for females. You can tell me whether I'm right, by and by."

He paused, thinking. "Is our future still up there? The one you came from? Or did you change things when you crashed? Or when you killed Brook. Even if it is, maybe you and I can change things with some new technology. Let's try."

Tamar sighed, and seemed to smile in her sleep. He bent over her to kiss her, his lips lightly brushing hers. "Is that why the crash was so bad that you could never get the ziggurat to fly again? Because just by crashing at all, or by killing my son, you destroyed the future you came from?"

In the movies, Emery reflected, people simply stepped into time machines and vanished, to reappear later or earlier at the same spot on Earth's surface, as if Copernicus had never lived. In reality, Earth was moving in the solar system, the solar system in the galaxy, and the galaxy itself in the universe. One would have to travel through space as well as time to jump time in reality.

Somewhere beneath the surface of the lake, the device that permitted such jumps was still functioning, after a fashion. No longer jumping, but influencing the speed with which time passed — the timing of time, as it were. The hours he had spent inside the ziggurat had been but a minute or two outside it; that had to be true, because the prints of his snowshoes coming in had still been sharp when he came out, and Aileen had spent half a day at least there in two hours.

He would burn the ziggurat tomorrow. He would have to, if he were not to lose everything he had taken from it, and be accused of the murder of the dead woman in the leaf bag, too — would have to, if he wished to keep Tamar.

But might not the time device, submerged who could say how deep in the lake, perhaps buried in mud at the bottom as well, survive and continue to function as it did now? Fishermen on Haunted Lake might see the sun stand still, while hours drifted past. Had the device spread itself through time to give the lake its name? He would buy up all the lakeside property, he decided, when the profits of the new company permitted him to.

"We're going to build a new cabin," he told the sleeping Tamar. "A house, really, and a big one, right on the shore there. We'll live in that house, you and me, for a long, long time, and we'll have children."

Very gently, her fingers tightened around his.

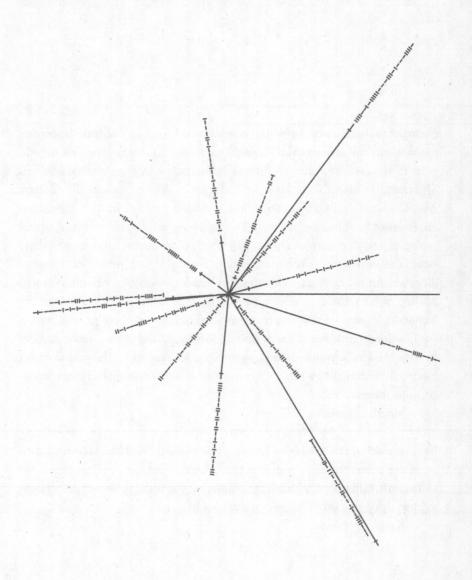

For what makes SF wonderful and complicated is that mix of speculation and the fabulous: SF is both think-fiction and dream-fiction. For the first 60-odd years of the century American fiction was deficient in exactly those qualities SF offered in abundance, however inelegantly. While fabulists like Borges, Abe, Cortázar, and Calvino flourished abroad, a strain of literary puritanism quarantined imaginative and surreal writing from respectability here. Another typical reflex, that anti-intellectualism which dictates that novelists shouldn't pontificate, extrapolate, or theorize, only show and feel, meant the novel of ideas was for many years pretty much the exclusive domain of, um, Norman Mailer. What's more, a reluctance in the humanities to acknowledge the technocratic impulse that was transforming contemporary culture left certain themes untouched. For decades SF filled the gap, and during those decades its writers added characterization, ambiguity, and reflexivity, helping it evolve toward something like a literary maturity, or at least the ability to throw up an occasional masterpiece.

—Jonathan Lethem

My intention was that the book [*Sarah Canary*] would read like a science fiction novel to a science fiction reader, and that it would read like a mainstream novel to a mainstream reader, which is the point, that you bring your own perceptions to everything in a very compelling sort of way.

—Karen Joy Fowler

THE HARDENED CRIMINALS
JONATHAN LETHEM

THE DAY WE went to paint our names on the prison built of hardened criminals was the first time I had ever been there. I'd seen pictures, mostly video footage shot from a helicopter. The huge building was still as a mountain, but the camera was always in motion, as though a single angle were insufficient to convey the truth about the prison.

The overhead footage created two contradictory impressions. The prison was an accomplishment, a monument to human ingenuity, like a dam, or an aircraft carrier. At the same time the prison was a disaster, something imposed by nature on the helpless city, a pit gouged by a meteorite, or a forest-fire scar.

Footage from inside the prison, of the wall, was rare.

Carl Hemphill was my best friend in junior high school. In three years we had graduated together from video games to petty thievery, graffiti, and pot smoking. It was summer now, and we were headed for two different high schools. Knowledge that we would be drawn into separate worlds lurked indefinably in our silences.

Carl involved me in the expedition to the prison wall. He was the gadfly, moving easily between the rebel cliques that rarely attended class, instead spending the school day in the park outside, and those still timid and obedient, like myself. Our group that day included four other boys, two of them older, dropouts from our junior high who were spending their high-school years in the park. For them, I imagined, this was a visit to one of their own possible futures. They must have felt that it was possible they would be inside someday. I was sure that for me it was not that but something else, a glimpse of a repressed past. My father was a part of the prison.

It was secret not only from the rest of our impromptu party, but from Carl, from the entire school. If asked, I said my father had died when I was six, and that I couldn't remember him, didn't know him except in snapshots, anecdotes.

The last part of the lie was true. I knew of my father, but I couldn't remember him.

To reach the devastated section that had been the center of the city we first had to cross or skirt the vast Chinese ghetto, whose edge was normally an absolute limit to our wanderings. In fact, there was a short buffer zone where on warehouse doors our graffiti overlapped with the calligraphs painted by the Chinese gangs. Courage was measured in how deep into this zone your tag still appeared, how often it obliterated the Chinese writing. Carl and one of the older boys were already rattling their spray cans. We would extend our courage today.

The trip was uneventful at first. Our nervous pack moved down side streets and alleys, through the mists of steaming sewers, favoring the commercial zone where we could retreat into some Chinese merchant's shop, and not be isolated in a lot or alley. The older Chinese ignored us, or at most shook their heads. We might as well have been stray dogs. When we came to a block of warehouses or boarded shops we found a suitable door or wall and tagged up, reproducing with spray paint those signature icons we'd laboriously perfected with ballpoint on textbook covers and desktops. Only two or three of us would tag up at a given stop before we panicked and hurried away, spray cans thrust back under our coats. We were hushed, respectful, even as we defaced the territory.

We were at a freeway overpass, through the gang zone, we thought, when they found us. Nine Chinese boys, every one of them verging on manhood the way only two in our party were. Had they been roaming in such a large pack and found us by luck? Or had one or another of them (or even an older Chinese, a shopkeeper perhaps) sighted us earlier and sounded a call to arms? We couldn't know. They closed around us like a noose in the shadow of the overpass, and instantly there was no question of fighting or running. We would wait, petrified. They would deliver a verdict.

It was Carl who stepped forward and told them that we were going to the prison. One of them pushed him back into our group, but the information triggered a fast-paced squabble in Chinese. We listened hard, though we couldn't understand a word.

Finally a question was posed, in English. "Why you going there?"

The oldest in our group, a dropout named Richard, surprised us by answering. "My brother's inside," he said. None of us had known.

He'd volunteered his secret, in the cause of obtaining our passage. I should chime in now with mine. But my father wasn't a living prisoner inside, he was a part of the wall. I didn't speak.

The Chinese gang began moving us along the empty street, nudging us forward with small pushes and scoffing commands. Soon enough, though, these spurs fell away. The older boys became our silent escort, our bodyguards. In that manner we moved out of the ghetto, the zone of warehouses and cobblestone, to the edge of the old downtown.

The office blocks here had been home to squatters before being completely abandoned, and many windows still showed some temporary decoration, ragged curtains, cardboard shutters, an arrangement of broken dolls or toys on the sill. Other windows were knocked out, the frames tarnished by fire.

The Chinese boys slackened around us as the prison tower came into view. One of them pointed at it, and pushed Carl, as though to say, *If that's what you came for, go.* We hurried up, out of the noose of the gang, towards the prison. None of us dared look back to question the gift of our release. Anyway, we were hypnotized by the tower.

The surrounding buildings had been razed so that the prison stood alone on a blasted heath of concrete and earth five blocks wide, scattered with broken glass and twisted tendrils of orange steel. Venturing into this huge clearing out of the narrow streets seemed dangerously stupid, as though we were prey coming from the forest to drink at an exposed water hole. We might not have done it without the gang somewhere at our back. As it was, our steps faltered.

The tower was only ten or eleven stories tall then, but in that cleared space it already seemed tremendous. It stood unfenced, nearly a block wide, and consummately dark and malignant, the uneven surfaces absorbing the glaring winter light. We moved towards it across the concrete. I understand now that it was intended that we be able to approach it, that striking fear in young hearts was the point of the tower, but at the time I marveled that there was nothing between us and the wall of criminals, that no guards or dogs or Klaxons screamed a warning to us to move away.

They'd been broken before being hardened. That was the first shock. I'd envisioned some clever fit, a weaving of limbs, as in an Escher print. It wasn't quite that pretty. Their legs and shoulders had been crushed into the corners of a block, like compacted garbage, and the fit was the simple, inhuman one of right angle flush against right angle. The wall bulged with crumpled limbs, squeezed so tightly together that they resembled a frieze carved in stone, and it was impossible to picture them unfolded, restored. Their heads were tucked inside the prison, so the outer wall was made of backs, buttocks, folded swollen legs, feet back against buttocks, and squared shoulders.

My father had been sentenced to the wall when it was already at least eight stories high, I knew. He wasn't down here, this couldn't be him we defaced. I didn't have to think of him, I told myself. This visit had nothing to do with him.

Almost as one, and still in perfect silence, we reached out to touch the prison. It was as hard as rock but slightly warm. Scars, imperfections in the skin, all had been sealed into an impenetrable surface. We knew the bricks couldn't feel anything, yet it seemed obscene to touch them, to do more than poke once or twice to satisfy our curiosity.

Finally, we required some embarrassment to break the silence. One of the older boys said, "Get your hand off his butt, you faggot."

We laughed, and jostled one another, as the Chinese gang had jostled us, to show that we didn't care. Then the boys with spray cans drew them out.

The prison wall was already thick with graffiti from the ground to a spot perhaps six feet up, where it trailed off. There were just a few patches of flesh or tattoo visible between the trails of paint. A few uncanny tags even floated above reach, where the canvas of petrified flesh was clearer. I suppose some ambitious taggers had stood on others' shoulders, or dragged some kind of makeshift ladder across the wastes.

We weren't going to manage anything like that. But our paint would be the newest, the outermost layer, at least for a while. One by one we tagged up, offering the wall the largest and most elaborated versions of our glyphs. After my turn I stepped up close to watch the paint set, the juicy electric gleam slowly fading to matte on the minutely knobby surface of hardened flesh.

Then I stepped back. From a distance of ten feet our work was already nearly invisible. I squinted into the bright sky and tried to count the floors, thinking of my father. At that height the bricks were indistinguishable. Not that I'd recognize the shape of my father's back or buttocks even up close, or undistorted by the compacting. I couldn't even be sure I'd have recognized his face.

A wind rose. We crossed the plain of concrete, hands in our pockets, into the shelter of the narrow streets, the high ruined offices. We were silent again, our newfound jauntiness expelled with the paint.

They were on us at the same overpass, the moment we came under its shadow. The deferred ambush was delivered now. They knocked us to the ground, displayed knives, took away our paint and money. They took Carl's watch. Each time we stood up they knocked us down again. When they let us go it was one at a time, sent running down the street, back into the Chinese commercial street alone, a display for the shopkeepers and deliverymen, who this time jeered and snickered.

I think we were grateful to them, ultimately. The humiliation justified our never boasting about the trip to the prison wall, our hardly speaking of it back at school or in the park. At the same time, the beating served as an easy repository for the shame we felt, shame that otherwise would attach to our own acts, at the wall.

In fact, we six never congregated again, as though doing so would bring the moment dangerously close. I only once ever again saw the older dropout, the one whose brother was in the prison. It was during a game of touch football in the park, and he went out of his way to bully me.

Carl and I drifted apart soon after entering separate schools. I expected to know him again later. As it happened I missed my chance.

"Stickney," the guard called, and the man on my right stepped forward.

By the time I entered the prison it was thirty-two stories high. I was nineteen and a fool. I'd finished high school, barely, and I was living at home, telling myself I'd apply to the state college, but not doing it. I'd been up all night drinking with the worst of the high-school crowd when I was invited along as an afterthought to what became my downfall, my chance to be a bystander at my own crime. I drove a stolen car as a getaway in a bungled armored-car robbery, and my distinction was that I drove it into the door of a black-and-white, spilling a lieutenant's morning coffee and crushing his left forearm. The trial was suffused with a vague air of embarrassment. The judge didn't mention my father.

"Martell."

I'd arrived in a group of six, driven in an otherwise empty bus through underground passages to the basement of the prison, and ushered from there to a holding area. None of us were there to be hardened and built into the prison. We were all first-time offenders, meant to live inside and be frightened, warned, onto the path of goodness by the plight of the bricks.

"Pierce."

We stood together, our bodies tense with fear, our thoughts desperately narrowed. The fecal odor of the prison alone overwhelmed us. The cries that echoed down, reduced to whispers. The anticipation of the faces in the wall. We turned from each other in shame of letting it show, and we prayed as they processed us and led us away that we would be assigned different cells, different floors, never have to see one another. We would rather face the sure cruelties of the experienced convicts than have our green terror mirrored.

"Deeds, Minkowitz."

I was alone. The man at the desk flicked the papers before him, but he wasn't looking at them. When he said my name it was a question, though by elimination it was the one of which he could have been certain. "Nick Marra?"

"Yes," I said.

"Put him in the hole," he said to the guards who remained.

I must have aged ten years by the time they released me from that dark nightmare, though it only lasted a week. But when the door first slammed I actually felt it was a relief that I was hidden away and alone, after preparing or failing to prepare for cellmates, initiations, territorial conflicts. I cowered down at the middle of the floor, holding my knees to my chest, feeling myself pound like one huge heart. I tried closing my eyes but they insisted on staying open, on trying to make out a hint of form in the swirling blackness. Then I heard the voices.

"Bad son of a bitch. That's all."

"— crazy angles on it, always need to play the crazy angles, that's what Lucky says —"

"C'mere. Closer. Right here, c'mon."

"Don't let him tell you what —"

"Motherfuck."

"— live like a pig in a house you can't ever go in without wanting to kill her I didn't think like that I wasn't a killer in my own mind —"

"Wanna get laid? Wanna get some?"

"Gotta get out of here, talk to missing persons, *man*. They got the answers."

"Henry?"

"Don't listen to him —"

They'd fallen silent for a moment as the guards tossed me into the hole, been stunned into silence perhaps by the rare glimpse of light, but they were never silent again. That was all the bricks were anymore, voices and ears and eyes; the chips that had been jammed into their petrified brains preserved those capacities and nothing more. So they watched and talked, and the ones in the hole just talked. I learned to plug my ears with shreds from my clothing soon enough, but it wasn't sufficient to block out the murmur. Sleeping through the talk was the first skill to master in the prison built from criminals, and I mastered it alone in the dark.

Now I went to the wall and felt the criminals. Their fronts formed a glossy, encrusted whole, hands covering genitals, knees crushed into corners that were flush against blocked shoulders. I flashed on the memory of that long-ago day at the wall. Then my finger slipped into a mouth.

I yelped and pulled it out. I'd felt the teeth grind, hard, and it was only luck that I hadn't really been bitten. The insensate lips hadn't been aware of my finger, of course. The mouth was horribly dry and rough inside, not like living flesh, but it lived in its way, grinding out words without needing to pause for breath. I reached out again, felt the eyes. Useless here in the hole, but they blinked and rolled, as though searching, like mine. The mouth I'd touched went on — "never want to be in Tijuana with nothing to do, be fascinating for about three days and then you'd start to go crazy" — the voice plodding, exhausted.

I'd later see how few of the hardened spoke at all, how many had retreated into themselves, eyes and mouths squeezed shut. There were dead ones, too, here and everywhere in the wall. Living prisoners had killed the most annoying bricks by carving into the stony foreheads and smashing the chips that kept the brain alive. Others had malfunctioned and died on their own. But in the dark the handful of voices seemed hundreds, more than the wall of one room could possibly hold.

"C'mere, I'm over here. Christ."

I found the one that called out.

"What you do, kid?"

"Robbery," I said.

"What you do to get thrown in *here?* Shiv a hack?"

"What?"

"You knife a guard, son?"

I didn't speak. Other voices rattled and groaned around me.

"My name's Jimmy Shand," said the confiding voice. I thought of a man who'd sit on a crate in front of a gas station. "I've been in a few knife situations, I'm not ashamed of that. Why'd you get thrown in the bucket, Peewee?"

"I didn't do anything."

"You're here."

"I didn't do anything. I just got here, on the bus. They put me in here."

"Liar."

"They checked my name and threw me in here."

"Lying motherfucker. Show some respect for your *fucking* elders." He began making a sound with his mummified throat, a staccato crackling noise, as if he wanted to spit at me. I backed away to the middle of the floor and his voice blended into the horrible, chattering mix.

I picked the corner opposite the door and away from the wall for my toilet, and slept huddled against the door. I was woken the next morning by a cold metal tray pressing against the back of my neck as it was shoved through a slot on the door. Light flashed through the gap, blindingly bright to my deprived eyes, then disappeared. The tray slid to the floor, its contents mixing. I ate the meal without knowing what it was.

"Gimme some of that, I hear you eating, you son of a bitch."

"Leave him alone, you constipated turd."

They fed me twice a day, and those incidental shards of light were my hope, my grail. I lived huddled and waiting, quietly masturbating or gnawing my cuticles, sucking precious memories dry by overuse. I quickly stopped answering the voices, and prayed that the bricks in the walls of the ordinary cells were not so malicious and insane. Of course, by the time I was sprung I was a little insane myself.

They dragged me out through a corridor I couldn't see for the ruthless light, and into a concrete shower, where they washed me like I was a dog. Only then was I human enough to be spoken to. "Put these on, Marra." I took the clothes and dressed.

The man waiting in the office they led me to next didn't introduce himself. He didn't have the grey deadness in his features that I already associated with prison staff.

"Sit down."

I sat.

"Your father is Floyd Marra?"

"Why?" I meant to ask why I'd been put in isolation. My voice, stilled for days, came out a croak.

"Leave the questions to us," said the man at the desk, not unkindly. "Your father is Floyd Marra?"

"Yes."

"You need a glass of water? Get him a glass of water, Graham." One of the guards went into the next room and came back with a paper cone filled with water and handed it to me. The man at the desk pursed his lips and watched me intently as I drank.

"You're a smart guy, a high-school graduate," he said.

I nodded and put the paper cone on the desk between us. He reached over and crumpled it into a ball and tossed it under the desk.

"You're going to work for us."

"What?" I still meant to ask *Why*, but he had me confused. A part of me was still in the hole. Maybe some part would be always.

"You want a cigarette?" he said. The guard called Graham was smoking. I did want one, so I nodded. "Give him a cigarette, Graham. There you go."

I smoked, and trembled, and watched the man smile.

"We're putting you in with him. You're going to be our ears, Nick. There's stuff we need to know."

I haven't seen my father since I was six years old, I wanted to say. *I can't remember him.* "What stuff?" I said.

"You don't need to know that now. Just get acquainted, get going on the heart-to-hearts. We'll be in touch. Graham here runs your block. He'll be your regular contact. He'll let me know when you're getting somewhere."

I looked at Graham. Just a guard, a prison heavy. Unlike the man at the desk.

"Your father's near the ceiling, left-hand, beside the upper bunk. You won't have anyone in the cell with you."

"Everybody's going to think you're hot shit, a real killer," said Graham, his first words. The other guard nodded.

"Yes, well," said the man at the desk. "So there shouldn't be any problem. And Nick?"

"Yes?" I'd already covered my new clothes with sweat, though it wasn't hot.

"Don't blow this for us. I trust you understand your options. Here, stub out the coffin nail. You're not looking so good."

I lay in the lower bunk trying not to look at the wall, trying not to make out differences in the double layer of voices, those from inside my cell, from the wall, and those of the other living prisoners that echoed in the corridor beyond. Only when the lights on the block went out did I open my eyes — I was willing myself back into the claustrophobic safety of the hole. But I couldn't sleep.

I crawled into the upper bunk.

"Floyd?" I said.

In the scant light from the corridor I could see the eyes of the wall turn to me. The bodies could have been sculpture, varnished stone, but the shifting eyes and twitching mouths were live, more live than I wanted them to be. The surface was layered with defacements and graffiti, not the massive spray-paint boasts of the exterior, but scratched-in messages, complex engravings. And then there were the smearings, shit or food, I didn't want to know.

"— horseshoe crab, that's a hell of a thing —"

"— the hardest nut in the case —"

"— ran the table, I couldn't miss, man. Guy says John's gonna beat that nigger and I say —"

The ones that cared to have an audience piped up. There were four talkers in the upper part of the wall of my cell. I'd soon get to know them all. Billy Lancing was a black man who talked about his career as a pool hustler, lucid monologues reflecting on his own cleverness and puzzling bitterly over his downfall. Ivan Detbar, who plotted breaks and worried prison hierarchies as though he were not an immobile irrelevant presence on the wall. And John Jones — that was Billy's name for him — who was insane.

The one I noticed now was the one who said, "I'm Floyd."

A muscle in my chest punched upward against my windpipe like a fist. Would meeting him trigger the buried memories? I felt a surge of powerful emotion, but it was virtual emotion. I didn't know this man. I should want to.

I was trembling all over.

My father was missing an eye. From the crushed rim of the socket it looked like it had been pried out of the hardened flesh of the wall, not lost before. And his arms, crossed over his stomach, were scored with tiny marks, as though someone had used him to count their time in the cell. But his one eye lived, examined mine, blinked sadly. "I'm Floyd," he said again.

"My name is Nick," I said, wondering if he'd recognize it and perhaps ask my last name. He couldn't possibly recognize me. After my week in the hole I looked as far from my six-year-old self as I ever would.

"Ever see a horseshit crap, Nick?" said John Jones.

"Shut up, Jones," said Billy Lancing.

"How'd you know my name?" said my father.

"I'm Nick Marra," I said.

"How'd you know my name?" he said again.

"You're a famous fuck," said Ivan Detbar. "Word is going around. 'Floyd is the man around here.' All the young guys want to see if they can take you."

"Horseshoe crab, horseradish fish," said John Jones. "That's a hell of a thing. You ever see —"

"Shut up."

"You're Floyd Marra," I said.

"I'm Floyd."

I turned away, momentarily overcome. My father's plight overwhelmed mine. The starkness of this punishment suddenly was real to me, in a way it hadn't been in the hole. This view out over the bunk and through the bars, into the corridor, was the only view my father had seen since his hardening.

"I'm Nick Marra," I said. "Your son?"

"I don't have a son."

I tried to establish our relationship. He agreed that he'd known a woman named Doris Thayer. That was my mother's name. His pocked mouth tightened and he said, "Tell me about Doris. Remind me of that."

I told him about Doris. He listened intently — or I thought that I could tell he was listening intently. Whenever I paused he asked a question to keep me on the subject. At the end he said only, "I remember the woman you mean." I waited, then he added, "I remember a few different women, you know. Some more trouble than they're worth. Doris I wouldn't mind seeing again."

Awkwardly I said, "Do you remember a boy?"

"Cheesedog crab," said Jones. "That's a good one. They'll nip at you from under the surf—"

"You fucking loony."

"A boy?"

"Yes."

"Yes, there was a boy —" All at once my father began a rambling whispered reminiscence, about *his* father, and about himself as a boy in the Italian ghetto. I leaned back on the bunk and looked away from the wall, towards the bars and the trickle of light from the hallway as he told me of merciless beatings, mysterious nighttime uprootings from one home to another, and abandonment.

Around us the other voices from the wall babbled on, as constant as televisions. I was already learning to tune them out like some natural background — crickets, or surf pounding. I fell asleep to the sound of my father's voice.

The next morning I joined the prison community. The two-tiered cafeteria called Mess Nine was a churning, teeming place, impossible not to see as a hive. Like the offices, it was on the interior, away from the living wall. I escaped notice until I took my full tray out towards the tables.

"Hey, lonely boy."

"He's not lonely, he's a psycho. Aren't you, man?"

"They're afraid of this skinny little guy, he's got to be psycho."

"Who you kill?"

I went and set my tray on an empty corner of a table and sat down, but it didn't stop. The inmate who'd latched on first ("lonely boy") followed and sat behind me.

"He needs his privacy, can't you see?" said someone else. "Let him eat and go back to his psycho cell."

"He can't socialize."

"I'll socialize him."

"He wants to fuck the wall."

"He was up late fucking the wall last night for sure. Little hung over, lonely boy?"

"Fuck the wall," I came to know, was an all-purpose phrase, in constant use either as insult or as an expression of rebellion, of yearning, of ironic futility. The standing assumption was that the dry, corroded mouths would gnaw a man's penis to bloody shreds in a minute. Stories circulated of those who'd tried, of the gangs who'd forced it on a despised victim, of the willing brick somewhere in the wall who encouraged it, got it round the clock and asked for more.

I survived the meal in silence. Better for the moment to truck on my reputation as a dangerous enigma, however slight, than expose it with feeble protests. The fact of my unfair treatment wouldn't inspire any more sympathy from the softer criminals than it had from Jimmy Shand, in the wall of the hole. I shrugged away comments, thrown bits of rolled-up bread, and a hand on my knee, and did more or less as they predicted by retreating to my cell. The television room, the gym, the other common spaces were challenges to be met some other day.

"Shoecat cheese!" said John Jones. "Beefshoe crab!"

"Quiet, you goddamn nut!"

"If you'd seen it you wouldn't laugh," said Jones ominously.

They were expecting me in the upper bunk. My father had been listening to Billy Lancing tell an extended story about a hustle gone bad in western Kansas, while they both fended off Jones.

"Nick Marra," said my father.

I was pleased, thinking he recognized me now. But he only said, "How'd you get sent up, Marra?" It occurred to me that he didn't remember his own last name.

"Robbery," I said. I still responded automatically with the minimum. My crime didn't get more impressive with the addition of details.

"You're in a rush?" said Floyd.

"What?"

"You haven't got all day? You're going somewhere? Tell your story, kid."

We talked. He drew the tale of my crime and arrest out of me. He and Billy Lancing laughed when I got to the collision, and Floyd said, "Fucking cop was probably jerking off with the other hand."

"He'll be telling it that way from now on," said Billy. "Won't you, Nick?"

"What?"

"Too good not to tell it like that," agreed Floyd.

And then he began to talk about his own crimes, and his punishments, before he was hardened. "— hadn't been sent upstairs to get the money he forgot I woulda been killed in that crossfire like he was. 'Course, my reward for living was the judge gave me all the years they wanted to give him —"

"Shit, you weren't more than a boy," said Billy.

"That's right," said Floyd. "Like this one."

"They all look like boys to me. Tell him how you used to work for the prison godfather, man."

"Jesus, that's a long time ago," said Floyd, like he didn't want to get into it. But he was just warming up.

The stories carried me out of myself, though I felt that I'd been warned that embellishments were not only possible, but likely. Floyd and Billy showed me that prison stories were myths, told in individual voices. What mattered were the universals, the telling.

I'd been using my story to show a connection between myself and Floyd, but the bricks were no longer interested in connections. Billy and Floyd might have been accomplices in the job that got them sent up or they might never have met; either way they were now lodged catty-corner to one another forever, and the stories they told wouldn't change it, wouldn't change anything. The stories could only entertain, and get them attention from the living prisoners. Or fail to.

So I let go of trying to make Floyd admit that he was my father, for the moment. It was enough to try to understand it myself, anyway.

On the way back from dinner Lonely Boy and two others followed me back to my cell. The hall was eerily empty, every adjoining cell abandoned. I learned later that such moments were no accident, but well orchestrated. The three men twisted my arms back, pushed me into the toilet stall, out of sight of the wall, and stripped down my pants.

I will not describe them or give them names.

What they did to me took a long time.

Lonely Boy stroked the nape of my neck all through the ordeal. What they did was seldom tender, but he never stopped stroking the small hairs of my neck and talking to me. His words were all contradictions, and I soon stopped listening to them. The sound was the point anyway, a kind of cooing interspersed with jagged accusations. Rhythm and counterpoint; Lonely Boy was teaching me about my loss, my helplessness, and the music of his words was a hook to help me remember. "Little special boy, special one. Why are you the special one? What did they choose you for? They pick you out for me? They send me a lonely one? You supposed to be a spy here, you want to in-fil-trate? How are you gonna spend your lonely days? You gonna think of me? I know I been thinking of you. This whole place is thinking of you. They'll kill you if I don't watch out for you. I'm your pro-tec-tor now —"

When I finally was alone I crawled into the lower bed and turned away from the wall. But I heard Ivan Detbar's voice from above. He was making sure to be heard.

"You don't have to go looking to find the top dog on the floor. The top dog finds you, that's what makes him what he is. He finds you and he's not afraid."

"Shit," said Billy Lancing.

"That's who you've got to take," said Detbar. "You've got to get on him like *thunder*. There is no other way."

"Shit," said Billy again. "First thing I learned in the joint is a virgin asshole's nothing to die for. It doesn't make the list."

Floyd wasn't talking.

Graham and another guard took me into an office the next day, an airless room on the interior.

"Okay," he said.

"Okay what?"

"Are you doing what we told you?"

"Talking? You didn't tell me anything more than that."

"Don't be smart. Your father trusts you?"

"Everything's great," I said. "So why don't you tell me what this is all about?" I didn't bother to tell him that Floyd didn't agree that he was my father, that we hadn't even established that after almost three days of talk.

I was feeling oddly jaunty, having grasped the depths of my situation. And I wasn't all that impressed with Graham on his own. There wasn't anything he could take away from me.

I wanted more information, and I suspected I could get it.

"There's time for that," said Graham.

"I don't think so. All this weird attention is going to get me killed. They think I'm a spy for you, or they don't know what to think. I'm not going to be alive long enough for you to use me."

I wasn't interested in telling him about the previous night. I knew enough to know that it wouldn't improve anything for me. The problem was mine alone. I didn't know whether I was ever going to confront Lonely Boy, but if I did it would be on prison terms. My priority now was to understand what they wanted from me and my father.

"You're exaggerating the situation," said Graham.

"I'm not. Tell me what this is about or I'll ask Floyd."

Graham considered me. I imagine I looked different than when they first dragged me out of the hole. I felt different.

He made a decision. "You'll be brought back here. Don't do anything you'll regret."

The other guard took me back to my cell.

It was a few hours later that I was standing in front of the man who didn't introduce himself the first time. He didn't again. He just told me to sit down. Graham stood to one side.

"Do you know the name Carl Allen Hemphill?" asked the man.

"Carl," I said, surprised.

"Very good. Have you been speaking with your father about him?"

"What? No."

"Did you know he was a prisoner here?"

"No." I'd heard he'd been a prisoner. But I didn't know he'd been a prisoner in the prison built of human bricks. "He's here now?" Somehow I was stupid enough to yearn for an old friend inside the prison, to imagine they were offering a reunion.

"He's dead."

I received it as a small, blunt impact somewhere in my stomach. It was muffled by the distance of years since I'd seen him, and by my situation, my despair. Sure he was dead, I thought. Around here everything is dead. But why tell me?

"So?" I said.

"Listen carefully, Nick. Do you remember the unsuccessful attempt on the President's life?"

"Sure."

"The assassin, the man that was killed — that was your friend."

"Bottmore," I said, confused. "Wasn't his name Richard Bottmore, or Bottomore, something like that —?"

"That wasn't his real name. His real name was Carl Allen Hemphill."

"That's crazy." I'd barely begun to struggle with the notion of Carl's having been here, his death. The assassination was too much, like being suddenly asked to consider the plight of the inhabitants of the moon. The point of this conversation, the answers I was seeking, seemed to whirl further and further out of my reach. "Why would he want to do that?"

"We'd very much like the answer to that question, Nick." He smiled at me as though he'd said enough, and thought I could take it from there. For a blind, hot second I wanted to kill him. Then he spoke again.

"He did his time quietly. Library type, loner. Nothing that was any indication.

He was released five months before the attempt."

"And?"

"He had your cell."

"That's what this is about?" It seemed upside down. Was he saying that my real connection with Floyd didn't interest them, wasn't the point?

"Floyd hasn't said anything?"

"I told you no."

This time it was the man at the desk who lit a cigarette, and he didn't offer me one. I waited while he finished lighting it and arranging it in his mouth.

When he spoke again his expression was oddly distanced. It was the first time I felt I might not have his full attention. "Hemphill left some papers behind. Very little of any value to the investigation so far. But he mentioned your father. It's one of the only interesting leads we have....

"The people I work with believe Hemphill didn't act alone. The more we dig up on his background, the more we glimpse the outlines of a conspiracy. You understand, I can't tell you any more than that or I'll be putting you in danger."

His self-congratulatory reluctance to "put me in danger" put a bad taste in my mouth. "You're crazy," I said. "Floyd doesn't know anything about that."

"Don't try to tell me my job," said the man behind the desk. "Hemphill left a list of targets. This is not a small matter. It was your father's name in his book. Not some other name. Floyd Marra."

I felt an odd stirring of jealousy. Carl and my father, my father who wouldn't admit he was. "Why don't you talk to Floyd yourself?"

"We tried. He played dumb."

What if he is dumb? I wanted to say. I was trying to square these bizarre revelations with the face in the wall, the brick I'd conversed with for the past three days. Trying to picture them questioning Floyd and coming away with the impression that he was holding something vital back.

"Can't bug the wall, either," said Graham. "Fuckers warn each other. Whisper messages."

"The wall doesn't like us, Nick. It doesn't cooperate. Floyd isn't stupid. He knows who he's talking to. That's why we need you."

He doesn't know who he's talking to when he's talking to me, I wanted to say.

"I'll ask him about Carl for you," I said. I knew I would, for my own reasons.

"Crabshit fish," interrupted Jones. "That's a hell of a thing."

It nearly expressed the way I felt. "He almost started a war," I said to Floyd, trying harder to make my point.

"He was a good kid," said Floyd. "Like you."

"Scared like you, too," said Ivan Detbar.

I had to remind myself that the bricks didn't see television or read newspapers, that Floyd hadn't lived in the world for over thirteen years. The President didn't mean anything to him. Not that he did to me.

"How'd you know him?" said Floyd. "Cellmates?"

It was an uncharacteristic question. It acknowledged human connections, or at least it seemed that way to me. Something knotted in my stomach. "We were in school together, junior high," I said. "He was my best friend."

"Best friend," Floyd echoed.

"After you were put here," I said, as though the framework were understood. "Otherwise you would have known him. He was around the house all the time. Mom — Doris — used to —"

"Get this cell rat," said Floyd. "Talking about the past. His mom."

"Hey," said Billy Lancing.

"That's a lot like that other one," said Ivan Detbar. "What's his name, Hemphill. He was a little soft."

"No wonder they were best friends," said Floyd. "Mom. Hey Billy, how's your *mom?*"

"Don't know," said Billy. "Been a while."

Now I hated him, though in fact he'd finally restored me to some family feeling. He'd caused me to miss Doris. She knew who I was, would remember me, and remember Carl as I wanted him remembered, as a boy. And besides, I knew her. I didn't remember my father and I was sick of pretending.

What's more, in hating him I recalled trying to share in Doris' hatred of him, because I'd envied her the strength of the emotion. She'd known Floyd, she had a person to love or hate. I had nothing, I had no father. There was the void of my memories and there was this scarred brick, and between them somewhere a real man had existed, but that real man was forever inaccessible to me. I wanted to go back to Doris, I wanted the chance to tell her that I hated him now, too. I felt that somehow I'd failed her in that.

I was crying, and the bricks ignored me, I thought.

"Hemphill sure got screwed, didn't he?" said Billy.

"The kid couldn't take this place," said Ivan Detbar.

"But he was a good kid," said Floyd.

"Wasn't his fault, something tripped him up bad," said Billy. "Something went down."

Through my haze of emotions — jealousy, bitterness, desolation — I realized they were offering me warnings, and perhaps some sort of apology.

And the talk of Carl made me remember my assignment.

"You guys talked a lot?" I said.

"I guess," said Floyd.

"Nothing else to do," said Billy. " 'Less I'm missing something. Floyd, you been holding out on me?"

"Heh," said Floyd.

"There wasn't any talk about what he was going to do when he got out?" I asked. My task might only be an absurd joke, but at the moment it was all I had.

"I don't hear you talking about what you're going to do when you get out, and you're only doing a three-year stretch," said my father.

"What?"

"That's the last thing you want to think about now, isn't it? Maybe when you get a little closer."

"I don't understand."

"That poor kid was here at the start of ten years," said Floyd. "Hey, Billy. You ever meet a guy at the start of a long stretch wants to talk about what he's gonna do when he *finishes?*"

"Not unless he's planning a break, like Detbar here. Hah."

"I'll do it, too," said Detbar. "And I ain't taking you with me, you motherfucker."

"But he got out," I said, confused. "Hemphill, I mean."

"Yeah, but all of a sudden," said Floyd. "He *thought* he was doing ten years."

"Why all of a sudden?" I said. "What happened?"

"Somebody gave him a deal. They had a job for him. Let him out if he did it."

"Yeah, but that just made him sorrier," said Billy. "He was one screwed-up cat."

"He was okay," said Floyd. "He just had to tough it out. Like Marra here."

It was as disconcerting to hear him use the last name as though it had nothing to do with him as it was to be linked again and again with Carl. The dead grown-up would-be assassin, and the lost child friend. It drew me out of my little investigation, and back to my own concerns.

I couldn't keep from trying again. "Floyd?" What I wanted was so absurdly simple.

"Uh?"

"I want to talk to you about Doris Thayer," I said. I wasn't going to use the word *mom* again soon.

"Tell me about her again."

"She was my mother, Floyd."

"I felt that way about her too," said Floyd. "Like a mother. She really was something." He wasn't being funny this time. His tone was introspective. It meant something to him, just not what I wanted it to mean.

"She was really my mother, Floyd. And you're my father."

"I'm nobody's father, Marra. What do I look like?"

That wasn't a question I wanted to answer. I'd learned that I didn't even want to watch his one eye blink, his lips work to form words. I always turned slightly away. If I concentrated on his voice he seemed more human, more real.

"Come on, Marra, tell me what you see," said Floyd.

I realized the face of the brick was creeping into my patched-together scraps of memory. For years I'd tried to imagine him in the house, to play back some buried images of him visiting, or with Doris. Now when I tried I saw the empty socket, the flattened skull, the hideous naked stone.

I swallowed hard, gathering my nerve, and pressed on. "How long ago did you come here?"

"Been a million years."

"Million years ago the dogshit bird ruled the earth," said John Jones. "Crawled outta the water, all over the place. It's *evolutionary.*"

"Like another life to me," said Floyd, ignoring him. His voice contained an element of yearning. I told myself I was getting somewhere.

"Okay," I said. "But in that other life, could you have been somebody's father?"

A shadow fell across the floor of my cell. I looked up. Lonely Boy was leaning against the bars, hanging there with his arms up, his big fingers inside and in the light, the rest of him in darkness.

"Looking for daddy?" he said.

The next day I told Graham I wanted another meeting. The man who never introduced himself was ready later that afternoon. I was getting the feeling he had a lot of time on his hands.

His expression was boredom concealing disquiet, or else the reverse. "Talk," he said.

"Floyd doesn't really know anything. He's never even heard of the assassination attempt. I can't even get him to focus on that."

"That's hard to believe, under the circumstances."

"Well, start believing. You have to understand, Floyd doesn't think about things that aren't right in front of him anymore. His world is — small. Immediate." Suddenly I felt that I was betraying my father, describing him like an autistic child, when what I meant was, *He's been built into a wall and he doesn't even know who I am.*

It didn't seem right that I should have to explain it to the men responsible. But the man behind the desk still inspired in me a queasy mixture of defiance and servility. All I said was, "I think I might have something for you anyway."

"Ah," he said. "Please."

I was going to tell him that he was right, there had been a conspiracy, and that Carl had been recruited from inside. An insipid fantasy ran in my mind, that he would jump up and clap me on my back, tell me I'd cracked the case, deputize me, free me. But as I opened my mouth to speak the man across the desk leaned forward, somehow too pleased already, and I stopped. I thought involuntarily: *What I'm about to tell him, he knows.* And I didn't speak.

I have often wondered if I saved my own life in that moment. The irony is that I nearly threw it away in the next. Or rather, caused it to be thrown.

"Yes?" he said. "You were going to say?"

"Floyd remembered Carl talking about some — group," I said, inventing. "Some kind of underground organization."

He raised his eyebrows at this. It was not what he was expecting. It seemed to take him a moment to find his voice. "Tell me about this — organization."

"They're called the Horseshoe Crabs," I said. "I don't really know more than that. Floyd just isn't interested in politics, I guess. But anyway, that should be enough to get you started."

"The Horseshoe Crabs."

"Yes."

"An *in-prison* underground?"

"No," I said quickly. "Something from before." I was a miserable liar.

I must have been looking at the floor. I didn't even see him leave his seat and come around the desk, let alone spot the fury accumulating in his voice or expression. He was just suddenly on me, my collar in his hand, his face an inch from mine. "You're fucking with me, Nick," he said.

"No."

"I can tell. You think I can't tell when I'm being fucked by an *amateur?*" He shoved me to the floor. I knocked over a trash basket as I fell. I looked at Graham. He just stood impassively watching, a foot away but clearly beyond appeal.

"What are the Horseshoe Crabs?" said the man. "Is Floyd a Horseshoe Crab?"

"He just said the name, that Carl used it. That's all I know."

"Stand up."

I got to my feet, but my knees were trembling. Rightly, since he immediately knocked me to the floor again.

Then Graham spoke. "Not here."

"Fine," said the man, through gritted teeth. "Upstairs."

They took me in an elevator up to the top floor, hustling me ahead of them roughly, making a point now. As they ran me through corridors, Graham pushing ahead and opening gates, living inmates jeered maliciously from their cells. They made a kind of wall themselves, fixed in place and useless to me as I went by. Graham unlocked the last door and we went up a stairway to the roof and burst out into the astonishing light of the sky. It was white, grey really, but absolutely blank and endless. It was the first sky I'd seen in two weeks. I thought of how Floyd hadn't seen it in thirteen years, but I was too scared to be outraged for him.

"Grab him," the man said to Graham. "Don't let him do it himself."

The roof was a worksite; they were always adding another level, stacking newly hardened bricks to form another floor. The workers were the first-timers, the still-soft. But there was nobody here now, just the disarray of discontinued work. A heap of thin steel dowels, waiting to be run through the stilled bodies, plastic barrels of solvent for fusing their side surfaces together into a wall. In the middle of the roof was a pallet of new human bricks, maybe twenty-five or thirty of them, under a battened-down tarp. In the roar of the wind I could still just make out the sound of their keening.

Graham and the man from behind the desk took me by my arms and walked me to the nearest edge. Crossing that open distance made me know again how huge the prison was. I kept my head down, protecting my ears from the cold whistle of the wind and my eyes from the empty sky.

The new story was two bricks high at the edge we reached. The glossy top side of the bricks had been grooved and torn with metal rasps, so the solvent would take. Graham held me by my arms and bent me over the short wall, just as Lonely Boy and the others had bent me over the toilet.

"Take a look," said the man.

"Looks like rain to me," said one of the nearby bricks chattily.

My view was split by a false horizon: the dark mass of the sheer face of the prison receding earthward below the dividing line, the empty acres of concrete and broken glass above. From the thirty-two-story height the ground sparkled like the sea viewed from an airplane.

Graham jammed me harder against the rough top of the bricks, and tilted me further towards the edge. I grunted, and watched a glob of my own drool tumble into the void.

"I hate to be fucked with," said the man. "I don't have time for that."

I made a sound that wasn't a word.

"Maybe we'll chop your father out of the wall and throw you both off," said the man. "See which hits the ground first."

I managed to think how odd it was to threaten a man in prison with the open air, the ultimate freedom. It was the reverse of the hole, all space and light. But it served their purposes just as well. Something I reflected on later was that just about anything could be turned to serve purposes like these.

"What are the Horseshoe Crabs?" he said.

I'd already forgotten how this all resulted from my idiotic gambit. "There are no Horseshoe Crabs," I gasped.

"You're lying to me."

"No."

"Throw him over, Graham."

Graham pressed me disastrous inches closer. My shirt and some of the skin underneath caught on the shredded upper surface of the wall.

"You're not telling me why I should spare you," said the man.

"What?" I said, gulping at the cold wind.

"You're not telling me why I should spare you."

"I'll tell you everything you want to know," I said.

Graham pulled me back.

"Are you lying to me again?" said the man.

"No. Let me talk to Floyd. I'll find out whatever you want."

"I want to know about the Horseshoe Crabs."

"Yes."

"I want to know anything he knows. You're my listening device, direct from him to me. I don't want any more noise in the signal. Do you understand?"

I nodded.

"Take him back, Graham. I'm going to have a cigarette."

Graham took me to my cell. I climbed into the top bunk and lay still until my trembling faded.

"The kid's getting ready to make his move," said Ivan Detbar.

"You think so?" said Floyd.

It was dinner hour. Inmates were shambling through the corridor towards Mess Nine.

My thoughts were black, but I had a small idea.

It seemed to me that one of my problems might solve the other. The way Graham had said "not here" to the man behind the desk made me think that the man's influence might not extend very far within the prison, however extensive and malignant it was in the world at large. I had never seen him command anyone besides Graham. Graham was in charge of my block, but the trip upstairs had made me remember the immensity of the prison.

My idea was simple, but it required physical bravery, not my specialty to this point. The cafeteria was the right place for it. With so many others at hand I might survive.

"Floyd," I said.

"Yeah?"

"What if you weren't going to see me anymore? Would that change anything?"

"What are you getting at?"

"Anything you'd want to say?"

"Take care, nice knowing ya," he said.

"How about 'Don't do anything I wouldn't do'?" said Billy Lancing.

Floyd and Billy laughed at that. I let them laugh. When they were done I said, "One last question, Floyd."

"Shoot."

I'd thought I was losing interest, growing numb. I guess in the longer term I was. But I was still pressing him. "Did you know your father?"

"You're asking me — what? My old man?" Floyd's eye rolled, like he thought his father had appeared somewhere in the cell.

"You knew him?"

"If I could get my hands around the neck of that son of a bitch —"

"You talk big, Floyd," said Ivan. "What about when you had your chance?"

"Fuck you," said Floyd. "I was a kid. I barely knew that motherfucker."

"The Motherfuck Dog," said John Jones. "He lives under the house —"

The tears were on my face again, and without choosing to do it I was beating my fist against the wall, against Floyd's petrified body. Once, twice, then it was too painful to go on. And I don't think he noticed.

I got down from the bunk. I had another place for the fury to go, a place where it might have a use. I only had to get myself to that place before I thought twice.

Dinner was meatballs and mashed potatoes covered with steaming greyish gravy. I took two cups of black coffee aboard my tray as well. I turned out of the food line and located Lonely Boy, sitting with his seconds at a table on the far side of the crowded room. Before I could think again, I headed for them.

"Hey, lonely boy, you want to sit?"

I flung the tray so it spilled on all three of them. I was counting on that to slow the other two; all my attention would be on Lonely Boy. I knew I'd lose any fight that was a contest of strategy or guile, lose it badly, that my only chance was blind, instantaneous rage. So I went in with my hands instead of picking up a fork or some other weapon. For my plan to work, Lonely Boy had to live. With what I knew was in me to unleash, his life seemed as much at risk as mine.

They pulled us apart before very long, but I'd already gotten my hands around his throat and begun hitting his head against the table, rhythmic revenge. One of his seconds had taken a tray and lashed open my scalp with it, and my blood was running into my opponent's eyes, and my own, and mixing with the coffee on the table. The voices around us roared.

Back in the hole for the night that followed, I screamed, bled, shat. I shoved the morning tray back out as it was coming through the slot. I attacked the men that came for me. How much was pretense I can't really say. Maybe none.

When they got me into the shower I calmed down somewhat. I didn't feel human, though. I felt mercenary and cold, like frozen acid.

They put six stitches in my scalp in the prison hospital and led me to another, larger office, with more file cabinets and chairs, more ashtrays. Graham was there, with two other men. One of the others did the talking.

Those others were my margin, I knew. My glint of light.

The one who spoke asked me about the fight.

"If I'm put back in the block with him one of us will have to die," I said simply.

I could see a look of satisfaction on the face of the other of the men, not Graham. I assumed Lonely Boy had been trouble to this man before. I assumed, too, that I'd done damage. I smiled back at this man, and I smiled at Graham.

Graham kept his face impassive.

The man who was talking explained to me that Lonely Boy was an established presence on Block Nine, that he had more support than might have been apparent — did I understand that?

"Move me upstairs," I said. "As far away as possible. If I see him again I'll have to kill him."

The one who was talking told me that I'd likely find men like Lonely Boy wherever I went in the prison.

Nobody said the word *rape*.

"I'll never be in this position again," I said. "I can promise you that. Nobody will ever be permitted to make the mistake he made."

The man raised his eyebrows. The other one, the smiling one, smiled. Graham sat.

"Just move me," I said.

"We don't let prisoners make our decisions for us, Mr. Marra," said Graham.

"Your unusual handling put me at a disadvantage in the situation, Mr. Graham. If you keep me on Block Nine I intend to be treated like the other prisoners."

The man who had been talking turned and looked at Graham, and in that moment I knew I would be transferred.

"Unusual handling?" said the man who'd smiled. He'd directed the question at me, but it was Graham who spoke.

"He presents unique difficulties," he said. "His father is in the prison. In the wall. I thought it was better to address it directly."

I took a leaf from Floyd's book. It was pure improvisation, but my skills at lying were improving rapidly. "He isn't my father."

The smiling man made an inquiring face.

"He knew my mother, I guess. But she told me later he wasn't my father. He's just some guy. Just another brick to me."

The smiling man smiled at Graham. "This doesn't seem to me to require special treatment."

"I had the impression —" Graham began.

The smiling man laughed. "Apparently mistaken, Graham."

Graham laughed along.

Graham never spoke to me again, though I lived in fear of some reprisal. I would see him moving through the corridors with the men in charge of my block or other blocks and think he was about to point a finger at me and say, *"Marra, come with me,"* but he never did. I don't think he cared enormously. It might have been some relief to him to be able to say to the man behind the desk that I'd slipped away. Graham was a man with a difficult job and dealing with the man behind the desk was clearly not an easy part of it.

I never saw the man behind the desk again.

He was a sadist and an idiot. The two were not mutually exclusive, I understood, after that day on the roof. The agency or service he worked for had assigned him the task of tracing a conspiracy he was a member of himself. Sending me in to question my father was just ritual activity. He might have been curious to know whether Hemphill had been talking about what was happening to him, but he wasn't worried. He hadn't even bothered to wire the cell, or he'd have known how I came up with "horseshoe crabs." Until I'd panicked him, triggered his paranoia with that bluff, he was just making a show of activity by torturing me. And keeping himself entertained, I suppose, killing time on an absurd assignment.

The only deeper explanation was that I'd become a kind of stand-in for Carl, the other young prisoner they'd had in their grasp. He'd been theirs, for a time, and then he twisted loose, became history. I don't know if what he did was a disastrous perversion of their plans, or whether it served them, but I sensed that either way they experienced a loss. The mechanism of control was more precious than any outcome. I'd become the new instrument, the new site where control was enacted. Until I broke the spell.

From then on, I became another prisoner in a cell, living out my hours, protecting my back. I spent days in the weight room, years in the television room. I told lies to make the time pass. The rest of my story was no different from anyone else's, so in the telling I made it as different as I could. I learned to use the phrase "fuck the wall," though like a million other cowards, I never tried it.

My thoughts rarely turned to Carl. I hadn't learned much about the tortured prisoner and would-be assassin, and I didn't have any interest in trying to learn more. The image of my thirteen-year-old friend had been obliterated without anything taking its place. I didn't object. He was just a ghost now, and there were plenty of more substantial ghosts available, in the wall.

I didn't see my father again until a week before I left the prison, when I was granted a minute in my old cell.

Billy Lancing was still the same. He looked me over when I came in and said, "Marra?"

"Yeah."

"I remember you. Where'd you go?"

"Upstairs."

"Well, I remember you."

I climbed up into the top bunk.

Ivan Detbar was dead, his eyes stilled. I recognized it instantly by now. John Jones was still raving, but more quietly, not looking for an audience anymore.

My father was still alive, if that's the word for it, but someone had pried out his other eye, splintering the stony bridge of his nose in the process.

His mouth was moving, but nothing was coming out.

"Floyd's not good," said Billy.

I went over and put my hand on him. He couldn't feel it, of course. I was touching my father, but it didn't matter to either of us.

I wondered if it had been Graham or the man behind the desk who'd removed the eye, in some offhand act of revenge. It could as easily have been a living prisoner, someone in that top bunk who'd taken offense at too much attention, or a joke.

Floyd, like Billy, had listened fairly well. That was the only real difference between him and the hundreds of other bricks I'd met by that time. What had happened between him and Carl was absurdly simple, but the man behind the desk was puzzled, because it wasn't supposed to happen to an assassin-in-training, or to a human brick. They'd become friends. Floyd had expressed his dim, blundering sympathy, and Carl had listened, and been drawn out of his fear.

Which was more or less all Floyd had done with me.

Had he been pretending not to know me, pretending not to make the connection between my stories, my family history, and his? I'd stopped wondering pretty quickly. I had more immediate problems, which was part of his point, I think, if he was making one.

Bricks only face one direction.

I let my hand slip from the wall, and left the cell.

…what I have loved most about science fiction is the short form. The short form fits science fiction in a beautiful way, and lends itself to the kind of science fiction I like, which is a cerebral, unsettling kind of fiction — a fiction that turns things you know into things that are strange, and turns things that are strange into things you are comfortable with. This kind of head-centered fiction is easier to accomplish in the short form. Novels for me are more about emotions and less about revelations.

    —Karen Joy Fowler

Realism is nonsense when you think of it. I mean, there is no such thing. Nobody writes realism, if realism is defined as "fiction that is objective and real and not distorted, but is just, you know, normal".… The nature of all fiction is distortion, exaggeration, and compression. So what we call realism is just distorting, exaggerating, and compressing with the intention of alluding to, or handwaving at — taking advantage of our fondness for — what I've heard called "consensus reality" — the sort of lazy, agreed upon "way things are."

    —George Saunders

STANDING ROOM ONLY
KAREN JOY FOWLER

ON GOOD FRIDAY 1865, Washington, D.C., was crowded with tourists and revelers. Even Willard's, which claimed to be the largest hotel in the country, with room for 1200 guests, had been booked to capacity. Its lobbies and sitting rooms were hot with bodies. Gas light hissed from golden chandeliers, spilled over the doormen's uniforms of black and maroon. Many of the revelers were women. In 1865, women were admired for their stoutness and went anywhere they could fit their hoop skirts. The women at Willard's wore garishly colored dresses with enormous skirts and resembled great inverted tulips. The men were in swallowtail coats.

Outside it was almost spring. The forsythia bloomed, dusting the city with yellow. Weeds leapt up in the public parks; the roads melted to mud. Pigs roamed like dogs about the city, and dead cats by the dozens floated in the sewers and perfumed the rooms of the White House itself.

The Metropolitan Hotel contained an especially rowdy group of celebrants from Baltimore, who passed the night of April 13 toasting everything under the sun. They resurrected on the morning of the 14th, pale and spent, surrounded by broken glass and sporting bruises they couldn't remember getting.

It was the last day of Lent. The war was officially over, except for Joseph Johnston's Confederate army and some action out West. The citizens of Washington, D.C. still began each morning reading the daily death list. If anything, this task had taken on an added urgency. To lose someone you loved now, with the rest of the city madly, if grimly, celebrating, would be unendurable.

The guests in Mary Surratt's boarding house began the day with a breakfast of steak, eggs and ham, oysters, grits and whiskey. Mary's seventeen-year-old daughter, Anna, was in love with John Wilkes Booth. She had a picture of him hidden in the sitting room, behind a lithograph entitled "Morning, Noon, and Night." She helped her mother clear the table and she noticed with a sharp and unreasonable disapproval that one of the two new boarders, one of the men who only last night had been given a room, was staring at her mother.

Mary Surratt was neither a pretty women, nor a clever one, nor was she young. Anna was too much of a romantic, too star- and stage-struck, to approve. It was one thing to lie awake at night in her attic bedroom, thinking of JW. It was another to imagine her mother playing any part in such feelings.

Anna's brother John once told her that five years ago a woman named Henrietta Irving had tried to stab Booth with a knife. Failing, she'd thrust the blade into her own chest instead. He seemed to be under the impression that this story would bring Anna to her senses. It had, as anyone could have predicted, the opposite effect. Anna had also heard rumors that Booth kept a woman in a house of prostitution near the White House. And once she had seen a piece of paper on which Booth had been composing a poem. You could make out the final version:

> Now in this hour that we part,
> I will ask to be forgotten never
> But, in thy pure and guileless heart,
> Consider me thy friend dear Eva.

Anna would sit in the parlor while her mother dozed and pretend she was the first of these women, and if she tired of that, she would sometimes dare to pretend she was the second, but most often she liked to imagine herself the third.

Flirtations were common and serious, and the women in Washington worked hard at them. A war in the distance always provides a rich context of desperation, while at the same time granting women a bit of extra freedom. They might quite enjoy it, if the price they paid were anything but their sons.

The new men had hardly touched their food, cutting away the fatty parts of the meat and leaving them in a glistening greasy wasteful pile. They'd finished the whiskey, but made faces while they drank. Anna had resented the compliment of their eyes and, paradoxically, now resented the insult of their plates. Her mother set a good table.

In fact, Anna did not like them and hoped they would not be staying. She had often seen men outside the Surratt boarding house lately, men who busied themselves in unpersuasive activities when she passed them. She connected these new men to those, and she was perspicacious enough to blame their boarder

Louis Wiechman for the lot of them, without ever knowing the extent to which she was right. She had lived for the past year in a Confederate household in the heart of Washington. Everyone around her had secrets. She had grown quite used to this.

Wiechman was a permanent guest at the Surratt boarding house. He was a fat, friendly man who worked in the office of the Commissary General of Prisons and shared John Surratt's bedroom. Secrets were what Wiechman traded in. He provided John, who was a courier for the Confederacy, with substance for his covert messages south. But then Wiechman had also, on a whim, sometime in March, told the clerks in the office that a Secesh plot was being hatched against the President in the very house where he roomed.

It created more interest than he had anticipated. He was called into the office of Captain McDavitt and interviewed at length. As a result, the Surratt boarding house was under surveillance from March through April, although, it is an odd fact that no records of the surveillance or the interview could be found later.

Anna would surely have enjoyed knowing this. She liked attention as much as most young girls. And this was the backdrop of a romance. Instead, all she could see was that something was up and that her pious, simple mother was part of it.

The new guest, the one who talked the most, spoke with a strange lisp and Anna didn't like this either. She stepped smoothly between the men to pick up their plates. She used the excuse of a letter from her brother to go out directly after breakfast. "Mama," she said. "I'll just take John's letter to poor Miss Ward."

Just as her brother enjoyed discouraging her own romantic inclinations, she made it her business to discourage the affections of Miss Ward with regard to him. Calling on Miss Ward with the letter would look like a kindness, but it would make the point that Miss Ward had not gotten a letter herself.

Besides, Booth was in town. If Anna was outside, she might see him again.

The thirteenth had been beautiful, but the weather on the fourteenth was equal parts mud and wind. The wind blew bits of Anna's hair loose and tangled them up with the fringe of her shawl. Around the Treasury Building she stopped to watch a carriage sunk in the mud all the way up to the axle. The horses, a matched pair of blacks, were rescued first. Then planks were laid across the top of the mud for the occupants. They debarked, a man and a woman, the woman unfashionably thin and laughing giddily as with every unsteady step her hoop swung and unbalanced her, first this way and then that. She clutched the man's arm and screamed when a pig burrowed past her, then laughed again at even higher pitch. The man stumbled into the mire when she grabbed him, and this made her laugh, too. The man's clothing was very fine, although now quite speckled with mud. A crowd gathered to watch the woman — the attention made her helpless with laughter.

The war had ended, Anna thought, and everyone had gone simultaneously mad. She was not the only one to think so. It was the subject of newspaper editorials, of barroom speeches. "The city is disorderly with men who are celebrating too hilariously," the president's day guard, William Crook, had written just yesterday. The sun came out, but only in a perfunctory, pale fashion.

Her visit to Miss Ward was spoiled by the fact that John had sent a letter there as well. Miss Ward obviously enjoyed telling Anna so. She was very near-sighted and she held the letter right up to her eyes to read it. John had recently fled to Canada. With the war over, there was every reason to expect he would come home, even if neither letter said so.

There was more news, and Miss Ward preened while she delivered it. "Bessie Hale is being taken to Spain. Much against her will," Miss Ward said. Bessie was the daughter of ex-senator John P. Hale. Her father hoped that a change of scenery would help pretty Miss Bessie conquer her infatuation for John Wilkes Booth. Miss Ward, whom no one including Anna's brother thought was pretty, was laughing at her. "Mr. Hale does not want an actor in the family," Miss Ward said, and Anna regretted the generous impulse that had sent her all the way across town on such a gloomy day.

"Wilkes Booth is back in Washington," Miss Ward finished, and Anna was at least able to say that she knew this, he had called on them only yesterday. She left the Wards with the barest of good-byes.

Louis Wiechman passed her on the street, stopping for a courteous greeting, although they had just seen each other at breakfast. It was now about ten A.M. Wiechman was on his way to church. Among the many secrets he knew was Anna's. "I saw John Wilkes Booth in the barbershop this morning," he told her. "With a crowd watching his every move."

Anna raised her head. "Mr. Booth is a famous thespian. Naturally people admire him."

She flattered herself that she knew JW a little better than these idolaters did. The last time her brother had brought Booth home, he'd followed Anna out to the kitchen. She'd had her back to the door, washing the plates. Suddenly she could feel that he was there. How could she have known that? The back of her neck grew hot, and when she turned, sure enough, there he was, leaning against the doorjamb, studying his nails.

"Do you believe our fates are already written?" Booth asked her. He stepped into the kitchen. "I had my palm read once by a gypsy. She said I would come to a bad end. She said it was the worst palm she had ever seen." He held his hand out for her to take. "She said she wished she hadn't even seen it," he whispered, and then he drew back quickly as her mother entered, before she could bend over the hand herself, reassure him with a different reading, before she could even touch him.

"JW isn't satisfied with acting," her brother had told her once. "He yearns for greatness on the stage of history," and if her mother hadn't interrupted, if Anna had had two seconds to herself with him, this is the reading she would have done. She would have promised him greatness.

"Mr. Booth was on his way to Ford's Theatre to pick up his mail," Wiechman said with a wink. It was an ambiguous wink. It might have meant only that Wiechman remembered what a first love was like. It might have suggested he knew the use she would make of such information.

Two regiments were returning to Washington from Virginia. They were out of step and out of breath, covered with dust. Anna drew a handkerchief from her sleeve and waved it at them. Other women were doing the same. A crowd gathered. A vendor came through the crowd, selling oysters. A man in a tight-fitting coat stopped him. He had a disreputable look — a bad haircut with long sideburns. He pulled a handful of coins from one pocket and stared at them stupidly. He was drunk. The vendor had to reach into his hand and pick out what he was owed.

"Filthy place!" the man next to the drunk man said. "I really can't bear the smell. I can't eat. Don't expect me to sleep in that flea-infested hotel another night." He left abruptly, colliding with Anna's arm, forcing her to take a step or two. "Excuse me," he said without stopping, and there was nothing penitent or apologetic in his tone. He didn't even seem to see her.

Since he had forced her to start, Anna continued to walk. She didn't even know she was going to Ford's Theatre until she turned onto Eleventh Street. It was a bad idea, but she couldn't seem to help herself. She began to walk faster.

"No tickets, Miss," James R. Ford told her, before she could open her mouth. She was not the only one there. A small crowd of people stood at the theater door. "Absolutely sold out. It's because the President and General Grant will be attending."

James Ford held an American flag in his arms. He raised it. "I'm just decorating the President's box." It was the last night of a lackluster run. He would never have guessed they would sell every seat. He thought Anna's face showed disappointment. He was happy, himself, and it made him kind. "They're rehearsing inside," he told her. "For General Grant! You just go on in for a peek."

He opened the doors and she entered. Three women and a man came with her. Anna had never seen any of the others before, but supposed they were friends of Mr. Ford's. They forced themselves through the doors beside her and then sat next to her in the straight-backed cane chairs just back from the stage.

Laura Keene herself stood in the wings awaiting her entrance. The curtain was pulled back, so that Anna could see her. Her cheeks were round with rouge.

The stage was not deep. Mrs. Mountchessington stood on it with her daughter, Augusta, and Asa Trenchard.

"All I crave is affection," Augusta was saying. She shimmered with insincerity.

Anna repeated the lines to herself. She imagined herself as an actress, married to JW, courted by him daily before an audience of a thousand, in a hundred different towns. They would play the love scenes over and over again, each one as true as the last. She would hardly know where her real and imaginary lives diverged. She didn't suppose there was much money to be made, but even to pretend to be rich seemed like happiness to her.

Augusta was willing to be poor, if she was loved. "Now I've no fortune," Asa said to her in response, "but I'm biling over with affections, which I'm ready to pour out all over you, like apple sass, over roast pork."

The women exited. He was alone on the stage. Anna could see Laura Keene mouthing his line, just as he spoke it. The woman seated next to her surprised her by whispering it aloud as well.

"Well, I guess I know enough to turn you inside out, old gal, you sockdologizing old man-trap," the three of them said. Anna turned to her seatmate who stared back. Her accent, Anna thought, had been English. "Don't you love theater?" she asked Anna in a whisper. Then her face changed. She was looking at something above Anna's head.

Anna looked, too. Now she understood the woman's expression. John Wilkes Booth was standing in the presidential box, staring down on the actor. Anna rose. Her seatmate caught her arm. She was considerably older than Anna, but not enough so that Anna could entirely dismiss her possible impact on Booth.

"Do you know him?" the woman asked.

"He's a friend of my brother's." Anna had no intention of introducing them. She tried to edge away, but the woman still held her.

"My name is Cassie Streichman."

"Anna Surratt."

There was a quick, sideways movement in the woman's eyes. "Are you related to Mary Surratt?"

"She's my mother." Anna began to feel just a bit of concern. So many people interested in her dull, sad mother. Anna tried to shake loose, and found, to her surprise, that she couldn't. The woman would not let go.

"I've heard of the boarding house," Mrs. Streichman said. It was a courtesy to think of her as a married woman. It was more of a courtesy than she deserved.

Anna looked up at the box again. Booth was already gone. "Let me go," she told Mrs. Streichman, so loudly that Laura Keene herself heard. So forcefully that Mrs. Streichman finally did so.

Anna left the theater. The streets were crowded and she could not see Booth anywhere. Instead, as she stood on the bricks, looking left and then right, Mrs. Streichman caught up with her. "Are you going home? Might we walk along?"

"No. I have errands," Anna said. She walked quickly away. She was cross now, because she had hoped to stay and look for Booth, who must still be close by, but Mrs. Streichman had made her too uneasy. She looked back once. Mrs. Streichman stood in the little circle of her friends, talking animatedly. She gestured with her hands like a European. Anna saw Booth nowhere.

She went back along the streets to St. Patrick's Church, in search of her mother. It was noon and the air was warm in spite of the colorless sun. Inside the church, her mother knelt in the pew and prayed noisily. Anna slipped in beside her.

"This is the moment," her mother whispered. She reached out and took Anna's hand, gripped it tightly enough to hurt. Her mother's eyes brightened with tears. "This is the moment they nailed him to the cross," she said. There was purple cloth over the crucifix. The pallid sunlight flowed into the church through colored glass.

Across town a group of men had gathered in the Kirkwood bar and were entertaining themselves by buying drinks for George Atzerodt. Atzerodt was one of Booth's co-conspirators. His assignment for the day, given to him by Booth, was to kidnap the Vice President. He was already so drunk he couldn't stand. "Would you say that the Vice President is a brave man?" he asked and they laughed at him. He didn't mind being laughed at. It struck him a bit funny himself. "He wouldn't carry a firearm, would he? I mean, why would he?" Atzerodt said. "Are there ever soldiers with him? That nigger who watches him eat. Is he there all the time?"

"Have another drink," they told him, laughing. "On us," and you couldn't get insulted at that.

Anna and her mother returned to the boarding house. Mary Surratt had rented a carriage and was going into the country. "Mr. Wiechman will drive me," she told her daughter. A Mr. Nothey owed her money they desperately needed; Mary Surratt was going to collect it.

But just as she was leaving, Booth appeared. He took her mother's arm, drew her to the parlor. Anna felt her heart stop and then start again, faster. "Mary, I must talk to you," he said to her mother, whispering, intimate. "Mary." He didn't look at Anna at all and didn't speak again until she left the room. She would have stayed outside the door to hear whatever she could, but Louis Wiechman had had the same idea. They exchanged one cross look, and then each left the hallway. Anna went up the stairs to her bedroom.

She knew the moment Booth went. She liked to feel that this was because they had a connection, something unexplainable, something preordained, but in fact she could hear the door. He went without asking to see her. She moved to the small window to watch him leave. He did not stop to glance up. He mounted a black horse, tipped his hat to her mother.

Her mother boarded a hired carriage, leaning on Mr. Wiechman's hand. She held a parcel under her arm. Anna had never seen it before. It was flat and round and wrapped in newspaper. Anna thought it was a gift from Booth. It made her envious.

Later at her mother's trial, Anna would hear that the package had contained a set of field glasses. A man named Lloyd would testify that Mary Surratt had delivered them to him and had also given him instructions from Booth regarding guns. It was the single most damaging evidence against her. At her brother's trial, Lloyd would recant everything but the field glasses. He was, he now said, too drunk at the time to remember what Mrs. Surratt had told him. He had never remembered. The prosecution had compelled his earlier testimony through threats. This revision would come two years after Mary Surratt had been hanged.

Anna stood at the window a long time, pretending that Booth might return with just such a present for her.

John Wilkes Booth passed George Atzerodt on the street at five P.M. Booth was on horseback. He told Atzerodt he had changed his mind about the kidnapping. He now wanted the Vice President killed. At 10:15 or thereabouts. "I've learned that Johnson is a very brave man," Atzerodt told him.

"And you are not," Booth agreed. "But you're in too deep to back out now." He rode away. Booth was carrying in his pocket a letter to the editor of *The National Intelligencer*. In it, he recounted the reasons for Lincoln's death. He had signed his own name, but also that of George Atzerodt.

The men who worked with Atzerodt once said he was a man you could insult and he would take no offense. It was the kindest thing they could think of to say. Three men from the Kirkwood bar appeared and took Atzerodt by the arms. "Let's find another bar," they suggested. "We have hours and hours yet before the night is over. Eat, drink. Be merry."

At six P.M. John Wilkes Booth gave the letter to John Matthews, an actor, asking him to deliver it the next day. "I'll be out of town or I would deliver it myself," he explained. A group of Confederate officers marched down Pennsylvania Avenue where John Wilkes Booth could see them. They were unaccompanied; they were turning themselves in. It was the submissiveness of it that struck Booth hardest. "A man can meet his fate or make it," he told Matthews. "A man can rise to the occasion or fall beneath it."

At sunset, a man called Peanut John lit the big glass globe at the entrance to Ford's Theatre. Inside, the presidential box had been decorated with borrowed flags and bunting. The door into the box had been forced some weeks ago in an unrelated incident and could no longer be locked.

It was early evening when Mary Surratt returned home. Her financial affairs were still unsettled; Mr. Nothey had not even shown up at their meeting. She kissed her daughter. "If Mr. Nothey will not pay us what he owes," she said, "I can't think what we will do next. I can't see a way ahead for us. Your brother must come home." She went into the kitchen to oversee the preparations for dinner.

Anna went in to help. Since the afternoon, since the moment Booth had not spoken to her, she had been overcome with unhappiness. It had not lessened a bit in the last hours; she now doubted it ever would. She cut the roast into slices. It bled beneath her knife and she thought of Henrietta Irving's white skin and the red heart beating underneath. She could understand Henrietta Irving perfectly. All I crave is affection, she said to herself, and the honest truth of the sentiment softened her into tears. Perhaps she could survive the rest of her life, if she played it this way, scene by scene. She held the knife up, watching the blood slide down the blade, and this was dramatic and fit her Shakespearian mood.

She felt a chill and when she turned around one of the new boarders was leaning against the doorjamb, watching her mother. "We're not ready yet," she told him crossly. He'd given her a start. He vanished back into the parlor.

Once again, the new guests hardly ate. Louis Wiechman finished his food with many elegant compliments. His testimony in court would damage Mary Surratt almost as much as Lloyd's. He would say that she seemed uneasy that night, unsettled, although none of the other boarders saw this. After dinner Mary Surratt went through the house, turning off the kerosene lights one by one.

Anna took a glass of wine and went to sleep immediately. She dreamed deeply, but her heartbreak woke her again only an hour or so later. It stabbed at her lightly from the inside when she breathed. She could see John Wilkes Booth as clearly as if he were in the room with her. "I am the most famous man in America," he said. He held out his hand, beckoned to her.

Downstairs she heard the front door open and close. She rose and looked out the window, just as she had done that afternoon. Many people, far too many people were on the street. They were all walking in the same direction. One of them was George Atzerodt. Hours before he had abandoned his knife but he too would die, along with Mary Surratt. He had gone too far to back out. He walked with his hands over the shoulders of two dark-haired men. One of them looked up. He was of a race Anna had never seen before. The new boarders joined the crowd. Anna could see them when they passed out from under the porch overhang.

Something big was happening. Something big enough to overwhelm her own hurt feelings. Anna dressed slowly and then quickly and more quickly. I live, she thought, in the most wondrous of times. Here was the proof. She was still unhappy, but she was also excited. She moved quietly past her mother's door.

The flow of people took her down several blocks. She was taking her last walk again, only backwards, like a ribbon uncoiling. She went past St. Patrick's Church, down Eleventh Street. The crowd ended at Ford's Theatre and thickened there. Anna was jostled. To her left, she recognized the woman from the carriage, the laughing woman, though she wasn't laughing now. Someone stepped on Anna's hoop skirt and she heard it snap. Someone struck her in the back of the head with an elbow. "Be quiet!" someone admonished someone else. "We'll miss it." Someone took hold of her arm. It was so crowded, she couldn't even turn to see, but she heard the voice of Cassie Streichman.

"I had tickets and everything," Mrs. Streichman said angrily. "Do you believe that? I can't even get to the door. It's almost ten o'clock and I had tickets."

"Can my group please stay together?" a woman toward the front asked. "Let's not lose anyone," and then she spoke again in a language Anna did not know.

"It didn't seem a good show," Anna said to Mrs. Streichman. "A comedy and not very funny."

Mrs. Streichman twisted into the space next to her. "That was just a rehearsal. The reviews are incredible. And you wouldn't believe the waiting list. Years. Centuries! I'll never have tickets again." She took a deep, calming breath. "At least *you're* here, dear. That's something I couldn't have expected. That makes it very real. And," she pressed Anna's arm, "if it helps in any way, you must tell yourself later there's nothing you could have done to make it come out differently. Everything that will happen has already happened. It won't be changed."

"Will I get what I want?" Anna asked her. She could not keep the brightness of hope from her voice. Clearly, she was part of something enormous. Something memorable. How many people could say that?

"I don't know what you want," Mrs. Streichman answered. She had an uneasy look. "I didn't get what *I* wanted," she added. "Even though I had tickets. Good God! People getting what they want. That's not the history of the world, is it?"

"Will everyone please be quiet!" someone behind Anna said. "Those of us in the back can't hear a thing."

Mrs. Streichman began to cry, which surprised Anna very much. "I'm such a sap," Mrs. Streichman said apologetically. "Things really get to me." She put her arm around Anna.

"All I want," Anna began, but a man to her right hushed her angrily.

"Shut up!" he said. "As if we came all this way to listen to *you.*"

Science fiction has been undergoing a kind of crisis of confidence. Some have worried that our stories are too often pitched at that narrowest of science fiction audiences, those who have spent lifetimes reading the stuff. The world building had gotten so complex that readers who are new to the genre get confused, then frustrated and then many give up. There has been a call for a more accessible science fiction, which still maintains the virtues of the genre.
   —James Patrick Kelly

I've thought about the domination of the literary arts by theory over the past twenty-five years — which I detest — and it's as if you have to be a critic to mediate between the author and the reader and that's utter crap. Literature can be great in all ways, but it's just entertainment like rock'n'roll or a film. It is entertainment. If it doesn't capture you on that level, as entertainment, movement of plot, then it doesn't work. Nothing else will come out of it. The beauty of the language, the characterization, the structure, all that's irrelevant if you're not getting the reader on that level — moving a story. If that's friendly to readers, I cop to it.
   —T. C. Boyle

10^{16} TO 1

JAMES PATRICK KELLY

> But the best evidence we have that time travel is not possible, and never will be, is that we have not been invaded by hordes of tourists from the future.
> —Stephen Hawking, "The Future of the Universe"

I REMEMBER NOW how lonely I was when I met Cross. I never let anyone know about it, because being alone back then didn't make me quite so unhappy. Besides, I was just a kid. I thought it was my own fault.

It looked like I had friends. In 1962, I was on the swim team and got elected Assistant Patrol Leader of the Wolf Patrol in Boy Scout Troop 7. When sides got chosen for kickball at recess, I was usually the fourth or fifth pick. I wasn't the best student in the sixth grade of John Jay Elementary School — that was Betty Garolli. But I was smart and the other kids made me feel bad about it. So I stopped raising my hand when I knew the answer and I watched my vocabulary. I remember I said *albeit* once in class and they teased me for weeks. Packs of girls would come up to me on the playground. "Oh Ray," they'd call and when I turned around they'd scream, "All beat it!" and run away, choking with laughter.

It wasn't that I wanted to be popular or anything. All I really wanted was a friend, one friend, a friend I didn't have to hide anything from. Then came Cross, and that was the end of that.

One of the problems was that we lived so far away from everything. Back then, Westchester County wasn't so suburban. Our house was deep in the woods in tiny Willoughby, New York, at the dead end of Cobb's Hill Road. In the winter, we could see Long Island Sound, a silver needle on the horizon pointing toward the city. But school was a half-hour drive away and the nearest kid lived in Ward's Hollow, three miles down the road, and he was a dumb fourth-grader.

So I didn't have any real friends. Instead, I had science fiction. Mom used to complain that I was obsessed. I watched *Superman* reruns every day after school. On Friday nights Dad used to let me stay up for *The Twilight Zone*, but that fall CBS had temporarily canceled it. It came back in January after everything happened, but was never quite the same. On Saturdays, I watched old sci-fi movies on *Adventure Theater*. My favorites were *Forbidden Planet* and *The Day the Earth Stood Still*. I think it was because of the robots. I decided that when I grew up and it was the future, I was going to buy one, so I wouldn't have to be alone anymore.

On Monday mornings I'd get my weekly allowance — a quarter. Usually I'd get off the bus that same afternoon down in Ward's Hollow so I could go to Village Variety. Twenty-five cents bought two comics and a pack of red licorice. I especially loved DC's *Green Lantern*, Marvel's *Fantastic Four* and *Incredible Hulk*, but I'd buy almost any superhero. I read all the science fiction books in the library twice, even though Mom kept nagging me to try different things. But what I loved best of all was *Galaxy* magazine. Dad had a subscription and when he was done reading them he would slip them to me. Mom didn't approve. I always used to read them up in the attic or out in the lean-to I'd lashed together in the woods. Afterwards I'd store them under my bunk in the bomb shelter. I knew that after the nuclear war, there would be no TV or radio or anything and I'd need something to keep me busy when I wasn't fighting mutants.

I was too young in 1962 to understand about Mom's drinking. I could see that she got bright and wobbly at night, but she was always up in the morning to make me a hot breakfast before school. And she would have graham crackers and peanut butter waiting when I came home — sometimes cinnamon toast. Dad said I shouldn't ask Mom for rides after five because she got so tired keeping house for us. He sold Andersen windows and was away a lot, so I was pretty much stranded most of the time. But he always made a point of being home on the first Tuesday of the month, so he could take me to the Scout meeting at 7:30.

No, looking back on it, I can't really say that I had an unhappy childhood — until I met Cross.

I remember it was a warm Saturday afternoon in October. The leaves covering the ground were still crisp and their scent spiced the air. I was in the lean-to

I'd built that spring, mostly to practice the square and diagonal lashings I needed for Scouts. I was reading *Galaxy*. I even remember the story: "The Ballad of Lost C'Mell" by Cordwainer Smith. The squirrels must have been chittering for some time, but I was too engrossed by Lord Jestocost's problems to notice. Then I heard a faint *crunch,* not ten feet away. I froze, listening. *Crunch, crunch*…then silence. It could've been a dog, except that dogs didn't usually slink through the woods. I was hoping it might be a deer — I'd never seen deer in Willoughby before, although I'd heard hunters shooting. I scooted silently across the dirt floor and peered between the dead saplings.

At first I couldn't see anything, which was odd. The woods weren't all that thick and the leaves had long since dropped from the understory brush. I wondered if I had imagined the sounds; it wouldn't have been the first time. Then I heard a twig snap, maybe a foot away. The wall shivered as if something had brushed against it, but there was nothing there. *Nothing.* I might have screamed then, except my throat started to close. I heard whatever it was skulk to the front of the lean-to. I watched in horror as an unseen weight pressed an acorn into the soft earth and then I scrambled back into the farthest corner. That's when I noticed that, when I wasn't looking directly at it, the air where the invisible thing should have been shimmered like a mirage. The lashings that held the frame creaked, as if it were bending over to see what it had caught, getting ready to drag me, squealing, out into the sun and….

"Oh, fuck," it said in a high, panicky voice and then it thrashed away into the woods.

In that moment I was transformed — and I suppose that history too was forever changed. I had somehow scared the thing off, twelve-year-old scrawny me! But more important was what it had said. Certainly I was well aware of the existence of the word *fuck* before then, but I had never dared use it myself, nor do I remember hearing it spoken by an adult. A spaz like the Murphy kid might say it under his breath, but he hardly counted. I'd always thought of it as language's atomic bomb; used properly the word should make brains shrivel, eardrums explode. But when the invisible thing said fuck and then *ran away,* it betrayed a vulnerability that made me reckless and more than a little stupid.

"Hey, stop!" I took off in pursuit.

I didn't have any trouble chasing it. The thing was no Davy Crockett; it was noisy and clumsy and slow. I could see a flickery outline as it lumbered along. I closed to within twenty feet and then had to hold back or I would've caught up to it. I had no idea what to do next. We blundered on in slower and slower motion until finally I just stopped.

"W-Wait," I called. "W-What do you want?" I put my hands on my waist and bent over like I was trying to catch my breath, although I didn't need to.

The thing stopped too but didn't reply. Instead it sucked air in wheezy, ragged *hooofs*. It was harder to see, now that it was standing still, but I think it must have turned toward me.

"Are you okay?" I said.

"You are a child." It spoke with an odd, chirping kind of accent. Child was *Ch-eye-eld*.

"I'm in the sixth grade." I straightened, spread my hands in front of me to show that I wasn't a threat. "What's your name?" It didn't answer. I took a step toward it and waited. Still nothing, but at least it didn't bolt. "I'm Ray Beaumont," I said finally. "I live over there." I pointed. "How come I can't see you?"

"What is the date?" It said *da-ate-eh*.

For a moment I thought it meant data. Data? I puzzled over an answer. I didn't want it thinking I was just a stupid little kid. "I don't know," I said cautiously. "October twentieth?"

The thing considered this, then asked a question that took my breath away. "And what is the year?"

"Oh jeez," I said. At that point I wouldn't have been surprised if Rod Serling himself had popped out from behind a tree and started addressing the unseen TV audience. Which might have included me, except this was really *happening*. "Do you know what you just…what it means when…."

"What, what?" Its voice rose in alarm.

"You're invisible and you don't know what year it is? Everyone knows what year it is. Are you…you're not from here."

"Yes, yes, I am. 1962, of course. This is 1962." It paused. "And I am not invisible." It squeezed about eight syllables into invisible. I heard a sound like paper ripping. "This is only camel." Or at least, that's what I thought it said.

"Camel?"

"No, camo." The air in front of me crinkled and slid away from a dark face. "You have not heard of camouflage?"

"Oh sure, camo."

I suppose the thing meant to reassure me by showing itself, but the effect was just the opposite. Yes, it had two eyes, a nose, and a mouth. It stripped off the camouflage to reveal a neatly pressed gray three-piece business suit, a white shirt, and a red and blue striped tie. At night, on a crowded street in Manhattan, I might've passed it right by — Dad had taught me not to stare at the kooks in the city. But in the afternoon light, I could see all the things wrong with its disguise. The hair, for example. Not exactly a crewcut, it was more of a stubble, like Mr. Rudowski's chin when he was growing his beard. The thing was way too thin, its skin was shiny, its fingers too long and its face — it looked like one of those Barbie dolls.

"Are you a boy or a girl?" I said.

It started. "There is something wrong?"

I cocked my head to one side. "I think maybe it's your eyes. They're too big or something. Are you wearing makeup?"

"I am naturally male." It — he bristled as he stepped out of the camouflage suit. "Eyes do not have gender."

"If you say so." I could see he was going to need help getting around, only he didn't seem to know it. I was hoping he'd reveal himself, brief me on the mission. I even had an idea how we could contact President Kennedy or whoever he needed to meet with. Mr. Newell, the Scoutmaster, used to be a colonel in the Army — he would know some general who could call the Pentagon. "What's your name?" I said.

He draped the suit over his arm. "Cross."

I waited for the rest of it as he folded the suit in half. "Just Cross?" I said.

"My given name is Chitmansing." He warbled it like he was calling birds.

"That's okay," I said. "Let's just make it Mr. Cross."

"As you wish, Mr. Beaumont." He folded the suit again, again and *again*. "Hey!"

He continued to fold it.

"How do you do that? Can I see?"

He handed it over. The camo suit was more impossible than it had been when it was invisible. He had reduced it to a six-inch square card, as thin and flexible as the queen of spades. I folded it in half myself. The two sides seemed to meld together; it would've fit into my wallet perfectly. I wondered if Cross knew how close I was to running off with his amazing gizmo. He'd never catch me. I could see flashes of my brilliant career as the invisible superhero. *Tales to Confound* presents: the origin of Camo Kid! I turned the card over and over, trying to figure out how to unfold it again. There was no seam, no latch. How could I use it if I couldn't open it? "Neat," I said. Reluctantly, I gave the card back to him.

Besides, real superheroes didn't steal their powers.

I watched Cross slip the card into his vest pocket. I wasn't scared of him. What scared me was that at any minute he might walk out of my life. I had to find a way to tell him I was on his side, whatever that was.

"So you live around here, Mr. Cross?"

"I am from the island of Mauritius."

"Where's that?"

"It is in the Indian Ocean, Mr. Beaumont, near Madagascar."

I knew where Madagascar was from playing *Risk,* so I told him that but then I couldn't think of what else to say. Finally, I had to blurt out something — anything — to fill the silence. "It's nice here. Real quiet, you know. Private."

"Yes, I had not expected to meet anyone." He, too, seemed at a loss. "I have business in New York City on the twenty-fifth of October."

"New York, that's a ways away."

"Is it? How far would you say?"

"Fifty miles. Sixty, maybe. You have a car?"

"No, I do not drive, Mr. Beaumont. I am to take the train."

The nearest train station was New Canaan, Connecticut. I could've hiked it in maybe half a day. It would be dark in a couple of hours. "If your business isn't until the twenty-sixth, you'll need a place to stay."

"The plan is to take rooms at a hotel in Manhattan."

"That costs money."

He opened a wallet and showed me a wad of crisp new bills. For a minute I thought they must be counterfeit; I hadn't realized that Ben Franklin's picture was on money. Cross was giving me the goofiest grin. I just knew they'd eat him alive in New York and spit out the bones.

"Are you sure you want to stay in a hotel?" I said.

He frowned. "Why would I not?"

"Look, you need a friend, Mr. Cross. Things are different here than...than on your island. Sometimes people do, you know, bad stuff. Especially in the city."

He nodded and put his wallet away. "I am aware of the dangers, Mr. Beaumont. I have trained not to draw attention to myself. I have the proper equipment." He tapped the pocket where the camo was.

I didn't point out to him that all his training and equipment hadn't kept him from being caught out by a twelve-year-old. "Sure, okay. It's just…. Look, I have a place for you to stay, if you want. No one will know."

"Your parents, Mr. Beaumont…."

"My dad's in Massachusetts until next Friday. He travels; he's in the window business. And my mom won't know."

"How can she not know that you have invited a stranger into your house?"

"Not the house," I said. "My dad built us a bomb shelter. You'll be safe there, Mr. Cross. It's the safest place I know."

I remember how Cross seemed to lose interest in me, his mission and the entire twentieth century the moment he entered the shelter. He sat around all of Sunday, dodging my attempts to draw him out. He seemed distracted, like he was listening to a conversation I couldn't hear. When he wouldn't talk, we played games. At first it was cards: Gin and Crazy Eights, mostly. In the afternoon, I went back to the house and brought over checkers and *Monopoly*. Despite the fact that he did not seem to be paying much attention, he beat me like a drum. Not one game was even close. But that wasn't what bothered me. I believed that this man had come from the future, and here I was building hotels on Baltic Avenue!

Monday was a school day. I thought Cross would object to my plan of locking him in and taking both my key and Mom's key with me, but he never said a word. I told him that it was the only way I could be sure that Mom didn't catch him by surprise. Actually, I doubted she'd come all the way out to the shelter. She'd stayed away after Dad gave her that first tour; she had about as much use for nuclear war as she had for science fiction. Still, I had no idea what she did during the day while I was gone. I couldn't take chances. Besides, it was a good way to make sure that Cross didn't skin out on me.

Dad had built the shelter instead of taking a vacation in 1960, the year Kennedy beat Nixon. It was buried about a hundred and fifty feet from the house. Nothing special — just a little cellar without anything built on top of it. The entrance was a steel bulkhead that led down five steps to another steel door. The inside was cramped; there were a couple of cots, a sink, and a toilet. Almost half of the space was filled with supplies and equipment. There were no windows and it always smelled a little musty, but I loved going down there to pretend the bombs were falling.

When I opened the shelter door after school on that Monday, Cross lay just as I had left him the night before, sprawled across the big cot, staring at nothing. I remember being a little worried; I thought he might be sick. I stood beside him and still he didn't acknowledge my presence.

"Are you all right, Mr. Cross?" I said. "I brought *Risk*." I set it next to him on the bed and nudged him with the corner of the box to wake him up. "Did you eat?"

He sat up, took the cover off the game and started reading the rules. "President Kennedy will address the nation," he said, "this evening at seven o'clock."

For a moment, I thought he had made a slip. "How do you know that?"

"The announcement came last night." I realized that his pronunciation had improved a lot; *announcement* had only three syllables. "I have been studying the radio."

I walked over to the radio on the shelf next to the sink. Dad said we were supposed to leave it unplugged — something about the bombs making a power surge. It was a brand new solid-state, multi-band Heathkit that I'd helped him build. When I pressed the on button, women immediately started singing about shopping: *Where the values go up, up, up! And the prices go down, down, down!* I turned it off again.

"Do me a favor, okay?" I said. "Next time when you're done would you please unplug this? I could get in trouble if you don't." I stooped to yank the plug.

When I stood up, he was holding a sheet of paper. "I will need some things tomorrow, Mr. Beaumont. I would be grateful if you could assist me."

I glanced at the list without comprehension. He must have typed it, only there was no typewriter in the shelter.

To buy:

- One General Electric transistor radio with earplug
- One General Electric replacement earplug
- Two Eveready Heavy Duty nine volt batteries
- One New York Times, Tuesday, October 23
- Rand McNally map of New York City and vicinity

To receive in change:

– Five dollars in coins
– twenty nickels
– ten dimes
– twelve quarters

When I looked up, I could feel the change in him. His gaze was electric; it seemed to crackle down my nerves. I could tell that what I did next would matter very much. "I don't get it," I said.

"There are inaccuracies?"

I tried to stall. "Look, you'll pay almost double if we buy a transistor radio at Ward's Hollow. I'll have to buy it at Village Variety. Wait a couple of days — we can get one much cheaper down in Stamford."

"My need is immediate." He extended his hand and tucked something into the pocket of my shirt. "I am assured this will cover the expense."

I was afraid to look, even though I knew what it was. He'd given me a hundred dollar bill. I tried to thrust it back at him but he stepped away and it spun to the floor between us. "I can't spend that."

"You must read your own money, Mr. Beaumont." He picked the bill up and brought it into the light of the bare bulb on the ceiling. "This note is legal tender for all debts public and private."

"No, no, you don't understand. A kid like me doesn't walk into Village Variety with a hundred bucks. Mr. Rudowski will call my mom!"

"If it is inconvenient for you, I will secure the items myself." He offered me the money again.

If I didn't agree, he'd leave and probably never come back. I was getting mad at him. Everything would be so much easier if only he'd admit what we both knew about who he was. Then I could do whatever he wanted with a clear conscience. Instead, he was keeping all the wrong secrets and acting really weird. It made me feel dirty, like I was helping a pervert. "What's going on," I said.

"I do not know how to respond, Mr. Beaumont. You have the list. Read it now and tell me please with which item you have a problem."

I snatched the hundred dollars from him and jammed it into my pants pocket. "Why don't you trust me?"

He stiffened as if I had hit him.

"I let you stay here. I didn't tell anyone. You have to give me *something*, Mr. Cross."

"Well then..." He looked uncomfortable. "I would ask you to keep the change."

"Oh jeez, thanks." I snorted in disgust. "Okay, okay, I'll buy this stuff right after school tomorrow."

With that, he seemed to lose interest again. When we opened the *Risk* board, he showed me where his island was, except it wasn't there because it was too small. We played three games and he crushed me every time. I remember at the end of the last game, watching in disbelief as he finished building a wall of invading armies along the shores of North Africa. South America, my last continent, was doomed. "Looks like you win again," I said. I traded in the last of my cards for new armies and launched a final, useless counter-attack. When I was done, he studied the board for a moment.

"I think *Risk* is not a proper simulation, Mr. Beaumont. We should both lose for fighting such a war."

"That's crazy," I said. "Both sides can't lose."

"Yet they can," he said. "It sometimes happens that the victors envy the dead."

That night was the first time I can remember being bothered by Mom talking back to the TV. I used to talk to the TV too. When Buffalo Bob asked what time it was, I would screech *It's Howdy Doody Time* just like every other kid in America.

"My fellow citizens," said President Kennedy, "let no one doubt that this is a difficult and dangerous effort on which we have set out." I thought the president looked tired, like Mr. Newell on the third day of a camp-out. "No one can foresee precisely what course it will take or what costs or casualties will be incurred."

"Oh my God," Mom screamed at him. "You're going to kill us all!"

Despite the fact that it was close to her bedtime and she was shouting at the President of the United States, Mom looked great. She was wearing a shiny black dress and a string of pearls. She always got dressed up at night, whether Dad was home or not. I suppose most kids don't notice how their mothers look, but everyone always said how beautiful Mom was. And since Dad thought so too, I went along with it — as long as she didn't open her mouth. The problem was that a lot of the time, Mom didn't make any sense. When she embarrassed me, it didn't matter how pretty she was. I just wanted to crawl behind the couch.

"Mom."

As she leaned toward the television, the martini in her glass came close to slopping over the edge.

President Kennedy stayed calm. "The path we have chosen for the present is full of hazards, as all paths are — but it is the one most consistent with our character and courage as a nation and our commitments around the world. The cost of freedom is always high — but Americans have always paid it. And one path we shall never choose, and that is the path of surrender or submission."

"Shut up! You foolish man, *stop this.*" She shot out of her chair and then some of her drink did spill. "Oh, damn!"

"Take it easy, Mom."

"Don't you understand?" She put the glass down and tore a Kleenex from the box on the end table. "He wants to start World War III!" She dabbed at the front of her dress and the phone rang.

I said, "Mom, nobody wants World War III."

She ignored me, brushed by and picked up the phone on the third ring.

"Oh thank God," she said. I could tell from the sound of her voice that it was Dad. "You heard him then?" She bit her lip as she listened to him. "Yes, but…."

Watching her face made me sorry I was in the sixth grade. Better to be a stupid little kid again, who thought grownups knew everything. I wondered whether Cross had heard the speech.

"No, I can't, Dave. No." She covered the phone with her hand. "Raymie, turn off that TV!"

I hated it when she called me Raymie, so I only turned the sound down.

"You have to come home now, Dave. No, you listen to *me*. Can't you see, the man's obsessed? Just because he has a grudge against Castro doesn't mean he's allowed to…"

With the sound off, Chet Huntley looked as if he were speaking at his own funeral.

"I am *not* going in there without you."

I think Dad must have been shouting because Mom held the receiver away from her ear.

She waited for him to calm down and said, "And neither is Raymie. He'll stay with me."

"Let me talk to him," I said. I bounced off the couch. The look she gave me stopped me dead.

"What for?" she said to Dad. "No, we are going to finish this conversation, David, do you hear me?"

She listened for a moment. "Okay, all right, but don't you dare hang up." She waved me over and slapped the phone into my hand as if I had put the missiles in Cuba. She stalked to the kitchen.

I needed a grownup so bad that I almost cried when I heard Dad's voice. "Ray," he said, "your mother is pretty upset."

"Yes," I said.

"I want to come home — I *will* come home — but I can't just yet. If I just up and leave and this blows over, I'll get fired."

"But, Dad...."

"You're in charge until I get there. Understand, son? If the time comes, everything is up to you."

"Yes, sir," I whispered. I'd heard what he didn't say — it wasn't up to *her*.

"I want you to go out to the shelter tonight. Wait until she goes to sleep. Top off the water drums. Get all the gas out of the garage and store it next to the generator. But here's the most important thing. You know the sacks of rice? Drag them off to one side, the pallet too. There's a hatch underneath, the key to the airlock door unlocks it. You've got two new guns and plenty of ammunition. The revolver is a .357 Magnum. You be careful with that, Ray, it can blow a hole in a car but it's hard to aim. The double-barreled shotgun is easy to aim but you have to be close to do any harm. And I want you to bring down the Gamemaster from my closet and the .38 from my dresser drawer." He had been talking as if there would be no tomorrow; he paused then to catch his breath. "Now, this is all just in case, okay? I just want you to know."

I had never been so scared in my life.

"Ray?"

I should have told him about Cross then, but Mom weaved into the room. "Got it, Dad," I said. "Here she is."

Mom smiled at me. It was a lopsided smile that was trying to be brave but wasn't doing a very good job of it. She had a new glass and it was full. She held out her hand for the phone and I gave it to her.

I remember waiting until almost ten o'clock that night, reading under the covers with a flashlight. The Fantastic Four invaded Latveria to defeat Doctor Doom; Superman tricked Mr. Mxyzptlk into saying his name backwards once again. When I opened the door to my parents' bedroom, I could hear Mom snoring. It spooked me; I hadn't realized that women did that, I thought about sneaking in to get the guns, but decided to take care of them tomorrow.

I stole out to the shelter, turned my key in the lock, and pulled on the bulkhead door. It didn't move. That didn't make any sense, so I gave it a hard yank. The steel door rattled terribly but did not swing away. The air had turned frosty and the sound carried in the cold. I held my breath, listening to my blood pound. The house stayed dark, the shelter quiet as stones. After a few moments, I tried one last time before I admitted to myself what had happened.

Cross had bolted the door shut from the inside.

I went back to my room, but couldn't sleep. I kept going to the window to watch the sky over New York, waiting for a flash of killing light. I was all but convinced that the city would burn that very night in thermonuclear fire and that Mom and I would die horrible deaths soon after, pounding on the unyielding steel doors of our shelter. Dad had left me in charge and I had let him down.

I didn't understand why Cross had locked us out. If he knew that a nuclear war was about to start, he might want our shelter all to himself. But that made him a monster and I still didn't see him as a monster. I tried to tell myself that he'd been asleep and couldn't hear me at the door — but that couldn't be right. What if he'd come to prevent the war? He'd said he had business in the city on Thursday; he could be doing something really, really futuristic in there that he couldn't let me see. Or else he was having problems. Maybe our twentieth century germs had got to him, like they killed H. G. Wells's Martians.

I must have teased a hundred different ideas apart that night, in between uneasy trips to the window and glimpses at the clock. The last time I remember seeing was 4:16. I tried to stay up to face the end, but I couldn't.

I wasn't dead when I woke up the next morning, so I had to go to school. Mom had Cream of Wheat all ready when I dragged myself to the table. Although she was all bright and bubbly, I could feel her giving me the mother's eye when I wasn't looking. She always knew when something was wrong. I tried not to show her anything. There was no time to sneak out to the shelter; I barely had time to finish eating before she bundled me off to the bus.

Right after the morning bell, Miss Toohey told us to open *The Story of New York State* to Chapter Seven, "Resources and Products," and read to ourselves.

Then she left the room. We looked at each other in amazement. I heard Bobby Coniff whisper something. It was probably dirty; a few kids snickered. Chapter Seven started with a map of product symbols. Two teeny little cows grazed near Binghamton. Rochester was a cog and a pair of glasses. Elmira was an adding machine, Oswego an apple. There was a lightning bolt over Niagara Falls. Dad had promised to take us there someday. I had the sick feeling that we'd never get the chance. Miss Toohey looked pale when she came back, but that didn't stop her from giving us a spelling test. I got a ninety-five. The word I spelled wrong was *enigma*. The hot lunch was American Chop Suey, a roll, a salad, and a bowl of butterscotch pudding. In the afternoon we did decimals.

Nobody said anything about the end of the world.

I decided to get off the bus in Ward's Hollow, buy the stuff Cross wanted, and pretend I didn't know he had locked the shelter door last night. If he said something about it, I'd act surprised. If he didn't…I didn't know what I'd do then.

Village Variety was next to Warren's Esso and across the street from the Post Office. It had once been two different stores located in the same building, but then Mr. Rudowski had bought the building and knocked down the dividing wall. On the fun side were pens and pencils and paper and greeting cards and magazines and comics and paperbacks and candy. The other side was all boring hardware and small appliances.

Mr. Rudowski was on the phone when I came in, but then he was always on the phone when he worked. He could sell you a hammer or a pack of baseball cards, tell you a joke, ask about your family, complain about the weather and still keep the guy on the other end of the line happy. This time though, when he saw me come in, he turned away, wrapping the phone cord across his shoulder.

I went through the store quickly and found everything Cross had wanted. I had to blow dust off the transistor radio box but the batteries looked fresh. There was only one *New York Times* left; the headlines were so big they were scary.

US IMPOSES ARMS BLOCKADE ON CUBA
ON FINDING OF OFFENSIVE MISSILE SITES;
KENNEDY READY FOR SOVIET SHOWDOWN
Ships Must Stop President Grave Prepared To Risk War.

I set my purchases on the counter in front of Mr. Rudowski. He cocked his head to one side, trapping the telephone receiver against his shoulder, and rang me up. The paper was on the bottom of the pile.

"Since when do you read the *Times,* Ray?" Mr. Rudowski punched it into the cash register and hit total. "I just got the new *Fantastic Four.*" The cash drawer popped open.

"Maybe tomorrow," I said.

"All right then. It comes to twelve dollars and forty-seven cents."

I gave him the hundred dollar bill.

"What is this, Ray?" He stared at it and then at me.

I had my story all ready. "It was a birthday gift from my grandma in Detroit. She said I could spend it on whatever I wanted so I decided to treat myself but I'm going to put the rest in the bank."

"You're buying a radio? From me?"

"Well, you know. I thought maybe I should have one with me with all this stuff going on."

He didn't say anything for a moment. He just pulled a paper bag from under the counter and put my things into it. His shoulders were hunched; I thought maybe he felt guilty about overcharging for the radio. "You should be listening to music, Ray," he said quietly. "You like Elvis? All kids like Elvis. Or maybe that colored guy, the one who does the Twist?"

"They're all right, I guess."

"You're too young to be worrying about the news. You hear me? Those politicians…." He shook his head. "It's going to be okay, Ray. You heard it from me."

"Sure, Mr. Rudowski. I was wondering, could I get five dollars in change?"

I could feel him watching me as I stuffed it all into my bookbag. I was certain he'd call my mom, but he never did. Home was three miles up Cobb's Hill. I did it in forty minutes, a record.

I remember I started running when I saw the flashing lights. The police car had left skid marks in the gravel on our driveway.

"Where were you?" Mom burst out of the house as I came across the lawn. "Oh, my God, Raymie, I was worried sick." She caught me up in her arms.

"I got off the bus in Ward's Hollow." She was about to smother me; I squirmed free. "What happened?"

"This the boy, ma'am?" The state trooper had taken his time catching up to her. He had almost the same hat as Scoutmaster Newell.

"Yes, yes! Oh, thank God, officer!"

The trooper patted me on the head like I was a lost dog. "You had your mom worried, Ray."

"Raymie, you should've told me."

"Somebody tell me what happened!" I said.

A second trooper came from behind the house. We watched him approach. "No sign of any intruder." He looked bored: I wanted to scream.

"Intruder?" I said.

"He broke into the shelter," said Mom. "He knew my name."

"There was no sign of forcible entry," said the second trooper. I saw him exchange a glance with his partner. "Nothing disturbed that I could see."

"He didn't have time," Mom said. "When I found him in the shelter, I ran back to the house and got your father's gun from the bedroom."

The thought of Mom with the .38 scared me. I had my Shooting merit badge, but she didn't know a hammer from a trigger. "You didn't shoot him?"

"No." She shook her head. "He had plenty of time to leave but he was still there when I came back. That's when he said my name."

I had never been so mad at her before. "You never go out to the shelter."

She had that puzzled look she always gets at night. "I couldn't find my key. I had to use the one your father leaves over the breezeway door."

"What did he say again, ma'am? The intruder."

"He said, 'Mrs. Beaumont, I present no danger to you.' And I said, 'Who are you?' And then he came toward me and I thought he said 'Margaret,' and I started firing."

"You did shoot him!"

Both troopers must have heard the panic in my voice. The first one said, "You know something about this man, Ray?"

"No, I-I was at school all day and then I stopped at Rudowski's…." I could feel my eyes burning. I was so embarrassed; I knew I was about to cry in front of them.

Mom acted annoyed that the troopers had stopped paying attention to her. "I shot *at* him. Three, four times, I don't know. I must have missed, because he just stood there staring at me. It seemed like forever. Then he walked past me and up the stairs like nothing had happened."

"And he didn't say anything?"

"Not a word."

"Well, it beats me," said the second trooper. "The gun's been fired four times but there are no bullet holes in the shelter and no bloodstains."

"You mind if I ask you a personal question, Mrs. Beaumont?" the first trooper said.

She colored. "I suppose not."

"Have you been drinking, ma'am?"

"Oh that!" She seemed relieved. "No. Well, I mean, after I called you, I did pour myself a little something. Just to steady my nerves. I was worried because my son was so late and…Raymie, what's the matter?"

I felt so small. The tears were pouring down my face.

After the troopers left, I remember Mom baking brownies while I watched *Superman*. I wanted to go out and hunt for Cross, but it was already sunset and there was no excuse I could come up with for wandering around in the dark. Besides, what was the point? He was gone, driven off by my mother. I'd had a chance to help a man from the future change history, maybe prevent World War III, and I had blown it. My life was ashes.

I wasn't hungry that night, for brownies or spaghetti or anything, but Mom made that clucking noise when I pushed supper around the plate, so I ate a few bites just to shut her up. I was surprised at how easy it was to hate her, how good it felt. Of course, she was oblivious, but in the morning she would notice if I wasn't careful. After dinner she watched the news and I went upstairs to read. I wrapped a pillow around my head when she yelled at David Brinkley. I turned out the lights at 8:30, but I couldn't get to sleep. She went to her room a little after that.

"Mr. Beaumont?"

I must have dozed off, but when I heard his voice I snapped awake immediately.

"Is that you, Mr. Cross?" I peered into the darkness. "I bought the stuff you wanted." The room filled with an awful stink, like when Mom drove with the parking brake on.

"Mr. Beaumont," he said, "I am damaged."

I slipped out of bed, picked my way across the dark room, locked the door and turned on the light.

"Oh jeez!"

He slumped against my desk like a nightmare. I remember thinking then that Cross wasn't human, that maybe he wasn't even alive. His proportions were wrong: an ear, a shoulder, and both feet sagged like they had melted. Little wisps of steam or something curled off him; they were what smelled. His skin had gone all shiny and hard; so had his business suit. I'd wondered why he never took the suit coat off and now I knew. His clothes were part of him. The middle fingers of his right hand beat spasmodically against his palm.

"Mr. Beaumont," he said. "I calculate your chances at 10^{16} to 1."

"Chances of what?" I said. "What happened to you?"

"You must listen most attentively, Mr. Beaumont. My decline is very bad for history. It is for you now to alter the time line probabilities."

"I don't understand."

"Your government greatly overestimates the nuclear capability of the Soviet Union. If you originate a first strike, the United States will achieve overwhelming victory."

"Does the President know this? We have to tell him!"

"John Kennedy will not welcome such information. If he starts this war, he will be responsible for the deaths of tens of millions, both Russians and Americans. But he does not grasp the future of the arms race. The war must happen now, because those who come after will build and build until they control arsenals which can destroy the world many times over. People are not capable of thinking for very long of such fearsome weapons. They tire of the idea of extinction and then become numb to it. The buildup slows but does not stop and they congratulate themselves on having survived it. But there are still too many weapons and they never go away. The Third War comes as a surprise. The First War was called the one to end all wars. The Third War is the only such war possible, Mr. Beaumont, because it ends everything. History stops in 2009. Do you understand? A year later, there is no life. All dead, the world a hot, barren rock."

"But you…?"

"I am nothing, a construct. Mr. Beaumont, please, the chances are 10^{16} to 1," he said. "Do you know how improbable that is?" His laugh sounded like a hiccup. "But for the sake of those few precious time lines, we must continue. There is a man, a politician in New York. If he dies on Thursday night, it will create the incident that forces Kennedy's hand."

"Dies?" For days, I had been desperate for him to talk. Now all I wanted was to run away. "You're going to kill somebody?"

"The world will survive a Third War that starts on Friday, October 26, 1962."

"What about me? My parents? Do we survive?"

"I cannot access that time line. I have no certain answer for you. Please, Mr. Beaumont, this politician will die of a heart attack in less than three years. He has made no great contribution to history, yet his assassination can save the world."

"What do you want from me?" But I had already guessed.

"He will speak most eloquently at the United Nations on Thursday evening. Afterward he will have dinner with his friend, Ruth Fields. Around ten o'clock he will return to his residence at the Waldorf Towers. Not the Waldorf Astoria Hotel, but the Towers. He will take the elevator to Suite 42A. He is the American ambassador to the United Nations. His name is Adlai Stevenson."

"Stop it! Don't say anything else."

When he sighed, his breath was a cloud of acrid steam. "I have based my calculation of the time line probabilities on two data points, Mr. Beaumont, which I discovered in your bomb shelter. The first is the .357 Magnum revolver, located under a pallet of rice bags. I trust you know of this weapon?"

"Yes." I whispered.

"The second is the collection of magazines, located under your cot. It would seem that you take an interest in what is to come, Mr. Beaumont, and that may lend you the terrible courage you will need to divert this time line from disaster. You should know that there is not just one future. There are an infinite number of futures in which all possibilities are expressed, an infinite number of Raymond Beaumonts."

"Mr. Cross, I can't...."

"Perhaps not," he said, "but I believe that another one of you can."

"You don't understand...." I watched in horror as a boil swelled on the side of his face and popped, expelling an evil jet of yellow steam. "What?"

"Oh *fuck*." That was the last thing he said.

He slid to the floor — or maybe he was just a body at that point. More boils formed and burst. I opened all the windows in my room and got the fan down out of the closet and still I can't believe that the stink didn't wake Mom up. Over the course of the next few hours, he sort of vaporized.

When it was over, there was a sticky, dark spot on the floor the size of my pillow. I moved the throw rug from one side of the room to the other to cover it up. I had nothing to prove that Cross existed but a transistor radio, a couple of batteries, an earplug and eighty-seven dollars and fifty-three cents in change.

I might have done things differently if I hadn't had a day to think. I can't remember going to school on Wednesday, who I talked to, what I ate. I was feverishly trying to figure out what to do and how to do it. I had no place to go for answers, not Miss Toohey, not my parents, not the Bible or the *Boy Scout Handbook,* certainly not *Galaxy* magazine. Whatever I did had to come out of me. I watched the news with Mom that night. President Kennedy had brought our military to the highest possible state of alert. There were reports that some Russian ships had turned away from Cuba; others continued on course. Dad called and said his trip was being cut short and that he would be home the next day.

But that was too late.

I hid behind the stone wall when the school bus came on Thursday morning. Mrs. Johnson honked a couple of times, and then drove on. I set out for New Canaan, carrying my bookbag. In it were the radio, the batteries, the coins, the map of New York, and the .357. I had the rest of Cross's money in my wallet.

It took more than five hours to hike to the train station. I expected to be scared, but the whole time I felt light as air. I kept thinking of what Cross had said about the future, that I was just one of millions and millions of Raymond Beaumonts. Most of them were in school, diagramming sentences and watching Miss Toohey bite her nails. I was the special one, walking into history. I was super. I caught the 2:38 train, changed in Stamford, and arrived at Grand Central just after four. I had six hours. I bought myself a hot pretzel and a coke and tried to decide where I should go. I couldn't just sit around the hotel lobby for all that time; I thought that would draw too much attention. I decided to go to the top of the Empire State Building. I took my time walking down Park Avenue and tried not to see all the ghosts I was about to make. In the lobby of the Empire State Building, I used Cross's change to call home.

"Hello?" I hadn't expected Dad to answer. I would've hung up except that I knew I might never speak to him again.

"Dad, this is Ray. I'm safe, don't worry."

"Ray, where are you?"

"I can't talk. I'm safe but I won't be home tonight. Don't worry."

"Ray!" He was frantic. "What's going on?"

"I'm sorry."

"Ray!"

I hung up; I had to. "I love you," I said to the dial tone.

I could imagine the expression on Dad's face, how he would tell Mom what I'd said. Eventually they would argue about it. He would shout; she would cry. As I rode the elevator up, I got mad at them. He shouldn't have picked up the phone. They should've protected me from Cross and the future he came from. I was in the sixth grade, I shouldn't have to have feelings like this. The observation platform was almost deserted. I walked completely around it, staring at the city stretching away from me in every direction. It was dusk; the buildings were shadows in the failing light. I didn't feel like Ray Beaumont anymore; he was my secret identity. Now I was the superhero Bomb Boy; I had the power of bringing nuclear war. Wherever I cast my terrible gaze, cars melted and people burst into flame.

And I loved it.

It was dark when I came down from the Empire State Building. I had a sausage pizza and a coke on 47th Street. While I ate, I stuck the plug into my ear and listened to the radio. I searched for the news. One announcer said the debate was still going on in the Security Council. Our ambassador was questioning Ambassador Zorin. I stayed with that station for a while, hoping to hear his voice. I knew what he looked like, of course. I knew Adlai Stevenson had run for President a couple of times when I was just a baby. But I couldn't remember what he sounded like. He might talk to me, ask me what I was doing in his hotel; I wanted to be ready for that.

I arrived at the Waldorf Towers around nine o'clock. I picked a plush velvet chair that had a direct view of the elevator bank and sat there for about ten minutes. Nobody seemed to care but it was hard to sit still. Finally I got up and went to the men's room. I took my bookbag into a stall, closed the door and got the .357 out. I aimed it at the toilet. The gun was heavy and I could tell it would have a big kick. I probably ought to hold it with both hands. I put it back into my bookbag and flushed.

When I came out of the bathroom, I had stopped believing that I was going to shoot anyone, that I could. But I had to find out for Cross's sake. If I was really meant to save the world, then I had to be in the right place at the right time. I went back to my chair, checked my watch. It was nine-twenty.

I started thinking of the one who would pull the trigger, the unlikely Ray. What would make the difference? Had he read some story in *Galaxy* that I had skipped? Was it a problem with Mom? Or Dad? Maybe he had spelled *enigma* right; maybe Cross had lived another thirty seconds in his time line. Or maybe he was just the best that I could possibly be.

I was so tired of it all. I must have walked thirty miles since morning and I hadn't slept well in days. The lobby was warm. People laughed and murmured. Elevator doors dinged softly. I tried to stay up to face history, but I couldn't. I was Raymond Beaumont, but I was just a twelve-year-old kid.

I remember the doorman waking me up at eleven o'clock. Dad drove all the way into the city that night to get me. When we got home, Mom was already in the shelter.

Only the Third War didn't start that night. Or the next.

I lost television privileges for a month.

For most people my age, the most traumatic memory of growing up came on November 22, 1963. But the date I remember is July 14, 1965, when Adlai Stevenson dropped dead of a heart attack in London.

I've tried to do what I can, to make up for what I didn't do that night. I've worked for the cause wherever I could find it. I belong to CND and SANE and the Friends of the Earth and was active in the nuclear freeze movement. I think the Green Party (www.greens.org) is the only political organization worth your vote. I don't know if any of it will change Cross's awful probabilities; maybe we'll survive in a few more time lines.

When I was a kid, I didn't mind being lonely. Now it's hard, knowing what I know. Oh, I have lots of friends, all of them wonderful people, but people who know me say that there's a part of myself that I always keep hidden. They're right. I don't think I'll ever be able to tell anyone about what happened with Cross, what I didn't do that night. It wouldn't be fair to them.

Besides, whatever happens, chances are very good that it's my fault.

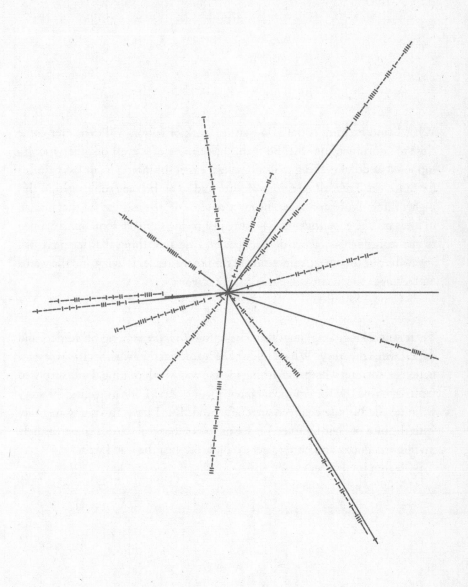

What I find exciting is the idea that no work of fiction will ever, ever come close to "documenting" life. So then, the purpose of it must be otherwise. It's supposed to do something to us to make it easier (or more fun, or less painful) for us to live. Then all questions of form and so on become subjugated to this higher thing. We're not slaves any more to ideas of "the real" or, for that matter, to ideas of "the experimental" — we're just trying to make something happen to the reader in his or her deepest places. And that thing that happens will always be due to some juxtaposition of the life the reader is living and the words on the page...the heart will either rise, or it won't.

    —George Saunders

There was a long, long, angry discussion on *Tangent* [among SF readers and critics] when my story "What I Didn't See" came out over whether it was science fiction or not, and whether anything I wrote was worth reading. I was surprised (and dismayed) by the emotional intensity of it. And I don't imagine the story winning the Nebula changed anyone's mind. But I have an issue sometimes with the idea of "hard science." It seems to me that real science is increasingly mythic and poetic and hard to get a handle on. Just the way I write.

    —Karen Joy Fowler

93990

George Saunders

A TEN-DAY acute toxicity study was conducted using twenty male cynomolgus monkeys ranging in weight from 25 to 40 kg. These animals were divided into four groups of five monkeys each. Each of the four groups received a daily intravenous dose of Borazadine, delivered at a concentration of either 100, 250, 500, or 10,000 mg/kg/day.

Within the high-dose group (10,000 mg/kg/day) effects were immediate and catastrophic, resulting in death within 20 mins of dosing for all but one of the five animals. Animals 93445 and 93557, pre-death, exhibited vomiting and disorientation. These two animals almost immediately entered a catatonic state and were sacrificed moribund. Animals 93001 and 93458 exhibited vomiting, anxiety, disorientation, and digging at their abdomens. These animals also quickly entered a catatonic state and were sacrificed moribund.

Only one animal within this high-dose group, animal 93990, a diminutive 26 kg male, appeared unaffected.

All of the animals that had succumbed were removed from the enclosure and necropsied. Cause of death was seen, in all cases, to be renal failure.

No effects were seen on Day 1 in any of the three lower-dose groups (i.e. 100, 250, or 500 mg/kg/day).

On Day 2, after the second round of dosing, animals in the 500 mg/kg/day group began to exhibit vomiting and, in some cases, aggressive behavior. This aggressive behavior most often consisted of a directed shrieking, with or without feigned biting. Some animals in the two lowest-dose groups (100 and 250 mg/kg/day) were observed to vomit, and one in the 250 mg/kg/day group (animal 93002) appeared to exhibit self-scratching behaviors similar to those seen earlier in the high-dose group (i.e. probing and scratching at abdomen, with limited writhing).

By the end of Day 3, three of five animals in the 500 mg/kg/day group had entered a catatonic state, and the other two animals in this dose group were exhibiting extreme writhing punctuated with attempted biting and pinching of their fellows, often with shrieking. Some hair loss, ranging from slight to extreme, was observed, as was some "playing" with the resulting hair bundles. This "playing" behavior ranged from mild to quite energetic. This "playing" behavior was adjudged to be typical of the type of "play" such an animal might initiate with a smaller animal such as a rodent, i.e. out of a curiosity impulse, i.e. may have been indicative of hallucinogenic effects. Several animals were observed to repeatedly grimace at the hair bundles, as if trying to elicit a fear behavior from the hair bundles. Animal 93110 of the 500 mg/kg/day group was observed to sit in one corner of the cage gazing at its own vomit while an unaffected animal (93222) appeared to attempt to rouse the interest of 93110 via backpatting, followed by vigorous backpatting. Interestingly, the sole remaining high-dose animal (93990, the diminutive male), even after the second day's dosage, still showed no symptoms. Even though this animal was the smallest in weight within the highest-dose group, it showed no symptoms. It showed no vomiting, disinterest, self-scratching, anxiety, or aggression. Also no hair loss was observed. Although no hair bundles were present (because no hair loss occurred), this animal was not seen to "play" with inanimate objects present in the enclosure, such as its food bowl or stool or bits of rope, etc. This animal, rather, was seen only to stare fixedly at the handlers through the bars of the cage and/or to retreat rapidly when the handlers entered the enclosure with the long poking stick to check under certain items (chairs, recreational tire) for hair bundles and and/or deposits of runny stool.

By the middle of Day 3, all of the animals in the 500 mg/kg/day group had succumbed. Pre-death, these showed, in addition to the effects noted above, symptoms ranging from whimpering to performing a rolling dementia-type motion on the cage floor, sometimes accompanied by shrieking or frothing. After succumbing, all five animals were removed from the enclosure and necropsied. Renal failure was seen to be the cause of death in all cases. Interestingly, these animals did not enter a catatonic state pre-death, but instead appeared to be quite alert, manifesting labored breathing and, in some cases, bursts of energetic rope-climbing. Coordination was adjudged to be adversely affected, based on the higher-than-normal frequency of falls from the rope. Post-fall reactions ranged from no reaction to frustration reactions, with or without self-punishment behaviors (i.e. self-hitting, self-hair-pulling, rapid shakes of head).

Toward the end of Day 3, all animals in the two lowest-dose groups (250 and 100 mg/kg/day) were observed to be in some form of distress. Some of these had lapsed into a catatonic state, some refused to take food, many had runny brightly colored stools, some sat eating their stool while intermittently shrieking.

Animals 93852, 93881, and 93777, of the 250 mg/kg/day group, in the last hours before death, appeared to experience a brief period of invigoration and renewed activity, exhibiting symptoms of anxiety, as well as lurching, confusion, and scratching at the eyes with the fingers. These animals were seen to repeatedly walk or run into the cage bars, after which they would become agitated. Blindness or partial blindness was indicated. When brightly colored flags were waved in front of these animals, some failed to respond, while others responded by flinging stool at the handlers.

By noon on Day 4, all of the animals in the 250 mg/kg/day group had succumbed, been removed from the enclosure, and necropsied. In every case the cause of death was seen to be renal failure.

By the end of Day 4, only the five 100 mg/kg/day animals remained, along with the aforementioned very resilient diminutive male in the highest-dose group (93990), who continued to manifest no symptoms whatsoever. This animal continued to show no vomiting, retching, nausea, disorientation, loss of motor skills, or any of the other symptoms described above. This animal continued to move about the enclosure normally and ingest normal amounts of food and water and in fact was seen to have experienced a slight weight gain and climbed the rope repeatedly with good authority.

On Day 5, animal 93444 of the 100 mg/kg/day group was observed to have entered the moribund state. Because of its greatly weakened condition, this animal was not redosed in the morning. Instead, it was removed from the enclosure, sacrificed moribund, and necropsied. Renal failure was seen to be the cause of death. Animal 93887 (100 mg/kg/day group) was seen to repeatedly keel over on one side while wincing. This animal succumbed at 1300 hrs on Day 5, was removed from the enclosure, and necropsied. Renal failure was seen to be the cause of death. Between 1500 hrs on Day 5 and 2000 hrs on Day 5, animals 93254 and 93006 of the 100 mg/kg/day dose group succumbed in rapid succession while huddled in the NW corner of the large enclosure. Both animals exhibited wheezing and rapid clutching and release of the genitals. These two animals were removed from the enclosure and necropsied. In both cases the cause of death was seen to be renal failure.

This left only animal 93555 of the 100 mg/kg/day dose group and animal 93990, the diminutive male of the highest-dose group. Animal 93555 exhibited nearly all of the aforementioned symptoms, along with, toward the end of Day 5, several episodes during which it inflicted scratches and contusions on its own neck and face by attempting to spasmodically reach for something beyond the enclosure. This animal also manifested several episodes of quick spinning. Several of these quick-spinning episodes culminated in sudden hard falling. In two cases, the sudden hard fall was seen to result in tooth loss. In one of the cases of tooth loss, the animal was seen to exhibit the suite of aggressive behaviors earlier exhibited toward the hair bundles. In addition, in this case, the animal, after a prolonged period of snarling at its tooth, was observed to attack and ingest its own tooth. It was judged that, if these behaviors continued into Day 6, for humanitarian reasons, the animal would be sacrificed, but just after 2300 hrs the animal discontinued these behaviors and only sat listlessly in its own stool with occasional writhing and therefore was not sacrificed due to this improvement in its condition.

By 1200 hrs of Day 5, the diminutive male 93990 still exhibited no symptoms. He was observed to be sitting in the SE corner of the enclosure, staring fixedly at the cage door. This condition was at first mistaken to be indicative of early catatonia but when a metal pole was inserted and a poke attempted, the animal responded by lurching away with shrieking, which was judged normal. It was also noted that 93990 occasionally seemed to be staring at and/or gesturing to the low-dose enclosure, i.e. the enclosure in which 93555 was still sitting listlessly in its own stool occasionally writhing. By the end of Day 5, 93990 still manifested no symptoms and in fact was observed to heartily eat the proffered food and weighing at midday Day 6 confirmed further weight gain. Also it climbed the rope. Also at times it seemed to implore. This imploring was judged to be, possibly, a mild hallucinogenic effect. This imploring resulted in involuntary laughter on the part of the handlers, which resulted in the animal discontinuing the imploring behavior and retreating to the NW corner where it sat for quite some time with its back to the handlers. It was decided that, in the future, handlers would refrain from laughing at the imploring, so as to be able to obtain a more objective idea of the duration of the (unimpeded) imploring.

Following dosing on the morning of Day 6, the last remaining low-dose animal (93555), the animal that earlier had attacked and ingested its own tooth, then sat for quite some time writhing in its own stool listlessly, succumbed, after an episode that included, in addition to many of the aforementioned symptoms, tearing at its own eyes and flesh and, finally, quiet heaving breathing while squatting. This animal, following a limited episode of eyes rolling back in its head, entered the moribund state, succumbed, and was necropsied. Cause of death was seen to be renal failure. As 93555 was removed from the enclosure, 93990 was seen to sit quietly, then retreat to the rear of the enclosure, that is, the portion of the enclosure farthest from the door, where it squatted on its haunches. Soon it was observed to rise and move toward its food bowl and eat heartily while continuing to look at the door.

Following dosing on Day 7, animal 93990, now the sole remaining animal, continued to show no symptoms and ate and drank vigorously.

Following dosing on Day 8, likewise, this animal continued to show no symptoms and ate and drank vigorously.

On Day 9, it was decided to test the effects of extremely high doses of Borazadine by doubling the dosage, to 20,000 mg/kg/day. This increased dosage was administered intravenously on the morning of Day 9. No acute effects were seen. The animal continued to move around its cage and eat and drink normally. It was observed to continue to stare at the door of the cage and occasionally at the other, now empty, enclosures. Also the rope-climbing did not decrease. A brief episode of imploring was observed. No laughter on the part of the handlers occurred, and the unimpeded imploring was seen to continue for approximately 130 seconds. When, post-imploring, the stick was inserted to attempt a poke, the stick was yanked away by 93990. When a handler attempted to enter the cage to retrieve the poking stick, the handler was poked. Following this incident, the conclusion was reached to attempt no further retrievals of the poking stick, but rather to obtain a back-up poking stick from Supply. As Supply did not at this time have a back-up poking stick, it was decided to attempt no further poking until the first poking stick could be retrieved. When it was determined that retrieving the first poking stick would be problematic, it was judged beneficial that the first poking stick was now in the possession of 93990, as observations could be made as to how 93990 was using and/or manipulating the poking stick, i.e. effect of Borazadine on motor skills.

On Day 10, on what was to have been the last day of the study, upon the observation that animal 93990 still exhibited no effects whatsoever, the decision was reached to increase the dosage to 100,000 mg/kg/day, a dosage 10 times greater than that which had proved almost immediately lethal to every other animal in the highest-dose group. This was adjudged to be scientifically defensible. This dosage was delivered at 0300 hrs on Day 10. Remarkably, no acute effects were seen other than those associated with injection (i.e. small, bright purple blisters at the injection site, coupled with elevated heart rate and extreme perspiration and limited panic gesturing) but these soon subsided and were judged to be related to the high rate of injection rather than to the Borazadine itself.

Throughout Day 10, animal 93990 continued to show no symptoms. It ate and drank normally. It moved energetically about the cage. It climbed the rope. By the end of the study period, i.e. midnight of Day 10, no symptoms whatsoever had been observed. Remarkably, the animal leapt about the cage. The animal wielded the poking stick with good dexterity, occasionally implored, shrieked energetically at the handlers. In summary, even at a dosage 10 times that which had proved almost immediately fatal to larger, heavier animals, 93990 showed no symptoms whatsoever. In all ways, even at this exceptionally high dosage, this animal appeared to be normal, healthy, unaffected, and thriving.

At approximately 0100 hrs of Day 11, 93990 was tranquilized via dart, removed from the enclosure, sacrificed, and necropsied.

No evidence of renal damage was observed. No negative effects of any kind were observed. A net weight gain of 3 kg since the beginning of the study was observed.

All carcasses were transported off-site by a certified medical waste hauler and disposed of via incineration.

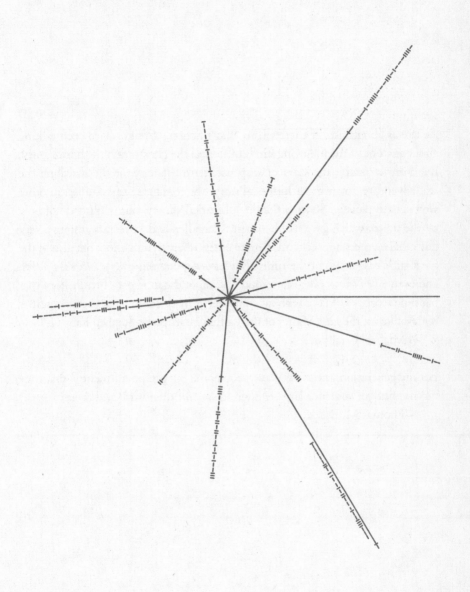

As late as about 1950, if I referred to "short fiction," I might have been talking about any one of the following kinds of stories: the ghost story; the horror story; the detective story; the story of suspense, terror, fantasy, or the macabre; the sea, adventure, spy, war, or historical story; the romance story. Stories, in other words, with plots.... Short fiction, in all its rich variety, was published not only by the pulps, which gave us Hammett, Chandler, and Lovecraft among a very few others writers now enshrined more of less safely in the canon, but also in the great slick magazines of the time: *The Saturday Evening Post, Collier's, Liberty,* and even *The New Yorker,* that proud bastion of the moment-of-truth story that has only recently, and not without controversy, made room in its august confines for the likes of the Last Master of the Plotted Short Story, Stephen King.

    —Michael Chabon

For my generation, the New Wave people, the big disappointment is that they did not find an audience large enough to sustain their work and their careers.

    —Thomas M. Disch

The Martian Agent, A Planetary Romance
Michael Chabon

'Tis theirs to sweep through the ringing deep where Azrael's outposts are,
Or buffet a path through the Pit's red wrath when God goes out to war,
Or hang with the reckless Seraphim on the rein of a red-maned star.
　　—Rudyard Kipling

I.

THE BROTHERS FIRST encountered a land sloop on the night, late in the summer of 1876, that one hunted their father down. It picked up their trail in Natchitoches country, two miles from Fort Wellington, at the ragged southwestern border of the Louisiana Territories and of the British Empire itself. The moon, as many sad partisans of the mutineer George Armstrong Custer were to record, hung fat in the sky, stained with an autumnal tinge of blood that, to some diarists, presaged hanging and debacle. Outside the windows of the coach in which the brothers and their parents rode lay the wilderness, flooded in black water and in a steady-flowing hubbub of night birds, insects, and amphibians. The coach bobbed and pitched as if borne on that current of bedlam and black water, down a road already ancient when the ancestors of these very insects had jabbed and goaded de Soto's men along it to their itching feverish deaths. The boot-heels of the coachman, a big, steady Vermonter named Haseltine, drummed against the front of the coach, just behind the boys' heads, with the random tattoo of a broken shutter in the wind. The timbers of the carriage groaned with each jolt and stone in the road. The respiration of the mosquito-mad team, a pair of spavined drays for which, two days earlier, they had exchanged the last of their sovereigns, rattled out behind the coach like a string of tin cans.

The first shrill call of the steel throat in the distance left a rippling wake of silence.

—Train, said the little one, or — no.

The cry had sounded too forlorn, too lupine for a train. Before the little boy even saw the knot of grief that deformed the hinge of the father's stubbled, powder-burnt jaw, he knew that whatever had uttered it was hungering for them.

—There are no trains, the older brother said. Not this deep into Indian country. Don't be a dolt.

—I'm not a dolt.

—A train.

—Please, the mother said, boys.

The little boy seized his brother's shoulder, gathering a scratchy wool handful of stained cadet gray. *He won't ever be a British officer now, nor will I.* Though he was a good forty pounds lighter and seven years the junior, the little boy sent the older brother lurching clear across the coach, slamming his head against a brass fitting. Before the older brother could retaliate there was another cry from the valve, louder, nearer, a blurred double-reeded blat less like the call of a wolf than of an implacable iron toad. At the sound of it the little boy scooted across the bench and buried his head in the brother's lap. The brother put an arm around him and stroked his hair. He pulled an old Ohio River Company trading blanket with its smell of dog and tallow, amid which they had huddled for most of the past week, up to their chins.

The mother turned to the father.

—Harry, she said. What is it? Could it be a train?

—Not here, said the father. Franklin is right. Not this close to Tejas.

They were less than ten miles now from the border and freedom — another fact which melancholy diarists of the failed rebellion would be inclined, in the days that followed, to record.

The father stood up and went to the door of the coach. The night and its furor of animals and bugs blew in and stirred the damp black strands of the mother's hair. Her cheeks were glinting, febrile. All the way from the Yalobusha River to the Red she had thrashed and dreamed fever dreams that to the little boy, whose name was Jefferson Mordden MacAndrew Drake, were unimaginably cavernous, lit with lamps of blood. The proximity of Tejas seemed to have revived her; reasoning conversely, her younger son was certain that if they did not make it across the Sabine River she would die. They were headed for the ferry at Beurre. Jefferson Drake had been in possession of this fact and little else for the past eleven days. The father hung half out of the door of the rocking coach and called upward into the night. The brothers could not hear what he inquired of the coachman, nor what reply he received. But when he sat down again, he hoisted the canvas haversack that had ridden between his feet all the way from Sulla, in the Ohio Territory, and began to take out his guns.

2.

Every lost cause has its sacred litany, each of whose plaints begins with the words "If only." If only Custer could have waited one week more for the road to Ashtabula to clear. If only Phil Sheridan had not been shot by the jealous husband of Mrs. Delaplane. And if only Cuyahoga Drake had made it to Tejas, surely the guns and gold promised by Lincoln...

In a telegram dispatched from Fort Wellington on the Sabine to the C-in-C of Her Majesty's Columbian Army, at Potomac, following the events whose successful conclusion raised him to Command of the Mississippi Army, Lieutenant General H. P. W. Hodge stated that Colonel Harry Drake, fleeing the ruin of the mutiny he had helped to foment, had been spotted by a native Natchitoches scout eleven miles from the Sabine River, eastern border of the Tejas Free Republic. The scout, a half-breed named Victor Piles, turned his mongrel pony toward the squat black turrets of the fort, raising a wild alarm. Word of Cuyahoga Drake's southwestern flight had followed him, more or less delayed by the intermittent drunkenness and indolence of the frontier courier corps, from the moment of his escape from the stockade at Sulla on the Ohio. General Hodge, sad, syphilitic, tormented by hidden sympathy with the mutineers, had been feeding the burners of his shining black pair of Mullock-Treadwell land sloops since early that morning, on the off-chance that Drake and his family might pass through the neighborhood on their way to the rusty yellow Sabine. Wellington was among the last of the southwestern stations to be equipped with steam wagons and had taken delivery of two brand-new Terror-class sloops, the *Dauntless* and the *Princess Louise,* only two weeks before. They had emerged from their crates, to the groaning of hot nails and navvies with crowbars, smelling of fresh paint, leather, packing oil, excelsior. Hodge had fallen in love them at once, with a helpless passion fostered by his remote and lonely billet. When Victor Piles came around crying about the rollicking carriage and dappled nags straining for Tejas down the old Natchitoches road, Hodge agonized over which of his darlings to risk and flaunt in pursuit of the renegade hero of Cleveland and Ashtabula.

In the end Hodge chose the *Dauntless*. She had been among the first wagons rolled out of Mullock-Treadwell's huge new Second Manchester Works, and she more than made up in style and speed what she lacked in seasoning or experience in the field. She was a Model 3 Terror, long and canine, a steel greyhound powered by a hundred-horsepower Bucephalus engine. The relative frailty of her armor-plating was more than compensated for by her maneuverability and by the range and mobility of her big .45 turret-mounted Gatling. Along with her crew of six she could carry a section of infantrymen, eight troopers of the 27th Cajun Fusiliers whom Hodge assigned to the pursuit. The question of whether there would be sufficient additional room in her acrid sweltering hold for a living prisoner remained unsettled as the *Dauntless* huffed, riveted leather treads clattering against the gangway of pine planking, out through the gates of Fort Wellington into the wilderness. The NCO in command of the Fusiliers, a Sergeant Swindell, had the foresight, in case space was wanting, to bring along a length of stout rope.

3.

In her haste to flee, after her husband's escape from the guardhouse at Sulla, Mrs. Drake, née Catherine Mordden, had endeavored to condense the wealth and history of her family into an Indiaman chest. Clean linens, a strand of Yalu pearls, her wedding dress, a Bible that had been the gift of her brother at their last parting. Mufflers and oilskins for the boys. Biscuit, wine, a small wheel of New York cheese. A plait of Iroquois wampum likely to have no value anywhere that her family might conceivably alight. A hundred-year-old flag of red and white stripes, with a quartered ring of yellowing stars on a blue field, that was her husband's most treasured possession; and a chromolithograph of Lieutenant General George Armstrong Custer, at the time of his accession to the Command of Her Majesty's Army of the Great Lakes, in a rosewood frame, which was her own. (Scurrilous rumors spread by the enemies of the Ohioists, and kept alive for decades afterward by the avid gossip of historians, would link Kitty Drake romantically to the Martyr of American Hopes, and even trace the younger of the two Drake boys to Custer's seed.) Half a mile from the ferry at Beurre Landing the sea chest, strapped to the roof of the rattling coach, worked itself out of its bindings and tumbled to the roadbed. It landed on one corner and split in two with the neat snap of a snuffbox springing open. Starry flag, lace, and biscuits were strewn across the road. Pearls skittered like water on a hot stove lid. The portrait of George Custer lay, glass glinting, in the lovely ill-betokening moonlight. For a moment, the expression of the Martyr in the portrait, that steady, slightly mad blue gaze which had always struck the portrait's owner as summarizing all that was brash, vainglorious, strong, fundamentally and conclusively un-English, about her husband's generation of solitary horsemen and wanderers and Indian fighters, took on a strangely plaintive air. Custer seemed to be remonstrating with the heavens he contemplated. Then, in a half-musical splintering of timber and glass, the *Dauntless's* left tread nosed its way onto and over the distilled patrimony of the Drakes, flattening what it did not tear or turn to dust and shards.

Then the *Dauntless* spoke.

—Colonel Drake.

It spoke in the voice of its chief engineer, a Sergeant Breedlove, who crouched in the dark roaring stink of its cabin, between the stack of metal rungs that climbed to the gun turret and a small transverse slot that permitted him to peer vaguely out into the Louisiana midnight, clutching a wooden funnel to his lips. The funnel was connected to a length of canvas-covered caoutchouc hose that ran up through a small eye in the roof of the land sloop, where it was joined to the narrow end of a large, slender horn or bell that opened beneath the Gatling like a lily, a black tin corsage.

—Colonel Drake, your mutiny is over. Custer has surrendered to the Crown.

The raspy, rather high-pitched tone of the *Dauntless* and its mushy Yorkshire accent carried easily across the narrowing gap between it and the carriage. The little boy looked at his brother, whose name was Franklin Mordden Evans Drake. Franklin Drake looked at their father.

—It's a trick, he said. Custer would never —

—You will not be permitted to reach the border, said the *Dauntless*. Please, Colonel. Do not force us to open fire.

The father rose from the bench once more to put his grimed face and staring eyes out into the uproar and moonlight of the bayou. He had a measuring gaze that could guess accurately at the weight of bullocks or the height of weather vanes or the wish, however pure or sinful, in the heart of an eight-year-old boy. He hung there for a long moment, leaning on the open door of the coach, estimating the chances and the outcomes. Then he closed the door and sat heavily down.

—Five hundred yards back, he said. A land sloop. Machine gun. A Gatling. A forty-five, I'd say.

—It's a Terror, said Frank with a hint of awe. Semi-amphibious. This late in the summer she could likely swim after us right into the river.

It was all the little boy could do to prevent himself from going to the door to see this marvel. The father noticed.

—No, he said.

The little boy sat back and looked at his brother, who was struggling with his own desire to see the thing that was running them to ground. The carriage rolled on, but its rocking had subsided and there was no question that Haseltine, the coachman, was losing his resolve. He had seen Gatlings and Nordenfeldts used on the Cayugas at Ashtabula and the Lakotas at Poudre and the Russians at Belokonsk. It was all too easy for him to imagine looking down to see the glaucous gray insides of his body lying steaming in his lap.

—Coward, said Cuyahoga Drake.

There was such universal disgust in his voice that for a moment the brothers were unsure whom the epithet was intended to damn. Then the father rose and went to the door once more.

—Haseltine! You damned milk-soaked —

—Harry.

The father turned to find the mother staring at him, her lips pressed together, worrying the worried kerchief tucked into the bodice of her shirtwaist dress.

Colonel Drake opened his mouth. He had sensibly and carefully and with only the most reasoning sort of bravery led the armies of the British Empire in victory after victory against Iroquois and Sioux and Alyeskan Tsarists before taking the first unmeasured step of his career and enlisting for eight brutal and glorious months in Custer's mad attempt to rekindle the extinguished Republic on the shores of Lake Erie. His sons waited for his next words.

—Colonel Drake, said the *Dauntless*, this is the final warning I will make.

In the end, the brothers would remember, their father merely nodded. When he drew his sword it was only to rap with the hilt, twice, against the ceiling of the coach.

Haseltine cursed and forgave the horses in a series of unintelligible barks. The carriage creaked and rumbled. The sand beneath its wheels sighed. Through the windows of the coach the clamor of the bayou, as if their forward progress had tended to slip them past or somehow through it like fingers cupped around a candle, now blew in, a steady, flame-snuffing gust. The mother winced and closed her eyes in pain, as if the discordant productions of nocturnal western Louisiana had triggered one of her megrims. Behind or within that clamor lay the grind of gears, the resolute, dumb, canine chuffing of the Terror's big Bucephalus. Up on the box, Haseltine coughed. There was the scratch of a lucifer.

More to his own surprise, perhaps, than that of those whom he addressed, who knew him better, Jefferson Drake found that he was moved by a spasm of profound outrage.

—We can't just sit here and wait for them to grab us!

Colonel Drake lit his own burled pipe. In more normal circumstances the business with match and tobacco might have served to veil his amusement with his younger son, who disdained generally to sit and wait for anything at all.

—What do you propose, Jefferson?

The boy looked at the two revolvers, two rifles, and eight boxes of cartridges that comprised the family arsenal. There were the pair of Webleys, a balky old single-shot Rigby won in a game of faro by the same seafaring maternal grandfather whose trunk had foundered on the Natchitoches road, and a captured Lebeau-Courally ten-gauge, its stock engraved with (Mrs. Drake had said) scenes from a book called *Atala* by Chateaubriand, and bearing the monogram of the late General Durmanov. It was exquisite but had been designed for the hunting of snipe and woodcock and could not be relied upon to kill a grown man.

Jefferson Drake was an inveterate reader of novels for boys. In these tales there were ever only three possible destinies available to those who found themselves in such a grave predicament. For Heroic Britons, there were the Fighting Martyrdom, guns blazing, and the Impossible Stand, holding out until help arrived. For a noble enemy — Russian, German, Pathan, the odd renegade Frenchman or Iroquois — there was only Defeat Without Surrender, choosing to end one's own life rather than face the ignominy of inevitable capture. (For "savage" enemies such possibilities rarely arose, for these traveled almost exclusively in Swarms or Hordes, and so never found themselves Surrounded.) Looking at their paltry armaments, and knowing from the grave listening expression on the face of his brother, who was keen on such things, that the approaching Terror must be a formidable piece of machinery indeed, the first two options seemed impracticable, in the first case, and in the second case ridiculous. Then too, they were no longer, for reasons the boy could have just managed to explain without truly understanding, Heroic Britons. They were rebels — mutineers. During those months of rapid victory, barbaric rains, and total failure, the Drake family had passed from that portion of the map of existence tinted proud and homely British red into a blank and hostile territory.

—Take our own lives, the little boy said.

It came out more of a question than he had intended, thin and grave and far too possible. He was hoping to be contradicted, and when the father said, "Nonsense," at once, without even taking his eyes off the glowing bowl of his pipe, the boy was so grateful that he burst into tears.

—Stop that blubbering, the father said.

He turned to the mother with a sharp tone and an air of giving her something useful to do. His tone was not unkind.

—Do button him up.

The mother sat forward and reached across the carriage toward him, trying to draw her son toward her fevered breast. But the boy pulled away, and wiped his eyes on his sleeve.

—I can button myself up.

He saw that his brother was watching him, with a peculiar empty expression that he knew well, and he sat back to wait, feeling obscurely comforted. Frank was always watching him, studying his words and behavior, not with envy or scorn or concern — though these were not unknown elements of his feelings for the little boy — but with a version of their father's measuring gaze that seemed to take Jeff's outbursts and ideas as a form of weather, phenomena that, correctly interpreted, could be exploited as the raw materials to which a masterly hand and chisel might be applied. All the currents of brotherly respect and imitation flowed in the usual direction between them: The younger idolized the older, nearly as devoutly as he did their father. But the impetus for their common undertakings as brothers — for all that it was the older one who arranged and directed them — nearly always derived from some wild remark, from the unreasoned hotheaded dissatisfaction, of the younger of the pair.

—Jeff's right. Give us a gun, Daddy. Let us go. They won't get us. I'll see to that.

—Oh, said the mother, Harry, no.

—We haven't got more than a few miles to go. It's hours yet until daylight.

Do you think I can't get myself and one little kid across a few miles of mud and frogs?

—He can, the little boy said. You know he can, Daddy.

The father sat a moment. Each time he drew on his pipe his long nose cast a flaring shadow up the high furrowed dome of his skull. The land sloop was close enough now that they could hear her crewmen shouting at one another to be heard over the racket of the machine they were laboring to control.

—Harry, the mother said. No. They will be cared for. They will not be harmed.

—They will be turned against us, said the father. Perhaps you do not consider this to be a form of harm.

He reached down and picked up one of the Webleys, opened the chamber, and checked it for the third time in ten minutes. Then he snapped it shut, and handed it to his older son.

—Your brother has never had the pleasure of meeting Mr. Lincoln, Franklin. See that you get him to San Antonio.

—Yes, sir. I will look after him, sir.

The boys slid from the bench and crouched down to fill their pockets with boxes of cartridges. Then the little boy went to the door. Afterward he would recall the way his heart pounded with the knowledge that he ought to go and throw his arms around his mother and father and bid them farewell. He was inclined, in later years, to excoriate himself for this omission. The truth, however, was that at the time his mind was such a jumble of agitation, apprehension, and the sheer blind desire to be free at last of that miserable rattletrap box, to be *doing something,* that it was not until he was already out of the coach, and scrambling across the road into a twisted thicket of dwarf-bearded oaks, that it occurred to him that he would never see his parents again. By then the land sloop was less than twenty yards from the coach, and it was too late. He crouched in an inch of sucking water, breathing hard, watching his brother's spidery form in the coach's open door. It was difficult to tell for sure but it looked as though Franklin and their father were gravely shaking hands. No doubt he had kissed their mother as well. Although it was Jefferson who concerned himself with the fine gesture and the act of panache, it was Franklin, who found such things laughable, who was always pulling them off.

There was a thud, a sharp huff of breath, and then Frank came scrambling into the trees, clutching the revolver to his chest. He found Jeff, and they squatted together in the foul-smelling mud, painting their backsides with swamp water, watching as the flame of the land sloop's lantern, mirrored and lensed, reached out to engulf the bayou in a swelling balloon of light.

—Get down, Frank said.

He pushed Jeff facedown into the mud and then lay beside him. The land sloop came, slowing, with a sound like an enormous box of nails and broken crockery falling down a flight of stairs. She stopped. In the moonlight Jeff could read the name, *Dauntless,* picked out in gilt letters on her flank. There was a flat chiming as her rear hatch rolled open, then the scrabble of boots, and then suddenly the roadbed seemed to fill with redcoats. They trotted, rifles aslant, to the carriage. Three of them pulled Haseltine from his seat and threw him to the ground. Several others dragged out Colonel Drake, and then with rough politesse assisted Mrs. Drake to step down. She stood slim and straight-backed, head held up, giving the soldiers a look the boys could not in fact see but could easily imagine. Their father struggled against them and was beaten, once, sharply, with the stock of a Martini. After that he stood, and suffered them to put him in irons.

—Colonel Henry Hudson Drake, in the name of Her Imperial Majesty, Queen Victoria, I place you under arrest on the charge of mutiny and treason against the Crown.

—Shoot! the little boy hissed. Shoot the gun.

—Quiet!

—Let me shoot it, then!

He reached for the revolver, kicking at his brother's shins, blind with rage or with the tears his rage incited. The older brother stuffed the gun into the waist of his pants and wrapped the boy up in his long arms that always seemed capable of encircling the younger one several times around. His left hand he clapped firmly, and for far from the first time in their lives, over the little boy's mouth.

The boy struggled for another moment, then just hung in his brother's embrace, and they watched as their parents and Haseltine were pushed toward the hatch of the *Dauntless.* Their mother was handed up into the hold at once, but the soldiers stood around the two male prisoners for some time, talking in low voices that occasionally broke out into angry hisses and, once, four words, shouted.

—I'll not permit it!

The boys recognized the thick Yorkshire burr in which the land sloop had called to them through the darkness. Then their father and Vernon Haseltine were heaved up into the *Dauntless,* like two buckling sacks of bricks. An order was given, and the iron hatch rolled shut, sealing up their parents within.

The older brother did not relax his grip, or remove his hand from the little boy's mouth, until the glow of the land sloop's lantern, handed from treetop to treetop in the eastern distance, dwindled and finally winked out, and the thump of her engine had been absorbed once more into the universal clangor of the swamp.

4.

At Tir-Na-Nog, the house on a Derbyshire hilltop, fifty miles from the sea, to which their maternal grandfather, Joseph Mordden, had retired at the end of his career as a ship's surgeon, there had stood an oak tree of great age and height. In the branches of this Khyber redoubt, storm-tossed yardarm, donjon, eyrie, pagoda, minaret, and pharos, both boys had spent a cumulative total of perhaps twenty-nine full, long August days during the course of their childhoods. And yet in all that time, it had never occurred to either of them — and certainly they would never have been permitted — to attempt to pass a night in the tree. But both of the boys had seen men under their father's command take off into the bush in a boiling cloud of dogs, in pursuit of deserters, fugitives from conscription, runaway spies. Frank suspected that it would be only a matter of time until a squad returned to look for the sons of Cuyahoga Drake. And so, after leading Jeff in a number of elaborate dog-baffling figures and hieroglyphs in and around the shallows of the bayou, he took hold of his younger brother, by the seat and waist of his breeches, and hoisted him up into the branches of a cypress for the night. The moon had set, and it was too dark for them to reconnoiter a way to the Sabine that would keep them off the road. He pulled himself up after Jeff, and they made their way carefully, dizzied by a medicinal odor, into the dark heart of the tree. The branches were coarse and slender and made an unpromising bed. They spent an hour that seemed like five hoping that the dawn would come and proving repeatedly to themselves and to one another that it was impossible to fall asleep while clinging. In the end they chanced the lower, broader boughs, and somehow fell asleep. Jeff's dreams were tormented by lurching and rocking, the creaking of old bones, the ghostly singing of frogs.

Frank hit him.

Jeff opened his eyes. The intervals among the foliage of the tree were filled with luminous needles and clusters of blue, and fringed with Spanish moss and tufts of mist. Jeff sat up, abruptly. If his brother had not caught hold of his arm he would have tumbled into the fly-rippled water below.

—They're coming.

He said it almost without voicing the words, rolling his eyes to the east. Jeff listened. The day lay in an interval of silence between the conversation of the night animals and that of the morning's birds. It was not long before Jeff heard the voices. He could hear that they were irritable and amused; he could hear that some were British and others bayou French. He could hear the labored, happy gasping of a hound. Frank stuck the revolver into the waistband of his uniform trousers, at the back, and lowered himself, hand under hand, down to the shallows. Jeff started after him.

—I thought you said we'd be safe up here, he whispered.

—Safe from alligators. Not redcoats. I just didn't want the dogs to find us before we had a chance to see where we were going.

—Where are we going?

Jeff nearly stumbled over the body of his brother, so quickly did he fall to the soft ground, and threw himself down alongside Frank. The voices had grown louder, the words intelligible; the men from Fort Wellington were coming their way, their boots sloshing and slurping in the mud. Now Jeff could make out the distant rumble of a steam wagon, idling perhaps, back on the Indian road. Perhaps a pair of wagons. No doubt the troops had been ordered to fan out into the bayou in all directions from the point at which the boys' parents had been taken. Frank was looking wildly around for a place to conceal themselves. The brush was thin, here; now Jeff could make out wavering patches of red moving toward them, beyond the clearing in which they had blindly landed the night before.

The expression on Frank's face was blank, thoughtless.

—Do something, Jeff said. Shoot them, swim for it, do something —

Frank seemed to come out of his fog.

—Give me your penknife, he said.

He cut a pair of the reedy stalks that grew all around them and investigated their cores, which proved to be not quite hollow but filled with a spongy mass through which, as he quickly demonstrated, sucking out his cheeks, a faint but steady breath could be drawn.

—What about the alligators?

—I just made them up.

Jeff looked at him. This was precisely the kind of lie that Frank excelled in; one which claimed that an earlier statement had been a lie. Often such a lie was followed by a third that claimed to invalidate it. Frank handed him a short length of reed, then started to crawl toward a deep pool on the other side of the tree in which they had waited out the night. He stopped and took the revolver from his waist, and tucked it lovingly into a hollow formed by the wild braiding of some thick old roots. Then he lowered himself, wincing broadly to cover the apprehension and disgust he felt at so doing, into the black water with its skin of slime.

5.

Buried in water, Franklin Drake clung to the bottom-mud, clutching a fistful of slick tangling tree roots for an anchor. Water hissed and whispered in his ears. Air came into his lungs only in recalcitrant sips that had a taste of stale bread. His circulatory system was protesting this ill treatment and at first, when he heard the water-muffled gunshots, he thought they were the pulse of his starved heart redounding in his ears. He let go of the roots, burst up into the light and air, and saw that his little brother had killed two men. The dead men lay facedown in an inch of brown water, near the plaiting of roots in which, five minutes earlier, Frank had hidden the gun. And Jeff was still shooting, taking careful aim as their father had taught him, both eyes open, one hand steadying the wrist of the other, as a dozen redcoats rushed him. A third fell backward, clutching his throat; then Jeff was swallowed up in scarlet wool. The gun was twisted from his hands, and he was hoisted into the air by the collar of his shirt.

—Jeff.

He thought they were going to kill his brother for what he had just done. Not five hours and I've already broken my promise, he thought. He waded out of the pool and up onto the slightly firmer mud, then lost his footing and went sprawling forward, hitting his head on an exposed root hard enough to render him almost senseless. There was shouting, and more shouting, red sleeves, spattered gaiters. Then a hand with very cold fingers grabbed him by the back of the neck and jerked him to his feet. Frank stumbled. There was blood in his right eye and then the smell of blood in his nostrils and finally the taste of it, like rawhide, in his mouth.

—Stand up, boy.

—I'm trying.

The soldier's knee found the seat of Frank's britches. Frank stumbled forward a few feet in the direction of his brother, reaching for him though he could no longer see him; though he could no longer see anything at all.

6.

A spatulate darkness, shaped like a shark, poured itself along the rues and alleys of the Vieux Carré. It splashed against the sides of houses and shops, then surged up walls of brick and clapboard to flood the Quarter's rooftops — drowning chimney pots, weather vanes, and tin flues — before brimming over the volutes of a cornice and ladling itself once more down an iron balcony into the street. The shadow, thrust by the angle of the rising sun several hundred feet ahead of its source, drifted west, toward the Place D'Armas and Government House. When it reached the pair of squat bell towers that flanked the dark brick barn or upended ark of the St. Ignatius Boys' Home, the shadow started up the side of the campanile, then hesitated, as if uncertain whether it would clear or be snagged on the tooth of the high black iron cross. After a moment, however, the shadow resumed its progress, inching its immense snout forward. It topped and descended the tower of St. Ignatius, drifted across the dairy and some other outbuildings, and flowed over the high stone wall that separated the home's grounds from those of the old Presbytère, which since the Declaration of Reunion had served as the territorial courthouse and bridewell. Here, as if having at last sniffed out what it sought, the great shadow came to a stop, falling halfway across the broad expanse of the jailyard, where it plunged into gloom the crew of Negro carpenters who were working there, effecting last-minute repairs to the old gallows that had once dangled the hooded carcasses of Andrew Jackson and the pirate Jean Lafitte.

In the office of the rector of St. Ignatius, the inveterate gloom, which served so well to cow the reprobate spirit of boyhood that was the ineradicable plague and evil genius of the institution, deepened to an almost nocturnal pitch. A faint aureole of dust bloomed around the globe of the gaslamp atop the escritoire at which the rector, in his dressing-gown, sat perched on a velvet stool. With his left hand Father Paul Joseph de St. Malo reached to turn up the flame in the lamp. His right hand went on scratching away at the page on his blotter. After a moment he looked up, and contemplated the dull patch on the carpet where, moments before, the morning sunlight slanting in through the leaded window had fallen in bright bars and chevrons. He smiled. He was engaged in the composition of a letter to the parents of an inmate who had died, and though he had written countless such missives over the twenty-odd years of his rectorship, and though the deceased boy had been a sniveler, a liar, and good-for-nothing, Father de St. Malo was nonetheless glad for the interruption, which had been foretold, the previous morning, in a cable from Savannah.

The old priest rose and passed through a stealthy door cut into the Spanish cedar wainscoting of his office. In his small, white bedchamber he washed his hands in the copper basin, emptied his bladder into the pot, and took off his dressing gown. He was still buttoning up his best shoes — from the workshop of Scapelli, the papal cordwainer — when Father Dowd, the rector's secretary, rapped softly on the hidden door.

—Did you put him in the garden?

—As you said.

—Did you offer him tea or coffee? Did you set out the *fraises des bois?*

—He declined them. He was not happy to be made to wait. He wanted to be taken directly to them.

The rector, having smoothed the scant hair of his pate with water and scrutinized his nostrils in the glass, opened the door. Father Dowd looked him over with professional detachment, and nodded. Suitable attire in which to meet a newly made O.B.E., a conqueror of the clouds, a hero of Empire and Science.

—I don't imagine he's very happy about anything just now, the rector said. Do you suppose he can have heard this morning's news?

—He said he has spent the last ten hours on his ship.

—Ah. Then I suppose I shall have to tell him myself.

They hurried, the gangly young priest from Cork and the stout Acadian rector, down the long corridor that led to the garden. The garden was the rector's only vanity, apart from his calfskin boots. He trained and reserved an elite crew of boys to turn its earth and pollard its fruit trees and sweep clean its sandy paths. Naturally these were the only boys ever permitted into its confines. The remainder of the wards of St. Ignatius found employment in the kitchen, the laundry, and in the shops, where they learned the manufacture of such useful items as bandages, laces, dippers and basins, simple furniture, toothpicks, and, lately, coffins. As they walked to the door that opened onto the garden, the priests passed — and inspected the labor of — five little boys on their knees, spread down the length of the corridor, going over the soft marble floor with buckets and chamois and rags.

—His ship, the rector said. You saw it?

—It's lovely, said Father Dowd. Looking at it, Father, I confess, it was difficult not to feel a desire to…

—Fly away? From this wonderful place?

They stepped out into the garden. The ponderous late-summer humidity of the last several weeks had diminished and the daylight had a touch of that delicate, wistful clarity that was perceptible only to natives of New Orleans as autumnal. The squash vines were effulgent as a horn section with brass-bright flowers, and a light, lightly rank breeze off the river stripped the petals from the last of the roses. It was, the rector thought, ideal weather for a hanging.

The inventor Sir Thomas Mordden stood beside a white-painted iron chair, his back to the garden door. A silver tray, with tea and coffee and cream from the teat of the home's own cow in silver pots, lay on a white iron table, beside an empty teacup and an appetizing red mound of wild strawberries that looked untouched. The inventor was gazing up at the windows of the dormitory. His hands were clasped behind his back with a suggestion of difficult restraint. He might have been trying to determine if he should call out to the boys he had come to redeem, or if he ought just to scale the wall with his bare hands and climb in through their window. He was a diminutive man, but his shoulders were broad, his legs thick, and the hands that labored to constrain one another behind his back looked capable of governing stone, of discovering fingerholds in the narrowest of chinks. At the sound of the priests' footsteps he spun and showed them a face that was sunburnt and wanted flesh. His pewter hair fell in lank strands, nearly to his collar; the breeze lifted and disarranged it. His suit, though it looked new, fit him poorly, as though it had been chosen in haste or disdain, The hair, the baggy suit, the enormous and snarled sideburns, the irritable cast of his haggard features were more in accordance with the proctor's notions of a Methodist pamphleteer, unkempt, idealistic, and doctrinaire, than of a savant, a renowned engineer, a man of considerable means.

—Father.

—Sir Thomas. May I say that however tragic and unfortunate the circumstances, you are most welcome in New Orleans.

—Thank you.

The aeronaut briefly weighed the hand the rector had offered him, then discarded it as if it suited no purpose of his.

—And may I say that it is with considerable interest and a sense of profound pride that I…that we all…have read of your wonderful experiments over these last several years. The newspapers —

—You may or may not, as you please.

—We read that you anticipate…

—Extraordinary things.

This in the same impatient, haughty tone, lips pursed, as if his nostrils burned with the saltpeter whiff of priestcraft. But Father de St. Malo saw something kindle in the aeronaut's eyes at the thought of the outlandish things he and his assistants were verging upon, in his laboratories in the wolds of Lincolnshire.

—Is it true, said Father Dowd, can it really be true, Sir Thomas, that you believe that it will one day be possible for men to travel to the moon?

Sir Thomas did not look at Father Dowd.

—Father, he said to the rector, I have not come four thousand miles to satisfy the idle curiosity of…of anyone. I am here as a private citizen, on personal business.

He gestured up to the windows of the dormitory. They were startling devices, his hands: large, long-fingered, smooth and nimble, with an unnerving suggestion of self-sentience.

—I wish to see my nephews and then be on our way. We spotted heavy weather off Biloxi. My weatherman believes it to be headed this way. I should like to avoid it if I can.

—You do not plan to pass even one night…

—Indeed I do not.

—But sir, Mrs. Drake…

—Naturally I intend to visit my sister before I leave New Orleans. Though I confess I fail to see that whether I do so or not is any affair of yours. Father.

—Sir Thomas. I regret that I must inform you. Mrs. Drake is dead.

Father de St. Malo turned to his secretary as if to have him confirm this information or to solicit further details, though the provost of the Hôtel-Dieu, Dr. Legac, was a boyhood friend. The rector knew as much as anyone about the death, that morning, of the traitor Cuyahoga Drake's wife.

—She suffered…she underwent a stroke, Sir Thomas. I am told that her end was swift and painless.

—Swift, perhaps, Sir Thomas said. Not painless. Oh, surely not.

—You have condolences of this house, sir, of the city, and of the whole Empire, I am sure.

Sir Thomas nodded. He took a handkerchief from his vest and dabbed at the corners of his eyes. Then he put the handkerchief away.

—Now I have less reason to tarry in this place than I had five minutes ago, he said.

He consulted his pocket watch, gold, fat as a biscuit, inscribed with tendrils and leaves that entwined the initials V. R.

—The storm may be here in an hour, he said, snapping the watch case shut. Time is short.

—I don't understand.

—It isn't necessary that you do.

—Do you not wish to see —? The, that is…the remains? And the arrangements, do you not—

—The arrangements have already been made. I made them by wire before I sailed from England, when it was made known to me that my sister might not survive.

—I see, the rector said. I suppose your work with engines has schooled you to be thorough in your plans.

—You satirize me.

—Not at all, I merely observe….

—You exhibit considerable interest in my affairs, Father. I take it that when I leave New Orleans, you will be careful to report each of my least little actions and statements to the gossips of the town.

—You do me great injustice, Sir Thomas.

—When you do so, Father, make sure you do not fail to report my wishes for the disposition of the second set of remains.

—The second…?

—Say that I wish that the body of Henry Hudson Drake be strung up as food for kites and buzzards, and that crows peck out his eyes.

He took out his handkerchief again, and dabbed a fleck of saliva from his lips.

—Sir Thomas.

—Will you not take that down, Father? Will you not forget?

—No, sir.

—Don't misquote me.

—I will not.

—Good, Sir Thomas said, turning toward the door. Now, take me to the boys.

7.

There was a fat white boy named Zebedee who sat on your head and broke wind into your mouth and nostrils, and a black boy named Hob Pistorus, all of whose modicum of unreasoning love was lavished on the shiv he had crafted from an iron bedslat. It could flay a live pig before the squeal was out the mouth, as he liked endlessly to repeat. Some of the so-called boys had rasp chins and hairy loins and were mean as Ohio keelmen. They drank themselves blind on cloudy stuff concocted from rainwater and sawdust, and boasted of having poisoned the predecessor of Father Dowd with rat bait. To the boys of St. Ignatius, Her Majesty the Queen-Empress was a fat, ancient she-toad who gaped from the wall with Jesus and Loyola as Father de Tant-Malodeur laid a whistling switch across their backs; her Empire was nothing more to them than the back of a constable's hand, the gates of the debtor's prison, the news that your father had succumbed to cholera with his entire troop in a cantonment on the Red River. Nonetheless the boys used the excuse of her betrayal by Cuyahoga Drake to plague the disgraced man's sons with taunts, blows, and wretched tricks, and with constant allusions, enigmatic and stark, to ropes, neck bones, hangman's hoods. Falling asleep at night, if it were not to be a fatal error, must be a work of forbearance and discipline; Jeff learned to distinguish and await the several snores and the varied nocturnal mutterings of every one of the twelve other boys who were locked into C Ward with him and Frank each night. After an early bad surprise from Zebedee Louch, Jeff schooled himself to tell the pattern of that boy's imitation snore from the more erratic trend of his real one. And yet if Jeff had been on his own —If it had been either one of the Drake boys left alone with the toughs, cranks, and arabs of St. Ignatius — he might have suffered a much harder fate than, as befell Frank, encountering with the ball of his naked foot the soft dead rat that someone had placed in his boot or, in Jeff's case, dwelling for an unbearable minute in the hot stench of Zebedee Louch's crotch. Each brother scouted the other's perimeters, stood picket on the other boy's flank, kept vigil, whistling outside the shit-house, as the other underwent his lonely tribulations in the sweltering hell of the jakes. They had been assigned to bunks at opposite ends of C Ward, but every night, as soon as the porter snuffed the lamps, Frank would make his way down the long row of iron bedsteads and climb in to lie, tensed, listening to the darkness, alongside Jeff. This was an infraction punishable by a jaunt on the strapping horse. Frank was obliged to rouse himself every morning before light showed in the sky, and creep back in the half-light to his own bare bunk.

The brothers felt themselves and their behavior scrutinized by the priests with a greater than usual degree of intensity, and to the extent that they attempted to baffle or elude inspection they might well have been pleased had they known that the weekly reports on their conduct sent by the Fathers of St. Ignatius to the military tribunal at Sulla were replete with puzzled apologies. Though their conversations were indeed diligently monitored, both by the priests and by Hob Pistorus, the usually reliable C Ward telltale, neither of the Drake whelps was ever heard to make reference — not once — to their parents, let alone to any other conspirator, putative accomplice, or hitherto unknown plan of the mutineers. This all-but-inhuman regimen of silence was broken only on Monday mornings at nine, as if according to some privately evolved protocol on the treatment due prisoners of war, when the older brother would appear before Father de St. Malo, shoulders back, head high, and make what he termed a formal petition that he and his co-captive be permitted to visit their mother in hospital, a request that each week, for a different arbitrary reason, was always denied. Beyond this weekly ceremony, however, it was as if the fate and disposition of their imprisoned and ailing parents meant nothing to them at all.

It was Jeff who had recalled reading, in the *Boys' Own Paper*, a ripping yarn, set in the time of Vortigern and Boadicea, in which shadowy druids spoke without speaking by means of a manual alphabet; it was Frank who had diagrammed their hands, assigning four letters to the tip, phalanges, and base of the thumb, five to each of the fingers, and Y and Z to the pair of knobby hinges at the heel of the palm. By this cumbersome, intimate means, lying beside each other on Jeff's cot in the gray eternity of a night on C Ward, they communicated slow and feverish plans of escape, itemizing careful lists of necessary materiel, alternate routes, means of creating disruptions. With great difficulty they consolidated geographic information gleaned from other boys to sketch on the flats of their bellies a map of New Orleans, locating at the navel the Presbytère where their father languished and just under the left breast the mournful pile of the Hôtel-Dieu. Against the skin and bones of their hands the boys dwelt constantly, if never at great length, on the physical and emotional state of their mother, and speculated, with urgent jabs of their forefingers, on the chances of their father's obtaining, and the likelihood of his accepting, the mercy of the court-martial. They remembered what they could of the history of Raleigh's first acquittal, and attempted to derive a kind of grim comfort from the stoical grace with which earlier rebels of the frontier, Jackson and Crockett and Clay, had gone to their deaths. If the boys fell asleep too soon or too deeply, they knew, they would be set upon, and so each labored to keep the other awake, quizzing him on the colors and orders of Imperial regiments; the stages, battles, and commanders of the great Yukon and Ohio campaigns; the names of dogs and horses their family had owned over the years; the genealogies of Morddens, MacAndrews, Evanses, and Drakes as far back as either could stretch them. They spoke and fretted and argued far into the stillness of the morning. They lay together on Jeff's narrow cot, holding hands.

On the day when the dogfish shadow came snuffling over the housetops of the Vieux Carré, the Drake boys took the extreme liberty of appearing for morning inspection as they had slept, side by side, sitting on the younger boy's bunk. This was grounds for caning but on this awful morning they sensed that for once they might be excused and if not then rules be damned and it would suit them to be caned. They had dressed themselves in the cadet's uniform and the broadcloth suit, laundered by Jeff and patched by Frank, in which the troop of Cajun Fusiliers had first dragged them onto the ward. Drawers, comb, stockings, and two suits of gray shoddy provided by the home lay rolled with regimental precision into a worn duffel on the floor.

The bolt was thrown back and the door to C Ward swung open. The brothers' gazes remained fixed on the tall windows opposite the younger boy's bunk. These windows overlooked the rector's garden but years of salt breeze and soot and some inherent light-denying property of the glass precluded a view of anything but an ashy residue of the morning. Frank sat perfectly still; Jeff swung his skinny legs back and forth, making a swishing sound with the tips of his boots against the rough canvas top of the duffel.

—Franklin, Jefferson, said the rector. Sir Thomas is here.

Jeff started to look toward the doorway but felt or rather struck against his brother's inertness, the inflexibility of his gaze on that impenetrable gray window. He stopped kicking at the duffel and just sat.

—He has come all the way from England to fetch you. That is far more than either of you deserves.

One of the boys snickered and Jeff could feel the steady hard examining stares of the others. The two men came down between the ranks of cots and stood before them. The black bulk of the uncle eclipsed the gray windows. His watch chain dangled before Jeff's eyes. Frank had met the uncle a few times before, at Tir-Na-Nog, but Jeff only once, and that when Jeff was an infant in a dress. Frank said that their father and the uncle had quarreled, then, over the murder of John Brown by the Kansas Separatists. They had come to blows, and parted with rancor and finality.

—Nephews. It is hard to be so ill-met after so long a separation.

Jeff's right hand crept across the blanket of the bunk and sought the fingers of his brother's left. They felt rough and cool and dry.

—Well, the rector demanded, have you nothing to say?

Have you? Jeff worked the words with his fingers against Frank's.

Not to a Tory bastard like him.

—Well? said the rector again.

Jeff looked up into the bony florid face of his mother's brother. The eyes were grave and held pity and fatigue. The lower lip of the mouth was like their mother's, full and sorrowing. The sight of it, the memory of her, of his failure to kiss her that night in the coach, filled Jeff with an obscure anger.

—God save the Ohio Rebellion! he cried.

The boys of C Ward whistled and hooted and crowed. There was the whiz of a hornet at Jeff's ear and then its sting. Jeff pitched forward and the hand he slapped to his temple came away shining with blood.

—Good heavens, the rector said.

The uncle caught hold of Jeff with his left hand, by the shoulder, and set him back upright on the bed, keeping a tight grip on him. He held out his big right hand, closed in a fist. The pale eyes were pink-rimmed, their whites stained yellow as if from exposure to some poisonous reagent or fumes.

—God save you, my boy, he said.

He opened the great white anemone of his hand, palm upward, revealing a smooth red stone.

—I assure you, Sir Thomas, the boy who threw that shall be punished, the rector said. None of them will eat today until he comes forward or is named.

There was a groan from the boys, and then silence. The rector worked at the silence with his glare and the twitching of his jaw. It would not give.

A damp cloth and a wad of bandage were found and applied to the jutting bone behind Jeff's ear, and then the uncle applied a plaster. His ministrations were brusque but patient and in the care he took Jeff sensed or perhaps even remembered a vein of tenderness.

—On your feet, the uncle said, both of you.

They went out of C Ward for the last time, followed by the rector, and stood in the great echoing central stair. It seemed dark for this hour. Jeff looked up to the ceiling of the stairwell, where an iron-ribbed skylight generally let in a portion of the fair sky that mocked, or the foul one that suited, the unvarying gray weather of an orphan boy's day. It was filled with something that Jeff took at first to be the shadow of the bell tower but which then moved — floated — to one side and seemed, ever so slightly somehow, to ripple.

The uncle's hand lay heavy on Jeff's shoulder.

—Let those boys not, he said to the rector, be punished for a display of patriotism, Father. I do not desire punishment.

The rector nodded. Then the uncle pushed Frank and Jeff toward the stairs.

—Up, boys, he said. We must hurry.

—Up? said Jeff.

He dug in his heels, gazing in uneasiness at the rippling shadow that filled the skylight. In spite of the gentle attention his cut had received, he felt a violent spasm of mistrust for the uncle now. Perhaps they were to be pushed from the roof, or thrown to a crowd of ruffians, or consigned to some unknown oubliette in the bell tower, like the poor little princes he remembered from his *Lamb's Shakespeare*.

—We go up?

—Quite a considerable way, the uncle said. As a matter of fact.

8.

Though he was to observe and ship out in dozens of them during the course of his life and career — from the world-spanning, titanic *Admiral Tobakoff*, with its concert hall and natatorium, to the worlds-spanning *Lancet,* hardly bigger than a racing scull, from the trim transpacific racer *Gulf of Sinkiang* to the sturdy, homely freight blimps of the Red Star line — Frank would never entirely lose the sense of melancholy majesty that stirred his heart when he first saw an airship, moored in the troubled sky a hundred feet above the St.

Ignatius Boys' Home. He was moved by her delicacy, by her massive silence, by the rich Britannic red of her silk gasbag. She was like a divot, bright as clay, cut into in the dull gray turf of the clouds. There was a wind in the southeast and she strained at the guy that moored her to the campanile, and once tossed her nose like a mare sniffing fire. An oblong car of silver and dark wood dangled from her underbelly, part Pullman sleeper, part clarinet, its windows haunted by dark mustached faces.

—The *Tir-Na-Nog*, Uncle Thomas said, as if she were a present he had brought along for his nephews. My own design.

He watched them watching his airship, pale eyes crinkling, face flushed. In the presence of the *Tir-Na-Nog* he seemed fonder of them; he draped his arms across their shoulders.

—There isn't another like her in the world.

A hatch opened in the forebelly of the black gleaming gondola. Two of the mustached lascars peered out. One raised an inquiring hand and the uncle nodded, and taking his arm from Frank's shoulders signaled, palm downward, twice. The blue-capped dark heads disappeared from the hatch and after a moment a large wicker basket dropped into sight and dangled, slowly falling.

Frank held his breath and pressed his lips together so hard they turned white. He suffered, with erotic intensity, from the signal passion of his age: engineering. He reverenced the men on whom was shed the peculiar glory of the second half of the century, when adventure went forth with gearbox, calipers, level, and chain. Thus he was mad to know the organization and capacity of the *Tir-Na-Nog*'s engines. He would gladly have indentured himself, for long years, to studying the system of cable, flap, and rudder that guided her, the science and finesse that regulation of her buoyancy and altitude required. He longed to subject his uncle to a close and niggling interrogation, as they had used to do on long July afternoons at Tir-Na-Nog, to draw fabulous facts and anecdotes out of Sir Thomas Mordden, pioneering aeronaut, penetrator of the trackless bush of the sky, deliverer, as the *Illustrated London News* had once phrased it, "of the key to making Britain the queen not merely of the land and sea but of all the vast empyrean girdle of the earth." But gazing up at the wondrous contraption in the sky in which, most wondrous of all, he was now evidently to take ship, Frank maintained a silence as absolute as that of the *Tir-Na-Nog* herself. Their uncle invited them to marvel; Frank refused. He wanted, if momentarily, then with all his heart, to see their uncle punished. Frank knew that this was unjust of him, that his uncle could not be held responsible for things that had transpired and decisions taken while he was sequestered with his assistants in the famous Mordden Laboratories. Frank knew that in holding his tongue he was only punishing himself.

—Is that the one you flew in to Africa? Jeff said.

—No, I fear the *Livingston* was destroyed upon my arrival there, Uncle Thomas said. He smiled. Hacked to bits by the Mtabebe.

—Can we fly all the way to England in that? Without even stopping? How high will we go?

Frank applied a furtive knee to his brother's bottom, hard. Jeff crumpled and then turned his traitor's gaze to Frank. For an instant he looked angry, but the reproach in Frank's eyes banked his fire and he rubbed at his backside with a sheepish air.

—We ain't going anywhere, Frank said.

The basket scraped the tiled cornice, bounced against the galvanized tin of the roof, and settled. Uncle Thomas took hold of Jeff under the arms, and hoisted him over the side of the basket. Frank stood, fighting against the longing to fly. He would not abandon his mother. He would ensure that there remained at least one man in New Orleans, in the Louisiana Territory, in all the vast Crown Colony of Columbia, to mourn the death of Cuyahoga Drake.

—We shall make London easily, my boy, Uncle Thomas said, as if to Jeff. We could make it as far as Istanbul. The Mordden Mark III is a dreadfully efficient engine.

He looked at Frank, fixedly, his womanly mouth curled at one corner, as if reading the hunger to know that underlay his nephew's stoical demeanor. He scattered specifications like crumbs to a reticent deer.

—There are a pair of them, he said. Four-cylinder compound engines. Vertical coil, parallel-flow flash boiler. Firebox above the boiler coils. Honeycomb condenser with vacuum pumps and complete automatic firing. One hundred and twenty horsepower apiece.

There was a burst of drum clatter from the yard of the old Presbytère, a workman's ragged laugh. Jeff reached for Frank's hand, but Frank would not take it. He did not want his brother distracting him with useless tappings at his palm.

—You won't be abandoning her, Franklin, their uncle said. There is no way that you could.

Frank caught his breath. The laughter of the workmen in the jailyard became general and merry. Down in the workshops of St. Ignatius he could hear the chiming hammers of a coffin being nailed.

—My poor boy, Sir Thomas said. You must accept that I am all the family you have left.

—That's a lie!

—Come aboard the *Tir-Na-Nog*, Frank. One day we shall sail her straight to the moon. To Venus or Mars.

Frank craned his head to try to catch a glimpse of the pale Presbytère; he envisioned his father waving from one of its stone window ledges, putting on a jaunty smile, saluting him. But all he could see was the high bell tower of St. Ignatius, part of a spike-topped stone wall, a rounded stucco corner of the prison, a dusty brown patch of tamped earth in the prison yard, a pair of colored workmen leaning on the handles of two pickaxes.

—Stay if you will, then, his uncle said curtly. He gave a signal, and with a jerk the basket rose off the pitted zinc of the roof.

—Frank!

Jeff threw himself against the side of the basket and tried to climb out, wild, in tears for the first time since the night of Custer's surrender. He managed to get one leg over the side. Sir Thomas caught him by the collar and hauled him back in.

—Frank!

Frank remembered the promise he had made to his father; surely to have broken it would be the greater abandonment.

The basket dragged, skipping, along the roof, and snagged against the cornice. In the instant before it would have freed itself and started upward, Frank crossed the roof and threw himself headlong into it, landing in a heap at his uncle's feet. He stood up, steadying himself. He wiped his hands against the knees of his patched cadet's uniform, and looked levelly at his uncle.

—You're a liar, he said. There is no atmosphere in interplanetary space.

Then he could see the bare tree, the scaffold, the platform with its neat square trapdoor. Sir Thomas gathered Jeff into his arms, and covered his face, hooding his eyes with his great hands.

—We're all liars, Franklin, he said. We lie, and then we wait and hope for time and hard work and the will of God to make us honest men.

They bumped up through the hatch of the *Tir-Na-Nog*, into the dark innards of her gondola. Strong arms hauled them from the basket. They were set on their feet in a bright room, trimmed in brass, paneled all around with windows and the glass faces of gauges.

Sir Thomas Mordden took a yachtsman's cap and settled it onto his head.

—London, sah? said the helmsman.

The captain of the *Tir-Na-Nog* nodded, his smile wistful and aimed curiously at his nephews. He might have been picturing them alighting, one day, on the dark red sand of Mars.

—At present, he said. Yes, London will do for now.

I don't want to define science fiction because there's a basic assumption when you ask somebody to define a genre. The word genre in French means species, and you can define a species, for example, by the fact that cats can't interbreed with dogs.... It's hard to imagine that a Chihuahua and a Great Dane are the same species and they can interbreed, but they can't breed with a fox.... That's not true of genres in literature. They aren't definable because they aren't fixed in the same way. Nonetheless, if you say science fiction to me, you and I can have a conversation in which we have a basic understanding. I'm not saying that genres don't exist. I'm just saying that they don't have defined edges.

—Maureen McHugh

Most of my short stories are science fiction. I never have quit writing science fiction; it's just that I only write [science fiction] short stories. My long works have been western stories. I have a book-length collection of science fiction short stories, but I'm not planning to publish it any time soon. I don't want to distract readers from who they think I am. If I came out with a collection of science fiction stories, they'd probably be baffled by it.

—Molly Gloss

Frankenstein's Daughter
Maureen F. McHugh

I'm at the mall with my sister Cara, doing my robot imitation. Zzzt-choo. Zzzt. Zzzt. Pivot on my heel stiffly, 45 degrees, readjust forward, headed towards Sears, my arms stiff and moving with mechanical precision.

"Robert!" Cara says. It's easy to get her to laugh. She likes the robot stuff a lot. I first did it about a year ago, and it feels a little weird to do it in public, in the mall. But I want to keep Cara happy. Cara is six, but she's retarded so she's more like three or four and she'll probably never be more than about four or five. Except she's big. She was born big. Big bones like a cow. Big jaw, big knuckles. Big blue eyes. Only her blond hair is wispy. You have to look really hard to see how she resembles Kelsey. Kelsey was my big sister. I'm fourteen. Kelsey was hit by a car when she was thirteen. She'd be twenty now. Cara is Kelsey's clone, except, of course, Kelsey wasn't retarded or as big as a cow. In our living room there's a picture of Kelsey in her gymnast's leotard, standing next to the balance beam. You can kind of see how Cara looks like her.

"Let's go in Spencer's," I say.

Cara follows me. Spencer's is like heaven for a retarded girl — all the fake spilled drinks and the black lights and the lava lamps and optical projections and Cara's favorite, the Japanese string lights. They're back with the strings of chili pepper lights and the Coca-Cola lights. They sort of look like weird Christmas lights. If you look right at them, all they do is flicker, but if you look kind of sideways at them, you see all these Japanese letters and shit. Cara just stares at them. I think it's the flicker. While she's staring, I wander towards the front of the store.

Spencer's is shoplifter paradise, so they've got really good security. There's this chubby guy in the back, putting up merchandise and sweating up a storm. There are the cameras. There's a girl at the front cash register who is bored out of her mind and fiddling with some weird Spencer's Gifts pen but who can pretty much see anything in the store if she bothers to look. But I've got Cara. That, and I understand the secret of shoplifting, which is to have absolutely no emotions. Be cold about the whole thing. I can switch off everything and I'm just a thinking machine, doing everything according to plan. If you're nervous, then people notice you. Iceman. That's my name, my tag. That's the nickname I use in chatrooms. That's me.

I look at the bedroom board games. I stand at the shelf so that I pretty much block anything anyone could see in a camera. I don't know exactly where the cameras are, but if I don't leave much space between me and the shelf, how much can they really see? I wait. After a minute or two, Cara is grabbing the light strings and after another couple of minutes, the girl who's watching from the cash register has called someone to go intercept Cara and I palm a deck of *Wedding Night Playing Cards*. They're too small to have an anti-theft thing. I don't even break a sweat, increase my heart rate, nothing. The Iceman. I head back to Cara.

Everyone's just watching the weird retarded girl except this one chubby guy who's trying to get her to put down the lights but who's afraid to touch her.

"Not supposed to touch those," he says. "Where's your mom? Is your mom here?"

"Sorry!" I say.

The chubby guy frowns at me.

"Cara," I say. "No hands."

Cara looks at me, looks at the lights. I gently try to take them.

"No!" she wails. "Pretty!"

"I'm sorry," I say, "I'm her brother. She's developmentally delayed. Cara! Cara, no. No hands."

She wails, but lets me disentangle her hands.

"I'm sorry," I say again, the concerned big brother. "I was just looking around and thought she was right with me, you know? Our mom's down at Dillard's."

Chubby guy kind of hovers until I get the lights away from Cara and as soon as I put them on the shelf he grabs them and starts straightening them out and draping them back over the display.

I herd Cara towards the front of the store, mouthing *sorry* at the front cashier. She's kind of pretty. She smiles at me. Nice big brother with retarded sister.

Back out in the mall, Cara is wailing, which could start an asthma attack, so to distract her I say, "You want a cookie?"

Mom has Cara on a diet, so of course she wants a cookie. She perks up the way Shelby, our Shetland Sheepdog does, when you say "treat." I take her to the food court and buy her an M&M cookie and buy myself a Mountain Dew and then while she's eating her cookie, I pull the deck of cards out of my pocket and unwrap it. We've got another fifteen minutes before we have to meet my mom.

The idea is to play fish except every time you get a match you're supposed to do what it says. *Tie partner's hands with a silk scarf. Kiss anywhere you like and see how long your partner can keep from moving or making any noise. The one who lasts the longest gets to draw an extra card.*

Tame, but pretty cool. I can't wait to show Toph and Len.

Cara has chocolate smeared on her mouth, but she lets me wipe her face off.

"You ready to go back to see Mom?" I say.

When we pass Spencer's again, she stops. "Uhhh," she says, pointing to the store. Mom always tries to get her to say what she wants, but I know what she wants and I don't want to fight with her.

"No," I say. "Let's go see Mom."

Cara's face crumples up and she hunches her thick shoulders. "Uhhh," she says, mad.

"It's okay." I say. "Come on."

She swings at me. I grab her hand and pull her behind me. She tries to sit down, but I just keep on tugging and she follows me, gulping and wailing.

"What did you do?" my mom says when she sees us. My mom had to buy stuff, like gym shorts for me and underwear for herself, so I told her that I'd take Cara with me while she bought her stuff. She's holding a Dillard's bag.

"She wanted to go in Spencer's," I say. "We went in but she kept grabbing stuff and I had to take her out and now she's upset."

"Robert," my mom says, irritated. She crouches down. "Ah, Cara mia, don't cry."

We trail out of the store, Cara holding Mom's hand and sniffling.

By the time we get to the car, though, Cara's wheezing. Mom digs out Cara's inhaler and Cara dutifully takes a hit. I tried it once and it was pretty dreadful. It felt really weird, trying to get that stuff in my lungs, and it made me feel a little buzzy but it didn't even feel good, so it's pretty amazing that Cara will do it.

Cara sits in her booster seat in the back of the car, wheezing all the way home, getting worse and worse, and by the time we pull in the driveway, she's got that white look around her mouth.

"Robert," Mom says, "I'm going to have to take her to the Emergency Room."

"Okay," I say and get out of the car.

"You want to call your dad?" Mom asks. "I don't know how long we'll be." Mom checks her watch. It's three something now. "We may not be home in time for dinner."

I don't want to call my dad who is probably with Joyce, his girlfriend, anyway. Joyce is always trying to be likable and it gets on my nerves after a while — she tries way too hard. "I can just make a sandwich," I say.

"I want you to stay at home, then," she says. "I've got my cell phone if you need to call."

"Can Toph and Len come over?" I ask.

She sighs. "Okay. But no roughhousing. Remember you have school tomorrow." She opens the garage door so I can get in.

I stand there and watch her back down the driveway. She turns back, watching where she's going, and she needs to get her hair done again because I can really see the gray roots. Cara is watching me through the watery glass, her mouth a little open. I wave good-bye.

I'm glad they're gone.

I watch my daughter try to breathe. When Cara is having an asthma attack she becomes still; conserving, I think. Her face becomes empty. People think Cara looks empty all the time, but her face is usually alive — maybe with nothing more than some faint, reflected flicker of the world around her, like those shimmers of light on the bottom of a pool, experience washing over her.

"Cara mia," I say. She doesn't understand why we won't pick her up anymore, but she weighs over sixty-five pounds and I just can't.

She doesn't like the Emergency Room but it doesn't scare her. She's familiar with it. I steer her through the doors, my hand on her back, to the reception desk. I don't know today's receptionist. I hand her my medical card. When Cara was born, we officially adopted her, just as if we had done a conventional in-vitro fertilization in a surrogate and adopted the child, so Cara is on our medical plan. Now, of course, medical plans don't cover cloned children, but Cara was one of the early ones.

The receptionist takes all the information. The waiting room isn't very full. "Is Dr. Ramanathan on today?" I ask. Dr. Ramanathan, a soft-spoken Indian with small hands, is familiar with Cara. He's good with her, knows the strange idiosyncrasies of her condition — that her lungs are oddly vascularized, that she sometimes reacts atypically to medication. But Dr. Ramanathan isn't here.

We go sit in the waiting room.

The waiting room chairs don't have arms, so I lay Cara across a chair with her head on my lap and stroke her forehead. Calming her helps keep the attack from getting too bad. She needs her diaper changed. I didn't think to bring any. We were making some headway on toilet training until about two months ago, but then she just decided she hated the toilet.

I learned not to force things when she decided to be difficult about dinner. She's big and although she's not terribly strong, when she gets mad she packs a wallop. The last time I tried to teach her about using a fork, I tried to fold her hand round it and she started screaming. It's a shrill, furious scream, not animal at all, but full of something terribly human and too old for such a little girl. I grabbed her hand and she hit me in the face with her fist and broke my reading glasses. So I don't force things anymore.

The nurse calls us at a little after five.

I settle Cara on the examining table. It's cold so I wrap her in a blanket. She watches me, terribly patient, her mouth open. She has such blue eyes. The same eyes as Kelsey and the same eyes as my ex-husband, Allan. I can hear the tightness in her chest. I sit down next to her and hum and she rubs my arm with the flat of her hand, as if she were smoothing out a wrinkle in a blanket.

I don't know the doctor who comes in. He is young and his face seems good-humored and kind. He has a pierced ear. He isn't wearing an earring, but I can see the crease where his ear is pierced and it cheers me a little. A little unorthodox, and kind. It seems like a good combination. His name is Dr. Guidall. I do my little speech — that she has asthma, that she had an attack and didn't respond to the inhaler, that she is developmentally delayed.

"Have you been to the Emergency Room before?" he asks.

"Many times," I say. "Right, Cara?"

She doesn't answer, she just watches me.

He examines her and he is careful. He tells her the stethoscope is going to be cold and treats her like a person, which is a good sign.

"She has odd pulmonary vascularization," I say.

"Are you a doctor?" he asks.

When Cara's sister Kelsey had her accident, I was in charge of the international division of Kleinhoffer Foods. Now I sell real estate. "No," I say. "I've just learned a lot with Cara. Sometimes we see Dr. Ramanathan. He's familiar with Cara's problems."

The doctor frowns. Maybe he doesn't care for Dr. Ramanathan. He's young. Emergency Room doctors are usually young, at least at the hospital where I take Cara.

"She's not Down's Syndrome, is she?" he says.

"No," I say. I don't want to say more.

He looks at me, and I realize he's pieced something together. "Is your daughter the clone?"

The clone. "Yes," I say. Dr. Ramanathan asked me if he could write up his observations of Cara to publish and I said yes, because he seems to really care about her. I get requests from doctors to examine her. When she was first born I got hate mail, too. People saying that she should never have been born. That she was an abomination in the sight of God. I'm upset that Dr. Ramanathan would talk about her with someone else.

Dr. Guidall is silent, examining her. I imagine his censure. Maybe I'm wrong. Maybe he's just surprised.

"Is she allergic to anything?"

"She isn't allergic, but she has atypical reactions to some drugs like leukotriene receptor antagonists." I keep a list of drugs in my wallet. I pull it out and hand it to him. The list is worn, the creases so sharp that the paper is starting to tear.

"Do you use a nebulizer?" he asks. "And what drug are you using?"

"Budesonide," I say. I'm not imagining it. He's curt with me.

The doctor puts a nebulizer — a mask rather than an inhaler so she won't have to do anything but breathe — on her face. He leaves to pull her chart from records.

I know we'll be here a long time. I've spent a lot of time in hospitals.

The doctor wants to punish me, I think. He does a thorough exam of Cara, who has fallen asleep as the asthma attack waned. He listens to her lungs and checks her reflexes and looks in her ears. He doesn't need to look in her ears. But how many cloned children will he get to examine? Cloning humans is illegal in the United States, although there's no law against having your child cloned in, say, Israel and then bringing the adopted child into the u.s.

"I don't like what I'm hearing in her breathing," he says. "I would like to run some tests."

He has gotten more formal, which means that something is wrong. I want to go home so bad, I don't want things to start tonight. *Things.* The crisis doesn't always come when you're tired and thinking about the house you're going to show tomorrow, but often it does.

The doctor is very young, and very severe. It's easy to be severe when you're young. I can imagine what he would like to ask. *Why the hell did you do it? How do you justify it?* Cara's respiratory defects will kill her, probably before she is twelve, almost certainly before she is eighteen.

He is perhaps furious at me. But Cara is right here. What would the angry people have me do, take her home and put a pillow over her face? How do I tell him, tell them, that when Cara was conceived, I wasn't sane? Nothing prepares you for the death of a child. Nothing teaches you how to live with it.

If he says anything I will ask him, *Do you have any children? I hope you never lose one,* I will say.

He doesn't ask.

Nobody is impressed with the wedding-night playing cards because Toph has scored really big. His dad took him along to Computer Warehouse so his dad could buy some sort of accounting software and while Toph was hanging out playing video games, some salesperson got out *Hacker Vigilante* to show to some customer, and then got paged and forgot to lock it back up. "So I just picked it up and slid it under my shirt," Toph says, "and then when my dad and me got to the car, I slid it under the seat before he got in."

We are in awe, Len and me. It's the biggest thing anyone has ever gotten away with. Toph is studying the box, like it's no big deal but we can tell he's really buggin' on the whole thing.

I'm not allowed to have *Hacker Vigilante*. In it, you have to do missions to track down terrorists and you do all these things to raise money, like steal stuff. My mom won't let me have it because one of the things that you can do to get money is pick up two teenaged girls at the bus station and get them to make a porn movie for you and then post it on the Internet. You don't really get to see anything, the girls just start taking off their shirts and the hotel room door closes but it's hysterical.

I am dying. I can't believe it. "Man, that was lucky," I say, because it was. No salesperson ever left anything that cool out in front of me.

"Hey," Toph says, "you just gotta know how to be casual."

"I'm casual," I say. "I'm way casual. But that just fuckin' fell in your lap."

"You loser," Toph says, laughing at me. "Fuck you." Len is laughing at me, too. I can feel my face turning red and my ears feel hot and I'm so mad I want to smash their faces in. Toph is just picking up stuff left lying around by dumbass salesdroids and I'm setting up scams in fucking Spencer's Gifts which everybody knows is really hard to score at because security is like bugfuck tight.

"You wait, asshole," I say. "You wait. I've got an idea for a score. You watch on the bus going to school tomorrow and you'll see."

"What?" Len says. "What are you going to do?"

"You'll see," I say.

By the time they check Cara into a room it's almost seven. I manage to get to a phone and call Allan. Joyce, his girlfriend, answers the phone. "Hi, Joyce," I say, "this is Jenna. Is Allan around?"

"Sure," she says. "Hold on, Jenna."

Joyce. Jenna. Allan likes "J" women. Actually, Allan likes thin women with dark hair and a kind of relentlessly Irish look. Joyce and I could be cousins. Joyce is prettier than I am. And younger. Every time I talk to her I use her name too much and she uses mine too much. We are working hard to be friendly.

"Jenna?" says Allan. "What's up?"

"I'm at the hospital with Cara," I say.

"Do you need me to come down?" he says, too fast. Allan is conscientious. He is bracing himself. *Is it a crisis?* is what he wants to know.

"No, it's just an asthma attack but the doctor in the emergency room didn't like her oxygen levels or something and they want to keep her. But Robert is home by himself and they want to do some more tests tonight..."

"Ah. Okay," he says. "Let me think a moment."

It's Sunday night? What can he be doing on a Sunday night? "Are you busy? I mean, am I calling at a bad time —"

"No, no." he says. "Joyce and I were supposed to meet some friends, but I can call them and let them know. It wasn't anything important."

I try to think of what they could be doing on a Sunday night.

"It's just Joyce's church." Allan says into the pause. "They have a social thing, actually a kind of study thing on Sunday nights."

I didn't know Joyce was religious. "Well," I say, "maybe you could just check in on him? I mean, will it take you too far out of your way?"

"No," Allan says, "I'll go over there."

"See how things are. If you think he's all right, maybe you can just call and make sure he's in bed by ten or something?"

"No," Allan says, "I can stay with him. You're going to be there for hours, I know."

"He's fourteen." I say. "Use your judgment. I mean, I hate to impose on you and Joyce."

"It's okay," Allan says. "They're my kids."

I feel rather guilty so I hang up without saying, "Church?" One Christmas my dippy older sister was talking about God protecting her from some minor calamity, some domestic crisis involving getting a dent in her husband's Ford pickup, and later, as we drove home, Allan said, grinning, "I'm so glad that God is looking after Matt's pickup. Makes up for whatever he was doing during, you know, Cambodia, or the Black Plague."

He's going to church for Joyce.

Well, he went through the whole cloning thing for me. I don't exactly have the moral high ground.

I go to bed early because my dad and his girlfriend have shown up to baby-sit for me. Toph and Len bug out as soon as Dad shows up. Joyce is being so nice it feels fake but she's acting weird towards my dad, really nice to him. They've brought a movie they rented and when my dad asks her if she wants popcorn with it she says things like, "That would be really nice, thank you." Like they barely know each other.

So I play computer games in my room for a while and then I go to bed. Shelby, our dog, leaps onto the bed with me. She usually sleeps at the foot of my bed. I get under the covers with my jeans on, and I don't mean to fall asleep, but I do. Shelby wakes me up when my mom gets home because she hears Mom and starts slapping the bed with her tail. My mom talks with my dad and Joyce for a few minutes — I can't hear what they're saying, but I can hear the murmur. I pretend to still be asleep when my mom checks in on me. Shelby is all curled up, but happy to see Mom and my mom comes in and says "shhh" and pets her a minute.

The hard part is staying awake after that. My clock says 11:18 when my mom leaves my room and I want to give her at least half an hour to be good and sound asleep. But I nod off and when I wake up with a jerk, it's 1:56 A.M.

I almost don't get up. I'm really tired. But I make myself get up. Shelby wakes up and leaps off my bed. Shelby is my big worry about sneaking out. If I lock her in my room she'll scratch and then she'll bark. So she follows me downstairs and I let her out back. Maybe Mom will just think that Shelby had to go out, although usually if Shelby has to go out I sleep right through it and she goes downstairs and pees in the dining room and then my mom gets really twisted at me the next morning.

I almost fall asleep on the couch waiting for Shelby to come back in. I could tell Toph and Len that my dad came over and I couldn't sneak out, and do it tomorrow night. But while Shelby is out I make myself go into the basement and get a can of black spray paint. My mom used black spray paint to repaint the patio furniture and most of this can is still left.

I have a navy hooded sweatshirt and I slide open the back door, let Shelby in and go out the back. That way the door only opened twice, once to let Shelby out, and then to let Shelby in.

The backyard is dark and the cold is kind of startling. Mom keeps saying that she can't believe that in four weeks it will be Memorial Day and the pools will be open, but I like the cold. I look up at the stars. The only constellation I know is Orion, but if it is up, it's behind the trees or on the other side of the house. I bet Shelby is watching me through the window when I come around the front of the house. I can't see her, but I know what she looks like 'cause she does it every time people go out in the car; she's standing on the couch so she can look out the window, but all we'd be able to see is just this little, miniature Lassie face with her ears up all cute.

I walk down the street and I feel like people are watching me out the windows, watching me like Shelby. But all the windows are dark. Still, anyone looking out would see me, and it's after curfew. I should cut through the yards, but they're too dark and people's dogs would bark and people would think I was stealing stuff and call the police — and mostly I just don't want to.

It's a couple of miles to the police station — which is past the middle school. After a while I stop feeling like people are looking at me. They're all in their beds and I'm out here. I'm the only one moving. I can picture them, all cocooned in their beds. Unaware.

I'm aware. All you sleeping people. I'm out here. And you don't know anything about me. I could do stuff while you sleep.

It's so cool. It's great. I'm like some sort of assassin or something. The Iceman. That's me. Moving out here in the dark. I'm a wolf and you're all just rabbits or something.

I'm feeling so good. I'm not cold because I'm walking and I'm feeling so good. By the time I get to the police station, I feel better than anything. Better than after I steal something, which up until now has been the best. But this is the best. The Iceman out moving in the dark. The dark is my friend. I watch the police station for a while but nothing's moving. I shake the paint can and the ball bearing in it sounds loud and for a moment my heart hammers, but then I'm okay again.

I'm casual. I'm better than casual. I'm Special Forces. I'm fucking terror in the streets.

I take a minute and look at the wall. I spray the words on the side, really big, big enough to be seen from the bus:

TO REPORT A CRIME CALL 425-1234

I sketch them fast, and then carefully fill them in. Then I sketch my tag — "Iceman." I make the letters all sharp and spiky. It's a bitch that I've only got black paint — it should be blue and white with black outline. I carefully start darkening the "I." Toph and Len will just die. It's so funny to me, that I've got this grin on my face. They're going to come by on the bus and there it will be. Tagging the fucking police station. 425-1234 really is the police phone number. First I was going to put PROTECTED BY NEIGHBORHOOD BLOCK WATCH, but I thought this was funnier.

Then the squad car coasts up behind me and turns the floodlights on and the whole world is white.

I had no idea that police stations had waiting rooms, but when I go to pick up Robert, that's where I end up. It's a room, with seats along the walls and fluorescent lights and a bullet-proof window. The window has one of those metal circles in it, like movie theaters. I tell the young woman that I'm Robert's mother and I got a call to come down and get my son and she picks up a phone to tell someone I'm here.

A cop comes out with Robert. Robert looks properly scared. The cop, who has sandy hair and a handlebar mustache and looks rather boyish, introduces himself as Bruce Yoder. Yoder is an Amish name, although Bruce Yoder obviously isn't Amish. I bet his parents are Mennonite, which is less strict than Amish. It's what you do if you're Amish and you don't have any high-school education but you want a car. You become Mennonite. And now their son is a cop, the route to assimilation of my Irish ancestors. Why am I thinking this while my son, who is almost as tall as the cop, stands sullen and afraid with his hands jammed in the front pocket of his sweatshirt?

We walk outside and around the building so I can survey Robert's handi-work.

The police station is pale sandstone — colored brick and the black letters, as tall as me, stand out even in the dim light. I don't know what to say. Finally I say, "What's 'Iceman'?"

When he doesn't answer I say, "Robert?"

"A nickname," he says.

The cop says to me, "You're the family with the little girl, the clone."

"Yes," I say. "Cara." When people call her "the clone," I always feel compelled to tell them her name. The cop looks a little embarrassed.

We go back inside, and I talk to the cop. Robert has been booked and he'll have a hearing in front of a family court referee. I say "I'm sorry" a number of times. A family court referee. That's what we need. That's what everyone needs, someone to tell us the rules. When the phone rang, I thought it was the hospital, that something had happened to Cara, and then I was washed with clear, cold rage. *How can you do this to me?* But it isn't about me, of course.

Allan walks in. I called him before I left the house and he said, as soon as he understood that it wasn't Cara, as soon as he understood what was going on, "He'll have to come live with me. You can't do this, not with Cara."

I am so glad to see him. There have been times I loved him, times I hated him, but now he is kin. For all his flaws and for all my flaws, seeing Allan walk in wearing an old University of Michigan sweatshirt, with his hair tousled so I can see how thin it is getting, and his poor vulnerable temples, I feel only relief and my eyes fill with tears. It's unexpected, this crying.

Allan talks to the cop, the ex-Amish cop, while I sniffle into a wadded-up and ancient Kleenex I found in the pocket of my jacket.

We walk back outside. "I think I should take him home with me tonight," Allan says. "We'll follow you to the house, get him some things. I'll call in tomorrow and start arranging for him to go to school in Marshall."

Robert says, "What?"

Allan says, "You're going to come live with me."

Robert says, his voice cracking across the syllables, "For how long?"

"For good, I suppose," Allan says.

"Is Joyce —" I almost say "Is Joyce at your place?" but I can't ask that.

"Joyce left early, she's got to go to work tomorrow," Allan says, and he looks off across the parking lot, his mouth pursed. This is a problem for him, a monkey wrench.

I start to reach out and say "I'm sorry" again, and tears well up, again.

"What about school?" Robert asks. "I've got to go to school tomorrow. I've got an algebra test on Tuesday!"

"That," Allan says quietly, "is the least of your problems."

"What about my friends!" Robert says. "You can't do this to me!" I can see his eyes glistening, too. The family that cries together.

"I can," Allan says, "and I will. Now you've put your mother and me through enough, get in the car."

"No!" Robert says, "You can't make me!"

Allan reaches for his arm, to grab him, and Robert slips away, dancing, tall and gangly, and then blindly turns and runs.

I open my mouth, drawing in the breath to shout his name, and he is running, long legs like his father's, full of health and desperation, running pointlessly. It's inescapable, what he is running from, but in the instant before I shout his name I am glad, glad to see him running, this boy of mine who will, I think, survive. "Robert!" I shout, exactly the same time as his father, but Robert is heading down the street, head up, arms pumping. He won't go far.

"Robert!" his father shouts again.

I am glad, oh so glad. *Run,* I think joyfully. *Run, you sweet bastard. Run!*

I'm fanatically reluctant to say that fiction ought to do one thing rather than another. I do know what I want from fiction. I want it to exhilarate me, to unbind my eyes, to murder and resurrect me, to harm me in some fruitful way. But that said, yes, the journey into intense feeling and the conquest of unknown emotional territory is something fiction can make possible.

—Steven Millhauser

THE WIZARD OF WEST ORANGE
STEVEN MILLHAUSER

OCTOBER 14, 1889. But the Wizard's on fire! The Wizard is wild! He sleeps for two hours and works for twelve, sleeps for three hours and works for nineteen. The cot in the library, the cot in Room 12. Hair falling on forehead, vest open, tie askew. He bounds up the stairs, strides from room to room, greeting the experimenters, asking questions, cracking a joke. His boyish smile, his sharp eye. Why that way? Why not this? Notebook open, a furious sketch. Another. On to the next room! Hurls himself into a score of projects, concentrating with fanatical attention on each one before dismissing it to fling himself into next. The automatic adjustment for the recording stylus of the perfected phonograph. The speaking doll. Instantly grasps the essential problem, makes a decisive suggestion. Improved machinery for drawing brass wire. The aurophone, for enhancement of hearing. His trip to Paris has charged him with energy. Out into the courtyard! — the electrical lab, the chemical lab. Dangers of high-voltage alternating current: tests for safety. Improved insulation for electrical conductors. On to the metallurgical lab, to examine the graders and crushers, the belt conveyors, the ore samples. His magnetic ore-separator. "Work like hell, boys!" In Photographic Building, an air of secrecy. Excitement over the new Eastman film, the long strip in which lies the secret of visual motion. The Wizard says kinetoscope will do for the eye what phonograph does for the ear. But not yet, not yet! The men talk. What else? What next? A method of producing electricity directly from coal? A machine for compacting snow to clear city streets? Artificial silk? He hasn't slept at home for a week. They say the Wizard goes down to the Box, the experimental room in basement. Always kept locked. Rumors swirl. Another big invention to rival the phonograph? Surpass the incandescent lamp? The Wizard reads in library in the early mornings. From my desk in alcove I see him turn pages impatiently. Sometimes he thrusts at me a list of books to order. Warburton's *Physiology of Animals*. Greene and Wilson,

Cutaneous Sensation. Makes a note, slams book shut, strides out. Earnshaw says Wizard spent three hours shut up in the Box last night.

OCTOBER 16. Today a book arrived: Kerner, *Archaeology of the Skin*. Immediately left library and walked upstairs to experimental rooms. Room 12 open, cot empty, the Wizard gone. On table an open notebook, a glass battery, and parts of a dissected phonograph scattered around a boxed motor: three wax cylinders, a recording stylus attached to its diaphragm, a voice horn, a cutting blade for shaving used cylinders. Notebook showed a rough drawing. Identified it at once: design for an automatic adjustment in recording mechanism, whereby stylus would engage cylinder automatically at correct depth. Wizard absolutely determined to crush Bell's graphophone. From window, a view of courtyard and part of chemical lab.

Returned to corridor. Ran into Corbett, an experimental assistant. The Wizard had just left. Someone called out he thought Wizard heading to stockroom. I returned down the stairs. Passed through library, pushed open double door, and crossed corridor to stockroom.

Always exhilarating to enter Earnshaw's domain. Those high walls, lined from floor to ceiling with long drawers — hides, bones, roots, textiles, teeth. Pigeonholes, hundreds of them, crammed with resins, waxes, twines. Is it that, like library itself, stockroom is an orderly and teeming universe — a world of worlds — a finitude with aspirations to allness? Earnshaw hadn't seen him, thought he might be in basement. His hesitation when I held up Kerner and announced my mission. Told him the Wizard had insisted it be brought to him immediately. Earnshaw still hesitant as he took out ring of keys. Is loyal to Wizard, but more loyal to me. Opened door leading to basement storeroom and preceded me down into the maze.

Crates of feathers, sheet metal, pitch, plumbago, cork. Earnshaw hesitated again at locked door of Box. Do not disturb: Wizard's strict orders. But Wizard had left strict orders with me: deliver book immediately. Two unambiguous commands, each contradicting the other. Earnshaw torn. A good man, earnest, but not strong. Unable to resist a sense of moral obligation to me, owing to a number of trifling services rendered to him in the ordinary course of work. In addition, ten years younger. In my presence instinctively assumes an attitude of deference. Rapped lightly on door. No answer. "Open it," I said, not unkindly. He stood outside as I entered.

Analysis of motives. Desire to deliver book (good). Desire to see room (bad). Yielded to base desire. But ask yourself: Was it only base? I revere the Wizard and desire his success. He is searching for something, for some piece of crucial knowledge. If I see experiment, may be able to find information he needs. Analyze later.

The small room well-lit by incandescent bulbs. Bare of furnishings except for central table, two armchairs against wall. On table a closed notebook, a copper-oxide battery, and two striking objects. One a long stiff blackish glove, about the length of a forearm, which rests horizontally on two Y-shaped supports about eight inches high. Glove made of some solid dark material, perhaps vulcanized rubber, and covered with a skein of wires emerging from small brass caps. The other: a wooden framework supporting a horizontal cylinder, whose upper surface is in contact with a row of short metal strips suspended from a crossbar. Next to cylinder a small electric motor. Two bundles of wire lead from glove to battery, which in turn is connected to cylinder mechanism by way of motor. On closer inspection I see that interior of glove is lined with black silky material, studded with tiny silver disks like heads of pins. "Sir!" whispers Earnshaw.

I switch off lights and step outside. Footsteps above our heads. I follow Earnshaw back upstairs into stockroom, where an experimental assistant awaits him with request for copper wire. Return to library. Am about to sit down at desk when Wizard enters from other door. Gray gabardine laboratory gown flowing around his legs, tie crooked, hair mussed. "Has that book —?" he says loudly. Deaf in his left ear. "I was just bringing it to you," I shout. Holding out Kerner. Seizes it and throws himself down in an armchair, frowning as if angrily at the flung-open pages.

OCTOBER 17. A quiet day in library. Rain, scudding clouds. Arranged books on third-floor gallery, dusted mineral specimens in their glass-doored cabinets. Restless.

OCTOBER 18. That wired glove. Can it be a self-warming device, to replace a lady's muff? Have heard that in Paris, on cold winter nights, vendors stand before the Opera House, selling hot potatoes for ladies to place in their muffs. But the pinheads? The cylinder? And why then such secrecy? Wizard in locked room again, for two hours, with Kistenmacher.

OCTOBER 20. This morning overheard a few words in courtyard. Immediately set off for stockroom in search of Earnshaw. E.'s passion — his weakness, one might say — is for idea of motion photography. Eager to get hold of any information about the closely guarded experiments in Photographic Building and Room 5. Words overheard were between two machinists, who'd heard an experimental assistant speaking to so-and-so from chemical lab about an experiment in Photographic Building conducted with the new Eastman film. Talk was of perforations along both edges of strip, as in the old telegraph tape. The film to be driven forward on sprockets that engage and release it. This of course the most roundabout hearsay. Nevertheless not first time there has been talk of modifying strip film by means of perforations, which some say the Wizard saw in Paris: studio of Monsieur Marey. Earnshaw thrives on such rumors.

Not in stockroom but down in storeroom, as I knew at once by partially open door. In basement reported my news. Excited him visibly. At that instant — suddenly — I became aware of darker motive underlying my impulse to inform Earnshaw of conversation in courtyard. Paused. Looked about. Asked him to admit me for a moment — only a moment — to the Box.

An expression of alarm invading his features. But Earnshaw particularly well qualified to understand a deep curiosity about experiments conducted in secret. Furthermore: could not refuse to satisfy an indebtedness he felt he'd incurred by listening eagerly to my report. Stationed himself outside door. Guardian of inner sanctum. I quickly entered.

The glove, the battery, the cylinder. I detected a single difference: notebook now open. Showed a hastily executed drawing of glove, surrounded by several smaller sketches of what appeared to be electromagnets, with coils of wire about a core. Under glove a single word: HAPTOGRAPH.

Did not hesitate to insert hand and arm in glove. Operation somewhat impeded by silken lining, evidently intended to prevent skin from directly touching any part of inner structure. When forearm was buried up to elbow, threw switch attached to wires at base of cylinder mechanism.

The excitement returns, even as I write these words. How to explain it? The activated current caused motor to turn cylinder on its shaft beneath the metal rods suspended from crossbar, which in turn caused silver points in lining of glove to move against my hand. Was aware at first of many small gentle pointed pressures. But — behold! — the merely mechanical sensation soon gave way to another, and I felt — distinctly — a sensation as of a hand grasping my own in a firm handshake. External glove had remained stiff and immobile. Switched off current, breathed deep. Repeated experiment. Again the motor turning the cylinder. Sensation unmistakable: I felt my hand gripped in a handshake, my fingers lightly squeezed. At that moment experienced a strange elation, as if standing on a dock listening to water lap against piles as I prepared to embark on a longed-for voyage. Switched off current, withdrew hand. Stood still for a moment before turning suddenly to leave room.

OCTOBER 21. Books borrowed by Kistenmacher, as recorded in library note-book, Oct. 7–Oct. 14: *The Nervous System and the Mind, The Tactile Sphere, Leçons sur la Physiologie du Système Nerveux, Lezioni di Fisiologia Sperimentale, Sensation and Pain.* The glove, the cylinder, the phantom handshake. Clear — is it clear? — that Wizard has turned his attention to sense of touch. To what end, exactly? Yet even as I ask, I seem to grasp principle of haptograph. "The kinetoscope will do for the eye what the phonograph does for the ear." Is he not isolating each of the five senses? Creating for each a machine that records and plays back one sense alone? Voices disembodied, moving images without physical substance, immaterial touches. The phonograph, the kinetoscope, the haptograph. Voices preserved in cylinders of wax, moving bodies in strips of nitrocellulose, touches in pinheads and wires. A gallery of ghosts. Cylinder as it turns must transmit electrical impulses that activate the silver points. Ghosts? Consider: the skin is touched. A firm handshake. Hello, my name is. And yours? Strange thoughts on an October night.

OCTOBER 24. This morning, after Wizard was done looking through mail and had ascended stairs to experimental rooms, Kistenmacher entered li-brary. Headed directly toward me. Have always harbored a certain dislike for Kistenmacher, though he treats me respectfully enough. Dislike the aggressive directness of his walk, arms swinging so far forward that he seems to be pulling himself along by gripping onto chunks of air. Dislike his big hands with neat black hairs growing sideways across fingers, intense stare of eyes that take you in without seeing you, his black stiff hair combed as if violently sideways across head, necktie straight as a plumb line. Kistenmacher one of the most respected of electrical experimenters. Came directly up to my rolltop desk, stopping too close to it, as if the wood were barring his way.

"I wish to report a missing book," he said.

Deeper meaning of Kistenmacher's remark. It happens — infrequently — that a library book is temporarily misplaced. The cause not difficult to wrest from the hidden springs of existence. Any experimenter — or assistant — or indeed any member of staff — is permitted to browse among all three tiers of books, or to remove a volume and read anywhere on premises. Instead of leaving book for me to replace, as everyone is instructed to do, occasionally someone takes it upon self to reshelve. An act well meant but better left undone, since mistakes easy to make. Earnshaw, in particular, guilty of this sort of misplaced kindness. Nevertheless I patrol shelves carefully, several times a day, not only when I replace books returned by staff, or add new books and scientific journals ordered for library, but also on tours of inspection intended to ensure correct arrangement of books on shelves. As a result quite rare for a misplaced volume to escape detection. Kistenmacher's statement therefore not the simple statement of fact it appeared to be, but an implied reproach: You have been negligent in your duties.

"I'm quite certain we can find it without difficulty," I said. Rising immediately. "Sometimes the new assistants —"

"Giesinger," he said. *"Musculo-Cutaneous Feeling."*

A slight heat in my neck. Wondered whether a flush was visible.

"You see," I said with a smile. "The mystery solved." Lifted from my desk *Musculo-Cutaneous Feeling* by Otto Giesinger and handed it to Kistenmacher. He glanced at spine, to make certain I hadn't made a mistake, then looked at me with interest.

"This is a highly specialized study," said he.

"Yes, a little too specialized for me," I replied.

"But the subject interests you?"

Hesitation. "I try to keep abreast of — developments."

"Excellent," he said, and suddenly smiled — a disconcerting smile, of startling charm. "I will be sure to consult with you." Held up book, tightly clasped in one big hand, gave a little wave with it, and took his leave.

The whole incident rich with possibility. My responsibility in library is to keep up with scientific and technical literature, so that I may order books I deem essential. Most of my professional reading confined to scientific journals, technical periodicals, and institutional proceedings, but peruse many books as well, in a broad range of subjects, from psychology of hysteria to structure of the constant-pressure dynamo; my interests are wide. Still, it cannot have failed to strike Kistenmacher that I had removed from shelves a study directly related to his investigations in Box. Kistenmacher perfectly well aware that everyone knows of his secretive experiments, about which many rumors. Is said to enjoy such rumors and even to contribute to them by enigmatic hints of his own. Once told Earnshaw, who reported it to me, that there would soon be no human sensation that could not be replicated mechanically. At time I imagined a machine for production of odors, a machine of tastes. Knows of course that I keep a record of books borrowed by staff, each with name of borrower. Now knows I have been reading Giesinger on musculo-cutaneous feeling.

What else does he know? Can Earnshaw have said something?

OCTOBER 26. A slow day. Reading. From my desk in alcove I can see Wizard's rolltop desk with its scattering of books and papers, the railed galleries of second and third levels, high up a flash of sun on a glass-fronted cabinet holding mineral specimens. The pine-paneled ceiling. Beyond Wizard's desk, the white marble statue brought back from Paris Exposition. Winged youth seated on ruins of a gas street-lamp, holding high in one hand an incandescent lamp. The Genius of Light. In my feet a rumble of dynamos from machine shop beyond stockroom.

OCTOBER 28. In courtyard, gossip about secret experiments in Photographic Building, Room 8, the Box. A machine for extracting nutrients from seaweed? A speaking photograph? Rumors of hidden workrooms, secret assistants. In courtyard one night, an experimental assistant seen with cylinders under each arm, heading in direction of basement.

OCTOBER 29. For the Wizard, there is always a practical consideration. The incandescent lamp, the electric pen, the magnetic ore-separator. The quadruplex telegraph. Origin of moving photographs in study of animal motion: Muybridge's horses, Marey's birds. Even the phonograph: concedes its secondary use as instrument of entertainment, but insists on primary value as business machine for use in dictation. And the haptograph? A possible use in hospitals? A young mother dies. Bereft child comforted by simulated caresses. Old people, lingering out their lives alone, untouched. Shake of a friendly hand. It might work.

NOVEMBER 3. A momentous day. Even now it seems unlikely. And yet, looked at calmly, a day like any other: experimenters in their rooms, visitors walking in courtyard, a group of schoolchildren with their teacher, assistants passing up and down corridors and stairways, men working on grounds. After a long morning decided to take walk in courtyard, as I sometimes do. Warmish day, touch of autumn chill in the shade. Walked length of courtyard, between electrical lab and chemical lab, nodding to several men who stood talking in groups. At end of yard, took a long look at buildings of Phonograph Works. Started back. Nearly halfway to main building when aware of sharp footsteps not far behind me. Drawing closer. Turned and saw Kistenmacher.

"A fine day for a walk," he said. Falling into step beside me.

Hidden significance of Kistenmacher's apparently guileless salutation. His voice addressed to the air — to the universe — but with a ripple of the confidential meant for me. Instantly alert. Common enough of course to meet an experimenter or machinist in courtyard. Courtyard after all serves as informal meeting place, where members of staff freely mingle. Have encountered Kistenmacher himself innumerable times, striding along with great arms swinging. No, what struck me, on this occasion, was one indisputable fact: instead of passing me with habitual brisk nod, Kistenmacher attached himself to me with tremendous decisiveness. So apparent he had something to say to me that I suspected he'd been watching for me from a window.

"My sentiment exactly," I replied.

"I wonder whether you might accompany me to Room 8," he then said.

An invitation meant to startle me. I confess it did. Kistenmacher knows I am curious about experimental rooms on second floor, just up stairs from library. These rooms always kept open — except Room 5, where photographic experiments continue to be conducted secretly, in addition to those in new Photographic Building — but there is general understanding that rooms are domain of experimenters and assistants, and of course of the Wizard himself, who visits each room daily in order to observe progress of every experiment. Kistenmacher's invitation therefore highly unusual. At same time, had about it a deliberate air of mystery, which Kistenmacher clearly enjoying as he took immense energetic strides and pulled himself forward with great swings of his absurd arms.

Room 8: Kistenmacher's room on second floor. On a table: parts of a storage battery and samples of what I supposed to be nickel hydrate. No sign of haptograph. This in itself not remarkable, for experimenters are engaged in many projects. Watched him close door and turn to me.

"Our interests coincide," he said, speaking in manner characteristic of him, at once direct and sly.

I said nothing.

"I invite you to take part in an experiment," he next remarked. An air of suppressed energy. Had sense that he was studying my face for signs of excitement.

His invitation, part entreaty and part command, shocked and thrilled me. Also exasperated me by terrible ease with which he was able to create inner turmoil.

"What kind of experiment?" I asked: sharply, almost rudely.

He laughed — I had not expected Kistenmacher to laugh. A boyish and disarming laugh. Surprised to see a dimple in his left cheek. Kistenmacher's teeth straight and white, though upper left incisor is missing.

"That," he said, "remains to be seen. Nine o'clock tomorrow night? I will come to the library."

Noticed that, while his body remained politely immobile, his muscles had grown tense in preparation for leaving. Already absolutely sure of my acceptance.

When I returned to library, found Wizard seated at his desk, in stained laboratory gown, gesturing vigorously with both hands as he spoke with a reporter from the *New York World*.

NOVEMBER 5. I will do my utmost to describe objectively the extraordinary event in which I participated on the evening of November 4.

Kistenmacher appeared in library with a punctuality that even in my state of excitement I found faintly ludicrous: over fireplace the big clock-hands showed nine o'clock so precisely that I had momentary grotesque sense they were the false hands of a painted clock. Led me into stockroom, where Earnshaw had been relieved for night shift by young Benson, who was up on a ladder examining contents of a drawer. Looked down at us intently over his shoulder, bending neck and gripping ladder-rails, as if we were very small and very far away. Kistenmacher removed from pocket a circle of keys. Held them up to inform Benson of our purpose. Opened door that led down to basement. I followed him through dim-lit cellar rooms piled high with wooden crates until we reached door of Box. Kistenmacher inserted key, stepped inside to activate electrical switch. Then turned to usher me in with a sweep of his hand and a barely perceptible little bow, all the while watching me closely.

The room had changed. No glove: next to table an object that made me think of a dressmaker's dummy, or top half of a suit of armor, complete with helmet. Supported on stand clamped to table edge. The dark half-figure studded with small brass caps connected by a skein of wires that covered entire surface. Beside it the cylinder machine and the copper-oxide battery. Half a dozen additional cylinders standing upright on table, beside machine. In one corner, an object draped in a sheet.

"Welcome to the haptograph," Kistenmacher said. "Permit me to demonstrate."

He stepped over to figure, disconnected a cable, and unfastened clasps that held head to torso. Lifted off head with both hands. Placed head carefully on table. Next unhooked or unhinged torso so that back opened in two wings. Hollow center lined with the same dark silky material and glittery silver points I had seen in glove.

Thereupon asked me to remove jacket, vest, necktie, shirt. My hesitation. Looked at me harshly. "Modesty is for schoolgirls." Turning around. "I will turn my back. You may leave, if you prefer."

Removed my upper clothing piece by piece and placed each article on back of a chair. Kistenmacher turned to face me. "So! You are still here?" Immediately gestured toward interior of winged torso, into which I inserted my arms. Against my skin felt silken lining. He closed wings and hooked in place. Set helmet over my head, refastened clasps and cable. An opening at mouth enabled me to breathe. At level of my eyes a strip of wire mesh. The arms, though stiff, movable at wrists and shoulders. I stood beside table, awaiting instructions.

"Tell me what you feel," Kistenmacher said. "It helps in the beginning if you close your eyes."

He threw switch at base of machine. The cylinder began to turn.

At first felt a series of very faint pin-pricks in region of scalp. Gradually impression of separate prickings faded away and I became aware of a more familiar sensation.

"It feels," I said, "exactly as if — yes — it's uncanny — but as though I were putting a hat on my head."

"Very good," Kistenmacher said. "And this?" Opened my eyes long enough to watch him slip cylinder from its shaft and replace with new one.

This time felt a series of pin-pricks in region of right shoulder. Quickly resolved into a distinct sensation: a hand resting on shoulder, then giving a little squeeze.

"And this?" Removed cylinder and added another. "Hold out your left hand. Palm up."

Was able to turn my armored hand at wrist. In palm became aware of a sudden sensation: a roundish smooth object — ball? egg? — seemed to be resting there.

In this manner — cylinder by cylinder — Kistenmacher tested three additional sensations. A fly or other small insect walking on right forearm. A ring or rope tightening over left biceps. Sudden burst of uncontrollable laughter: the haptograph had re-created sensation of fingers tickling my ribs.

"And now one more. Please pay close attention. Report exactly what you feel." Slipped a new cylinder onto shaft and switched on current.

After initial pin-pricks, felt a series of pressures that began at waist and rose along chest and face. A clear tactile sensation, rather pleasant, yet one I could not recall having experienced before. Kistenmacher listened intently as I attempted to describe. A kind of upward-flowing ripple, which moved rapidly from waist to top of scalp, encompassing entire portion of body enclosed in haptograph. Like being repeatedly stroked by a soft encircling feather. Or better: repeatedly submerged in some new and soothing substance, like unwet water. As cylinder turned, same sensation — same series of pressures — recurred again and again. Kistenmacher's detailed questions before switching off current and announcing experiment had ended.

At once he removed headpiece and set it on table. Unfastened back of torso and turned away as I extracted myself and quickly began to put on shirt.

"We are still in the very early stages," he said, back still turned to me as I threw my necktie around collar. "We know far less about the tactile properties of the skin than we do about the visual properties of the eye. And yet it might be said that, of all the senses" — here a raised hand, an extended forefinger — "touch is the most important. The good Bishop Berkeley, in his *Theory of Vision,* maintains that the visual sense serves to anticipate the tangible. The same may be said of the other senses as well. Look here."

Turned around, ignoring me as I buttoned my vest. From his pocket removed an object and held it up for my inspection. Surprised to see a common fountain pen.

"If I touch this pen to your hand — hand, please! — what do you feel?"

Extended hand, palm up. He pressed end of pen lightly into skin of my palm.

"I feel a pressure — the pressure of the pen. The pressure of an object."

"Very good. And you would say, would you not, that the skin is adapted to feel things in that way — to identify objects by the sense of touch. But this pen of ours is a rather large, coarse object. Consider a finer object — this, for example."

From another pocket: a single dark bristle. Might have come from a paintbrush.

"Your hand, please. Concentrate your attention. I press here — yes? — and here — yes? — and here — no? No? Precisely. And this is a somewhat coarse bristle. If we took a very fine bristle, you would discover even more clearly that only certain spots on the skin give the sensation of touch. We have mapped out these centers of touch and are now able to replicate several combinations with some success."

He reached over to cylinders and picked one up, looking at it as he continued. "It is a long and difficult process. We are at the very beginning." Turning cylinder slowly in his hand. "The key lies here, in this hollow beechwood tube — the haptogram. You see? The surface is covered with hard wax. Look. You can see the ridges and grooves. They control the flow of current. As the haptogram rotates, the wax pushes against this row of nickel rods: up here. Yes? This is clear? Each rod in turn operates a small rheostat — here — which controls the current. You understand? The current drives the corresponding coil in the glove, thereby moving the pin against the skin. Come here."

He set down cylinder and stepped over to torso. Unfastened back. Carefully pulled away a strip of lining.

"These little devices beneath the brass caps — you see them? Each one is a miniature electromagnet. Look closely. You see the wire coil? There. Inside the coil is a tiny iron cylinder — the core — which is insulated with a sleeve of celluloid. The core moves as the current passes through the coil. To the end of each core is attached a thin rod, which in turn is attached to the lining by a fastener that you can see — here, and here, and all along the lining. Ah, those rods!"

He shook his head. "A headache. They have to be very light, but also stiff. We have tried boar's bristle — a mistake! — zinc, too soft; steel, too heavy. We have tried whalebone and ivory. These are bamboo."

Sighing. "It is all very ingenious — and very unsatisfactory. The haptograms can activate sequences of no more than six seconds. The pattern then repeats. And it is all so very — clumsy. What we need is a different approach to the wax cylinder, a more elegant solution to the problem of the overall design."

Pause — glance at sheet-draped object. Seemed to fall into thought. "There is much work to do." Slowly reached into pocket, removed ring of keys. Stared at keys thoughtfully. "We know nothing. Absolutely nothing." Slowly running his thumb along a key. Imagined he was going to press tip of key into my palm — my skin tingling with an expected touch — but as he stepped toward door I understood that our session was over.

NOVEMBER 7. Last night the Wizard shut himself up in Room 12: seven o'clock to three in the morning. Rumor has it he is still refining the automatic adjustment for phonograph cylinder. Hell-bent on defeating the graphophone. Rival machine produces a less clear sound but has great practical advantage of not requiring the wax cylinder to be shaved down and adjusted after each playing. The Wizard throws himself onto cot for two hours, no more. In the day, strides from room to room on second floor, quick, jovial, shrewd-eyed, a little snappish, a sudden edge of mockery. A university man and you don't know how to mix cement? What do they teach you? The quick sketch: fixed gaze, slight tilt of head. Try this. How about that? Acid stains on his fingers. The Phonograph Works, the electrical lab, the Photographic Building. Alone in a back room in chemical lab, quick visit to Box, up to Room 5, over to 12. The improved phonograph, moving photograph, haptograph. Miniature phonograph for speaking doll. Ink for the blind, artificial ivory. A machine for extracting butter directly from milk. In metallurgical lab, Building 5, examines the rock crushers, proposes refinements in electromagnetic separators. A joke in the courtyard: the Wizard is devising a machine to do his sleeping for him.

I think of nothing but the haptograph.

NOVEMBER 12. Not a word. Nothing.

NOVEMBER 14. Haptograph will do for skin what phonograph does for ear, kinetoscope for eye. Understood. But is comparison accurate? Like phonograph, haptograph can imitate sensations in real world: a machine of mimicry. Unlike phonograph, haptograph can create new sensations, never experienced before. The upward-flowing ripple. Any combinations of touch-spots possible. Why does this thought flood my mind with excitement?

NOVEMBER 17. Still nothing. Have they forgotten me?

NOVEMBER 20. Today at a little past two, Earnshaw entered library. Saw him hesitate for a moment and look about quickly — the Wizard long gone, only Grady from chemical lab in room, up on second gallery — before heading over to my desk. Handed me a book he had borrowed some weeks before: a study of the dry gelatin process in making photographic plates. Earnshaw's appetite for the technical minutiae of photography insatiable. And yet: has never owned a camera and unlike most of the men appears to have no desire to take photographs. Have often teased him about this passion of his, evidently entirely mental. He once said in reply that he carries two cameras with him at all times: his eyes.

Touché.

"A lot of excitement out there," I said. Sweeping my hand vaguely in direction of Photographic Building. "I hear they're getting smooth motions at sixteen frames a second."

He laughed — a little uncomfortably, I thought. "Sixteen? Impossible. They've never done it under forty. Besides, I heard just the opposite. Jerky motions. Same old trouble: sprocket a little off. This is for you."

He reached inside jacket and swept his arm toward me. Abrupt, a little awkward. In his hand: a sealed white envelope.

I took envelope while studying his face. "From you?"

"From" — here he lowered his voice — "Kistenmacher." Shrugged. "He asked me to deliver it."

"Do you know what it is?"

"I don't read other people's mail!"

"Of course not. But you might know anyway."

"How should — I know you've been down there."

"You saw me?"

"He told me."

"Told you?"

"That you'd been there too."

"Too!"

Looked at me. "You think you're the only one?"

"I think our friend likes secrets." I reached for brass letter-opener. Slipped it under flap.

"I'll be going," Earnshaw said, nodding sharply and turning away. Halfway to door when I slit open envelope with a sound of tearing cloth.

"Oh there you are, Earnshaw." A voice at the door.

Message read: "Eight o'clock tomorrow night. Kmacher."

It was only young Peters, an experimental assistant, in need of some zinc.

NOVEMBER 20, LATER. Much to think about. Kistenmacher asks Earnshaw to deliver note. Why? Might easily have contrived to deliver it himself, or speak to me in person. By this action therefore wishes to let Earnshaw know that I am assisting in experiment. Very good. But: Kistenmacher has already told Earnshaw about my presence in room. Which means? His intention must be directed not at Earnshaw but at me: must wish me to know that he has spoken to Earnshaw about me. But why? To bind us together in a brotherhood of secrecy? Perhaps a deeper intention: wants me to know that Earnshaw has been in room, that he too assists in experiment.

NOVEMBER 21, 3:00. Waiting. A walk in the courtyard. Sunny but cold: breath-puffs. A figure approaches. Bareheaded, no coat, a pair of fur-lined gloves: one of the experimenters, protecting his fingers.

NOVEMBER 21, 5:00. It is possible that every touch remains present in skin. These buried hapto-memories capable of being reawakened through mechanical stimulation. Forgotten caresses: mother, lover. Feel of a shell on a beach, forty years ago. Memory-cylinders: a history of touches. Why not?

NOVEMBER 21, 10:06 P.M. At two minutes before eight, Earnshaw enters library. I rise without a word and follow him into stockroom. Down stairway, into basement. Unlocks door of experimental room and leaves without once looking at me. His dislike of Box is clear. But what is it exactly that he dislikes?

"Welcome!" Kistenmacher watchful, expectant.

Standing against table: the dark figure of a human being, covered with wires and small brass caps. On table: a wooden frame holding what appears to be a horizontal roll of perforated paper, perhaps a yard wide, partially unwound onto a second reel. Both geared to a chain-drive motor.

A folding screen near one wall.

"In ten years," Kistenmacher remarks, "in twenty years, it may be possible to create tactile sensations by stimulating the corresponding centers of the brain. Until then, we must conquer the skin directly."

A nod toward screen. "Your modesty will be respected. Please remove your clothes behind the screen and put on the cloth."

Behind screen: a high stool on which lies a folded piece of cloth. Quickly remove my clothes and unfold cloth, which proves to be a kind of loincloth with drawstring. Put it on without hesitation. As I emerge from behind screen, have distinct feeling that I am a patient in a hospital, in presence of a powerful physician.

Kistenmacher opens a series of hinged panels in back of figure: head, torso, legs. Hollow form with silken lining, dimpled by miniature electromagnets fastened to silver points. Notice figure is clamped to table. Can now admit a man.

Soon shut up in haptograph. Through wire mesh covering eyeholes, watch Kistenmacher walk over to machine. Briskly turns to face me. With one hand resting on wooden frame, clears throat, stands very still, points suddenly to paper roll.

"You see? An improvement in design. The key lies in the series of perforations punched in the roll. As the motor drives the reel — here — it passes over a nickel-steel roller: here. The roller is set against a row of small metallic brushes, like our earlier rods. The brushes make contact with the nickel-steel roller only through the perforations. This is clear? The current is carried to the coils in the haptograph. Each pin corresponds to a single track — or circular section — of the perforated roll. Tell me exactly what you feel." Throws switch.

Unmistakable sensation of a sock being drawn on over my left foot and halfway up calf. As paper continues to unwind, experience a similar but less exact sensation, mixed with prickles, on right foot and calf. Kistenmacher switches off current and gives source reel a few turns by hand, rewinding perforated paper roll. Switches on current. Repeats sensation of drawn-on socks, making small adjustment that very slightly improves accuracy in right foot and calf.

Next proceeds to test three additional tactile sensations. A rope or belt fastened around my waist. A hand: pressing its spread fingers against my back.

Some soft object, perhaps a brush or cloth, moving along upper arm.

Switches off current, seems to grow thoughtful. Asks me to close eyes and pay extremely close attention to next series of haptographic tests, each of which will go beyond simple mimicry of a familiar sensation.

Close my eyes and feel an initial scattering of prickles on both elbows. Then under arms — at hips — at chin. Transformed gradually into multiple sensation of steady upward pushes, as if I've been gripped by a force trying to lift me from ground. Briefly feel that I am hovering in air, some three feet above floor. Open my eyes, see that I haven't moved. Upward-tugging sensation remains, but illusion of suspension has been so weakened that I cannot recapture it while eyes remain open.

Kistenmacher asks me to close eyes again, concentrate my attention. At once the distinct sensation of something pressing down on shoulders and scalp, as well as sideways against rib cage. A feeling as if I were being shut up in a container. Gradually becomes uncomfortable, oppressive. Am about to cry out when suddenly a sensation of release, accompanied by feeling of something pouring down along my body — as though pieces of crockery were breaking up and falling upon me.

"Very good," says Kistenmacher. "And now one more?"

Again a series of prickles, this time applied simultaneously all over body. Prickles gradually resolve themselves into the sensation — pleasurable enough — of being lightly pressed by something large and soft. Like being squeezed by an enormous hand — as if a fraternal handshake were being applied to entire surface of my skin. Enveloped in that gentle pressure, that soft caress, I feel soothed, I feel more than soothed, I feel exhilarated, I feel an odd and unaccountable joy — a jolt of well-being — a stream of bliss — which fills me to such bursting that tears of pleasure burn in my eyes.

When sensation stops, ask for it to be repeated, but Kistenmacher has learned whatever it was he wanted to know.

Decisively moves toward me. Disappears behind machine. Unlatches panels and pulls them apart.

I emerge backward, in loincloth. Carefully withdraw arms from torso. Across room see Kistenmacher standing with back to me. Yellowish large hands clasped against black suit-jacket.

Behind screen begin changing. Kistenmacher clears his throat.

"The sense of sight is concentrated in a single place — two places, if you like. We know a great deal about the structure of the eye. By contrast, the sense of touch is dispersed over the entire body. The skin is by far the largest organ of sense. And yet we know almost nothing about it."

I step out from behind screen. Surprised to see Kistenmacher still standing with back to me, large hands clasped behind.

"Good night," he says: motionless. Suddenly raises one hand to height of his shoulder. Moves it back and forth at wrist.

"Night," I reply. Walk to door: turn. And raising my own hand, give first to Kistenmacher, and then to haptograph, an absurd wave.

NOVEMBER 22. Mimicry and invention. Splendor of the haptograph. Not just the replication of familiar tactile sensations, but capacity to explore new combinations — pressures, touches, never experienced before. Adventures of feeling. Who can say what new sensations will be awakened, what unknown desires? Unexplored realms of the tangible. The frontiers of touch.

NOVEMBER 23. Conversation with Earnshaw, who fails to share my excitement. His unmistakable dislike of haptograph. Irritable shrug: "Leave well enough alone." A motto that negates with masterful exactitude everything the Wizard represents. And yet: his passion for the slightest advance in motion photography. Instinctive shrinking of an eye-man from the tangible? Safe distance of sight. Noli me tangere. The intimacy, the intrusiveness, of touch.

NOVEMBER 24. Another session in Box. Began with several familiar sensations, very accurate: ball in palm, sock, handshake, the belt. One new one, less satisfactory: sensation of being stroked by a feather on right forearm. Felt at first like bits of sand being sprinkled on my arm; then somewhat like a brush; finally like a piece of smooth wood. Evidently much easier for pins to evoke precise sensations by stimulating touch-spots in limited area than by stimulating them in sequence along a length. Kistenmacher took notes, fiddled with metallic brushes, adjusted a screw. Soon passed on to sensations of uncommon or unknown kind. A miscellaneous assortment of ripples, flutters, obscure thrusts, and pushes. Kistenmacher questioned me closely. My struggle to describe. Bizarre sensation of a pressure that seemed to come from inside my skin and press outward, as if I were going to burst apart. At times a sense of disconnection from skin, which seemed to be slipping from my body like clothes removed at night. Once: a variation of constriction and release, accompanied by impression that I was leaving my old body, that I was being reborn. Immediately followed by sensation, lasting no more than a few seconds, that I was flying through the air.

NOVEMBER 26. Walking in courtyard. Clear and cold. Suddenly aware of my overcoat on my shoulders, the grip of shoe leather, clasp of hat about my head. Throughout day, increased awareness of tactile sensations: the edges of pages against my fingers, door handle in palm. Alone in library, a peculiar sharp impression of individual hairs in my scalp, of fingernails set in their places at ends of my fingers. These sensations vivid, though lasting but a short time.

NOVEMBER 27. The Wizard's attention increasingly consumed by his ore-separating machinery and miniature mechanisms of speaking doll. The toy phonograph — concealed within tin torso — repeatedly malfunctions: the little wax cylinders break, stylus becomes detached from diaphragm or slips from its groove. Meanwhile, flying visits to the Box, where he adjusts metallic brushes, studies take-up reel, unhinges back panels, sketches furiously. Leaves abruptly, with necktie bunched up over top of vest. Kistenmacher says Wizard is dissatisfied with design of haptograph and has proposed a different model: a pine cabinet in which subject is enclosed, except for head, which is provided with a separate covering. The Wizard predicts haptograph parlor: a room of cabinet haptographs, operated by nickel-in-slot mechanism. Cabinet haptograph to be controlled by subject himself, by means of a panel of buttons.

NOVEMBER 28. Another encounter with Earnshaw. Distant. Won't talk about machine. So: talked about weather. Cold today. Mm hmm. But not too cold. Uh-huh. Can't tell what makes him more uncomfortable: that I know he takes part in experiment, or that he knows I do. Talked about frames per second. No heart in it. Relieved to see me go.

NOVEMBER 29. Fourth session in Box. Kistenmacher meticulous, intense. Ran through familiar simulations. Stopped machine, removed roll, inserted new one. Presented theory of oscillations: the new roll perforated in such a way as to cause rapid oscillation of pins. Oscillations should affect kinesthetic sense. At first an unpleasant feeling of many insects attacking skin. Then: sensation of left arm floating away from body. Head floating. Body falling. Once: sensation of flying through air, as in previous session, but much sharper and longer lasting. My whole body tingling. Returned to first roll. Skin as if rubbed new. Heightened receptivity. Seemed to be picking up minuscule touches hidden from old skin. Glorious.

NOVEMBER 29, LATER. Can't sleep for excitement. Confused thoughts, sudden lucidities. Can sense a new world just out of reach. Obscured by old body. What if a stone is not a stone, a tree not a tree? Fire not fire? Face not face? What then? New shapes, new touches: a world concealed. The haptograph pointing the way. Oh, what are you talking about? Shut up. Go to bed.

NOVEMBER 30. Kistenmacher says Earnshaw has asked to be released from experiment — the Wizard refuses. Always the demand for unconditional loyalty. In it together. The boys. "Every man jack of you!"

Saw Earnshaw in courtyard. Avoiding me.

DECEMBER 1. This morning the Wizard filed a caveat with Patents Office, setting forth design of haptograph and enumerating essential features. A familiar stratagem. The caveat protects his invention, while acknowledging its incompleteness. In the afternoon, interviews in library with the *Herald,* the *Sun,* and the *Newark News.* "The haptograph," the Wizard says, "is not yet ready to be placed before the public. I hope to have it in operation within six months." As always, prepares the ground, whets the public appetite. Speaks of future replications: riding a roller coaster, sledding down a hill. Sensations of warmth and cold. The "amusement haptograph": thrilling adventures in complete safety of the machine. The cabinet haptograph, the haptograph parlor. Shifts to speaking doll, the small wax cylinders with their nursery rhymes. In future, a doll that responds to a child's touch. The Wizard's hands cut through the air, his eyes are blue fire.

The reporters write furiously.

Kistenmacher says that if three more men are put on job, and ten times current funds diverted to research, haptograph might be ready for public in three years.

DECEMBER 2. Lively talk in courtyard about haptograph, the machine that records touch. Confusion about exactly what it is, what it does. One man under impression it operates like phonograph: you record a series of touches by pressing a recording mechanism and then play back touches by grasping machine. Someone makes a coarse joke: with a machine like that, who needs a woman? Laughter, some of it anxious. The Wizard can make anything. Why not a woman?

DECEMBER 3. Arrived early this morning. Heard voices coming from library. Entered to find Wizard standing at desk, facing Earnshaw. Wizard leaning forward, knuckles on desk. Nostrils flared. Cheek-ridges brick-red. Earnshaw pale, erect — turns at sound of door.

I, hat in hand: "Morning, gentlemen!"

DECEMBER 5. Fifth session in Box. Kistenmacher at work day and night to improve chain-drive mechanism and smooth turning of reels. New arrangement responsible for miracles of simulation: ball in palm, handshake, the sock, the hat. Haptograph can now mimic perfectly the complex sensation of having a heavy robe placed on shoulders, slipped over each arm in turn, tied at waist. Possible the Wizard's predictions may one day be fulfilled.

But Kistenmacher once again eager to investigate the unknown. Change of paper rolls: the new oscillations. "Please. Pay very close attention." Again I enter exotic realms of the tactile, where words become clumsy, obtuse. A feeling — wondrous — of stretching out to tremendous length. A sensation of passing through walls that crumble before me, of hurtling through space, of shouting with my skin. Once: the impression — how to say it? — of being stroked by the wing of an angel. Awkward approximations, dull stammerings which cannot convey my sense of exhilaration as I seemed to burst impediments, to exceed bounds of the possible, to experience, in the ruins of the human, the birth of something utterly new.

DECEMBER 6. Is it an illusion, a trick played by haptograph? Or is it the revelation of a world that is actually there, a world from which we have been excluded because of the limitations of our bodies?

DECEMBER 6, LATER. Unaccustomed thoughts. For example. Might we be surrounded by immaterial presences that move against us but do not impress themselves upon the touch-spots of our skin? Our vision sharpened by microscopes. Haptograph as the microscope of touch.

December 7. Ever since interview, the Wizard not once in Box. His attention taken up by other matters: plans for mining low-grade magnetite, manufacture of speaking dolls in Phonograph Works, testing of a safe alternating current. The rivalry with Westinghouse. Secret experiments in Photographic Building.

December 8. My life consumed by waiting. Strong need to talk about haptograph. In this mood, paid visit to stockroom. Earnshaw constrained, uneasy. Hasn't spoken to me in ten days. I pass on some photographic gossip. Won't look me in the eye. Decide to take bull by horns. So! How's the experiment going? Turns to me fiercely. "I hate it in there!" His eyes stern, unforgiving. In the center of each pupil: a bright point of fear.

December 9. There are documented cases in which a blind person experiences return of sight. Stunned with vision: sunlight on leaves, the blue air. Now imagine a man who has been wrapped in cotton for forty-five years. One day cotton is removed. Suddenly man feels sensations of which he can have had no inkling. The world pours into his skin. The fingers of objects seize him, shake him. Touch of a stone, push of a leaf. The knife-thrust of things. What is the world? Where is it? Where? We are covered in cotton, we walk through a world hidden away. Blind skin. Let me see!

December 10. This afternoon, in courtyard, looked up and saw a hawk in flight. High overhead: wings out, body slowly dipping. The power of its calm. A sign. But of what? Tried to imagine hawkness. Failed.

December 11. Long morning, longer afternoon. Picked up six books, read two pages in each. Looked out window four hundred times. Earnshaw's face the other day. Imprint of his ancestors: pale clerics, clean-cheeked, sharp-chinned, a flush of fervor in the white skin. Condemning sinners to everlasting hellfire.

December 12. A night of terrors and wonders. Where will it end?

Kistenmacher tense, abrupt, feverish-tired. Proceeded in his meticulous way through familiar mimicries. Repeated each one several times, entered results in notebook. Something perfunctory in his manner. Or was it only me? But no: his excitement evident as he changed rolls. "Please. Tell me exactly." How to describe it? My skin, delicately thrummed by haptograph, gave birth to buried powers. Felt again that blissful expansion of being — that sense of having thrown off old body and assumed a new. I was beyond myself, more than myself, un-me. In old body, could hold out my hand and grasp a pencil, a paperweight. In new body, could hold out my hand and grasp an entire room with all its furniture, an entire town with its chimneys and saltshakers and streets and oak trees. But more than that — more than that. In new skin I was able to touch directly — at every point on my body — any object that presented itself to my mind: a stuffed bear from childhood, wing of a hawk in flight, grass in a remembered field. As though my skin were chock-full of touches, like memories in the brain, waiting for a chance to leap forth.

Opened my eyes and saw Kistenmacher standing at the table. Staring ferociously at unwinding roll of paper. Hum and click of chain-drive motor, faint rustle of metallic brushes. Closed my eyes...

...and passed at once into wilder regions. Here, the skin becomes so thin and clean that you can feel the touch of air — of light — of dream. Here, the skin shrinks till it's no bigger than the head of a pin, expands till it stretches taut over the frame of the universe. All that is, flowing against you. Drumming against your skin. I shuddered, I rang out like a bell. I was all new, a new creature, glistening, emerging from scaly old. My dull, clumsy skin seemed to break apart into separate points of quivering aliveness, and in this sweet cracking open, this radiant dissolution, I felt my body melting, my nerves bursting, tears streamed along my cheeks, and I cried out in terror and ecstasy.

A knock at the door — two sharp raps. The machine stopped. Kistenmacher over to door.

"I heard a shout," Earnshaw said. "I thought —"

"Fine," Kistenmacher said. "Everything is fine."

DECEMBER 13. A quiet day, cold. Talk of snow. The sky pale, less a color than an absence of color: unblue, ungray: tap water. Through the high arched windows, light traffic on Main. Creak of wagons, knock of hooves. In library fireplace, hiss and crackle of hickory logs. Someone walking in an upper gallery, stopping, removing a book from a shelf. A dray horse snorts in the street.

DECEMBER 14. A sense within me of high anticipation, mixed with anxiousness. Understand the anticipation, but why the other? My skin alert, watchful, as before a storm.

December 15. A new life beckons. A shadow-feeling, an on-the-vergeness. Our sensations fixed, rigid, predictable. Must smash through. Into what? The new place. The there. We live off to one side, like paupers beside a railroad track. The center cannot be here, among these constricting sensations. Haptograph as a way out. Over there. Where?

Paradise.

December 17. Disaster.

On evening of sixteenth, Kistenmacher came to fetch me at eight o'clock. Said he hadn't been in Box for two days — a last-minute snag in automatic adjustment of phonograph required full attention — and was eager to resume our experiments. Followed him down steps to basement. At locked door of Box he removed his ring of keys. Inserted wrong one. Examined it with expression of irritable puzzlement. Inserted correct one. Opened door, fumbled about. Switched on lights. At this point Kistenmacher emitted an odd sound — a kind of terrible sigh.

Haptograph lay on floor. Wires ripped loose from fastenings. Stuck out like wild hair. Back panels torn off, pins scattered about. On the floor: smashed reels, a chain from the motor, a broken frame. Wires like entrails. Gashed paper, crumpled lumps. In one corner I saw the dark head.

Kistenmacher, who had not moved, strode suddenly forward. Stopped. Looked around fiercely. Lifted his right hand shoulder-high in a fist. Suddenly crouched down over haptograph body and began touching wires with great gentleness.

Awful night. Arrived at library early morning. Earnshaw already dismissed. Story: On night of December 16, about seven o'clock, a machinist from precision room, coming to stockroom to pick up some brass tubing, saw Earnshaw emerging from basement. Seemed distracted, fidgety, quite unlike himself. After discovery of break-in, machinist reports to Wizard. Wizard confronts Earnshaw. E. draws himself up, stiff, defiant, and in sudden passionate outburst resigns, saying he doesn't like goings-on "down there." Wizard shouts, "Get out of here!" Storms away. End of story.

Kistenmacher says it will take three to five weeks to repair haptograph, perforate a new roll. But the Wizard has ordered him to devote himself exclusively to speaking doll. The Wizard sharp-tempered, edgy, not to be questioned. Dolls sell well but are returned in droves. Always same complaint:

the doll has stopped speaking, the toy phonograph concealed in its chest has ceased to operate.

DECEMBER 18. No word from Kistenmacher, who shuts himself up in Room 8 with speaking doll.

DECEMBER 19. The Wizard swirling from room to room, his boyish smile, a joke, laughter. Go at it, boys! Glimpse of Kistenmacher: drooping head, a big, punished schoolboy. Can Wizard banish disappointment so easily?

DECEMBER 20. Earnshaw's destructive rage. How to understand it? Haptograph as devil's work. The secret room, naked skin: sin of touch. Those upright ancestors. Burn, witch!

DECEMBER 20, LATER. Saw Kistenmacher walking in courtyard. Forlorn. Didn't see me.

DECEMBER 20, LATER. Or did he?

DECEMBER 20, STILL LATER. Worried about fate of haptograph. Felt we were on the verge. Of what? A tremendous change. A revolution in sensation, ushering in — what, exactly? What? Say it All right. A new universe. Yes! The hidden world revealed. The haptograph as adventure, as voyage of discovery. In comparison, the phonograph nothing but a clever toy: tunes, voices.

Haptograph: instrument of revelation.

Still no word.

DECEMBER 21. The Wizard at his desk, humming. Sudden thought: Is that a disappointed man? The haptograph destroyed, Kistenmacher broken-hearted, the Wizard humming. A happy man, humming a tune. How could I have thought? Of course only a physical and temporary destruction. The machine easily reconstructed. But no work ordered. Takes Kistenmacher off job. Reign of silence. Why this nothing? Why?

Perhaps this. Understands that haptograph is far from complete. Protected by caveat. Sees Kistenmacher's growing obsession. Needs to wrest his best electrical experimenter from a profitless task and redirect his energies more usefully. So: destruction of machine an excuse to put aside experiment. Good. Fine. But surely something more? Relief? Shedding of a tremendous burden? The machine eluding him, betraying him — its drift from the practical, its invitation to heretical pleasures. Haptograph as seductress. Luring him away. A secret desire to be rid of it. No more. Consider: his sudden cheerfulness, his hum. Ergo.

And Earnshaw? His hostility to experiment serves larger design. By striking in rage at Wizard's handiwork, unwittingly fulfills Wizard's secret will. Smash it up, bash it up. Earnshaw as eruption of master's darkness, emissary of his deepest desire. Burn! Die! The Wizard's longing to be rid of haptograph flowing into Earnshaw's hatred of haptograph as wicked machine. Two wills in apparent opposition, working as one. Die! Inescapable conclusion: arm raised in rage against Wizard's work is the Wizard's arm.

Could it be?

It could be.

Kistenmacher entombed with speaking doll. The Wizard flies from room to room, busies himself with a hundred projects, ignores haptograph.

No one enters the Box.

DECEMBER 30. Nothing.

FEBRUARY 16, 1890. Today in courtyard overheard one of the new men speak of haptograph. Seemed embarrassed when I questioned him. Had heard it was shaped like a life-size woman. Was it true she could speak?

Already passing into legend. Must harden myself. The experiment has been abandoned.

Snow in the streets. Through the high windows, the clear sharp jingle of harness bells.

Perhaps I dreamed it all?

Have become friendly with Watkins, the new stockroom clerk. A vigorous, compact man, former telegraph operator, brisk, efficient, humorous; dark blond side-whiskers. His passion for things electrical. Proposes that, for a fee, the owner of a telephone be permitted to listen to live musical performances: a simple matter of wiring. The electric boot, the electric hat. Electric letter opener. A fortune to be made. One day accompanied him down to storeroom, where he searched for supply of cobalt and magnesium requested by an assistant in electrical lab who was experimenting on new storage battery. Saw with a kind of sad excitement that we were approaching a familiar door. "What's in there?" — couldn't stop myself. "Oh that," said Watkins. Takes out a ring of keys. Inside: piles of wooden crates, up to ceiling. "Horns and antlers," he said. "Look: antelope, roebuck, gazelle. Red deer. Walrus tusks, rhino horns." Laughter. "Not much call for these items. But heck, you never can tell."

A dream, a dream!

No: no dream. Or say, a dream, certainly a dream, nothing but a dream, but only as all inventions are dreams: vivid and impalpable presences that haunt the mind's chambers, escaping now and then into the place where they take on weight and cast shadows. The Wizard's laboratory a dream-garden, presided over by a mage. Why did he abandon the haptograph? Because he knew in his bones that it was commercially unfeasible? Because it fell too far short of the perfected phonograph, the elegant promise of kinetoscope? Was it because haptograph had become a terrible temptress, a forbidden delight, luring him away from more practical projects? Or was it — is it possible — did he sense that world was not yet ready for his haptograph, that dangerous machine which refused to limit itself to the familiar feel of things but promised an expansion of the human into new and terrifying realms of being?

Yesterday the Wizard spent ten hours in metallurgical lab. Adjustments in ore-separator. "It's a daisy!" Expects it to revolutionize the industry. Bring in a handsome profit.

The haptograph awaits its time. In a year — ten years — a century — it will return. Then everyone will know what I have come to know: that the world is hidden from us — that our bodies, which seem to bring us the riches of the earth, prevent the world from reaching us. For the eyes of our skin are closed. Brightness streams in on us, and we cannot see. Things flow against us, and we cannot feel. But the light will come. The haptograph will return. Perhaps it will appear as a harmless toy in an amusement parlor, a playful rival of the gustograph and the odoroscope. For a nickel you will be able to feel a ball in the palm of your hand, a hat sitting on your head. Gradually the sensations will grow more complex — more elusive — more daring. You will feel the old body slipping off, a new one emerging. Then your being will open wide and you will receive — like a blow — like a rush of wind — the in-streaming world. The hidden universe will reveal itself like fire. You will leave yourself behind forever. You will become as a god.

I will not return to these notes.

Snow on the streets. Bright blue sky, a cloud white as house paint. Rumble of dynamos from the machine shop. Crackle of hickory logs, a shout from the courtyard. An unremarkable day.

It seems to me that SF is standing, these days, in a doorway. The door is open, wide open. Are we just going to stand there, waiting for the applause of the multitudes? It won't come; we haven't earned it yet. Are we going to cringe back into the old safe ghetto room and pretend that there isn't any big, bad multitude out there? If so, our good writers will leave us in despair, and there will not be another generation of them. Or are we going to walk through the doorway and join the rest of the city? I hope so. I know we can and I hope we do, because we have a great deal to offer — to art, which needs new forms like ours, and to critics who are sick of chewing over the same old works and above all to readers of books, who want and deserve better novels than they mostly get. But it will take not only courage for SF to join the community of literature, but strength, self-respect, the will not to settle for the second rate. It will take genuine self-criticism. And it will include genuine praise.

—Ursula K. Le Guin

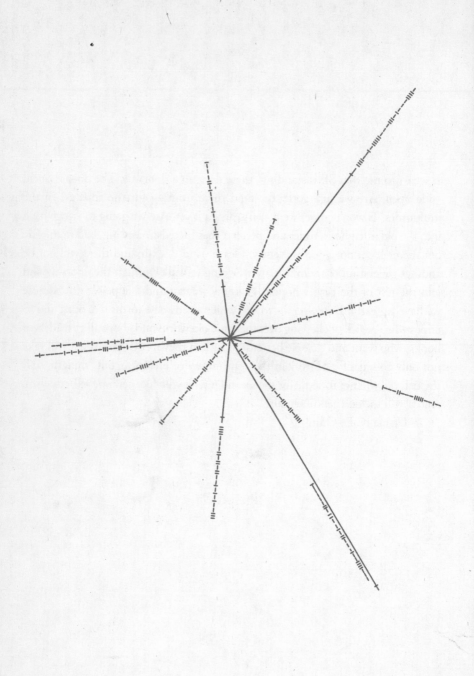